It's clever, funny, and sweet. It deals ...   s, but the author does a brilliant job of lightening the mood through witty dialogue, and humorous anecdotes.

-The Lesbian Review

It's pure Noyes storytelling, and fans won't want it to end!

-Women Using Words

Ms. Noyes once again delivers us a balanced storyline that contributes to a winning reading experience that will appeal to fans of both romance and suspense genres.

-Carol C., *NetGalley*

Integrity

Noyes writes in first-person point of view like no other. This author made me see and feel everything through Lexie's eyes. Noyes' writing is beautiful and real, I loved getting lost in the main character's head and re-read several paragraphs because they were so poignant.

Noyes always writes witty, funny heartfelt dialogue and this book has all of that in bucket loads.

-The Lesbian Review

Noyes never fails to impress me with her talent. She is fearless in her storytelling, never hesitating to flesh it out and let the story take her where it will. Because she does, it feels organic to the reader. ... Book one of the Halcyon Division Series is a fantastic beginning; I have no doubt readers are going to enjoy this journey and sign up for more. This is heart-pumping, non-stop, page-flipping fun, and one heck of a ride! My recommendation: don't miss out!

-Women Using Words

Schuss

This is an absolutely charming first-love, new-adult romance between characters that I had already bonded with. Seeing how they have grown and matured in the four years is a treat and watching the two struggle with their feelings for each other just melted my heart… *Schuss* could be read as a standalone novel, but honestly, I think you should read both books together. They are wonderful stories, and I highly recommend them.

-Betty H., *NetGalley*

E. J. Noyes has this way of writing characters that you get completely absorbed into. When we were left with the Gemma and Stacey cliffhanger in *Gold*, I was hoping we'd get their story and it was phenomenal.

-Les Bereading, *NetGalley*

If I Don't Ask

If I Don't Ask adds a profound depth to Sabine and Rebecca's story, and slots in perfectly with what we already knew about the characters and their motivations.

-Kaylee K., *NetGalley*

Overall, another winner by E. J. Noyes. An absolute pleasure to read. 5 stars.

-*Lez Review Books*

Go Around

Noyes excels at writing both romance and intrigue and it shows in this book. Her characters might as well be real they are so well-written. I'm a pretty big fan of second-chance love stories, and I love the way this one is done. You get the angst you expect from the two women trying to get past the pain of their separation and work their way back to being a couple in love. The outside forces that had a role in their breakup are still around and have to be dealt with. Add in a nasty bad guy (or guys) who are physically and psychologically stalking Elise and you get a tale full of danger, excitement, intrigue, and romance. I also love the Easter egg the author included for her book *Alone*. I actually laughed out loud at that little scene. E. J. Noyes' works always get my highest praise and recommendation, and this novel is no different. You really need to read this book.

-Betty H., *NetGalley*

In *Go Around*, E. J. Noyes has dipped her toes in the second-chance romance pool and was masterful in blending angst, enduring love and suspense in it. The chemistry and dynamics between the pair were thick and palpable but what stood out for me throughout the book was the type of love everyone wished they had; fierce and protective, grounded in loyalty, passionate yet to be able to just be when you are with the other. Noyes also made Bennet, Avery's dog, another highlight for me. He was the tension breaker and a giant darling.

-Nutmeg, *NetGalley*

Pas de deux

Pas de deux doesn't disappoint: the writing is excellent, the pace is ideal, the characters are layered and, yes, relatable, including the secondary characters, from Caitlyn's groom Wren, to Addie's friend Teresa and, of course, Dewey the horse. One of the many things I loved in this book is the way the MCs deal with problems. They do this very adult and very rare-in-lesfic thing: they talk to each other. This book is proof that miscommunication isn't required for drama. Neither is a breakup. Well-fleshed characters with very human hang-ups bring all the angst and drama necessary. It's all the more interesting here as *Pas de deux* is part enemies-to-lovers romance, part second chance, depending on whose point of view is playing.

-Les Rêveur

This story is not the traditional enemies-to-lovers romance, and I love that. Noyes really puts emphasis on how skewed memories can become as you get older, and how an experience may appear different to another person who had the exact same one. Even if you are unfamiliar with dressage, Noyes' writing is still spot-on and delivers the same compelling, fun, and intriguing story with loveable characters of both the two-legged and four-legged kind. This love letter to a sport she obviously has a passion for is so evident, and I felt honored to have her share her passion with me and every reader who picks it up. If you love horses, enemies-to-lovers, or even just Noyes' stories in general, this one will definitely be a favorite on your list.

-*The Lesbian Review*

Reaping the Benefits

The story is quite eccentric with its paranormal context but in fact is a pure romance at heart with a nice dose of humor. The book is written in third person, from the point of view of both protagonists, which is not common for Noyes, but it is executed perfectly. With all main elements done well, this makes an awesome read which I could easily recommend to all romance fans.

-Pin's Reviews, *goodreads*

I've read many love stories that entertain the idea of soul mates, but this one does something even more interesting. This one explores the depth of love and its ability to transcend death. This story plays with the idea that love has no limits or boundaries. Its exploration provides a unique setting for this heartfelt romantic tale. At its core it remains a romance. The love story between Jane and Morgan is tender and sweet. It's so cleverly and delightfully done; I've never read anything quite like it before. Noyes possesses the ability to see a story where others don't and turn that into something unique and captivating. She uses rich storytelling and engaging characters to enthrall and delight us.

It's fresh and original. It's everything you crave when you want to dig into a great romance. I highly recommend it.

-Deb M., *NetGalley*

If you're looking for a lesbian romance, but with a twist of something different, I recommend *Reaping the Benefits*. It's sweet, sexy, and fun.

-*The Lesbian Review*

If the Shoe Fits

When we pick up an E. J. Noyes book we expect intensity, characters with issues (circumstantial and/or internal), and a romance that builds believably. Considering this is *Ask, Tell* #3 we expected all of the above layered with epic seriousness. We were pleasantly surprised and totally floored by the humor in addition to what was already expected!

-*Best Lesfic Reviews*

Alone

E. J. Noyes is easily one of the most gifted writers pulling us into whatever world she creates making us live and feel every emotion with her characters. Definitely, loudly, vehemently recommended.

-Reviewer@Large, *NetGalley*

Alone is an absolutely stunning book. This book is not a 5-star, it is well above that. You don't see books like this one very often. Truly a treasure and one that will stay with you long after the final page.

-Tiff's Reviews, *goodreads*

There are only a few books out there so compelling they seem to take control of you and force you to read them as quickly as possible. You can't put them down. You just want the world to go away and leave you alone until you can finish this story. *Alone* by E. J. Noyes is that book for me. This novel is absolutely wonderful.

-Betty H., *NetGalley*

Not only is this easily one of the best books of 2019, but it has worked its way onto my personal all-time top 10 list. There is not one formulaic thing going on, and it's "unputdownable."

-Karen C., *NetGalley*

I cannot give this anything more than five stars, but damn I wish I could. I would give it 15.

-Carolyn M., *NetGalley*

Ask Me Again

Not every story needs a sequel. *Ask, Tell* demanded it, and Noyes delivers in spectacular fashion. Sabine and Rebecca show us their fortitude and their strength in their love for each other…Thank you, Noyes, for giving us a great story, a great series, and amazing women that teach us the best things in life are worth fighting for.

There really is only one way to tell this story, and Noyes executes it perfectly. She gives us events from the first-person perspective. However, she alternates each chapter between Sabine's point of view and Rebecca's point of view. You're able to get the full perspective of their inner feelings and turmoil they hide from one another. In addition, you're able to get the complete picture of the unconditional love Sabine and Rebecca have for each other. It's this little light of love that propels the reader to keep going and hope these women will finally reach the end of the darkness.

-*The Lesbian Review*

Gold

This is Noyes' third book, and her writing just keeps getting better and better with each release. She gives us such amazing characters that are easy for anyone to relate to. And she makes them so endearing that you can't help but want them to overcome the past and move forward toward their happily ever after.

-*The Lesbian Review*

This book is exactly the way I wish romance authors would get back to writing romance. This is what I want to read. If you are a Noyes fan, get this book. If you are a romance fan, get this book. I didn't even talk about the skiing… if you are a skiing fan, get this book.

-Lex Kent's Reviews, *goodreads*

Turbulence

Wow… and when I say 'wow' I mean… WOW. After the author's debut novel *Ask, Tell* got to my list of best books of 2017, I was wondering if that was just a fluke. Fortunately for us lesfic readers, now it's confirmed: E. J. Noyes CAN write. Not only that, she can write different genres... Written in first person from Isabelle's point of view, the reader gets into her headspace with all her insecurities, struggles, and character traits. Alongside Isabelle, we discover Audrey's personality, her life story and, most importantly, her feelings. Throughout the book, Ms. Noyes pushes us down a roller coaster of emotions as we accompany Isabelle in her journey of self-discovery. In the process, we laugh, suffer, and enjoy the ride.

-Gaby, *goodreads*

The entire story just flowed from the first page! E. J. Noyes did a superb job of bringing out Isabelle's and Audrey's personalities, faults, erratic emotions, and the burning passion they shared. The chemistry between both women was so palpable! I felt as though the writer drizzled every word she wrote with love, combustible desire, and intense longing.

-*The Lesbian Review*

Ask, Tell

This is a book with everything I love about top-quality lesbian fiction: a fantastic romance between two wonderful women I can relate to, a location that really made me think again about something I thought I knew well, and brilliant pacing and scene-setting. I cannot recommend this novel highly enough.

-*Rainbow Book Reviews*

Noyes totally blew my mind from the first sentence. I went in timidly, and I came away awaiting her next release with bated breath. I really love how Noyes is able to get below the surface of the DADT legislation. She really captures the longing, the heartbreak, and especially the isolation that LGBTQ soldiers had to endure because the alternative was being deemed unfit to serve by their own government. I applaud Noyes for getting to the heart of the matter and giving a very important representation of what living and serving under this legislation truly meant for LGBTQ men and women of service.

-*The Lesbian Review*

E. J. Noyes was able to deliver on so many levels… This book is going to take you on a roller-coaster ride of ups and downs that you won't expect but it's so unbelievably worth it.

-Les Rêveur

Noyes clearly undertook a mammoth amount of research. I was totally engrossed. I'm not usually a reader of romance novels, but this one gripped me. The personal growth of the main character, the rich development of her fabulous best friend, Mitch, and the well-handled tension between Sabine and her love interest were all fantastic. This one definitely deserves five stars.

-CELEStial books Reviews

LOYALTY

BOOK THREE
IN THE
HALCYON DIVISION SERIES

E. J. NOYES

Other Bella Books by E. J. Noyes

Ask, Tell
Turbulence
Gold
Ask Me Again
Alone
If the Shoe Fits
Reaping the Benefits
Pas de deux
Go Around
If I Don't Ask
Schuss
Integrity
Leverage

About the Author

E. J. Noyes is an Australian transplanted to New Zealand, which may be the awesomest thing to happen to her. She lives in the South Island with her wife and the world's best and neediest cat, and is enjoying the change of temperature from her hot, humid homeland.

An avid but mediocre gamer, E. J. lives for skiing (which she is also mediocre at), enjoys arguing with her hair, pretending to be good at things, and working the fact she's a best-selling and award-winning author into casual conversation.

LOYALTY

BOOK THREE
IN THE
HALCYON DIVISION SERIES

E. J. NOYES

2024

Copyright © 2024 by E. J. Noyes

Bella Books, Inc.
P.O. Box 10543
Tallahassee, FL 32302

All rights reserved. No part of this book may be reproduced or transmitted in any form or by any means, electronic or mechanical, including photocopying, without permission in writing from the publisher.

This is a work of fiction. Names, characters, businesses, places, events and incidents are either the products of the author's imagination or used in a fictitious manner. Any resemblance to actual persons, living or dead, or actual events is purely coincidental. The publisher does not have any control over and does not assume any responsibility for author or third-party websites or their content.

First Edition - 2024

Editor: Cath Walker
Cover Designer: Heather Honeywell

ISBN: 978-1-64247-540-1

PUBLISHER'S NOTE

The scanning, uploading, and distribution of this book via the Internet or via any other means without the permission of the publisher is illegal and punishable by law. Please purchase only authorized print or electronic editions, and do not participate in or encourage electronic piracy of copyrighted materials. Your support of the author's rights is appreciated.

Acknowledgments

And so here we are—Book Three in the Halcyon Division Series. Is Book Three the end of the series? I honestly don't know. *For now*, this story has reached a natural stopping point, but not a hard stopping point. If there's one thing Lexie Martin has taught me, it's that there's always hope.

I loved writing *Loyalty* (a.k.a. *The Book Formerly Known As Fortitude*), and I loved it from start to finish, which is a rare thing indeed. Normally any snippets of manuscript love and ease are gobbled up like they're the rarest thing in the world, but this one fell from my fingertips like it couldn't get out fast enough. And if my readers love it even a fraction as much as I do, then I'll be a happy author.

Writing book acknowledgements has always been a funny thing for me, and also an exercise in "Have I said this in an earlier acknowledgments?" Usually I'll start a document early in the writing process and jot down names and anything relevant I want to say, building upon it as more people pop in with help, before I add the usual suspects at the end of editing and then write out the little intro. Doing acknowledgments over time like this makes for an interesting study in the progression of my life because things happen, like could-have-been-super-serious medical events.

So, please indulge me if some of these thank-yous seem incongruously emotional. Because that's where I'm at right now. Emotional and grateful for a lot of things. I'm grateful to my family and friends and all the people on the Internet, who I've never met, sending me their good vibes. I'm *so* grateful I'd finished this manuscript well before my medical drama, and that if anything went awry, at least I wouldn't leave you all on that cliffhanger at the end of *Leverage*. And, of course, I'm grateful to have a list of people to thank for their help with this novel.

Abbie, cheers for popping in on another of my random "Can anyone help" tweets to teach me about how long it takes to crack passwords, especially because I'm a complete stranger. And if you, the reader, are wondering how long it'll take someone to brute-force your password? A very long time, if you've got a good one. Here's your friendly reminder to check and update your passwords, friends.

Big thank you to Jude, who is far better than Google Translate, and also managed to come up with something suitably weird for me after I gave them *very* specific requirements.

Claire, your excitement and support for each new project is infectious. In a good way. Not a "you should get that checked out" way.

Lee, thanks for helping me shovel some dirt. That sounds nefarious. Nobody was harmed during the production of this book.

Eternal, groveling thanks to Gay Sam, Cyber Expert, who is the perfect Venn diagram. We're just not sure of what yet.

Kate, my shitty-alpha-draft reader and this-isn't-what-an-American-would-say expert extraordinaire. I adore you. Thanks for sending me those new comfy compression socks. I cannot wait to see you in person again.

Betsy, I truly cannot express the depth of my gratitude for your help. Gratitude not only for reading through cruddy drafts and sharing your expertise, but also for your willingness to brainstorm ideas with me. Thank you for helping me round out Lexie's world. You've given me three books' worth of your time and expertise, and all after a weird tweet I put out asking if someone with experience in your field would share that experience with me (I'm sensing a pattern here with me tweeting into the void for assistance). I loathe asking people for help, but you made it so easy to ask for help. Thank you.

Cath. What can I say? This one was a bit of a bumpy ride through edits, with my badly timed health drama (though is any health drama well-timed?) and my badly timed eleventh-hour plot realizations. But your support—both with edits and the "other stuff"—got me through the times when I just really didn't feel like dealing with edits on this one. I'm honoured to have you as my editor, but I'm mostly grateful to call you a friend.

Bella Books. All of you (the people, not the books). Thanks, legends.

Pheebs. Pheebs… Bebe… I don't even know what to say. I'm currently in my post-PE/I diagnosis crying-at-everything stage, so trying to think of what to say is just a lip-trembling, eye-stinging exercise in writing futility. So…I love you. More than I have words for (said the author, yet again). We're totally awesome together.

Author's Note

Yep, it's all fiction.

PROLOGUE

Here we are again, but…how did we get here exactly?

I've had a really strange eight months.
 If you already know what I've been up to, I won't be offended if you don't want to hear my take on what's happened. Oh, sorry, who am I? I'm Lexie Martin. I'm an intelligence analyst, and I also work for Halcyon Division, which is an important part of the whys and hows of how I got to this point in my life. But because nobody except Halcyon knows who Halcyon is, I'll brief you. Halcyon Division works as a very secret system of checks and balances for the government, like a hidden antivirus making sure the people in charge aren't working against the country's best interests.
 Late last year, I received intelligence—let's call it the Kunduz Intelligence—that powerful people didn't want investigated. Halcyon told me to hide so I could figure it out. I did figure it out, and I also figured out I was head-over-heels into Sophia Flores, the woman I'd just started dating, who I'd brought along with me on my intelligence-figuring-out road trip as a kind of security blanket.
 And that intelligence? It proved the vice president was involved with Russia, in the bad, I'm-selling-American-secrets-to-the-enemy way. Not that there's a good way to be involved with Russia, especially not when you're the VP. Halcyon "convinced" him to resign, with the

president's blessing and also the president's denial of all knowledge about his VP's extracurricular activities. And instead of showing an ounce of remorse for picking such a shitty ally, the president blamed *me* for the fact he'd lost his political BFF, because I'd been the one who'd received the intelligence. And he made it very clear that he didn't like me.

If I liked the president and craved his approval, I'd be bothered. But I don't, so I wasn't. The problem with being hated by the president is that he has the power to be a complete dick to you. And he was. I returned to work just in time for him to reassign me overseas for six months as punishment. What was my new essential and vital assignment? To receive intelligence and investigate it—kindergarten stuff that so many others could do; that *I* could do while safe at home in the States.

I said thanks but no thanks, and was reminded that technically I'd been a Very Bad Girl and it was either accept this reassignment overseas, or accept a reassignment to jail.

No brainer, right?

My first favorite part of the new assignment was packing up the comfortable, stable life I was building with Sophia to work in the country where six years earlier I'd been held hostage and stabbed multiple times. My second favorite part was how they gave me a partner: Jeffrey Burton, the guy who'd debriefed me after the Kunduz Intelligence adventure. Talk about mind games.

Long story short—it sucked. I missed Sophia. She missed me. And to add a fun little twist, I discovered Elaheh, a woman I knew (and when I say knew, I mean that I'd been sleeping with) from my last assignment in the region, was now a terrorist. Did not see that one coming.

Another thing I didn't see coming was Sophia dropping a bombshell on me a few months into my overseas assignment, when she told me the relationship I thought was kind of perfect—except for the me being away working for six months thing—wasn't working for her and she wanted to break up. Talk about blindsided. If you've ever wondered what it'd be like to get dumped during an unexpected long-distance portion of your relationship—your relationship that you'd thought was pretty good—I can say with certainty that it's fucking awful.

Adding to the fucking awful part of it was that I wasn't sure if she really didn't want to be with me, or if someone, say a president with a vendetta, had threatened her and forced her to do it to punish me even more. Yeah I know, I made it all about me. But being in a terrorist hotbed tends to make one a little selfish and self-absorbed.

Once I realized Sophia wasn't joking, I did what I do best—shove it down for later and bury myself in work. Unfortunately, that work involved meeting with my now-terrorist ex-(or, with Sophia gone, is that technically my ex-ex?)-sleeping-with-regularly person and teasing out information about her other life while pretending I wasn't trying to do just that. It didn't go so well, but we still managed to break down part of her little terrorist team. Go, us.

I thought my pointless assignment would end with a whimper. But as it turns out, it ended with a bang when I barely escaped being killed in a suicide bomb attack. The only reason I'm still alive is because Jeffrey noticed something was wrong, dragged me out of there, and saved my life. Seconds after I'd left the building, Elaheh blew up a café she knew I frequented, killing herself and most of the occupants inside. She almost murdered me. I don't know if her timing was intentional or not, and I'm still trying to unpack how I feel about that whole mess.

All in all, the assignment left me with more minuses than pluses. But, it turns out Jeffrey wasn't a bad guy—I lost a girlfriend, but gained a trustworthy friend.

By the time I came home, I'd accepted Sophia's decision and had worked my way through all stages of post-separation emotions to a point where I could say I'd made peace with it and moved on. Then I found a cryptic note from her hidden in a pocket of one of my work suits. It led me to a book blurb about a woman sacrificing happiness to save her family and kingdom, confirming my suspicions that Sophia had broken up with me because someone "guided" her toward that, not because she didn't want our relationship.

I went back to work and met the new head of the agency. And, color me shocked, the new agency director was Lennon.

A.k.a the head of Halcyon Division.

A.k.a (unbeknownst to me until that moment) my father's best friend from when I was a child.

So, yeah. Strange. And confusing. But I'm hoping it'll get less strange and confusing from now on…

CHAPTER ONE

I guess it runs in the family

I was pretty sure my internal "What the actual fuck is going on here?" could be heard from Mars.

As I stared at the newly appointed agency director, I wondered how exactly I'd ended up in this position. Every time I thought things couldn't get weirder, or worse, or harder, they did. I really needed to stop tempting fate by thinking that.

I leaned back in the chair I'd collapsed into, hoping feigning relaxation would result in some actual relaxation. "So, should I call you Lennon? Or Mr. Lennon, or Uncle Michael, or Michael, or… what?" He wasn't my uncle by blood, but as a kid I'd always called him Uncle Michael, probably because he and my father were best friends, and he was the closest thing I'd have to an uncle with both my parents being only children.

I was still trying to wrap my head around that revelation. Lennon, the man I'd never met but had spoken to countless times in his role as head of Halcyon Division, was actually my father's good friend, and was also now the head of the agency for which I worked. Talk about coming out of left field.

With far more grace than I'd shown, Lennon sat down across from me at his ornate mahogany desk. His smile was both benevolent and condescending, as if he'd expected me to ask that inane question. "Lennon if we're talking about Halcyon business. Mr. Lennon if we're discussing agency business." No mention of anything involving his first name. So we're super professional. Got it. I wasn't bothered—calling him "Uncle Michael" as an adult felt strange, almost uncomfortable, as did calling him that when my dad wasn't around. Actually, now that I thought about it, calling him Uncle Anything when we weren't actually related was strange, but that's how Dad had always referred to him and it'd stuck.

I'd had enough of the inside-out, upside-down bullshit that had been thrown at me in the last eight months, and decided to cut right to the core and ask the questions I wanted answered. "How did you get installed as the new director of the agency?" It felt a little off to me, almost a little too convenient. Or maybe I was just incredibly cynical and suspicious after six months in a hostile environment as punishment by the government for doing my job. "And when?"

Lennon's sigh was theatrically over-the-top, as if he couldn't believe I'd dare to question his qualifications. But given I knew absolutely nothing about him except for his name and job, I thought it was a fair question. "Because I am eminently qualified for this role. I have the ability to ensure the strength and security of the agency, especially as it pertains to the Intelligence Community's relationship with Halcyon. As to when, it was very last-minute. I only accepted the role over the weekend."

"What about Halcyon Division? Who's running it now that you're heading up this agency?" Leaving Halcyon unhelmed, or inadequately helmed, could be disastrous.

"I am," Lennon said firmly. "If it becomes apparent that I cannot execute both roles to the standards required of both the agency and Halcyon, then someone capable will take over Halcyon." The unspoken "but that's unlikely" was woven into his statement.

"Will you leave Halcyon if you step down as the…" I had to think hard on the word I wanted. I'd always just called Lennon my boss—*one of* my bosses—but I honestly didn't know his official title at Halcyon. After an eternal thinking pause, I finally just said, "Leader?"

"No. I would remain on the leadership team, providing relevant consulting as needed, just no longer as the head of the Division."

He rested his hands on top of his desk, palms down. He had strong, masculine hands, but the skin seemed almost incongruously soft and his nails were manicured. It was so weird seeing him, Lennon, in person like this and observing all these human things, things that I'd never paid any attention to as a child. His eyes were hazel-ish, piercing and serious. He wore his blondish-brown hair with a militant side part. He didn't smile much. "But enough about me, Alexandra. We'll have ample time to talk about my relocation. How are you? You've had quite an experience these past eight months."

Quite an experience… That was one way to put it. Apparently Lennon was into understatements.

Lennon's expectant stare prompted me to stop thinking and start answering. "I've never been better," I lied.

The slight lift of his eyebrow told me he didn't believe me, but he didn't push. Feeling suddenly antsy, likely due to his probing, I stood up and walked to the wall where, amongst a group of framed pictures, hung a photo of him with my father. I tried so hard to recall any interactions I'd had with Lennon, this man my dad had said was his best friend, but nothing came to mind. He was an intermittent shadow hovering in the periphery of my childhood.

I studied the other photos, which were mostly Lennon with important government figures, and then one incongruous one of him fly fishing, before I returned to the photo of him and my dad. Dad looked to be in his fifties, so it was likely taken in the early or mid-2000s, at an indeterminate location. Both men were in suits, standing close in a way that suggested they'd been instructed to pose. The photograph had captured a moment of levity and they were leaning in toward each other like one of them had whispered something that made them both laugh.

My dad had a dry, biting wit and if you asked me to list his character traits, "humor" would be quite low on the list. I had to scramble to find memories that were of him laughing, and the disconnect between this image and the one in my head of my father was discomforting. It made me realize that parents have whole lives and are whole people before they have kids. And that made me feel weird, especially now that my parents were dead.

That thought blossomed and one of the many things that had been niggling since I'd first seen Lennon finally hit me. I looked over my shoulder, finding Lennon still at his desk, watching me. "You weren't at my parents' memorial service." Dad hadn't mentioned his friend "Uncle" Michael in years but it hadn't registered because not mentioning something wasn't unusual for my father, especially not anything personal. Still, you'd think your supposed best or even good friend would come to your funeral.

Lennon's expression was a curious mix of aloofness and regret. "No, unfortunately I was detained out of the country on Halcyon business and couldn't return in time. Did you get my condolence card and flowers?"

Frowning, I admitted, "I…honestly don't remember." There had been so much happening after my parents died in a light-aircraft crash in the middle of 2021, so many cards from people I didn't know, and well-wishers at the service that I'd lost track. "It was all a blur."

"I can understand that, and I am very sorry I couldn't be there. Why don't you have a seat, Alexandra," Lennon offered, gesturing across the desk to the chair I'd occupied before.

Everyone knew "have a seat" was code for "I'm about to tell you something you won't like." I'd heard so many things already that I didn't like and had never needed to sit down for any of them. I turned around, crossing my arms over my chest. "I'm fine standing, thanks. Any chance we'll ever get to that thing you've been dangling over my head since the Kunduz Intelligence? My 'importance'?" If I prodded him about it, maybe I'd get thrown a bone.

At first it'd been interesting, exciting even, to be told I was so irreplaceable that they would bend unbendable rules for me. That I would be freed instead of imprisoned, that my security clearance would be returned, despite what I'd done. Then it became tedious, having it held just out of my reach like a kid taunting that they knew something I didn't but that they'd tell me soon. Now…well, now I just wanted to know what was going on so I could move forward without this carrot Halcyon was dangling in front of me.

Lennon nodded briskly. "I suppose that's one way of framing it." He gave me a look that told me he thought I'd made a mistake not taking him up on the sitting, but he didn't offer again. Instead, he just came right out and told me, "Your father wasn't just a diplomat, Alexandra. He was also an undercover American intelligence officer. His service for this country was extensive. He obtained intelligence from places most thought inaccessible, from people thought untouchable, in a career spanning over forty years."

Um…

My legs quit in shock at Lennon's revelation. "You know," I said breathily, "I might sit down after all." I fumbled my way back to the chair, my shaking legs grateful when I sat heavily. A *spy*? A legit spy? What the—? I finally managed to stop my spinning thoughts for long enough to exclaim, "You are shitting me."

"I assure you I'm not. Your father was undercover for most of his working life," Lennon said steadily. "And he had been doing the most important work—compiling dossiers of all foreign operatives working in this country."

Foreign operatives. I'd thought the news my dad was an undercover intelligence officer was huge, but this new information smothered that. "Foreign operatives in the US?" My thoughts went back and forth, spinning over what he'd just told me, not settling on any one thing.

"Yes. Back then, and still now."

I couldn't help the incredulity that seeped into my tone. "Foreign operatives in our country? Really?" There'd been a number of foreign operatives found and weeded out over the years, and I was fairly confident there weren't any more lurking in the shadows—our counterintelligence was almost unbeatable. As soon as I thought it, I realized my arrogance and naivety. Hadn't I recently worked with intelligence that placed our ex-vice president, Randolf Berenson, in Russia's pockets? He wasn't a foreign operative, but he'd definitely been working with a foreign entity. If that had happened under our noses… Oh fuck.

"Yes, really. Your father's intelligence has provided the basis for removing most of the operatives to date."

"Who continued the work after he died?"

"Nobody. But, before his death, he gave the hard drive containing his life's work to me for safekeeping. I believe that, among other things, it contains the dossiers of the foreign operatives we haven't managed to uncover yet."

Interesting. That stopped my frenetic thoughts. I wondered why Dad hadn't passed it to his handler at the agency. I guess Lennon was a more trusted friend, who obviously worked in intelligence and had clearance. Maybe Dad suspected his handler was sideways. Whatever, the reason didn't matter. "Okay. And what does that have to do with me? Are you going to make me work my dad's old cases?" I asked grumpily. I wasn't a spy. I didn't want to be a spy. That sounded like another punishment, and I was so done with being punished. I shook my hands out. "Sorry, I'm just trying to process this."

"I know this must be shocking," he said soothingly. "But let me assure you that revealing the truth about your father isn't for shock value, Alexandra."

"Then what value *is* it for?"

"Because we need you."

I stared at him and hoped I didn't look as skeptical as I felt. "For what?"

"The hard drive is encrypted with a password. And despite working on decrypting it for over a year, we have been unable to break it." Lennon leaned back in his chair. "Alexandra, it's possible you may know the password."

"Me?" It came out embarrassingly squeaky. Blame shock. It wasn't every day you were told your dad was an undercover intelligence officer and that he'd spent most of his diplomatic career gathering intelligence on foreign operatives hiding in our country. "How could *I* possibly know the password? Are you sure?"

"No, we're not sure. But all our attempts to access the data have failed, so we need to try something new." Lennon smiled. "*Your* father compiled this intelligence. He knew your job and thought very highly of your personal and professional skills. It's not outside the realm of possibility that he gave the key to you as a safeguard of sorts. Isn't that a logical conclusion?"

"I…yes, I suppose so, but it still makes no sense," I said, suddenly so wired I couldn't stand being seated anymore. I paced back and forth in front of his desk. "I didn't even know about this hard drive until a minute ago, so how could he have given me the password?" Frowning, I added, "Nor did he give me anything that could be used to store an encryption key." And there had been nothing in my father's personal effects that even seemed remotely like it could be a key. No external computer media, no secret diaries with weird scribbles, no hidden compartments in desks.

Lennon was emphatic. "He must have told you what it is, either overtly or subtly."

My laugh burst out so fast, I almost choked on it. "He definitely did not. My father never shared anything personal with me, as evidenced by the fact I only *just* found out he was actually an intel officer. What do you think he did? That one night as he was tucking me into bed, he just casually said 'Daddy's working on something very important so here's a password for you to remember for the next thirty years,' and that's what I've done?" I tapped my temple. "Just kept it up here, waiting for you to ask me for it?" What a ludicrous notion.

"There's no need to be facetious, Alexandra."

Oh there was every reason. I ignored everything Lennon had said so far to ask an important question. "Do you think my mom knew what my father really did?" I didn't know why I was so bothered by the thought that she'd been duped too—it's not like she would have told me, even if she'd known.

"It's doubtful. Your mother would have just thought she was a diplomat's wife. A diplomat is the perfect cover for an undercover operative, and he would have been functioning well under that guise. Your father was a very good diplomat."

"Why didn't you approach me about this hard drive before if it's so important?" And if my dad had given it to Lennon, shouldn't he have told him how to access it? Unless he assumed he had more time and was planning on passing it along separately like a good spy not keeping all their eggs in one basket. Most people probably don't assume they're going to die in a light-plane crash.

"Your parents died, Alexandra," he said gently. "It didn't seem particularly kind to badger you about this. And, we've been trying, since your parents' death, to brute-force the encryption. But, as I said, we've had no success. It's time to stop messing around. Accessing this information is a pressing issue, as I'm sure you can appreciate."

"Right. I know *I* don't want foreign operatives moving freely through our country, fucking with things they shouldn't."

An expression of distaste moved over his face the moment I said "fucking." Interesting. Given I'd never had a face-to-face conversation with him, I had no idea he had an aversion to expletives. Unfortunate for him, given how often I'd used expletives during our phone conversations over the years. "None of us want that," he said firmly. "I'm sure I don't need to tell you how important this is, not only to the security of our country, but that of our allies as well."

Oh, no, I got that part. "Was my dad Halcyon?"

"No. He knew of it, and knew you were Halcyon. We asked him to join, but he declined. But, he suggested you for the Division."

"Why?"

"Because he knew you'd be excellent at this work. And you are."

I didn't know why, but the revelation that my dad may have used his friendship with Lennon to get me into Halcyon made me feel sick. "Has my entire working life just been manipulation?"

"No. Halcyon knew you had the qualities of an excellent analyst, and that's the only reason you were offered the role. Your father and I were very close, but he had nothing to do with Halcyon, so you may rest assured that nepotism had nothing to do with your recruitment."

I sat back down, slumping into the chair. "This is…a lot to work through. I've only been home a week and thought my life might get back to some semblance of normal." Whatever my next version of normal was.

"I understand. But I need you to process it. This is your father's life's work, Alexandra. There's rot, hidden deep. We're going to find the core of that rot and all the branches spreading from it, and we're going to cut it out so we can rebuild something the country, the *world*, has faith in." Good speech. I'd vote for him. Lennon leaned forward. "But to do that, I need your father's intelligence, which means I need you to figure out the password."

"Why isn't brute-forcing working?" I didn't know much about the inner workings of computers, but surely the country's best computer people could figure it out. Hackers hacked people's passwords all the time.

"Brute-forcing is just running through infinite possibilities, hoping one of them works. We do not have infinite time." Lennon sighed. "There is also the issue of security. This is not something I want too many eyes upon, so I have limited who can work with it."

"So I'm just supposed to do…what? Think really hard until it comes to me?"

"Yes. As well as looking at everything we have from your father's hard-copy files to see if something triggers a memory or possibly leads you to where he may have hidden the code. Perhaps he gave you something that could lead you to it. You need to approach this from every angle, Alexandra."

Thanks for telling me how to do my job. "Will this be my sole focus, or do I have to work on it in my free time around my agency work?" Because if that was the case, I was going to insist Halcyon put in some sort of overtime clause into my contract.

"Your sole focus," he said immediately, firmly.

"And is this an agency task, or a Halcyon task?"

"Technically Halcyon, but you will be operating under the agency umbrella for security and ease of access to your father's files." His eyes softened at the edges. "I know this is a lot to take in. And a huge burden to put upon you. But your loyalty to Halcyon and the agency is not going unnoticed, Alexandra."

Great?

The fact I was apparently pleasing my bosses didn't change the fact I'd received yet another assignment where I had no choice about whether I accepted it. But…maybe something like this was exactly what I needed to reset my life after the past eight months of mental, physical, and emotional highs and lows. "Okay, obviously I'm in. But I'm going to need a lot of resources."

"Whatever you need, it will be made available to you."

"Does Derek know?" Derek Wood, my agency boss and another Halcyon agent, was clued in on almost everything. "About my dad, and this hard drive, I mean."

"Yes. You'll meet with him today to discuss a cover story for why you've been moved to another agency team."

"Again," I pointed out. My workmates were going to think I was a lunatic or very special. I was going to push the "special" angle. Leaving for a few weeks because of the Kunduz Intelligence, coming back for a month, leaving for six months on the president's shitty reassignment, coming back for…a day, then moving to yet another team. "I'll need a private space to work, obviously. And I need a secure laptop and a bunch of other things. I'll let you know as soon as I've made a list of necessary equipment."

"We can do that. Obviously the laptop will have to remain offline, even from the internal agency network. I can't risk anyone with access to the network seeing this."

"Sure. I'll just go out to my car and get my phone from its lockbox in the trunk every time I need to Google something," I said dryly. "I think I'll also need a team, or an assistant or something, someone with the clearance to help me." Lennon nodded, so I decided to go all-in. "I want Jeffrey Burton." At his raised eyebrows, I elaborated, "I trust him, and I trust his ability to not only help with the decryption but with obtaining anything I might need to move forward."

Jeffrey was going to owe me for keeping him employed. As a contractor with a wide skill set and clearance to work just about anywhere, I knew he had the luxury of picking and choosing jobs. But he'd also told me Halcyon paid extremely well, so why not offer him another well-paying assignment? I owed him for keeping me alive, so I supposed my suggesting him for another job, one with no physical danger, was a fair trade, maybe skewed slightly in his favor.

Lennon nodded once, briskly. "Consider it done. I'll find an office in this building for you. And I trust you to brief Burton on what you think he needs to know."

Oh, he'd need to know everything. "Good. That means I can come into my usual office to socialize with my team, or everyone is going to get suspicious about how much time I've been away and why I've suddenly got *another* new thing in a new location to do."

"That sounds like a solid plan. The last thing we need is any more attention drawn to this than absolutely necessary."

I took a deep breath, and asked for a long shot. "Can you read Jeffrey Burton in to Halcyon Division? Or something? Even just let him know it exists and what our basic function is?" I ignored the tightening around Lennon's mouth and barreled on. "Constant mental gymnastics with him while I'm trying to figure this out is a no-go. Offer him a job or something, I don't care what you do, but please don't make me exert more mental effort on lying and roundabout explanations while I'm trying to explain things to Jeffrey."

"We don't have any job openings."

"Then create one, make it temporary, or put him on the books as a contractor. I don't care," I repeated. "This is going to be hard enough already, and I need it to be as easy as it can be. I know he has the clearance. And he already suspects that being hired by 'Mr. Lennon' to protect me during my reassignment—thanks, by the way—means there's more to this whole thing than appears on the surface."

His thinned lips relaxed ever so slightly. "I'll see what I can do."

"Thank you. And I obviously need the hard drive."

"I can't do that," Lennon said immediately.

A little alarm bell dinged quietly in my head and I tried a bluff. "Then I can't work on it. I'm not going to come running to you every time I have a breakthrough to ask you to check if it's right." I'd uncovered the former VP's treachery, so you'd think I'd have clearance to view dossiers on current foreign operatives, or whatever was on my dad's hard drive. Not to mention, this entire building was a SCIF—sensitive compartmented information facility—which meant nobody outside could see or hear inside to view or listen to anything, and any super-classified information would remain that way.

"Okay, you'll be given a copy," he agreed, again without hesitation. "And your father's files will be delivered to your new office."

Oh yay. I couldn't wait to read about my father's double life.

CHAPTER TWO

Lexie's Code Cracking Club

I'd spent hours at work liaising with Derek about my new role, and when I wasn't at work, I was Googling passwords, pass phrases, encryption, brute-forcing encryption, and everything else I could think of that might pertain to my new task. And in my scant free time, I'd tried to wrangle my feelings about my father's secret life. A secret life that was adjacent to my professional life. So far, my feelings had slipped the lasso every single time.

Half of Wednesday was spent getting my tickets to give me access to this new program, which was basically staring at a classified computer, reading documents about what I'd be working on, then signing more documents to pinkie swear I wouldn't disclose what I knew. Of course I had, and had had, access to other Secret and Top Secret programs, but because this was an entirely new one—a new one that had files about my father that were still classified—I had to be read in to it.

On Thursday morning, I'd given Lennon a list of equipment for my new workspace, and by Friday morning, he'd delivered. When I let myself into the fifth-floor office, piles of brand-new furniture, electronics, kitchen amenities, and tech equipment were stacked neatly around the room. Geez, couldn't have had the office set up for me, could you, Lennon? And given Jeffrey's uncooperative spine, I'd be dragging these desks into position by myself. Don't mind me, just the lead on one of the most important tasks of the century and I'm doubling as a mover.

Because it'd been converted from one of the smaller conference rooms, my office had a fridge/freezer in the tiny kitchenette, as well as plenty of space for desks, conferencing, and even a spot I'd designated my Zen Zone for meditation—hard to do yoga in work clothes. When Lennon first showed me the space on Wednesday afternoon, I'd raised an eyebrow at him. "Are you trying to keep me in here all day by giving me everything I want?"

And Lennon had chuckled. "Of course not. We just thought it would be nice for you to have whatever you might need in here. Being comfortable and relaxed results in good work."

And he'd done everything to ensure just that. I checked off everything on my list—all accounted for—then decided it was time to get down to business. If I'd known I'd be spending most of the day moving heavy things around, I would have dressed down a little. I pulled off my blazer and rolled up the sleeves of my seafoam-green linen button-up, ready to haul around and arrange some furniture. And there was a lot of furniture to haul around and arrange. The only thing already in place was a safe—big enough to hold a few file boxes—bolted to the wall in the corner. The door was open and instructions for setting biometric and numerical locks rested on top.

I'd just unwrapped my new leather executive chair and plonked down in it—hey, if I was going to be responsible for uncovering possibly one of the biggest cadres of foreign operatives in the United States, my ass and back deserved comfort—when someone knocked on the door. Given the office was unmarked (shame, I could have had *Lexie's Code Cracking Club* on the door), it could only be one of three people. I was surprised to see Lennon rather than Derek or Jeffrey, because "I thought you had an access card for this office," I said once I'd closed the door behind him.

He set a file box onto the kitchenette counter. "I do, but this is your workspace and unless I need to access it in an emergency, I will respect that."

I wondered what constituted an emergency in this assignment. "Okay, thanks. The less people interrupting my brainstorming, the better."

"That's what I thought." He looked around the room, more like a construction site than an office at the moment. Lennon passed me the tape-sealed file box. "These are the files from your father's career."

"Wow," I said as I took custody of the box. I quickly set it down on one of the plastic-wrapped desks. It was heavy—clearly my dad was a prolific intel officer. "Well, isn't this old-school cool. Shouldn't these have been digitized?"

"They have been, but I thought you might want to see the originals."

I'd had no real opinion either way, but now I thought about it, it was kind of cool to see the physical information on, and collected by, my father. Especially now I knew he was actually an undercover operative, not just a diplomat. I fingered the security tape holding the box closed. "And do you have the hard drive he gave you?"

He looked like I'd just asked him to give me a kidney, but dipped into his inner jacket pocket and handed me a USB thumb drive. "This is a cloned copy," he said, as if that were the most important thing about this external media, that he really wanted me to know I wasn't allowed to handle the master.

"I'd expected nothing less." I held it up and mocked out a salute with it. "Thanks. Being able to see what I'm supposed to be getting the pass phrase for should help." It was a long shot, but maybe there was a password hint or something that would pop up when I tried to open whatever was on the drive. *Long* long shot—if there was a hint or a prompt, Lennon would have seen that already and figured it out.

"One more thing." He went to the door and opened it to a late-thirties guy I'd never seen before. Wonder how long he'd been creeping outside my door, holding on to that cart with a computer tower and monitor on it. Lennon didn't introduce us, which I took to mean I didn't need to know who this was. "Here's your PC from downstairs so you can access your agency emails. And my technician is going to whitelist the thumb drive you'll be working with on the laptop, and block access to all others."

I shrugged. "Okay." It was a logical precaution, and one I didn't take personally. Any sort of external drive in my place of employment could be…problematic. To avoid leaks, our work computers didn't have USB ports, but obviously I needed one in the laptop to access the drive.

After quickly setting up my work PC and reconnecting it to the agency network, Mr. No-name took the cloned drive, plugged it in to the laptop, and did some tech stuff while Lennon and I stared at each other. Then he gave me back the drive and left without saying a word. Friendly guy.

I turned the thumb drive over in my hand. "I assume cloning an encrypted drive hasn't caused problems?"

"My technician assured me that the software is highly sophisticated. And the encryption is definitely still in place on your copy," he added ruefully, like he'd expected cloning the drive might strip away any encryption and solve all his problems. Lennon's expression shifted, and I watched him, trying to figure out where he might take the conversation. Though I would say I knew him well enough, our time together hadn't been face-to-face until this week, and I was still working out his expressions. Out of the blue, he urged, "Speaking of technicians. Alexandra, I'm afraid you cannot ask Scott to help you with this."

Shit. I'd been planning on doing exactly that, because if anyone could get somewhere they weren't supposed to inside computer spaces, it was my old pal Bianca "Bink" Scott. They'd helped me out with the Kunduz Intelligence, copying files from the agency server for me when I'd been locked out. Bink had worked in naval intelligence, but now they freelanced, including for the government, and could get into basically any place that was built of 1s and 0s. "Well, that makes it a lot harder."

Lennon's expression was unapologetic. "The only people, other than me and the person I've been working with to brute-force the encryption, who may have eyes on this, are you and Burton. No exceptions."

"Seems a little extreme."

His face closed off. "Extreme is what keeps us safe. We don't know who these operatives are, Alexandra, what we might find behind the encryption. Exercise the highest level of caution."

"I will."

Lennon's eye contact turned intense. "And, Alexandra, I know I don't need to tell you this, but if you break the encryption on that drive, the contents are not for your eyes."

I held back a sigh. "Yes, I know." While I'd been read in, I'd noted my tickets didn't give me clearance to view the contents of the drive, only my dad's career files.

He nodded once, decisively, before his expression smoothed back to his usual blank impassivity. "Burton is downstairs being read in to this program, and once he's done and gets his new credentials organized he should come right up."

"Great. I need someone to help me move all this furniture into a proper feng shui arrangement," I deadpanned.

No reaction, not even a chuckle. I used to get chuckles all the time during our phone conversations. Lennon had apparently lost what little sense of humor he had since taking up his new role as agency director. Or I was losing my wit. No, that wasn't it. I was funny. The problem was him. "As you requested, Burton has been brought up to speed on Halcyon. Not everything about us, obviously," he hastened to add. "Just our existence and mission statement, the information that we give all prospective Halcyon agents. So you're free to discuss Halcyon's operations with him, but obviously without revealing classified specifics."

"Thank you."

"If you need me to clarify anything, you know where to find me. Otherwise, I'll leave you to it."

A little before ten thirty a.m., after I'd denuded both desks, the conference table, and chairs of all packaging, I discovered the beep of the card reader outside was audible inside. Good to know I had an alarm of sorts to alert me to visitors.

Jeffrey flung the door wide and dumped his leather messenger bag on the kitchenette counter before closing the door. He grinned. "Well, well, well, if it isn't my favorite person." He opened his arms for a hug and I went to him immediately. "Sorry I couldn't get here earlier. Dominique and I were in Mallorca." He gave me a tight squeeze as he teased, "I needed a vacation after that last job with you." The last job where he had been assigned to protect me, and had done just that.

"Shit, I'm so sorry about dragging you away from a vacation." I let go of him and instantly missed the comfort. Damn, now I was single, I was starved for hugs. I shoved the thought into a back corner of my mind because I couldn't do anything about it. "Your wife must really hate me." First I'd taken him away from home for Thanksgiving and Christmas and kept him away for six months, then put him in physical danger, and now I'd interrupted a vacation they'd probably planned well in advance to reconnect after being separated for half a year because of me.

Jeffrey shrugged. "Mallorca will still be there once this assignment is done. And with all the money I'll make from this gig, fuck, I might just take a year off, rent a villa in Tuscany for twelve months, and we'll have a real vacation."

"Thanks for rubbing it in," I said dryly. I was well paid too, especially by Halcyon, but I wasn't quite "take a yearlong vacation and rent a Tuscan villa" well paid. My Halcyon salary was paid into a high-interest offshore account, where I'd decided to leave it untouched until I retired.

"You're welcome." Jeffrey checked out the fridge. "This needs to be stocked," he pointed out.

"I know. Work-kitchen shopping is on my list of things to do over the weekend." I'd already collected my most important work accessories—my Oolong tea stash and strainer from the common break room down on my old floor. "You can bring in whatever coffee you want for the pod machine." Pod machine instead of drip. I really was a big deal.

"Will do." Jeffrey straightened the electric kettle. It was the first thing I'd unboxed and set up—tea breaks were life. "So, who's actually in charge of this assignment?"

"I am."

He let out an exaggerated sigh. "Obviously. I meant is it an agency task or…someone else's task?"

"Someone else's," I said, playing along with his crypticness.

"I see. And do you do things like this for 'someone else' a lot?"

"Not exactly like this, no. But 'someone else' keeps me busy."

"I suppose you're their star employee." At my eye-rolly nod, he grinned. "Not that I'm complaining. Halcyon is keeping me employed again, though I didn't know it was Halcyon before." He shook his head, whistling through his teeth. "All that, right under our noses. Almost makes you wonder what else we don't know about, doesn't it."

"It does."

"So, why you?"

"Because apparently I'm the only one who can do this. So it's all on me. Or…on us now."

He chuckled. "You've come a long way, kid."

"Don't I know it," I mumbled. "Now come on and help me get everything set up. I'll do all the heavy lifting and you can unpack your laptop and get it set up. There's no network functionality, at all, they're just plain workhorse machines for notes and whatnot, so if we need to research anything, we have to go out to our cars and use our phones."

"Wow. Serious secret-squirrel business."

"You could say that. I figure we set things up today, then get into the actual assignment fresh on Monday."

Jeffrey saluted sharply. "Yes, boss."

"Call me that again and I'm going to have you removed from the assignment. Also, touch my Oolong and I'll have you removed. Interrupt my meditation and I'll—"

"Have me removed," he finished with another broad grin. "You seem to forget we lived together for six months. And you also seem to have forgotten that I don't like plain tea."

"Oh that's right. But I converted you to the local chai, didn't I?" I mused, feigning thoughtfulness. "And eggplant, and—"

"Yeah, yeah." He bumped me with his shoulder. "You're a hero."

"Don't forget it. Now, come on, let me show you around."

Jeffrey followed me while I pointed things out. There wasn't much to point out.

"This desk will be yours." He dumped his bag on it. "And so is this." I passed over the laptop box with BURTON written on it in Sharpie. "How much convincing did it take for you to accept this assignment, especially without actually being told what it was you were doing?"

"None," he said instantly. "Apart from lazing on a Mediterranean beach with my beautiful wife, I had nothing to do after our last adventure together except relax and wait for job offers. When Lennon called and asked me to step in, I didn't hesitate. They pay really *really* well, I'm working close to home, so who cares what it is? Not to mention, it's working with you. No reason to say no."

"You'd better not be getting paid more than I am."

He grinned as he opened the sealed laptop box. "I'm a contractor, so of course I am."

I narrowed my eyes at him, until an unpleasant realization struck. Halcyon, or rather, Lennon, had employed Jeffrey to accompany me on my failed overseas assignment. I'd assumed he was working for the agency in the same context as I was but as it turned out, his main role was, unbeknownst to me at the time, to protect me. Which he had. Maybe Halcyon or Lennon had employed him before that. "Were you contracted by *them* to debrief me?"

Jeffrey paused, and I knew him well enough to know he'd picked up on the fact I was avoiding saying *Halcyon*. Though, given Lennon was Halcyon, not saying Halcyon seemed kind of silly. "Back in October?"

"Mhmm, back in October."

"No, that was government work."

"Okay. Good." Knowing Halcyon had contracted someone to debrief and humiliate me, and then forced me to live and work with that someone for six months would make me seriously reconsider my second employer.

"So are you actually going to tell me what the assignment is? I just finished being read in, but aside from the usual classified secrecy don't share or you're in trouble, it was…vague, and basically defers everything to you. So, you, what's my assignment? Or is it just setting up this big office? Because you picked the wrong person there, Lexie." He pointed at his lower back.

"I know. You're the last person I'd have chosen for that." Jeffrey Burton may have back issues, but he also had access to some of the most closely held compartmented programs in intel, and I didn't hesitate to explain why I'd dragged him away from his vacation that I hadn't even known about. "Remember that conversation we had at the airport when we came home, about why I'd been released after the Kunduz Intelligence with no real ramifications? And you said I must have something they want." He nodded. "You were right. Turns out, my dad wasn't just a diplomat, he was also an undercover intelligence officer."

Jeffrey didn't blink, so I kept explaining. "And his lifelong mission was finding foreign operatives within America so they could be removed."

Still no blink.

"Dad gave someone a hard drive of his work, and they think it contains information on those foreign operatives who are still here. But the drive is encrypted, obviously, and he neglected to share the password or pass phrase with the person he entrusted the drive to." I was still wrapping my head around the logistics of that oversight. "All other options to decrypt it have failed, and they think I might know the key to unlocking it. But I have no idea what it could be because obviously it's not really something my dad discussed with me, like 'Good night, Lexie, and by the way I'm actually an American spy and remember this special password until you'll need it one day in the maybe distant or maybe not-so-distant future.'"

Jeffrey snorted. "Of course not, that would make everything far too easy."

"Right? So, yeah, I might somehow know the key, or how to work out the key, that will unlock it. Or maybe I don't. But it seems like I'm their last resort, so that's why I'm so special."

"I'll say." He rubbed his hands together. "So we're codebreaking? Excellent."

"Pretty much. But also not codebreaking so much as me just… brainstorming and trying anything we can to figure it out. So I need an assistant of sorts to help me go through whatever mountains of intelligence I happen to come across, chase up leads, that sort of thing."

He clasped his hands in front of his chest. "And you thought of lil ol' me? I'm flattered."

"Don't be," I said instantly, but I was smiling as I burst his bubble. "The list of people with the clearance for this task who are also on my list of people I could stand working with and also trust to see some of my family history and secrets is a Venn diagram with a one-person overlap. You."

"Ouch." Jeffrey's furrowed eyebrows softened out. "But also, still flattering. Have you had any thoughts about what the password could be?"

"Not really. I was only assigned this on Monday, when I was also told my dad had lied to me my whole life, so most of my thoughts have been about how my already complicated feelings regarding my parents have become way more complicated." I loved my parents. I missed my parents. But my parents weren't what I would class as affectionate, and though I'd never wanted for material things growing up, I'd always felt like I'd missed out on something I couldn't even name. Maybe it was the product of moving so much because of Dad's work. Maybe it was just my parents, moderate with everything, including affection. "And I've spent this week getting read in, researching passwords, and explaining without explaining to my colleagues why I'm leaving my cozy cubicle for yet another weird assignment."

"Understandable. So, if you *do* know the password, it's either a word or phrase you know because of your dad, or you've been given the things you need to discover what it is, which only you can do because only you know what to look for."

"Right. My Googling says the most secure passwords are long ones with mixes of upper and lower case, numbers, and symbols. But even more secure is a bunch of random words, like…purple monkey space helicopter, and that's called a pass phrase. Given they've been trying to brute-force the encryption for over a year with no success, I think it's a random jumble of words making a pass phrase."

"Okay, so we just need to find a bunch of random words?"

"I *think* so? But I also can't be sure it's not a password like… Alexandra!123." I leaned back against the desk, crossing my feet at the ankles. "But, knowing my father, and now knowing what he really did, I believe that if he wanted me to know the pass phrase he would have given me all the tools I needed to figure it out. Because I'm absolutely certain he didn't tell me outright in some way."

Jeffrey rubbed his freshly shaven chin. "Okay. Then let's start with that angle."

"I honestly have no idea where to start, except to read these classified documents about his life and work," I said, gesturing to the file box.

He nodded slowly, thoughtfully, as he cast his eye toward the box. "I think that's as good a place to start as any, get some notes down, a feel for his state of mind and what he might have been thinking when he locked that hard drive up good and tight. Did he ever give you anything as a gift that seemed odd? Like a codebreaking book? Because that would be really helpful."

The Longines watch on my wrist suddenly felt like it weighed a ton, and I fought to not react to the phantom sensation. My father had given me the flashy, not-really-my-style wristwatch for my thirtieth birthday. He'd also had *Little Mouse* and *XXX* engraved on two of the metal bands. I knew the meaning of both, but they didn't seem unusual or portentous in any way. An old nickname, and the Roman numerals for thirty.

For some reason, I wasn't quite ready to share this with Jeffrey, so I rolled my eyes, trying to project mild exasperation and amusement. "All my dad's gifts were odd, but no codebreaking books unfortunately. This weekend, I'll start compiling everything he ever gave me, but I guess I'll also have to go into the storage unit and have a dig around in my parents' personal effects. See if there's anything that screams 'I'm useful.'" I still hadn't been in there since I'd emptied out their house before selling it, mostly because those things were just things, not my parents. And there honestly wasn't much, due to their spartan, itinerant lifestyle. I had a sudden pang of panic that my dad might have engraved something onto one of the pieces of furniture I'd donated to Goodwill. Just as quickly, I dismissed the thought. He would never be so careless.

"Ohh, like a real-life *Storage Wars*. Count me in."

"Maybe later. Right now, it'd be a show called *Set Up This Office Wars*."

Jeffrey's expression fell. "Boring. That's not a show I want to watch, Lexie."

"Well, you're not watching our fake television show. You're participating in it."

"Fun." He bounced his eyebrows comically. "Dominique is thrilled we're working together again, and she's already mentioned having you over for dinner a couple of times." He'd said something about that when we'd said our goodbyes at the airport a few weeks ago, and I was comforted to know his wife was also on board with his invitation.

"Even after what happened the last time you were assigned to support me? How is your ass, by the way?" When he'd shielded me from the explosion, he'd taken a fuckton of glass and metal in his back, butt, and legs. I'd had to pick out each piece, and treat the wounds.

He looked behind himself. "Healing well. As is the rest of the back of me. There's just those few large shrapnel wounds that haven't fully healed yet, but no pain, so it's a win."

"Have you healed well enough to help me set up the rest of this stuff?"

"Assuming you remember our heavy-lifting arrangement, then yes, I have."

By one p.m., we'd unpacked all the furniture and set it up in a way we were both happy with, decided after much rational discussion and utilizing the knowledge about each other we'd gained from six months living and working in an apartment together. The desks were set up facing each other with a long table between them so the workspace looked like a large capital I. We could use the table between our desks to sprawl our work out a little, or even have meetings if need be.

We set up the laptops with our respective private security credentials, and I noted that we had different models. Mine had one USB port, presumably because I'd demanded access to my dad's hard drive. But Jeffrey's was a slim machine with no ports at all—in fact, it was so slim it looked like it barely contained essential computing functions. Lennon was clearly controlling who had access to my dad's data, though given Jeffrey and I worked in close proximity, it wasn't like he couldn't look over my shoulder. But I knew he wouldn't unless I invited him to.

The Zen Zone in the back corner was closed off with Japanese privacy screens for me to have a quiet space if I needed to meditate. It was amazing what you could get when you were important. I'd have to bring in a few things to Zen up the space, and make sure I wore work clothes that were easy to sit on the ground in, but I knew Jeffrey would leave me alone and be quiet if I ever went into the Zone.

We'd been through a list of break-room food and beverage essentials, and I'd agreed to purchase what we needed over the weekend so we could have the best-stocked kitchenette in the entire building. Lennon had someone come in to clear the environmental-nightmare amount of packaging, which meant the room finally looked like an actual office. Jeffrey gave himself a literal pat on his fragile back.

After eating a late lunch in the ground-floor cafeteria, we came back up to dive into the box of my dad's classified life. Even though I'd had days to come to terms with it, I still felt nervous and uneasy about what I might find. Jeffrey and I rolled our chairs around to opposite sides of the long side of the table between our desks.

"We should go into office design," he said. "This is genius."

"When I said I've spent most of the week WTF-ing over my dad, I wasn't exactly truthful. I've also been mentally building my dream office." I dragged the file box to the middle of the table and fiddled with it until its sides were parallel with the table's. Stalling, by any chance, Lexie?

"Do you need a moment?" Jeffrey asked gently.

"No, I don't. I don't know why I feel weird about reading these." I took a deep breath, cut the security tape and pulled the lid off my father's secret life. After laying out the folders, I decided his secret life actually looked pretty boring.

We spent thirty minutes going through the dossiers and sorting them by date. Each one had a big bold CLASSIFIED coversheet, and then a newer stamp with the initials MAL—Michael A. Lennon perhaps?—on it. The folders were well-thumbed. I wondered why my dad's files had been handled so much, and by whom. Probably Lennon, trying to do the task he'd assigned to me, and clearly failing.

I discovered my dad had been active as an undercover officer from 1978 until 2019, when he moved into a handler role. Who better to handle undercover intelligence officers than a former undercover intelligence officer? My parents had died in July 2021, and Dad supposedly retired in 2019. Retired my ass. Try retired from his diplomat-slash-spy job so he could take up another job as a handler. After that "retirement," he and my mom vacationed overseas a few times a year, all over the globe, usually for a week or so at a time. Now I wondered if he wasn't actually making contact, handling his assets. Or maybe he was still gathering intelligence. And if Mom was unaware of his true occupation, how the hell was he doing this right under her nose? And I thought I was a good liar. Guess it was genetic.

We'd given each folder a cursory look to make sure we had every year, when I decided I'd had enough. Emotionally and physically. The best thing about this assignment was that I didn't technically have set office hours, but I'd decided to stick roughly to my normal work schedule. Roughly. After almost fifteen years in this job, I knew what worked for me. I pulled off my glasses and put them in their case. "Let's start fresh on Monday." I rubbed my eyes, but the grit stubbornly refused to budge. "I'm going to start making lists of all 'Dad gifts' and whatnot over the weekend and maybe I'll get the urge to start looking into them. If the inspiration to dig deep into the items doesn't strike, then at least we'll have a list."

"Sounds good." Jeffrey glanced at the time. "Are we not working regular hours?"

"We're working whatever needs to be worked. Or at a least I am. And if my brain is fried and useless by four on a Friday afternoon, then that's when I'm finishing up. If you want to stay here and stare at the walls, be my guest."

"No way. Getting home before dinner? Lexie, my wife is going to love you. And I'm going to give you the highest rating on that employer-rating website."

"Wait until you hear about our job benefits," I joked.

We locked the laptops and the dossiers in the safe and gathered our things. Jeffrey checked the door was locked, and we walked in step to the elevators. The ride down was comfortably silent, and I kept my thoughts away from what remained upstairs in my office. If I let myself get too caught up in everything I'd discovered about my family, I was going to lose my shit. So, like a normal person with a normal job, I let myself think about being home at a reasonable hour for my hypothetical future girlfriend. A nice thought.

I wished the security staff a good evening and nice weekend, and stepped out into the gorgeous late-spring afternoon. We'd walked twenty meters away from the building when Jeffrey placed his hand on my shoulder and pulled me to a stop. "Hey. If you're worried someone might be listening in there, or you just want me to trust you, then ask me out for a drink, and I'll know we need to talk about something." He squeezed lightly then dropped his hand.

"Will we actually be getting a drink, or just talking while we walk to our cars or something?"

He grinned. "We can absolutely get a drink. We can get a couple of drinks. Maybe even some food if you're nice."

"Thank you. My social life is abysmal and drinking over discussing state secrets might just fill that void." The void left when my girlfriend, my gorgeous, fabulous, funny, kind girlfriend, the one I thought I'd be with forever, broke up with me.

Jeffrey laughed. "If having drinks and snacks with me gets you excited, then yeah, your social life really is abysmal." He gave me a quick hug. "See you Monday. Don't think too hard this weekend, Lexie. You don't get paid to think on weekends."

CHAPTER THREE

I have promises to keep

I spent Friday night lingering over a bottle of excellent pinot noir I'd been saving. It was not only delicious, but lowered my guard enough to aid my conclusion that I was really fucking lonely. It seemed obvious—drinking at home *alone* to start my weekend—but my loneliness went beyond that. Even during the breakup, when I was overseas, Jeffrey had been there 24/7. I wasn't alone. But now I was home, coming back to my empty apartment each night, I was clobbered by how much I wished it wasn't empty. Add to that the bombshell of my father's true occupation, and I felt like I was walking a tightrope and had forgotten to clip on a safety line.

Thanks, Dad.

I shook the thought out. It wasn't his fault. Actually, it was nice to imagine that he might have trusted me with the information to unlock his most important work. And it was a good change of pace and distraction from the shit show of my life. Case in point? In the maelstrom of the past week, I'd totally forgotten about Sophia's hidden message. But now I was still and silent and alone and had time to think, thoughts of Sophia barreled to the forefront. I stared at the bottle on the coffee table, unsurprised by the sadness that swamped me. I'd been planning on opening this bottle with her for an anniversary.

I swapped my book for my phone and opened the tab with the blurb for *Sinka's Sacrifice*, the novel Sophia had led me to with a code—an ISBN—on a piece of paper hidden in one of my work suits. The novel was unavailable for purchase, which made me think that everything I needed had already been given to me in that blurb. As far as hidden messages went, it was a good one, and as I skimmed the text for what felt like the hundredth time, I tried to reconcile this story, of a woman sacrificing herself to protect her kingdom and her family, with what Sophia had done.

It seemed obvious, didn't it? That she'd broken up with me to protect herself, or me, or her family, or all of us, rather than because she didn't want to be in a relationship with me. Blaming external forces rather than accepting the fact that I was flawed made me feel marginally better, but it wasn't an absolute truth. She had many ways to contact me, with no one knowing, to tell me the truth about the breakup. And she hadn't. She'd broken up with me, broken off contact with me, and left me broken.

Maybe I should call her. Tell her I was home. Ask her to explain.

Oh that's a *great* idea, *exactly* what someone in a weird headspace who's been drinking should do. The problem was that I just didn't know what I should do. I'd absolutely accepted our breakup, months ago, but I hadn't entirely moved on. I still loved her and wanted to be with her. But the circumstances around the breakup were muddying the waters because I didn't have a clear answer about her motivation. The book-blurb clue pushed me slightly more toward the "she was manipulated into breaking up with me" side of the scale. And that hope that it wasn't me who'd caused the breakup felt nice. But was hope enough? I thought it was, but I'd been tricked before, hoping desperately the breakup wasn't real and thinking hope might sustain me until I could fix whatever the problem was. But it was real and there had been no hope.

You need to talk to her, Lexie. Just…not right now. Maybe when I'd figured out all this shit with my dad's work, I'd reach out to Sophia. If nothing else, I was insanely curious about what her reference to *Sinka's Sacrifice* really meant. And giving myself some time to work on myself could only be a good thing. But, fuck, I really wished I had someone right now to go to bed with, sit on the couch and talk or not talk with, eat with, laugh with, cry with…

Desperate for human connection, I decided on an early-morning yoga class. An hour of Vinyasa, surrounded by people, sharing their energy, was exactly what I needed to reenergize. If I was going to go to an early yoga class in the morning, drinking a whole bottle of wine wasn't a great idea. I corked the pinot with a little less than half left. And then I went to bed alone.

* * *

Yoga with a mild hangover is both horrendous and helpful. I breathed my way through my discomfort, absorbing the atmosphere and energy and allowing my body to guide me into the spaces it needed. By the time the class had wound down and I'd lowered myself onto my back for Savasana, I felt like I could do anything, or nothing, and it would all be okay.

My yoga teacher's voice floated around the room, low, melodic, and soothing. "Good, good. Relax, focus on your breath. Draw it deep into your belly, feel it nourish your body, then exhale out any negative energy. Deep breaths, in…and out…Now begin to wiggle out those fingers and toes as you come back into your body."

I lay still for a few extra seconds after the class ended before I rolled onto my side and pushed myself up. Low chatter surrounded me as everyone packed up their mats and props. A woman I'd seen in a few weekday evening classes smiled at me, holding eye contact, and I smiled back. She'd been smiling at me after class a lot. Was she trying to flirt…without actually saying anything? Or was I just reading into nothing more than friendly good vibes?

A year ago, I wouldn't have thought anything more of it beyond what I saw at face value. But since Sophia…and then no Sophia, I'd let myself become more open to emotional possibilities. So, maybe cute yoga woman was flirting, maybe she was just being nice, maybe she thought I was a basket case. But whatever her reason, the brief moment of connection had felt good. I rolled my mat, looped the strap around each end, then slung it over my shoulders and across my chest like a cosplayer's scabbard. After collecting my phone and keys from my small locker, I exited the studio to a slew of cheerful goodbyes and promises to see each other in another class.

My weekend yoga routine was to walk the two miles to the studio and back, but after my class, I'd detour for coffee and maybe a sweet treat. Okay, always a sweet treat. Now we were right at the beginning of summer, the warmth was hovering at "pleasant" but would soon edge into "unbearable," and I let myself enjoy the weather as I wandered along the sidewalk.

The café a block from the studio was its usual Saturday morning crowded, and unless I wanted to share a table, which I didn't, it'd have to be a to-go order today. I slipped into the takeout line behind a couple in their sixties, and unlocked my phone for some mindless waiting scrolling.

Weather looked good for a hike tomorrow. Maybe I should suck it up, wake up before dawn and head out to—

A woman's laugh froze my thoughts.

I hadn't heard that laugh since January, and it made every hair on my body stand up. I spun around without thinking—because why not act on impulse when you've just heard something you thought you'd never hear again—and tried to isolate where the sound had come from. About fifteen feet away, a woman with dark, curly hair up in a loose bun sat with her back to me. She sat opposite another woman with a reddish-blond bob, very attractive, also laughing. Now I was homed in, I could hear the conversation and that voice—low, husky like she'd just woken up—and I wanted to pass out and cry and throw up and run away and go over there. The dark-haired woman facing away from me laughed again and reached across the table to grip the other woman's hand, confirming my sick suspicion. Not that I needed it confirmed.

Oh my god. I turned away from them, my mind spinning a million revolutions a minute. What in the actual fuck was Sophia doing *here*? With her girlfriend. The new girlfriend that wasn't me, because she'd broken up with me. This café wasn't close to her apartment, and she'd never once mentioned it while we were together, and she'd mentioned a lot of cafés. She loved cafés. I loved cafés. Oh my god. I dragged my runaway thoughts back to the here and now, back to the woman who'd dumped me—maybe or maybe not because she'd been forced to—and the fact she was right near me with her new girlfriend.

Be smart, Lexie. You haven't been together for over four months. People change. People go places they didn't before and freak you out because your previously safe ex-free place is now no longer safely ex-free. Well, this cemented it. I needed a new post-yoga coffee and sweet-treat spot. Maybe I needed to find a new yoga studio. Actually, maybe I just needed a whole new city. Or country.

Sweat ran down my spine, pooled under my armpits, and cooled on my bare arms and shoulders in the air-conditioned café. I shuddered. Do I stay and ignore her? Stay and approach her? Leave as fast as I can? Vaporize into thin air to escape what might be the world's most awkward scenario? The line moved and I shuffled forward automatically, too close to the couple in front, so I shuffled back, earning a quiet, "Hey" from the guy behind me when I bumped him with my yoga mat.

"Sorry," I mumbled. The heat tendrilling up my neck reached my ears, heating them until I was sure all my skin was turning beet red.

Oh god. I can't do this. I need to leave. But I couldn't make my feet move. Until I heard Sophia's low, amused laugh again.

Okay. Leave. Leave now.

I spun around to slip out of line, carelessly I'll admit, and again lightly tapped the man behind me with my mat.

"Watch it," he grumbled. "Yoga jerk."

"Sorry," I said again, as sincerely as I could while trying to be quiet and inconspicuous.

"Yeah, well, sorry's great but maybe watch where you're swinging that thing. No fucking manners," he added under his breath.

I straightened up, drawing my shoulders back. "It was an accident, obviously," I said evenly. "And again, I'm very sorry for accidentally tapping you very lightly on your elbow with a soft foam mat." I shouldn't be having this conversation with him. I should leave. Quietly. Calmly. But this dickface was pressing my buttons. I layered on the sarcasm. "I promise I'll never do it again."

Whatever he said in response didn't register, because the last person in the world I wanted to turn around turned around, and all I heard was her soft gasp, the quick inhalation, the whispered, "Lexie?"

Oh no, oh no no no no. Not this. Not now.

I rushed past Mr. Don't Touch Me With Your Yoga Mat, not caring if he got another tap or even a whack, and toward the exit as quickly as I could. The sound of a chair scraping roughly on the floor was followed quickly by Sophia calling, "Lexie!" from behind me as I pushed through the door.

I ignored her, hoping to get outside and vaporize into the atmosphere before I had to look at her again, before I had to talk to her, before I forgot everything that'd happened and touched her. I wasn't prepared for this. My feelings were so close to the surface and it would take nothing for them to spill out into the world for everyone to see.

Sophia's voice was even louder now, carrying over the noise of people and cars swirling around me. "Lexie! Stop! Wait."

I didn't want to stop. I didn't want to wait. But a firm hand on my bicep shut my legs down and I stopped dead on the sidewalk. Sophia's firm grip held me in place, and she pulled gently until I turned around. She looked like she'd seen a dead person, her hands moving up and down my arms as if testing I was actually there. Without saying anything, she yanked me closer and wrapped her arms around me, burying her face into my shoulder the way she always did…always *had* when we hugged.

And for just one second, I let myself imagine that nothing between us had changed, and relaxed into her embrace. Until the unfortunate reality of everything having changed quickly stiffened my body again. Sophia, apparently registering that my arms remained firmly by my sides instead of stealing around her, dropped me like my skin had burned her. Her expression contorted from pleasure to confusion to anxiety. "Sorry," she said breathlessly. "I didn't mean to—I just…I didn't expect—" She inhaled slowly, pushing her hands into the front pockets of her jeans. "My god. I…you look great. It's so good to see you. When did you get back?"

That quick, but fierce, one-sided hug had left me trembling, and I wrapped my arms around myself, desperately trying to stop the shiver. "Two weeks ago." I mentally patted myself on the back for not only answering, but getting it out without stammering or spewing.

Her expression contorted into upset. "Why didn't you let me know? You said you would."

"I did," I agreed, carefully keeping my tone neutral. "But then you broke up with me completely out of nowhere and I guess I just didn't feel like texting to tell you I was home when we weren't even together. You also didn't contact me at all, so I assumed that we're no longer even classed as friends." I hadn't meant to say it, and I hated myself for the cruelty, especially after I'd decided less than twelve hours ago that I was going to reach out to her. But having her right there put a sledgehammer through my carefully constructed plan.

Sophia's mouth fell open. She slowly closed it again. Without breaking eye contact she said steadily, "I deserve that."

I stared at her, as if I could see what she really thought just by looking at her. But there was nothing except a carefully cultivated blankness to her expression. I wanted to tell her she *did* deserve that. That she deserved my anger and my upset and so much more. But, like a mute idiot, I said nothing.

Sophia raised a hand as if to touch my face, then snatched it back. "Your eyebrow. It's been cut. What happened?"

"I ran into the ground at high speed." Assisted by an explosion. An explosion caused by a woman I'd once been intimate with, a long, long time ago.

Sophia gave me a look that told me she knew I was being evasive. A look I knew too well. "Are you hurt?" she asked, with only the slightest waver in the question.

"No," I said honestly. I wasn't hurting anymore, in any sense of the word.

She exhaled noisily. "Good. Listen, about what happened, I—"

Thankfully we were interrupted before I could interrupt her to tell her I couldn't do this, not here, not now. The woman who'd been sitting opposite my ex-girlfriend appeared like she'd teleported from inside to ask, "Sophia? Everything okay?"

Sophia spun around to face her incredibly attractive companion. Who was I kidding? She spun around to face her incredibly attractive girlfriend. "Yeah, everything's fine. Sorry. I'll be right in."

The unknown woman eyed me dubiously, but acquiesced with a nod. "Sure, I'll just be inside then. If you need me, let me know," she added, a protective note lacing the words. That tone made my stomach queasy, and I didn't care to examine all the reasons why at that moment.

Sophia lightly touched the woman's arm. "I will. Thanks." The moment we were alone again, she turned her focus back to me. Her intense focus. I wanted to squirm and wilt under it, but I kept myself upright, standing tall, breathing steadily. Sophia smiled. "Maybe we could meet up for coffee, or—"

I cut her off, even though I'd spent the last four and a half months desperate to hear her say something exactly like what she was saying, even though I'd made plans to contact her so one of us could say those words. I just…I wasn't ready. I needed to prepare. I needed to better myself. My voice quavered slightly when I said, "Sophia, look, I can't do this right now. I'm sorry. It…was…nice seeing you. You look—" I faltered. Incredible, amazing, beautiful, like you're totally over me and completely unaffected by the breakup. "Good," I finished lamely.

"Thanks?"

It took an immense effort, but I forced my mouth into a smile. "So, I really have to go, but it was nice seeing you." You already said that, dumbass. But I couldn't make myself say anything else, anything meaningful. Because if I said something meaningful I was going to lose my shit and I couldn't do that there where I was so exposed.

"Lexie…" She sounded as if she was on the verge of tears and I gripped the strap of my yoga mat firmly to stop myself from physically comforting her.

And I felt like a fucking monster for just leaving her standing there about to cry while I walked away with nothing more than a mumbled, "Bye, take care," because if I did or said anything more, I was going to fall to the sidewalk right there and bawl my eyes out.

I did bawl, just a little, in my shower at home after class. Post-yoga showers were usually high on my list of relaxing events, but as I sobbed into my facewash, I felt anything but relaxed. I was all for things that built character. All for karmic give-and-take. But I was starting to wonder why exactly I'd had so much shit thrown at me during the past eight months. At this rate I was going to have built so much character I could carry a movie on my own.

After a calming cup of tea, I had a sudden urge to text Sophia to apologize for acting like an emotional mute. To explain she'd totally surprised me and I'd been too busy trying to cope with my feelings and panic to be open to talking with her. To tell her to come around, sans attractive girlfriend please, that I wanted to clear the air and find out the truth. So I locked my phone in my safe which was a totally mature and rational response to wanting to text your ex.

To distract myself, I decided to go through all my possessions and set aside everything my dad had given me as a "special" gift—something different from the usual parents' gifts for my birthday or Christmas. It was a great way to kill a few hours and distract myself from the unsettling meeting with my ex-girlfriend.

When I was done sorting through my things, I had a watch and some hardcover books. Inventive gift giver, that was my father. I'd never read any of the books because they were thick tomes that didn't align with my literary tastes. And now I thought about it, he'd never asked me if I'd read them, nor wanted to discuss the prose, which was...odd for my dad.

Dad was intelligent and loved cerebral discussions, but I'd always felt like these gifts were just gifts for the sake of gifts, because who expects anyone to appreciate *War and Peace*? Now, that strangeness made me think they were more important than just a father giving his daughter something. Or maybe I was simply allocating more importance to them now I knew who he really was.

I already knew what was inscribed on the metal band of my wristwatch, so I laid out the books on my coffee table, in date-gifted order.

Moby Dick
1984
Don Quixote
War and Peace
Ulysses
Anna Karenina
The Odyssey

Lord of the Flies
Little Women
Madame Bovary
Great Expectations

Starting in 2001, Dad had given me one book every two years, always on the same date. The tenth of January. I'd discerned the pattern after three books—that every two years he would gift me with some unwieldy novel that I would never read. I guess the fact I never read the book was part of whatever joke he had going on in his head. The date, and its apparent significance was not significant to me, and I'd always just put it down to yet another of my dad's quirks. But now? It felt weighted.

I sat on the couch with my laptop, opened up a browser and typed in "important historical events January 10" and went right to Wikipedia—the fount of all knowledge. Most of what happened on that day was boring, and in my opinion, didn't warrant a mention. But a few events stood out.

Julius Caesar crossing the Rubicon River into Rome—the event that started a civil war, which led to the downfall of one of the greatest historical empires. Or so the Internet said. Seemed portentous. Especially if the hard drive contained, as Lennon thought, files on all the foreign operatives currently active in the United Sates who would be working to undermine our democracy…and more.

I unsnapped my watch and stared at the engravings. The inner workings of the watch were visible through the back face, so the engravings were on the back of the metal links of the band, one each side of the watch. *Little Mouse* and *XXX*.

Little Mouse. I bit my lower lip.
Have you finished your homework, Little Mouse?
That's a great drawing, Little Mouse.
Not now, I'm busy, Little Mouse.
Do you want chocolate or vanilla ice cream, Little Mouse?

There was no significance in a pet name that Dad started calling me when I was barely talking. It was just a pet name. But my brain was stuck on this nugget of affection. I'd been putting that watch on my wrist every day for over a decade and never gave it any thought. Now it was all I could think about.

Focus.

Obviously XXX in Roman numerals was for my thirtieth birthday. Or did it mean something else? Roman numerals. The date in the books, the tenth of January, led me to Caesar. Was Dad leading me to something encrypted with a Caesar cipher? Logical. It was a simple substitution cipher, using a key to shift letters by a fixed number of places through the alphabet. All the decoder needed was that key to determine which letter replaced the one they had in their working text.

But what he'd actually encrypted and the shift he'd used were as yet, totally unknown. And a Caesar cipher was *so* basic and easy to break—especially if the person trying to break it had both the encrypted and unencrypted texts. It was also easy to brute-force the answer through trial and error, and not secure if the person trying to break it had modern, AI-based decryption.

But nobody had been able to decode the encryption.

My dad was a lot of things, but he wasn't stupid. So if he'd used a basic cipher like a Caesar, he had to have hidden the encrypted base text for the pass phrase somewhere nobody else would find it. Maybe split up in multiple locations. Like, for instance…eleven books he'd given his daughter?

I wrote a quick list of each tenth of January historical event into a document (who was I to say which were significant and which weren't when it came to breaking a code), typed out the titles of the books into another document, then sent both to my printer so I could show Jeffrey on Monday. Wandering across the room to the printer on the desk I never used in the corner of the living room was a welcome, albeit far too short, break from my thoughts.

I opened *Moby Dick* and flicked through to the copyright and publisher information page, where Dad had written the date in his fine script. *10th January 2001*. I turned the pages, hoping to come across something that might tell me how to figure out the pass phrase (or, miracle of miracles—tell me the pass phrase). On the blank left page before the first chapter began, my dad had inscribed:

"*The woods are lovely, dark and deep,*
But I have promises to keep,
And miles to go before I sleep,
And miles to go before I sleep."
-Robert Frost, Stopping by Woods on a Snowy Evening

I leafed through the book, but didn't see another handwritten thing. That didn't mean they weren't there, but a thorough examination would have to wait until I had an assistant. I picked up *1984* and checked beyond the page where Dad had written *10th January 2003*. Yep, the same inscription from Robert Frost's poem on the same page as the one in *Moby Dick*.

Well, isn't this starting to look like a pattern?

I hurriedly checked every book. The same date on the same page, then the same inscription on that blank page. Two simultaneous emotions hit me like an out-of-control train. Excitement that I might have found something, then guilt that I'd never looked at these books.

I slumped back onto the couch. Hello, Significance, nice to see you.

CHAPTER FOUR

Nike-ing it

A minute after I'd finished unpacking the kitchen stores I'd bought over the weekend, Jeffrey sauntered into the office with two coffees.

"You have the most impeccable timing," I said as I accepted the almond-milk latte with one raw sugar. It was comforting to know that he remembered how I took my coffee. Though, he remembered everything. Even things I wished he'd forget.

"Because you were dying of caffeine withdrawal and I arrived just in time to perform coffee CPR?"

"I really need to dial up my sarcasm. I meant, you arrived just as I was done dealing with this annoyingly heavy box of things for our kitchen. But, thanks for the coffee."

"You're welcome. And if you'd told me you needed help, I would have been here to help." He grinned. "But it's nice to know that your passive-aggressive snark is still in there."

My shoulders dropped. "I'm so sorry," I said, injecting every ounce of sincerity I could into those three words. It'd been a while since we'd snarked at each other—living together in a terrorist hotbed for six months and bonding over missing your partner or spouse and then having your life saved (mine) or your shrapnel wounds tended to (his) makes it hard to maintain the status quo of your early, snark-laden interactions.

Jeffrey smiled and waved me off. "You're forgiven. How was your weekend? Or need I ask if you're snarking first thing on a Monday morning?"

"Fine," I answered quickly. If you defined *fine* as seeing your ex and her new girlfriend, freaking out about it, then distracting yourself from that hot mess by digging into your father's secret life, then yeah—it'd been fine. I knew he'd pick up on both my tone and the one-word answer, so to hold off any delving into what was up with me, I asked, "What about you? Get up to anything exciting?" I took a long sip of my coffee.

There was the faintest twitch at the edge of his mouth, but it seemed the urge to tell me about his weekend took precedent over digging into mine. "Good. Took Benjamin for a long walk then gave him a bath and brush. Dominique and I pored over paint samples for our living room, and alabaster with a peacock-blue accent wall won. So, we went paint shopping ready for next weekend's painting adventures. And we had a romantic dinner and planned our next vacation to replace our aborted Mallorca one."

"Sounds great." And so lovey-dovey and adorable that I felt simultaneously gooey and jealous.

"It was. And if you want to talk about how your weekend *really* was, you know where to find me." Sipping his coffee, Jeffrey turned and walked over to the kitchenette to inspect the new loot.

Goddamn his perceptiveness. Now that I had some separation from Saturday morning, I realized that I'd maybe overreacted with Sophia. Maybe overreacted? Definitely overreacted. I sat at my desk, watched his childlike glee at what I'd bought, and tried not to get myself down at how I'd acted on Saturday.

"I may never go home," Jeffrey enthused. "I might just stay here all the time drinking gourmet pod coffee and eating fancy-ass cookies." He pulled out a choc-caramel chunk cookie from the jar on the counter and bit into it, chewing as he opened the cupboards underneath the sink. "Do you have shares in the company that makes Cheddar Cheese Pretzel Combos? I knew you liked them, but this is a little obscene."

He was right. I'd bought out the entire stock, and would do it again in a heartbeat. "I wish I did. I'd make myself a millionaire buying so many for myself."

"I have one word for you, Lexie. Wholesale. You'll save yourself a ton of money. And given you said you'd do the shopping to stock us up, I'm assuming you're paying for this out of pocket and not with some office budget."

"Noted. And yes, I am." But now I was absolutely going to bug Lennon about an office snacks budget.

Jeffrey grabbed another cookie. "Let me know what I owe you for half. Because I'm going to devour these."

"Will do."

After finishing my coffee, I felt ready to tackle the box of my dad's working life. Jeffrey and I liberated our laptops and the dossiers we'd date-sorted on Friday and got right into it.

I was surprised, and moderately annoyed, to discover parts of each folder had been redacted, and left the office to go blast Lennon about it. "How am I supposed to figure this out if you're withholding information on my dad?"

Lennon looked at me impassively. "Those segments were redacted years ago, Alexandra. I'm afraid you'll just have to figure it out without that information because even I don't know what's behind those redactions."

"Fine." I turned to leave, then remembered the other thing I needed to bug him about. "Also, can we find a budget for snacks for my office? The other floors have agency-supplied snack baskets and tea and coffee for the break rooms."

"Sure," he said testily. "I'll have my secretary get a budget form for you."

I noted his pissy tone. "Not loving the paperwork side of being the agency director, huh?"

"Not when I'm being harassed about minor issues like this, no I'm not."

I raised an eyebrow. "You told me I would have anything I needed to get this task completed. I need snacks. So does Jeffrey. If I were still in my old team, I'd have access to the break-room snacks and beverages. I shouldn't have to supply my own. It's not like I'm asking you for a full meal allowance for every day I'm in the office."

I hoped my argument had landed, because all he said was, "Is there anything else you needed, Alexandra? I'm quite busy. And now I have another item to deal with. Your snack allowance."

Real-life Lennon was a much bigger bore than phone-only Lennon. I smiled as cheerily as I could. "Nope, that's all. Thanks."

While I'd been out of the office, Jeffrey hadn't moved from his place at our middle table. Or so I thought, until I noticed a conspicuous pile of cookie crumbs in front of him. "No judging," he mumbled.

I raised my hands. "I wouldn't dream of it."

We sat opposite each other on the long side of the I, with my dad's yearly dossier folders laid out in front of us. I stared. Jeffrey stared.

"Did you have any revelations over the weekend about how to approach these files?" he finally asked.

"Not a single one. Aside from Nike-ing it."

"Nike-ing?"

"Just do it?"

So we did.

I opened up the 1978 folder again and after reading the first paragraph, all I could think about was that I wasn't even born, and my dad was off being all undercover-operative-spy guy and stuff. That single thought blossomed into a million others, like: did he think about me while he was gone or was he worried about dying and leaving me and my mother or did he not care because he was all about the job?

An uncomfortable sensation settled in the pit of my stomach. I knew my dad well enough to know he probably didn't think or worry about his family at all while he was off playing super spy. Or, at least I assume he was a super spy because he was an overachieving, type A, anally retentive person for everything he did. Why would this be any different?

Suddenly, the last thing I felt like doing was reading about my dad's secret life, which was unfortunate because that was my allocated, important, time-sensitive task. I set my pen down on the legal pad by my forearm and just blurted out, "I ran into Sophia on Saturday morning after yoga."

Jeffrey looked up immediately, dropping the 1979 folder. He inhaled deeply, then folded his hands together on top of the document. His entire postured screamed "I want to ask you everything and I'm dying to know, but I'm going to be calm." Nodding slowly, he said, "That sounds awkward. How are you?"

"It *was* awkward. Extremely. And then it felt…sad. And I'm not sure how I am. I freaked out a little and I feel stupid."

"It was an unexpected meeting, I'm not surprised you freaked out. How many times have you texted her?"

"Not once and I'm very proud of myself." But I'd had some seriously itchy fingers for the rest of the weekend, even though I knew nothing good would come of opening up the healed wound of our breakup when I hadn't had time to work on myself.

"That's some serious restraint," he said, his voice laced with teasing.

"You're telling me. So after that fun experience, I decided to distract myself with the reminder of my dad's secret, because what better way to make yourself feel better than to remind yourself that people lie to you."

"Please tell me you're kidding, because I detected no sarcasm."

"Sorry, forgot the sarcasm. I spent a while pulling out every gift my dad ever gave me, aside from birthdays and Christmas which were shared parental gifting occasions."

"You kept all the gifts he gave you?" There was both incredulity and hopefulness in the question.

"Yes, all of them. There weren't many. It was such a strange occurrence, so they were sentimental. And he was a little weird about them, which I realized over the weekend when I thought about those occasions. I think he was giving them weight, but without trying to make me feel uneasy or alarmed."

"Lexie, never have I been so grateful to be in the presence of a sentimental hoarder. So, what do you have?"

"I made an inventory." I passed over the sheet of paper with the book titles.

He looked at the paper, then back at me with an eye roll. "You could have just said 'books.'"

"Pretty much. I thought about it, and these are really the only things he gave me, as something separate from my mom. Every two years on the same day, from 2001, he gave me a book. The books are all inscribed with the date, the tenth of January, on the copyright info page, as well as an inscription on the final blank page before the book begins—it's the final stanza of the Robert Frost poem *Stopping by Woods on a Snowy Evening*." I quoted it for him.

His eyebrows arched. "An interesting coincidence."

"I thought so too."

"We don't believe in coincidences, do we?" Jeffrey said slyly.

"No, we don't. I've been trying to think of why he'd use that particular stanza. Is he saying his work wasn't done, but he's tired of trying to complete it? Or…" I had to pause to swallow nervously. "I know some people think that poem has suicidal ideation in it." Shit. Had my father deliberately crashed his personal plane? I dismissed the thought almost as soon as it came to me. My mother was with him.

"I'm not sure," Jeffrey said carefully. "I suppose we should keep an eye out for things in your father's dossiers that hint that he may have struggled with his mental health or suicidal thoughts."

"I know it's ridiculous to say this, and me not seeing it doesn't mean it wasn't there, but I don't think he had mental health issues." I didn't even know how I'd feel if it turned out I was wrong.

Jeffrey nodded, and thankfully let it be for now. "Okay, then either you're right that he's hinting that his work is not done, or maybe there's something else in that poem that's relevant. How about the tenth of January? Does that date hold any personal meaning to you?"

"None. Not personal. But"—I passed over another sheet of paper—"thanks to Wikipedia, I do know that it's the date Caesar and his army crossed the Rubicon River into Rome and started a civil war. Also the date of the end of the Han Dynasty. Some guy was beheaded in the Tower of London. Florida seceded from the Union. And a bunch of other shit."

"Your dad didn't tell you the significance of the date?"

"No, of course not. He…wasn't big on sharing in that fashion. I asked him a couple of times, kind of whiny because he was being weird and these books felt stupid, and he just laughed and said it was a good date. And I promptly forgot about it until now."

"A good date?" Jeffrey's forehead wrinkled. "Those were his words?"

"Verbatim." I raced back through my memories, trying to find anything else significant he may have said about the books. But I found nothing. Except my own feelings of idiocy that I'd never considered them to be important. But I consoled myself with the knowledge that unless someone was in my position and had reason to think the books were anything more than a present from their dad, they wouldn't have looked any further.

"Interesting." He studied the tenth of January events list.

"I haven't looked inside the books properly yet, to see if he's marked any passages. I thought we could do that together. Share the workload and all that."

Jeffrey looked up instantly, his eyebrows bouncing upward in surprise. "You never read them? Even though they were a gift?"

"No," I said, not bothering to disguise my indignation. "Have *you* read *War and Peace*? *The Odyssey*? *Ulysses*?"

"Of course I have…n't." He grinned at his clever pun, before exchanging the grin for a piercing look. "You said these are *really* the only things he gave you. That implies there's other things."

Shit. I hadn't even realized my slightly evasive, untruthful wording. I undid the clasp on my watch and passed it to Jeffrey.

"Nice watch. Are you giving it to me?"

"No. Turn it over. My dad gave me this on my thirtieth birthday, just another gift apart from the usual parents' gift." I frowned. "I never understood why, but it was so typical of him to gift me things like this, like books I had no interest in." Now, I was beginning to think there was method to his madness.

He flipped the watch over, staring at the metal band. "Was Little Mouse something important to you?"

"A nickname for me that only he used," I said, pleased that it came out without my voice cracking.

"And Roman numerals for thirty," Jeffrey mused. "Did he like Roman history and whatnot?"

"Not that I know of. But he rarely did anything without careful consideration. Why use Roman numerals instead of just three and zero? My gut makes me feel like I'm being led to a Caesar cipher. The tenth of January, Caesar and his big political action. And I don't know, maybe the XXX is significant in another way too? Thirtieth page on each book? Relevant passages marked with XXX? The Roman civil war is maybe a warning? I really don't know. And I *hate* that I don't know."

"Maybe, to all that. Or maybe not." He passed me back my watch and I put it back on. "Okay, so one big issue I see with these books being part of determining his code is that it's a constantly evolving gift. If there's something in these books that forms the basis for deciphering the pass phrase, then that means every two years when he gave you a book, he would have had to update the encryption to include whatever new information is in the new book. And if the watch is important, then he risked something happening and you not getting the watch on your thirtieth birthday."

"I've already thought about that. And yeah, I agree. But it's not exactly like that would be difficult, updating password encryption. And don't they say you should change your passwords frequently?"

He laughed. "I think that's more for your Netflix account, not your hiding-deep-cover-foreign-operatives intelligence."

"Same concept."

Jeffrey tapped the list of books. "This as the basis for unlocking the password also assumes that you would keep these books forever, just in case."

"I know. But I feel like he was guiding me toward keeping them. I'm not a hoarder, but I keep sentimental things. Whenever he came over, he always went to my bookshelves. Maybe he was actually checking all his books were still there? Maybe he would have replaced one if I lost it, or all if I tossed them." I held up my hands. "Look, I'm not locked on to the book idea, but it's the only place I have to start right now. It's logical to think he'd make figuring this out as easy as he could for me."

"I agree that it seems like a good lead. A logical lead. But until we actually find something in these books that tells us they're not just a quirky paternal offering, I'm not getting my hopes up."

"Me either." I blew out a long breath. "I guess we'll finish reading these dossiers and unless something in there jumps out at us that says it's definitely not the books, I'll bring them in, and we can see if there's something hopeful on the other pages."

Jeffrey nodded decisively. "Then I'll make a note to bring my magnifying glass." He shook his head. "Damn, I wish I'd met your dad, he sounds pretty fucking smart. Gather intelligence, and split the key to accessing it over multiple parts that first need to be put together before you get anywhere near what the key is."

"It is smart. But it's also dumb. If what's on this hard drive is as important as Lennon said, me not finding these clues or not being able to put them together properly means I'm the weak link. And like you said, it all hinges on me actually keeping his books and maybe the watch too. And if I haven't done all of those things then it means that this intelligence will never be accessed. Seems like a massive point of failure to me."

"Then he must have known you would never fail." Jeffrey smiled gently. "Maybe you're actually the strong link."

"Maybe," I agreed, though it wasn't with much conviction. I didn't feel like a strong link. I felt like I was flailing.

He rested his elbows on the table, bringing his hands together. "I'm just going to come out and say it. You don't seem like you were close to your father."

"Astute observation," I said dryly. "I wasn't what you'd call close to either of my parents." After a deep breath, I decided to elaborate, but only because it might be relevant to our case. "I loved them. I know they loved me, in their own way, but it was never a television-nuclear-family scenario in our house. We moved a lot because of Dad's job, which I now know was *intel officer* as well as *diplomat*. And they always felt…preoccupied, is probably the best way to describe it, like I was an afterthought once they had met my basic needs of food, shelter, clothing, education and all that." I shrugged. "But compared to many people, I had an idyllic childhood so I always feel like a shithead for being resentful that they didn't shower me with physical or emotional affection."

"Just because you didn't have a"—he air-quoted his next words—"*traditionally* abusive, horrible upbringing doesn't mean your experience wasn't shitty."

"I know. It's…I…my relationship with my parents is just one of those things. I can't change it and I don't understand it. And my dad always felt more like he was trying to be one of my teachers instead of my dad, which is ironic because Mom actually was a school teacher. Now I'm wondering if he wasn't trying to prepare me for something." I reached for the 1978 folder again, though my concentration had not miraculously returned. I just didn't really feel like discussing the complicated feelings I had toward my parents.

Thankfully Jeffrey seemed to realize I'd reached my limit and redirected the conversation, though maybe not for the better… "So. Ms. Flores—"

I cut him off. "You don't have to call her Ms. Flores." He'd always done it. Something to do with respect because he'd never met her, and probably lingering from when he was assigned to figure where I was and what I was doing with the Kunduz Intelligence while hiding with Sophia.

He shook his head, as I'd expected. "How do you feel about that?"

Smiling, I asked him to, "Please remove your psych hat when you're around me, Jeffrey."

It wasn't an aimless jibe—he had a psychology degree. I knew that during his military career he'd been special ops, sometimes utilizing his psych skills to help his colleagues deal with what they saw during deployments, but mostly to "obtain information" from suspected terrorists. He hadn't needed to elaborate about how he "obtained" information. I knew what happened at black sites. He'd used those psych skills on me when we'd first met and he'd been assigned to debrief me about my time with the Kunduz Intelligence. He was good at it, and I'd hated him for it.

"Sorry." He mimed removing a ball cap and then putting on a wide-brimmed hat. "Friend hat is firmly in place. Are you sure you're okay?" he repeated, grinning like an idiot.

"Yeah, I'm okay. Confused and embarrassed, but okay. Thanks for asking," I added belatedly.

"Why embarrassed?"

"Because like I said—I freaked out when I saw her. I spent Friday night enjoying some introspection, and had decided I was going to contact her to talk about what happened, but in the future, you know? When all this shit was done and I'd worked on some things. And then I ran into her and I was so unprepared and I panicked."

"What made you decide to get in touch with her on Friday night?" he asked neutrally.

"Wine, mostly," I admitted. Jeffrey snorted, and some of the tension eased. "I…I didn't tell you, but I found a coded message in my dry-cleaning when I got back. From Sophia."

His eyebrows jumped up. "Coded? She encodes stuff? Maybe you should offer her a job helping us with this…" he said slyly.

Despite myself, I smiled. "She's a mystery-puzzle nut. I'm sure she'd figure this out in ten seconds. And it wasn't an especially hard code to break."

"Details, please."

"It was an ISBN for a book, some weird fantasy sci-fi new adult romance I think. I read the blurb, and it's about a woman doing something she doesn't want to in order to save her dad and her kingdom."

"Interesting," he mused. "I wonder why she sent you that." Jeffrey's eyebrows bounced up and down comically.

"We both know why. She was trying to tell me something. I think it tells me I was right, she broke up with me because someone pressured her to." I obviously didn't know what they'd held over her head to convince her to go along with it.

Jeffrey raised victorious fists high into the air. "I *knew* it! I knew she still loved you. This is great news." He'd been a little more devil's advocate than me when I'd told him I thought Sophia had been coerced, and it was nice to know he was just helping me see all angles and really was in my corner.

"Yeah…" I'd known it too. Or I'd suspected it, hard, until she hadn't contacted me after breaking up with me, and that suspicion had given way to self-doubt and I'd become convinced that the problem was actually me. On the plus side, it'd make me realize I needed to work on myself as a person, as a girlfriend, and that could only be beneficial.

"You sound like you don't think it's great news."

"I'm not sure what it is. Aside from seeing her setting me back emotionally to the day she broke up with me? She said she wants to talk."

"Talking is good. Are you going to call her?"

"Why would I call her? Just to say 'hey'?" What a ridiculous notion. "If she was forced into breaking up with me then she'd want to stay far away from me. And if she wasn't, well…she's had four and a half months to contact me to explain."

Jeffrey's forehead wrinkled. "This makes no sense. I thought you'd be running victory laps with phone in hand, her number ready to dial."

"I just don't think there's any point."

"The *point* is that this bump-into-each-other opened the door for you to get back together!" For a person who'd never actually met Sophia, Jeffrey had always seemed rather invested in my being in a relationship with her. I set that aside as something to think about later.

"No, it hasn't."

He all but spluttered, "Did you suddenly get over her? Fall *out* of love with her?"

I fought the urge to cross my arms over my chest. "No. But that's not the issue."

"Then what is? Because I am ten shades of confused right now. She basically told you, in a roundabout way, granted, that she didn't want to break up with you."

"Right, but she still broke up with me. Out of nowhere. Without even a courtesy 'things are not great' talk. So I spent months feeling fucking terrible about that, wondering if she really meant it or not, convincing myself she didn't and then eventually convincing myself she did. But now I know someone's obviously held her toes over the fire, and for all I know—they could still be doing that, so why would she want to get back with me when they're leveraging something to keep her away from me?" They'd leveraged her against me, leveraged something against her. For once, I wished I was the one with the leverage. Though, now that I thought about it, my being the only person who could unlock this important drive seemed like fucking good leverage.

"Uh. Love?" Happily married for twenty-six years, he had an adorable, but also frustratingly simple way of looking at it.

"It's not enough in this instance, and you know that."

"Maybe it is. She said she wanted to talk. What could she possibly want to talk about? If she was truly forced into breaking up with you, then I'd imagine she's dying to explain that. If she broke up with you because of personal reasons, then wouldn't she be actively avoiding further contact?"

"I think 'can we talk?' is just the polite thing you say to your ex when you run into them unexpectedly. I don't think it means she actually wants to talk."

"Usually avoidance is key in unexpected ex run-ins. You really haven't had a lot of exes, have you…" Jeffrey said dryly. He held up both hands in a conciliatory gesture, which was unnecessary because he was right.

"No." I picked up my pen and turned it over and over. Finally I looked up. "Do you really think I should contact her?"

"It doesn't matter what I think. What matters is what you want to do."

I rolled my eyes. "Humor me."

"Why?" he asked, a hint of the snide, snarky bastard he'd been in the early days of our…whatever our relationship was peeking through.

"Because I'm scared," I finally admitted, hating myself for feeling so vulnerable.

Jeffrey's expression softened. "Of what?"

"Of everything." Realizing my broad "everything" would send him off on a psychoanalytic tangent, I verbalized my two greatest fears about opening the door to Sophia being in my life again. "Being hurt. Rejection."

"Understandable fears. I know you want me to tell you what to do, which I can't. But…if I were you? I would take the whole 'secret message' thing, and the fact she explicitly said during the accidental meeting that she wanted to talk as a sign that she genuinely wants to reconnect with you. It's up to you in what capacity. I think you should contact her." He reached over and patted my hand. "If nothing else, you could finally get some closure."

"I already have closure," I rebutted.

Laughing, he shook his head. "No you don't. If you had closure, you wouldn't be agonizing over this."

Then the asshole got up and left the office before I could come back at him.

We'd read my dad's career dossiers up to 1989—he was a diligent and productive intelligence officer; I'd give him that—when Jeffrey declared he needed a break. "Sorry," he said. "I know we were going to do dossiers, then look at the other evidence, but I'm going to die if I have to read any more agency-speak."

I put a Post-it in the folder to mark my place at the start of the 1990 folder, then set it off to the side. The dossiers weren't long, each about twenty pages at most, but it was dense reading and required a lot of concentration rather than a lot of time. "Okay. I'm not sure there is a right way of approaching this, so whatever you want. I honestly don't know what's germane and what's not."

"Wow, big word."

"Blame my father. Reading about his life is putting him in my head." Now I was up to a time period where I was a kid, I felt like I should be madder at my dad for dragging me and my mom everywhere to new diplomatic posts, and all the while being undercover. But hadn't I done that exact thing with Sophia in the beginning? Sophia. Dammit. Was she just going to pop up everywhere in my thoughts now?

Jeffrey made a show of capping his pen and dropping his 1988 folder into the "completed" box. "Obviously we need to look into each of these January tenth events, but I'm just going to start with the most logical one, based on the Roman numerals on your watch." He paused for a dramatic beat then, gesticulating wildly, boomed, "Caesar!" Jeffrey picked up a pen and notepad, then collected his car keys. "If you'll excuse me, I need to go Google something. And get some air." He absently patted his chest where his credentials hung on a lanyard. "I shall return. Hopefully victorious."

I let him research his butt off while I ate a late lunch and stared at the wall, wishing there was a window so I could indulge in some aimless staring. I'd finished lunch, washed my lunch container, put the kettle on for tea, and poured some Cheddar Cheese Pretzel Combos into a bowl, when Jeffrey came back.

He sat down, spun his chair around, raised the notepad, and like a schoolteacher reading to their class, intoned, "Caesar crossing the Rubicon, January tenth, 49 BC. From Wikipedia. 'According to Suetonius, Caesar uttered the famous phrase *ālea iacta est—the die has been cast.* The phrase *crossing the Rubicon* has survived to refer to any individual or group committing itself to a risky or revolutionary course of action, similar to the modern phrase *passing the point of no return.*'" Jeffrey raised his eyebrows. "Interesting. I think I need to brush up on my history."

"I think I do too." Sighing, I put my glasses back on. "But first, I need to read about what my dad was up to in 1990."

Not a lot, as it turned out. We'd been living in Poland. I'd made a friend at school, Jadwiga, and then I'd had to leave her when we'd come back to the States. We'd tried to keep up pen pal status, but she'd found a new friend within two months of my leaving, a friend who was actually there in person. And so she'd friend-dropped me. I'm pretty sure I was devastated in that nine-year-old way, when everything feels so huge. Poland… Close to Russia. Was Dad gathering information?

Probably.

We made it to 1993 before mutually agreeing it was time to pack up for the day. This was far more brain-intensive than my usual work and I was cerebrally fatigued. Jeffrey slung his messenger bag over his shoulder. "Have I told you how much I love leaving the office before five p.m.?" He checked his watch. "Before four p.m. even. Because I really love it."

"I know. So do I." I just wished I had someone to go home to so I could enjoy my extra few hours per day of not being at work.

We said our goodbyes, and I strolled to my car, relishing the fresh air after yet another day inside.

Sophia's ears must have been burning during the day, because when I liberated my phone from its thermal lockbox bolted to the chassis in my trunk, there was a text message from her. Nervous excitement twisted through my stomach as I read it.

Hey, hope you're okay. It was really good to see you Saturday. I meant what I said, I'd like to talk and just explain some things if you're open to it. But I totally understand if you're not ready or just don't want to. I really miss you.

I really miss you… Oh that was a low blow.

The problem was, I really missed her too.

CHAPTER FIVE

Just a few regrets

Okay, let's talk.
It was just three words, nothing deep or confrontational, but I'd been sitting on the couch since I'd arrived home, with that completed text message on my phone screen for what felt like an eternity before pressing the send button.

Sophia's response was lightning fast. *Thank you. Whenever and wherever you want is fine with me.*

When and where I wanted. Obviously I couldn't have such a personal conversation in public, and going to her house felt too raw. Being at my place would make me more settled, and also give me an emotional upper hand. I also didn't want to spend all tomorrow, or the rest of the week thinking about meeting up with her, so before I could second-guess myself, I typed out: *How about now, my place?*

Sounds good. Have you had dinner?

It was approaching six p.m. and I hadn't eaten yet, but the idea of her bringing over takeout, or us ordering a meal, or me cooking—hell, even just us sitting down for a meal the way we used to—felt wrong. So I typed out a lie. *Yes I have. See you soon.* A lie. Slipping back into old habits there, Lexie. I deleted the unsent text, and instead sent: *I'm good, thanks. See you soon.*

The typing dots appeared. Disappeared. Appeared again. Disappeared again. Eventually, a text landed. *Sounds great, see you soon.*

Assuming she left right away without fretting over her appearance the way I was going to, Sophia would be here in about twenty minutes. I was sure she wouldn't fret, aside from putting on eyeliner, without which she generally refused to leave the house. Maybe she'd already left the house today and already had eyeliner on. Maybe she didn't have that must-wear-eyeliner-in-public habit anymore. I had no idea, and for some reason, that thought bothered me.

I would have loved to have a massive panic about the fact my ex-girlfriend was coming by to talk about fuck knows what, but I only had time for a little panic. And it would have to be while I showered because there was no time to melt down fully. I stripped in a hurry and jumped into the shower before the water had heated. I wanted to be showered, dressed—what to wear?—and relaxing (hahaha, yeah, sure) when she arrived.

The icy blast shocked a little of the panic out of me, and while the water warmed, I gave myself a minute of anxiety. Then, as the hot water rained over me, I let it soothe the anxiety away. As best I could around washing my face free of work makeup and scrubbing my body, I deep-breathed my way through some of the angst. I had no illusions that I'd be completely relaxed when she arrived, but at least I wasn't going to be vibrating with nerves.

After a quick bout of staring at my wardrobe, wondering what would convey to Sophia that I was confident, calm, and totally over her, I ended up pulling on a pair of old, comfy jeans and a casual button-up. Rolling the sleeves up made me feel even better, like… look at me, I don't care how I look, I'm totally over you and not at all desperate to know what you need to tell me.

I let my hair out of its French braid and fluffed it out. There'd been no time to wash it, but I wished I had anyway. Then I finally looked at myself in the mirror. And immediately wished I hadn't. I'd looked worse, but I'd definitely looked better. Why now, when I was trying to appear calm and put-together, did I look like I'd spent a week working at a fright house?

I was about to put some makeup on to smooth the weird splotchiness of my cheeks and cover some of my pallor, but then I decided fuck it—I wasn't trying to impress anyone and whether or not I was over her was none of Sophia's business. Maybe this was a bad idea. But the desperate-for-answers side of me was charging ahead. As was the I-want-to-be-a-better-person-for-my-next-girlfriend side of me. A tiny voice in my head said that next girlfriend *could* be Sophia, then just as quickly, it reminded me that she'd been at the café with a women with whom she looked very cozy.

If nothing else, the breakup had forced me to confront the parts of myself that weren't good for relationship bliss and stability. And for that, I had to admit I was grateful to her, even as I struggled to reconcile my emotions and the knock-on effects of the breakup.

The expected knock on my apartment door still made me flinch. I checked the time. 6:22 p.m. She'd come right over. I pushed myself up from the couch where I'd been staring at my blank television and walked slowly to the door. Inhale for four seconds. Exhale for six.

I peeked into the peephole, and Sophia must have caught the flash of movement because she raised her hand immediately, smiling an excited smile. I'd seen that smile so many times before. I'd missed that smile, and every other smile Sophia had in her repertoire. Oh god. My stomach lurched. Not in an I'm-going-to-vomit-imminently kind of way, but in a yeah-I'm-not-actually-over-you kind of way. No surprises there. You're good at lying to other people, Lexie, not so good at lying to yourself.

I stuck a smile on my face, flung open the door and stepped aside. "Hi." Good good, nice and cheerful, not too exuberantly deranged.

Sophia looked like she'd been holding her breath the entire drive over, and all her air rushed out along with her, "Hey." She was dressed casually in tight dark-blue jeans, suede sneakers, and the brick-red scoop-necked tee I'd always thought made her beautiful light-brown eyes look radiant. And she looked amazing.

"Come on in," I said unnecessarily. Great start. Closing, deadbolting, and chaining the door gave me a moment to reset. "Would you like something to drink?"

"Water would be great, thanks."

I held out my hand, and Sophia stared at it for a moment before she shrugged out of her light jacket and passed it to me. BB—before breakup—she would have taken it off the moment she got inside and flung it over one of the high-top chairs at my breakfast bar. "Thanks for letting me come around," she said, a little of her excitement dissipating.

"No problem." I slipped into the kitchen, poured her a glass of cold water and set it on the counter. After a moment, I pushed it closer to her. "Was your girlfriend okay with you coming to meet with me?" I hadn't meant to say anything about her girlfriend, but my mouth had bypassed my brain.

Sophia's eyebrows rocketed up, the water pausing halfway to her mouth. "My what?"

"Your girlfriend?" I had a sudden feeling I'd made a huge assumption. A logical assumption, based on what I'd seen, but maybe it'd been a wrong assumption. The little voice in my brain hoped it was a wrong assumption. "The woman at the café with you on Saturday morning?"

Sophia's mouth fell open. She snapped it closed again, but a laugh burst through her lips. "That's Amanda. Steph's girlfriend. We're planning a surprise birthday party for Steph next month."

Steph's girlfriend. Not Sophia's girlfriend. I was embarrassed by the enormity of my relief, and tried very hard to sound a normal amount of relieved not massively relieved. "Oh. Okay. I just thought… you guys seemed really friendly. To an outsider it kind of looked like a relationship." An outsider who was paying far too much attention and analyzing far too much.

"We are really friendly, because we're friends, because she's dating one of my best friends." Apparently satisfied I'd been set straight and she didn't have to babysit my feelings about her not-actually-girlfriend, she drank a quarter of the glass of water in a few swallows then set the glass down again.

"Friends," I repeated. I filled up the glass again, itching to pour a glass of wine or make myself a gin and tonic to blunt the edges of my tension, my anticipation, my…hope.

"Mhmm. I'm not seeing anyone, Lexie," Sophia said earnestly. "I haven't seen anyone since—" She cleared her throat. "Since we broke up."

We broke up. I crossed my arms over my chest and bit back the antagonistic urge to remind her *we* didn't break up. She broke up with me. Against my will. There was a huge difference.

"Me either. Obviously." I pulled one arm out to enforce my point with a vague gesture. "Because I've been overseas." In a place where I'd have been murdered if anyone had discovered I was a lesbian.

"Mmm." Sophia picked up her water. "Can we go sit on the couch? Next to each other instead of staring at each other with this countertop as a barrier," she said teasingly, smiling across at me.

I wasn't surprised she'd picked up on the unconscious protection I'd put up between us. "Sure," I agreed.

I waited until she'd put her drink on the coffee table and sat down before I took a seat on the couch too, putting as much space between us as I could without being rude. And I tried not to notice how incredible she smelled, how beautiful she was, the way her eyes softened when she looked at me. A question. I needed a question to stop her from looking at me like she wanted to touch me. "So, how have you been? How's work? Pickleball?" That should keep her talking for a little while, enough time for me to settle my nerves, still anxiously firing.

"Work's good, it's been really busy the past couple of months, with the usual mix of clients."

"Good, bad, annoying, demanding, sweet?" Smiling, I rattled off the usual suspects she always seemed to have.

Sophia laughed. "That's exactly it. Pickleball is great. Alana never came back to play, so Gina stepped in." It took me a minute to put all those dots together. Her pickleball partner, Alana, had broken her ankle in a mountain biking accident just before New Year's. She shrugged. "Gina's a much better player, so I'm not too broken up about Alana's deflection."

"I see. I suppose it all worked out then." She'd neglected to answer my first question, and I didn't know if it was deliberate, or she just thought of answers to the others first. "You didn't tell me how you've been," I said gently.

She held eye contact with me, even as she admitted, "Honestly? Up and down. More down than up. I've really missed you, Lexie." Her face contorted and she took a deep breath. "I've missed you so much. It's been awful without you."

It took every bit of willpower I possessed to not get up and move to the other side of the room where it was safe. But I'd invited her here because I wanted to talk. I wanted to give her the opportunity to explain, even if I was scared of what she was going to say. And of what I was going to say. "I've missed you too. I didn't want to…hope. I never thought I'd go down this path with you again. You told me that it was over, and I didn't understand it, but I'd accepted it. But when I saw you on Saturday, part of me wanted to grab your hand and pull you with me, down that path again, wherever it might take us."

She leaned toward me. "Lexie."

I held up both hands to keep her from leaning any closer. "Just a moment, please. That's what I *want* to do. But I can't pretend that what happened didn't happen. Because it did. And it hurt me." I frowned, and decided to go ahead and say what I needed to. "*You* hurt me. Badly. And I'm still so fucking confused, and I thought I was over it, over you, but now I know I'm not. And your book blurb message just confused me even more. And you being here, acting like nothing happened is really messing with my head. And having my head messed with is the last thing I need at the moment."

Sophia exhaled loudly, clearly relieved. Then she skipped over everything I'd laid out, and said, "I wondered if you'd found my clue. I knew you'd figure it out if you did."

"I almost didn't find it. My dry-cleaner did."

"I wasn't sure if someone would come into your apartment and see a note, even one hidden under a pillow or in a book or your…bedside drawer." The brief flash of desire in her eyes told me why she hadn't gone to my bedside table. "I thought I should be careful. I wanted to tell you, but I couldn't, obviously."

"Smart." I paused before admitting something embarrassing. "When I got home, I looked everywhere, desperately hoping you'd left me a secret note telling me the breakup wasn't real. But I didn't find anything." I swallowed hard, remembering those hours where I'd searched frantically, and the emptiness as I'd realized there was nothing. "So I decided it must have been real."

"It wasn't," she said quietly. So quietly I wasn't sure I'd heard her. But the desperate look in her eyes told me I had.

"It felt real to me," I said, unable to project that thought as anything more than a loud whisper.

"I'm sorry." She sucked in a deep breath, but instead of explaining, she said, "I was hoping that note would be enough to get you to contact me. But you didn't. You didn't even tell me you'd come home."

"I only found it the day before I went back to work, when I picked up my dry cleaning, like…just over a week ago, and work has been beyond crazy since." I drew circles with my fingertips on the arm of the couch. "And honestly? I didn't know what to think. Because…" And I didn't even know how to express it.

"Because what, Lexie?"

"Because it doesn't change anything!" I said, unable to hold back my exasperation. "And I'm hurt and angry and have been trying to not be those things for months, but now those feelings are pushing back to the surface again."

"I understand that. Would it help you be less angry and hurt and those things if I could explain why I had to break up with you?"

Had to break up with you. *Had to…*

"I don't know," I said quietly, pushing down the urge to wring my hands and fidget. Because I did know. I wanted her to explain it all. To explain how she could break up with me so easily. How she could break me so easily. But I was so scared to hear it.

"Okay," she said on an exhale. "Then I'm going to start talking and we'll see how helpful it is. And if you want me to stop and leave at any time, I will."

I bit my lower lip hard, and nodded. The fear wasn't unexpected, but I was still stunned by its intensity. How could I want so badly to know the truth but be so afraid of it at the same time?

Sophia drank a little more water, then tucked a leg underneath herself, turning to face me on the couch. "The first thing I want to say is that breaking up with you was not my choice. But I did it because I was convinced that it was the right thing for you, the thing that could keep you safe."

Keep me safe… It was a noble thought, but I couldn't honestly believe that she would blow up our lives on a suspicion that it was "keeping me safe." I just couldn't. "Is that the only reason?" I asked, forcing my voice to remain calm.

Sophia shifted uneasily. "It was one of the reasons," she said carefully.

By her expression I knew what she was going to say. And I didn't know if I felt sick or triumphant that I'd correctly suspected someone had threatened her family as a way to get her to break up with me, to punish me. Relief fought with rage, guilt fought with distress. "So if it wasn't your choice, then whose choice was it?"

"Honestly, I don't know exactly." Her eyebrows drew in, furrowing her forehead. "Do you remember how someone was following me while you were gone?"

I nodded, forcibly unclenching my jaw. I'd been furious when I'd learned the government had someone shadowing her, and had demanded it stop immediately. And I thought it had, until she spoke again.

"That same man came to see me. Just knocked on my door and scared the shit out of me." Sophia inhaled tremulously. "I thought he was going to take me away for some sort of questioning or something to do with the road trip to Tampa. But then he told me he was your boss."

She'd assured me that the person following her had gone away, and I'd believed her. But now, the realization that she'd lied felt awful, even if she'd been trying to protect me. "Which boss?" The question had slipped out, and I hoped Sophia took it as a fumbled question rather than me letting slip that I had two bosses because I worked for two departments. "Why would my boss come to see you? Are you sure? Did he say who he represented? Like…maybe he was actually from the White House or something?" Maybe it was someone doing the president's bidding, pretending to be my boss so Sophia would trust him more readily.

"No. Nothing like that." She eyed me askance. "He never gave me a name, and I didn't ask because it didn't seem odd for an intelligence person to not share details. And he showed me a government ID which looked legitimate." I set aside some of my annoyance, because she was right and the only reason she'd have had that thought would be from my justified paranoia during our road trip. "He told me a lot of things about you and your current assignment overseas that made me feel confident that he was who he said he was."

"What did he look like?"

"Maybe mid to late sixties? About six-one. Blond-brown hair, parted on the side. Hazel-ish eyes. Kind of…intense-looking, if that makes sense? Like he takes everything he does really seriously. Well-dressed, a super-expensive suit and loafers." My suspicions had been growing based on those descriptions, but when she said, "And he wore Faberge Brut cologne" I almost lost my shit. Sophia frowned. "It really threw me off, because that's what my dad wears when he's going somewhere fancy."

"Sonofabitch," I snarled. I clenched my teeth tightly. Tomorrow morning, I was going to confront someone. Wasn't that going to be a fun work conversation. I had to unclench my teeth to assure her, "Not you. Sorry. But yes, I know who that is, and yes, he is my boss. And now I'm absolutely furious. Do you want a glass of wine? Because I do."

Sophia's eyebrows settled from where they'd shot up at my tirade. "Sure. Thanks."

I went to the kitchen, and Sophia was silent while I poured the remainder of Friday's bottle into two glasses. "And he came to see you to give you specific instructions to break up with me?"

She slung both arms over the back of the couch, resting her chin on her forearms, her eyes tracking me as I moved around the kitchen. "Not exactly in those words. We talked a little about you and me, nothing specific, but just how we'd met and how things were going." Sophia spun back around as I approached.

"That didn't seem weird to you?" I passed her a wineglass.

"Thanks." Her hand shook a little as she drank. "A little, but again, he seemed so…trustworthy. He knew things about you, things I didn't think some random person would know, which made me think he knew you pretty well. And the stuff about us wasn't creepy, freaky, peeping Tom type stuff, just things I would have thought someone you worked with would know. So I listened. And then he just came right out and told me that our relationship put you in danger. That not only was I distracting you, but that people were watching you, and looking for anything they could use against you. Like me. Us." She swallowed visibly.

"And you believed him?"

"I had no reason not to," she said quietly. "Everything he said sounded plausible, and like I said—he convinced me that he knew you. Knew you well. Knew what was good for you, especially while you were gone." Sophia raised the wineglass and after an indulgent mouthful, murmured, "This is really good."

That segue softened me a little and made me feel like this could just be any other night, me and her together, talking, watching television with snacks and drinks. "I know. I'd been saving it for us, but I decided to just open the bottle on Friday night." I tilted my glass and peered into the pinot. "It nearly made me call you." Looking up, I smiled. "Aaand, that's when I decided it was time to close the bottle."

She snickered. "I've had quite a few of those nights myself."

I wished she had just given in and contacted me then. It would have saved so much heartbreak. I pushed down my lingering outrage at what they'd done to us, even though there wasn't an us anymore. "So what did you do? Say 'thanks for that, I'll call her right now and break up with her'?"

Her eyebrows bounced upward. "Actually, I told him to get fucked, in nice words, and that I trusted you to tell me if there was something I should know, especially about our relationship. And then he—" She cleared her throat, leaned over to place the wine on the coffee table, then sat back, folding her hands in her lap. "He told me he was trying to keep me and my family safe as well. He insinuated that what had happened with my dad, the fake 'immigration mix-up,' might happen again."

I almost choked on my outrage. How fucking *dare* Lennon. How dare he contact Sophia and tell her these lies. My whole body was coiled so tightly I was afraid I wouldn't be able to contain it. I drank a long, slow mouthful of wine, holding it in my mouth for a few seconds before trickling it down my throat. Sophia, probably sensing my fury, watched me calmly as I inhaled and exhaled, letting each breath settle in my belly before pushing it out again.

After almost a minute, I'd tamped down my feelings enough to continue the conversation. "And you believed him? Even though I'd assured you that your family was protected." I'd done everything I could, even threatening the president with my noncooperation if he harassed Sophia's family again. "He had *no* right, no basis with which to make that assertion. It's completely false." I wondered what else Lennon might have done to interfere in my life, or my dad's, and had to push those thoughts away so I wouldn't explode.

"I—" Sophia frowned. "It's…I mean…they used my family to make you comply once before, Lexie." There was something I'd never heard in her voice when we'd talked about our government threatening her father with deportation back to Mexico to get me to turn myself in with the Kunduz Intelligence.

It sounded like accusation.

"And you believed him?" I asked again. "Instead of talking to me about something so monumental?"

"Yes. Because it's not outside the realm of possibility. You… you don't have a normal job. And he made incredibly convincing arguments, so calmly, and for every question or doubt or rebuttal I had, he had an answer. I was trying to protect you. He insinuated that if I told you, you would deny it and things would be worse and you'd have to keep lying. He told me not to tell you. Actually, it felt more like a warning, not to tell you."

"So why have you told me?"

Smiling sadly, Sophia shrugged. "Because I couldn't help myself. Because I saw you right here, home safe, and I just had to tell you. Because I needed to know if it was all a lie."

I swallowed hard, but my question still came out hoarsely. "Did it feel like a lie when we made love?"

She didn't hesitate, and her answer was equally hoarse. "No."

"Did it feel like a lie every time I told you I loved you?"

"No."

"So why did you believe him and not *us*? Why didn't you believe *me*, every time I told you it was okay, that I would protect you and your family, that I could handle things?"

"Because…because then I started thinking about it all, thinking about you not telling me about the semiregular terrorist attacks because you wanted to protect me, and I started spiraling pretty hard. Second-guessing myself about us and if I was taking your focus away. And then I started to get upset with you for not being honest, even as I was rationalizing that I knew you were trying to stop me from worrying. Because I was struggling with myself, Lexie. With reconciling everything that'd happened since we started seeing each other. And the more I reconciled, the more uncomfortable I felt. I realized how naïve I was, just…going along with you in Tampa, trusting you."

That felt like a slap in the face. "You don't trust me?"

Sophia huffed out a frustrated breath. "No, that's not it. I *do* trust you. I did. It's…I felt stupid, because the whole time we were in Florida, I knew something was off and I ignored it. It didn't seem like a bad thing that was off, just that something was off, and I kept rationalizing what I felt. And the worst thing was that I didn't feel it in the moment, while we were on the road trip. I realized later that if I'd taken a step back then I would have seen that I skimmed over the things that didn't suit my loved-up narrative of us, together, getting to know one another while I helped you with your job." She reached for her wine. "Once I agreed with your boss, thinking that I was doing the right thing for you, I started to have these little niggling doubts about everything."

"Why didn't you tell me? We could have avoided all of this if you'd just told me. Even if we did break up, I wouldn't have been flailing around in the dark." I. I. I. "And you wouldn't have been second-guessing everything that had happened."

"I don't know. I guess because I was scared of what you'd say. And because I realized that what he was telling me wasn't outside the realm of realistic."

"But you could have contacted me afterward to explain," I rebutted. "I gave you that secret email address. It was safe."

She blinked rapidly. "I didn't contact you because contacting you was too damn hard. Don't you see that? I *had* to go cold turkey, it was the only way to keep my sanity. Little trickles of contact that couldn't go anywhere were just too fucking painful for me."

"So you hurt yourself, hurt me, thinking you were protecting me."

Sophia raised her chin defiantly. "I thought I was doing the right thing," she said. "And then it just felt so wrong and so painful. And now I'm here with you and I just want what we had before."

God I wanted that too. But… "I need to figure some things out first. About me. And just about all of this. Because what's to stop this happening again? I told you repeatedly that I'd protect your family. And I just told you that the man who came to see you lied. But what if you can't move past that fear? You'll be constantly wondering if it's going to happen again, and nothing I say will ease that if you don't trust me."

Her mouth twitched at the edges, lips trembling. "I honestly don't know. And I do trust you. It's everyone else at the periphery of your professional life that I don't trust." She squared her shoulders, took in a deep breath. "If you can't be in a relationship with me, I understand.

If you're scared, I understand." Despite her assertion, it looked like she'd barely managed to choke the words out.

"I *am* scared. I never want to go through that again. I can't."

"I know. Me either. But, if we can't move past this then I at least want to be your friend, Lexie. I don't think I can *not* be something in your life. If you're okay with that."

"Is that all you want?" I asked, surprised by my boldness.

"I think you're telling me that's all we can be, for now," she said carefully. "But I still want more, even if it's later."

"I just don't know if I can give you more later." I wanted to. Fuck, I wanted to. But first I needed to figure a few things out, like myself. Also, I needed to remove an obstacle named Lennon, because there was no way I was going to let him come between me and a partner again. I was furious, insulted, disgusted, and a million more emotions about the fact he'd had the temerity to even think he could, let alone actually, interfere in my personal life so enormously. I needed to make sure that nothing like this could ever happen again.

Sophia tried to mask her disappointment, but gave up and let it show. "Well, I'd rather have friendship than nothing at all." She smiled, and there was sadness in it. "And if you ever change your mind, and we're both in a place to do something about it, then maybe we can revisit how we feel."

"Okay," I said quietly. "That sounds good. I'm on board."

Her shoulders dropped. "Great. No pressure, obviously, from either of us. We'll just see how things turn out. But in the meantime, do you want to grab coffee or something this weekend?" There was no disguising the hopeful note in her question. "Test out that new friends thing?"

I was about to decline, simply because the thought of spending more time with Sophia in a setting where we weren't together felt uncomfortable. And that word—friend—hung thickly between us. I didn't want to be her friend. But, I needed friends. I needed people I could rely on, turn to when I needed support. Because right now I could count the number of best friends I had on a closed fist, the number of grab-a-coffee friends on one hand, and the number of close I-trust-you-but-we-haven't-been-friends-for-long friends on one finger. "That also sounds good. Why don't you text me with details in the next few days."

"Will do." Sophia gave me a long, searching look, but it seemed she'd either exhausted everything she wanted to say, or decided whatever she was about to say wasn't a good idea. So she said something I didn't want her to say. "Okay. I think I'd better go." She drank the rest of her wine and stood up before I'd even thought of how to respond. "I think we've talked enough for one day about what happened, and you need to have dinner."

I rocketed to my feet. "How do you know I haven't had dinner?"

"Because I know you would have only just gotten home when you texted me. And you never eat in your car, nor would you have had time to make dinner before I arrived. So, I'm assuming, and am confident in my assumption, that you haven't eaten yet." She managed to look both smug and concerned. I almost told her I'd been home for a while because I had a new assignment, but didn't feel like adding "talking about my dad" to tonight's emotional evisceration.

I crossed my arms over my chest, trying to block out the uncomfortable sensation that she still knew me well enough to know my habits. "Right. Thanks. For thinking of me needing to eat, that is."

"You're welcome. Thanks for letting me come around and try to explain what happened. And thanks for listening without being judgey about it all."

You're welcome. No worries. Sure thing. Every platitude-laden response that came to mind felt wrong. So I went with honesty. "Thanks for reaching out. I appreciate it." As I spoke, I felt the lightness of that honesty.

I followed her to the front door, my arms still crossed, keeping my eyes on the heels of her shoes. New shoes. I wondered what else had changed. She shrugged into her jacket then turned to face me. Sophia took a step toward me, then stopped abruptly, a nervous laugh bursting out of her mouth. "I just went to hug you. Reflex. Sorry."

"That's okay. I think," I added. "A hug is fine. Maybe even good." Great. A hug would be great.

Sophia smiled indulgently as she gently grasped my wrists. "Then you'll need to free up your arms," she said lightly, teasingly.

"Yeah, I know." But no matter how hard I tried to release the grip I had on myself, my arms had locked up.

"We don't have to hug," she said quietly, and I felt the tinge of disappointment.

"No, it's not that. I want to. But I'm just…" I laughed. "I don't even know what I am."

"Well, why don't we just…try." She carefully peeled my arms open from where they were still crossed protectively over my chest, opening the space to get inside. Sophia paused, her eyes locked with mine as if checking I was really sure. I was. She stepped closer then slowly wrapped her arms around my waist.

I exhaled shakily and hugged her back, keeping my arms above her waist. I relaxed into the hug, but not quite enough for tight, full-frontal body contact the way we used to hug. Clichés tumbled through my head. Dozens of them. She felt like coming home after being away for months. She felt like safety. She felt like the only place I was supposed to be, yet at the same time, she felt like a dangerous place.

I loosened my grip and thankfully Sophia read the movement and pulled back too. After inhaling deeply, she said, "I'll text you about coffee this weekend."

"Sounds good," I agreed.

She stretched up, and at the last second I realized she was about to kiss my cheek. We didn't kiss cheeks when we were together, but maybe that's what friends did? When I realized what was happening, I turned my head awkwardly and her featherlight kiss landed on the edge of my mouth. More off than on, barely there, yet still enough that I felt the heat. The sound Sophia made was somewhere between pleasure and concern, low and throaty.

Before I could tell my lips it was a bad idea, they'd sought hers out, and when I found her mouth, I couldn't help it—I kissed her. And she kissed me back. I gulped in a deep breath as Sophia reached up to thread her fingers through my hair, her lips parting and her tongue gently searching. That changed the kiss from soft and borderline chaste to passionate and desperate. Sophia moaned quietly when my tongue found hers, and in that instant I forgot every reason why I shouldn't be kissing her. I gripped her hips to pull her more tightly against me, but even as I pulled her to me I knew I should have pulled away. Should push her away.

But with every soft caress of her lips and tongue and tightening of her hands in my hair, I fell deeper into her. I wanted to drag her into my bedroom, *could* pull her away from the front door and to my bedroom, and I was sure she'd consent. That thought was enough to make me realize it felt all wrong. It was too soon and more importantly, we weren't even together.

We weren't even together.

So why were we kissing like lovers who'd been starved for each other's touch? Because, technically, that's what we were? No, we weren't. We'd broken up. That thought was like running headfirst into a brick wall and it dragged me out of my mindless enjoyment of her. I broke the kiss and took a step backward for extra security, because all I wanted was to press myself to her and taste her mouth again and again.

Sophia pressed her fingertips against her lips, her eyes wide, her cheeks flushed. I fought back my swirling emotion and swallowed hard to push down the tight lump of desire so I could force out, "I'm sorry. I shouldn't have done that." Though my apology was sincere, I didn't want to be sorry for kissing her. I wanted to embrace it, and do it again and again, even though I knew it was a terrible idea.

"Me too. And neither should I," she said hoarsely. She dropped her hand from her mouth and shuffled backward, toward the door. When her back bumped against it, Sophia fumbled behind herself for the handle. "I'll text you?" The question made it clear she was as unsure as I was about where we were and what should come next after that brain-melting kiss.

The only thing I could get out was a whispered, "Okay."

I secured the door behind her and slumped against it. My pulse still hammered in my ears, excitement still churned in my belly. And another sensation fought for recognition—not arousal exactly, not guilt, not hope.

Certainty.

And I wondered how the hell I was supposed to meet up with her for coffee, as just friends, without kissing her again…

Just friends. Right.

CHAPTER SIX

*Screaming at your boss probably isn't good
for career advancement*

So I'd kissed my ex-girlfriend. In the scheme of things, it wasn't exactly a big deal—I'm sure that sort of thing happened all the time. But…it felt like a huge deal. A huge deal in amongst a bunch of big deals crowding my life. The biggest of those big deals was Lennon's interference into my personal life. I pushed down my simmering anger about what he'd done, because if I let it simmer it would boil and then boil over and I needed to stay calm so I could deal with it strategically. If Sophia and I had any chance of moving forward, either with friendship or a relationship, I needed to deal with Lennon.

A relationship. With Sophia. Twenty-four hours ago, that wasn't even on my radar as possible. But now? Now it was pinging all over the place. I'd lain awake last night, going over our conversation, dissecting everything she'd said. The revelation that she'd been pushed toward breaking up with me didn't feel like as much of a relief as I'd thought it would. When we'd broken up, I'd convinced myself she'd been coerced (nice to know I was right) and was certain we could just jump back into things once I came home from my pointless assignment.

But now I wasn't so sure.

The months after the breakup had shown me that I needed to work on being more open with my partner. And if she'd caved so easily after just a suggestion that I'd been a lying liar who lies about *everything*, rather than that I was simply withholding information about work things I couldn't share, and that her family was always going to be on the table as leverage against me, then was that going to be a constant thorn in our sides?

Obviously there was more to the nuance of her conversation with Lennon, and I couldn't begin to unpack how she would have felt about his visit. It would have been frightening and confusing, and knowing she'd felt those things only added to my rage at him. And though I could guess, I still couldn't fully understand his motives for interfering, for lying.

But I was going to find out.

I didn't bother making an appointment with the director's secretary, and when I charged past her desk at nine a.m., greeting her surprised look with nothing more than an, "Is he in?" I knew she wouldn't stop me. I did, however, knock because barging in on an important or classified meeting or phone call wasn't great for my employment prospects.

"Come in?" was the response to my fist hammering. Lennon glanced up, his expression mildly interested. I closed the door and strode up to his desk. He closed the folder he was reading and put it into a drawer. "How may I help you, Alexandra?"

I took a deep breath. I hadn't really thought about how I was going to approach this, so I just went with my gut feeling and unleashed with all barrels. "How dare you!"

Lennon had the grace to look concerned. "How dare I…what?"

"Did you think I wouldn't find out it was you who was following Sophia while I was gone? That it was *you* who told Sophia to break up with me? How fucking dare you!" I spat out.

Lennon sighed. "Please sit down, Alexandra. And try to calm down before you say something you might regret."

I did as he'd asked—the sitting, not the not saying something I might regret. "I'm *dying* to know how you're going to explain this."

He clasped his hands on top of the desk, and thankfully didn't skirt around the answer. "I was trying to protect you, Alexandra. Now that your father is gone, I consider it my duty to him. We were friends. He would have wanted me to protect you."

What a fucking joke. "Protecting me is respecting my privacy. Protecting me is not doing something that almost ruined my life and my work and someone else's life. Someone I love and care about. Protecting me is realizing that Sophia makes me a better person and in turn, a better analyst. So in future, if you'd kindly stay the fuck out of my personal business, I'd appreciate it. Because you stepped where you have no right stepping and I don't even have the words to express how infuriated I am with what you did."

His jaw tightened, but he didn't admonish me. It was amazing what you could get away with when your dad was BFFs with the director of the agency and you might hold the key to the nation's safety somewhere in the dark recesses of your brain. "I was trying to protect you," he repeated. "You don't understand what's at stake here. And you were blinded by your relationship with her, you couldn't see how important your work was. You'd lost your focus."

I heard what he was saying. I really did. But with every word that was supposed to appease me, I just grew angrier. Lennon, for all his years of being in charge of people, clearly had no idea of human nature and emotions. "You're wrong," I said emphatically. "I wasn't blinded, nor had I lost my focus. And I know my dad. Both he and my mom would have wanted me to be happy. My dad would never have done this and he wouldn't have wanted you to do it either. He was many things, and maybe not the most emotionally expressive father but I know he supported and respected me enough to never try to push me away from someone I love. So you have *zero* right to go against what we both know he would have wanted for me, spouting bullshit about protecting me, when what you're really protecting is Halcyon's interests."

"You're right. Halcyon's interests. You're being naïve, Alexandra. And petulant. Neither of those things are good character traits."

"Do you do this to all Halcyon and agency employees? Try to break up relationships so people focus on nothing but their work?" I raised my eyebrows at his silence, silence because of course he didn't. When he pressed his lips together, I confirmed, "No. So you don't get to do it to me. I don't care who you were to my father. I barely know you as 'Uncle Michael,' you were only that because that's what my dad called you to me. You have no right to my personal life."

Lennon was apparently allergic to apologies. All he said was, "I did what needed to be done."

"And you were wrong," I said simply. "If I wasn't working on something so important, I'd tell Halcyon to go fuck itself. Stay out of my business or I'm finished. I don't care how important my dad's work is."

"You'd put your personal life ahead of your obligations to your country? Do I need to remind you what's at stake here? The very integrity of our nation."

Of course I knew what was at stake, but I ignored his obvious statement. I shook my head. "You know, all this time, I thought it was the president interfering, trying to make my life miserable to punish me. But it was you. Did you make him send me on that assignment? To get me away from Sophia?"

"No," Lennon said instantly, forcefully. "I was vehemently opposed to it. I wanted to start on *this*, and with you away we could not. Then there was the danger of you being overseas, the possibility of you being harmed or worse. Without you, I don't think we can break into your father's files."

"The danger." I almost choked on my incredulity. "You made me so upset that my focus was completely shot. Because of her breaking up with me, not because we were together. I could have been killed if not for Burton. So, well done." I golf-clapped him.

"I did what I thought I had to do," he said again. "I tried everything I could think of, everything that wouldn't physically harm either of you, that is. Hampering your communication in an attempt to temper your bond didn't work, so I had to intervene." He was completely confident in his actions, no remorse or guilt. Lennon's Way was the right way. And that was that. And that was fine, he could be like that, but I'd never trust him completely ever again. I was always going to be suspicious of his motives.

I ground my molars. All those times our video calls had cut out while I was overseas. Every missed message, every call that just wouldn't go through. And then cutting the phone and Internet services on Christmas. What fucking asshole would do that? Well, now I knew it was "You," I seethed. "And here I was blaming the president this whole time, but it was you. Do you always make other people take the blame for you, Lennon?"

His eyes bore holes into me. "Be careful, Alexandra."

Fair point. I dialed myself back a notch. "Well, it's done the opposite of what you thought. Sophia and I are still talking. We still care about each other. You can't just tell someone to stop feeling." I stopped myself there, before I told him intimate personal details.

His jaw bunched. Finally, a reaction. "I didn't count on the strength of your connection, on Ms. Flores's tenacity."

"You're lucky she's tenacious. You have *no* idea what you did to me, or if you do, you obviously don't care. Nor do you understand. You almost fucked everything up for me, personally and professionally. Why didn't you drop it when I asked you to?"

"I don't need to explain myself any further," he said evenly.

"No? Okay then, let *me* explain myself. My relationships outside of work, with Sophia or anyone else, are off-limits to you, Halcyon, the agency. My personal life is No Man's Land. Or I'm done, with all of this. I mean it."

Lennon's expression remained neutral. So neutral that it felt unnatural. And all he did was nod.

My stomach dropped. What else had he done? What else was he planning? "What? Please don't tell me you're actually my real dad or something, and that's why you're so fucking intrusive into my personal life. Because that would just about top me off."

"No, I am certainly not your father, in any sense of the word. And yes, I understand. It won't happen again." His tone was so impassive that I didn't know if he was being truthful. If he wasn't, if I caught a whiff that he was even *thinking* about me and Sophia, then I was done with Halcyon.

"Good," I said crisply. "Why do you care so much about Sophia? What is it about her specifically that has you so worked up? It's not like I've been single my whole life." Just most of it…

"I have nothing against Sophia Flores personally. But she appeared in your life at a very tumultuous time, and I feel she made it more so. I would have had the same misgivings about any woman at that time. You know what happened with Berenson. And you risked the integrity of that investigation for what? A woman?"

I snorted. "Misgivings." My mild amusement turned sharply, and I had to grip the armrests tightly to keep myself from launching out of the chair at him. "I'd slap you but I've had a taste of incarceration and I didn't like it." I stood up abruptly. "And I'm too fucking polite. But if you even so much as hint at anything to do with my relationships other than something along the lines of 'Congratulations, Alexandra, on your happiness,' you'll have my resignation from both the agency and Halcyon within an hour and I don't care if I haven't finished breaking my dad's encryption. Are we clear?"

I wondered if he knew I was bluffing. Mostly bluffing. I wasn't going to tolerate any more interference from him or the president in my personal life, but I also couldn't turn my back on the biggest investigation this side of the Kunduz Intelligence.

He nodded once, briskly. "Yes, we are."

I stood up and smoothed my hands down my blouse, surprised they were steady and not trembling with outrage. "Excellent." Smiling tightly, I told him to, "Have a nice day, Lennon."

I patted myself on the back for not slamming the door.

How do you process something like this? I'm honestly not sure you can. And how do you rid yourself of fury when someone betrays you so deeply? I'd never considered myself a person with a bad temper. Sure, I'd been mad plenty of times. Furious here and there. Utterly outraged once or twice (mostly recently). But I'd never felt this seething, hot, I-want-to-physically-hurt-someone-for-what-they-did rage before.

I needed air. Instead of stopping at my floor, I took the elevator all the way down to the lobby. The security personnel looked up as I charged toward them, and I forced aside my foul mood as I went through the mag arch with my badge held out for inspection.

"Forget something in your car, Dr. Martin?" Kevin asked, not hiding his surprise.

I smiled. "No. Just need a little fresh air."

He nodded slowly. "I hear ya. Breathe some in for me."

"Will do."

I walked out of the building, wishing I'd remembered that it was gray and breezy outside. Ah well. Wrapping my arms about my midsection, I conjured up a mental image of warm sun on my face. I wandered by the concrete bollards with flowers spilling from the top that stood guard in front of the front doors of the building. Both decorative and protective. After walking by the bollards, I backtracked to smell the blooms, disappointed that they had no scent.

As I followed the path to the parking lots, I was moving away from the flow of employees. After a few near misses, and too many interactions for my current mood, I stepped off the path and continued my brain-cleansing walk through the first parking lot. The masses of assault-rifle-wielding security guys were undoubtedly watching me.

Some of my anger at Lennon had abated, and my thoughts inevitably turned to Sophia. And last night. Was being in love with someone enough to rekindle a relationship? It *felt* like it was, but then I remembered her email after she'd broken things off. What was one of the lines? *I wish being in love was enough, but I don't think it is.*

But was that email even really her? If it'd been Lennon pressuring her, then every word in it, every word she'd said when she'd called me to end things had been untruthful. I had to believe love was enough, especially now that I'd removed one of the major issues that'd come between us. Fuck, my head was a mess. And running through all the maybes and what-ifs wasn't helping. I had to trust that if Sophia and I were meant to get back together, then we would.

When we met up for coffee this weekend, I was going to tell her exactly how I felt, and what I had done with Lennon to ensure nothing like what had happened would ever happen again. And hope she'd accept me for who I was and who I was trying to be.

But now? Now I needed to get back inside and figure out what the hell my dad had hidden for me. If he had at all. Maybe this whole thing was a wild goose chase. But it was still my goose to chase down.

"I wondered where you were. You look like you've had a horrible morning," Jeffrey observed when I came back into the office. I'd told him I just had to duck out for a few minutes. And that was almost an hour ago…

I flicked on the electric kettle. "That's an astute observation. But I'd say less horrible and more just…antagonistic," I said as I filled my tea strainer with Oolong. "Actually, no. It was cleansing."

He spun around fully on his chair and folded his hands in his lap. "Is this something I should know about, or something you want to share?"

Sharing sounded amazing. Maybe Jeffrey would have some idea about what I should do. I blew out a loud breath. "Do you remember when I was telling you that the president was punishing me by sending me overseas for that assignment? Then he was fucking with my life, having people follow Sophia, messing with our communication services and all that just to remind me that he's the guy with power?"

"I remember."

"Turns out, that following Sophia and fucking with my life by interrupting comms part? It was actually Lennon. The president had nothing to do with anything except demanding I be sent away for our assignment at the end of last year."

His mouth fell open. "Lennon as in the director of this agency and part of the Halcyon Division Lennon?" Interesting. I wondered why Lennon hadn't told Jeffrey that he actually ran Halcyon. But if Lennon hadn't clarified his role, then I wasn't going to spill the beans.

"The very one," I confirmed. "And there's more. It was Lennon who told Sophia to break up with me. Apparently it was for my own good, my safety, but I fail to see the connection."

"I don't see it either." Jeffrey frowned. "But Ms. Flores seems to be an intelligent woman. Why would she go along with this?"

"Yes she is. And she went along with Lennon's breakup plot because she's been through this shit with me before, and Lennon knew exactly what buttons to push. He implied that remaining with me would forever keep her family in the government's crosshairs. I feel like I should send the president an apology bouquet for wishing he'd die in a pit of lava for messing with my life." I shrugged. "But, he did mess with it, just not quite as much as I'd thought, so you know what? Fuck him too."

Jeffrey looked aghast. "Jesus. Why would Lennon do that?"

"He *claimed* to have my best interests at heart. Said Sophia was making me lose focus, which is absolute bullshit. Aaaand…Don't go all 'you're a nepotism baby' on me, but Lennon and my dad were best friends." At that revelation, Jeffrey's eyebrows shot up, but quickly settled. "I knew him from when I was a kid, but I only really saw him a few times when we were back in the States between my dad's diplomatic postings. I don't know him well at all in his role as Dad's BFF." Though I wouldn't say I knew him well in his role as Halcyon Lennon, either. "His view was that my dad would have wanted him to intervene, for my *safety*, which is also bullshit." I placed my hands flat on my desk. "So now I'm furious at him. Just another emotion to add to all the others I'm currently enjoying."

Jeffrey frowned, but it was more a frown of working things out than of displeasure. "This just gets more interesting. Maybe we need to ask him about his relationship with your father. Given they both worked in intelligence, surely he could be of some use."

"I don't know if Lennon and my dad ever worked together, though the connection is obvious." I gestured to the 1994 folder on my desk. "There's no mention of Lennon thus far, not even a code name that I would attribute obviously to him. And wouldn't Lennon have told me everything he thought pertinent?"

"You would think so," Jeffrey mused. "But given his behavior, I have doubts. He may be protecting his own interests, things he did if he was undercover. Or his dealings may still be classified." He shrugged. "We have no way of knowing."

"Search the databases? Either we'll find nothing, something, or something that leads to nothing."

Jeffrey nodded. "We can. Then at least we've covered another base."

I bit my lower lip until the pain was too much. "Can you please do it? I'm pissy at him and really need a break from his power trips." I huffed out a frustrated breath. "I still cannot fucking believe he did that. The audacity is astounding."

Jeffrey seemed unconcerned by my rant. And then he made an excellent point, one I hadn't considered. "People in a position of power want to control things that they think belong to them. He thought you were his because of your dad I guess, and because he needed you for something and he helped you remain free. He thinks you owe him. Or that's my best guess." He held up both hands. "That doesn't make it right though."

"No, it doesn't."

"So how did you figure out it was Lennon, not the president, who'd been interfering in your romantic life?"

"I asked Sophia to come around last night to talk."

"And?" he said, his voice pitching up two octaves over the three seconds he took to draw the word out.

"She came around and we talked."

"And?" he said again, his voice going higher this time.

"She told me the guy who'd been following her had come to her apartment, said he was my boss, and told her she should break up with me. When she described him, I knew who it was. And I confronted him about"—I checked my watch—"forty-five minutes ago. He didn't bother denying it. So I tore him a new asshole about it, and told him to stay the fuck out of my personal life."

He air-clapped. "Nice."

"I thought so." Inhaling a quick breath, I blurted, "And I kissed Sophia. Or, she kissed me." I waved impatiently. "Whatever. We kissed." Excited butterflies began flitting around my stomach at the memory. It had felt so natural, yet so wrong.

"I see," Jeffrey said, his calm expression at odds with the almost manic excitement in those two words. "And how do you feel about that?"

"I'm not sure," I said honestly. "But I know I don't feel bad about it. We're going to meet up for coffee or something this weekend and talk some more." And definitely not kiss again. "We can see where we're both at and maybe where to go from here." I exhaled loudly. "I can tell she wants to get back together. She basically said as much."

"Is that what you want?"

I didn't hesitate. "Yes. Of course. But I don't know if it's the right thing to do." Preempting his "Why the fuck not?" I said, "I need to be sure we won't have the same issues again, with me unconsciously, or consciously, not telling her things I should tell her." I didn't need to elaborate—Jeffrey was well aware of the requirement, the…*duty* of people in our line of work to withhold information from significant others. My problem was that I hadn't quite figured out where the line of what I *could* share was. "And then of course, I need to be sure she's not thinking that someone is going to come for her dad again just to stir up trouble to keep me under control."

"Not wanting to go down the same road again is a good start for changing your direction toward happiness, don't you think?"

"Yes. But not wanting to and being able to are two completely separate things."

"Well, for what it's worth, I'm rooting for you two."

I smiled. "Thanks, personal cheerleader. Now, what say we read some more about my dad's other life."

Jeffrey fluttered his eyelashes. "I thought you'd never ask."

CHAPTER SEVEN

Almost as fun as a black-light rave

We'd finished reading through Dad's dossiers on Wednesday, and after comparing notes and making lists of anything that stood out—such as repeated mentions of assets beyond usual interactions, odd events and the like—it was time to move on. There was only one thing that made me really pay attention: the repeated mention of someone code-named "Frost," and the fact most information about this person was redacted. I had no idea if they were an asset, a target, or a partner. And all I could think about when I saw that name was the excerpt from the Robert Frost poem in every book my dad gave me. No such thing as a coincidence…

I brought in all my dad's books on Thursday morning, ready for us to pore over, and I could not express how unenthused I was by the prospect of looking through thousands and thousands of pages, searching for some clue. If there even was a clue.

"Are you starting a workplace library, Dr. Martin?" Kevin asked as I handed him everything to feed through the x-ray. I positioned myself to see the screen, and stared intently, hoping for a hidden compartment or something in the books. So far, nothing.

Laughing, I held up *War and Peace*. "Do you know anyone who'd want to trudge through this brick during their lunch breaks?"

"I would," he said brightly, as he set the final book on the belt. "I might finish it by Christmas."

"Then you're a better reader than me," I said, moving to the other end of the belt to gather up my stack of reading material. "Speaking of reading…" I'd anticipated him commenting on my books this morning and had tailored my fact of the day for it. "The Guinness World Record for the fastest reader is from 1990, a guy who can read more than twenty-five thousand words per minute. For comparison, the average is around two to four hundred words per minute."

Kevin whistled through his teeth. "The Bugatti of readers. But I'm perfectly happy reading at my beat-up Honda level."

Laughing, I agreed, "Same. Though I wouldn't mind a little Ferrari boost to get through this stack."

Kevin helped me pack up my tomes back into the cardboard box, then wished me good luck with my reading, and a good day.

Up in the office, I set the eleven books out on the middle table in age order left to right. Jeffrey rubbed his hands together. "All right. Time to get educated." He picked up *Moby Dick*, and opened to the page that held the inscription, murmuring, "'The woods are lovely, dark and deep, But I have promises to keep, And miles to go before I sleep, And miles to go before I sleep.' Robert Frost, *Stopping by Woods on a Snowy Evening*." He looked up. "It's kind of melancholy, but also… staunch, isn't it? Like haven't we all felt like just giving up at one point or another, but then we trudge on because we have to?"

"Mmm. I remember the poem from high school English, but I read through it again to refamiliarize myself. It doesn't feel relevant as a whole, but this final stanza really does."

Jeffrey grabbed a random book—*Anna Karenina*—and opened it to my dad's writing. As he turned it this way and that, and flicked through the pages, I recited the rest of *Stopping by Woods on a Snowy Evening* for him from memory. Thanks, Mrs. Lowen, for hammering that into my brain as a teenager. "I know my dad feeling suicidal isn't off the table but my gut feeling is that he was tired, but devoted, and quoting this poem was his way of passing the task to me. But I also think there must be something relevant in those words. My father rarely did anything without deep, conscious thought or meaning. And I don't think this inscription would be any different."

"Yeah," Jeffrey agreed. "Then let's see what we can figure out."

Jeffrey and I spent the day slowly turning the pages of the first two novels—*Moby Dick* and *1984*—until I felt cross-eyed, and I'm sure Jeffrey did too. But so far, there was nothing. I'd imagined Xs marking the spots my dad wanted to draw me to, or lines of text in the margins, or…*something* to tell me I was on the right track. But there was absolutely nothing. Which just made me feel like I was on the wrong track.

After I finished *1984*—we'd each taken one then swapped to make sure we hadn't missed anything—I dropped it onto the table and pulled my glasses off, setting them on top of the book. "Is it just me, or does this feel pointless?"

He stretched both arms above his head, twisting left and right. "I wouldn't say pointless, but at the moment I'm struggling to connect the dots. What are we missing here?"

"A crystal ball?"

Jeffrey snorted out a loud laugh. "And your dad's cipher codebook."

"Knowing him, that would all be up here." I tapped my temple. "I know I've said it before, but fuck, I wish he'd told me about this. Left me some sort of clue as to where and how I should be looking."

"I think he wouldn't want to risk you knowing until you needed to know. In case you got compromised."

"Mmm." I wrinkled my nose. "And him telling me means he would have had to come clean about the whole undercover intel officer thing."

Jeffrey laughed. "That's true. And I know I've said it before, but knowing you, Lexie, I'm sure your dad had all the faith in you, and gave you all the tools you needed for this task."

"I hope so." A quick check of my watch told me it was approaching the time I had to leave for an appointment. I'd finally managed to snag a spot with my personal therapist to supplement my professional one—thanks to my brush with death overseas, I'd been rushed up the waiting list to see my agency-appointed therapist my first week back at work. I'd left that work session feeling, well…*revitalized* was probably the best way to describe it.

But also, thanks to being on the run, incarcerated, then deployed overseas for six months, I hadn't seen my personal therapist since before the Kunduz Intelligence. Over eight months. And I was desperate to talk to him. I usually felt good after therapy, even if I'd emotionally eviscerated myself or been given some hard truths, but now I was ready for more therapy, ready to feel like a new person. A person on the path to being a better person.

Lennon apparently had a radar for the worst possible times to come check in, as evidenced by the firm knock on the door as I was packing up my laptop for the day. I would have thought after Tuesday morning's little angry tête-à-tête, he'd give me some space. No such luck. I'd thought the knock might be Derek—I hadn't seen him since my first week back—and when I opened the office door and saw Lennon, I almost just closed the door again.

He moved into the open doorway before my lizard brain slammed the door in his face, and I stepped out of his way after he'd stepped into my way. His demeanor was casual, almost relaxed. "Alexandra. Jeffrey." He closed the door behind him.

I crossed my arms over my chest. "Hello."

Lennon looked between the two of us. "I'm just here to check in on your progress."

Jeffrey gathered his coffee mug and empty protein bar wrapper and stood. "I'll leave you two to it."

"No need," I said cheerfully. "You're part of the team too. It's your progress as much as mine." I knew he'd understand the look I sent his way. I didn't want to be alone with Lennon right now. I'd had enough of his bullshit for one week. For one lifetime.

Jeffrey gave me the slightest nod, but instead of sitting back at his desk, he moved to the kitchenette and began making coffee, eating a cookie to sustain him through the pod process. He was still in the room, here if I needed him, but in the unobtrusive way he seemed to have perfected.

Lennon turned away from Jeffrey and sat at one of the chairs on the long side of the I. He directed his question to me, apparently taking the mindset that if he ignored Jeffrey, he wasn't there. "And how is your task coming along, Alexandra?"

"Slowly. *We*"—I made sure to emphasize that word—"finished reading all my dad's career dossiers. We have some notes, a few overlapping events and players, but nothing that I'd class as groundbreaking." Because I was still pissy with him, I didn't want to tell him the direction I was taking, but I kind of had to. "I have some books Dad gave me, and that's all. So far, there's nothing obvious in them, but that's our next step. Reading. Hopefully, between his dossiers and the books, something will stand out."

Lennon looked dubious. You try finding a pass phrase out of thin air, then, if you don't like my methods, pal.

"Did your parents have a rented storage locker? Is there anywhere your father might have stored anything that hinted at the code? Something that might lead you there faster than reading some novels?" He glanced at *War and Peace*. "Long novels at that."

Lennon's pushiness was both annoying, and confusing. I mean, yeah, this was a big deal, but he'd also been sitting on it for how many months? Years even. Me taking a week or more to sort through some things wasn't outside the scope of timeliness. Skepticism and caution were in my analyst DNA, and something felt off. Two major things about my dad's hard drive were still stumbling blocks for me: why would he give it to Lennon but not provide the tool to unlock it, and why had Lennon held off telling me about Dad's work for so long? So I decided to keep some things to myself.

I shook my head. "Nope. There was nothing in their estate that hinted at anything like that. No storage unit payments, no keys, no weird words. Nothing," I lied smoothly. There *was* a storage unit, but I hadn't been inside yet. Also, what kind of idiot intel officer would have written down keys to anything, just scribbled in a book, just sitting around for anyone to find?

"That's unfortunate," he murmured.

"You're telling me," I said lightly. "It would make this a whole lot easier if I had a map to what I was looking for." Laughing in an attempt to pull his focus away from possible hidden treasures, I said, "This whole thing is just like Dad though, to make me use my brain for something like this. He never let me have anything easily."

Lennon smiled, but it didn't quite touch his eyes. "Yes, it sure is, but I believe his way taught you to be a better analyst."

I played along. "Yes it did."

"Okay then. Thank you for the status update." Lennon stood, buttoning his suit jacket. "I'll let you get back to it."

"Actually, I'm done for the day," I said breezily. "I have a therapy appointment this afternoon. I have some personal things to get off my chest." The pointed look I sent his way had no effect, but I heard Jeffrey's quiet snort.

Lennon smiled tightly. "I hope it's beneficial. Anything that helps you stay on top of things is important."

Thankfully, Jeffrey came over with his fresh coffee and cookies, because otherwise I would have said something I might have regretted. As soon as the office door closed behind Lennon, Jeffrey sat down and spun his chair toward me. He widened his eyes comically. "Tense."

As I packed up my things, I rambled, "You're telling me. I just…I don't trust him now. And I know it's ridiculous to let something personal seep into this, but I can't help it. He overstepped in a massive way, and made a bad judgment call. It makes me wonder what other things he's fucking up."

Jeffrey shrugged. "You don't have to explain to me, Lexie. You know I'm all about following gut feelings."

"Thanks. You almost done for the day too?"

He quickly chewed a mouthful of cookie. "I'm going to read back through a few things in your dad's dossiers, then call it a day too."

I squeezed his shoulder. "Don't stay too late. It's against the rules of Lexie's Code Cracking Club."

He held up his hand, pinkie outstretched. "I won't. Pinkie promise. I'll make sure all this stuff gets into the safe."

I hooked my pinkie with his, then left him to his reading. On my way down to the lobby, the elevator stopped on my old floor, opening the doors to my good work friend, Sam. His mouth fell open. "Girl," he deadpanned. "You look so fucking tired." He stepped in and folded me into a hug. "I've missed you. Nobody else on our team can gossip for shit." What he really meant was—nobody else listened to his gossip like I did. "How's the new fancy taskforce going?"

"It's nice being the boss," I said, deliberately evading the question. I knew Sam would pick up on it, and also not push me about it.

"I'm sure it is. Speaking of bosses, you've missed some interesting stuff with ours."

I frowned. "Derek?"

"Mhmmmm." He drew the sound out over three seconds. At my "don't leave me hanging, asshole" look, Sam elaborated, "The director is in his office almost every day and let me tell you—there's been some arguments. I think our boss's boss is upset with him about something."

Interesting. I feigned a smile and a shrug and spat out the first thing that came to mind. "Maybe Derek's just trying to get you guys some pay raises and the director is resistant."

"Maybe. And it's *us* guys," he corrected, pointing at me. "You're still one of us."

"I know," I assured him. "How's Muffin?" It was weird not having Sam's constant cat updates, and I was interested, but this was also the surest way to redirect his attention from having to talk about Lennon and Derek. Lennon and Derek who were part of Halcyon. It was logical they'd be talking, right?

Sam took the bait immediately. "Gorgeous as ever. I bought her a new collar and she looks *stunning*."

"I'm sure she does."

"Don't be a stranger," he said as he headed toward the ground-floor café, likely for his afternoon ham and cheese croissant.

"I'll try not to be," I promised.

I spent the first twenty minutes of my therapy session hastily explaining my life since we'd last spoken. To his credit, my therapist just sat there calmly taking notes and occasionally asking me to expand on a point (when I could). It would be so much easier if I could combine my personal and professional therapists and not omit parts of my personal that weren't particularly relevant to my work therapist, and parts of my professional that I just couldn't tell anyone who didn't have clearance.

When I was finally done blurting, he smiled, folding his hands on top of his crossed legs. "Well, that's a lot to unpack. I'm going to reschedule an appointment so I can slot you in again in a few days." Oh dear. Even I knew it was bad when your therapist wanted to see you more frequently. He straightened his glasses, smiling a smile I knew all too well. "Now, let's see where this takes us."

We delved into the nitty-gritty, which obviously led to me telling him about seeing Sophia again, me kissing Sophia—which earned me a disappointed-but-supportive dad-like look—and the coffee meetup (not a date!) this weekend. I'd told him the face-value reason Sophia had first given for breaking up with me, which worked well enough for therapy purposes. My therapist asked me what had changed between us, aside from me being home, for me to consider getting back together with her.

It was easy enough to explain. The love had never left, it was just the external factors (a polite way to put it) and my being away from her that'd caused the breakup. Those external factors were gone, so why not think about getting back together? That'd earned me a hmm and a few lines of scribble on his notepad.

When I shared my thoughts about my natural disinclination toward sharing information, which spilled into a disinclination toward sharing personal information that *should* be shared, and how I wanted to change that, it was like a lightbulb pinged over his head. "Making positive changes to your life can help lead you toward feeling better. And if that leads to a change in a relationship, then that's excellent. But you should make the changes for yourself first, Lexie, because if you change for a person and they don't receive that change in a positive way, you risk feeling like the change was for nothing, or, worst-case scenario, unravel the good and hard work you've put into your mental space."

Made sense. "Do you think I should wait until I've fixed myself before I start a relationship with Sophia again? Potential relationship," I amended. It felt silly to dance around it when both Sophia and I seemed to be moving toward romantic reconciliation. She'd basically said she was on board, and really—there was no reason for us to not get back together, now that Lennon wouldn't be interfering. But I didn't want to rush into it without being sure what we'd build the second time around would last. "Because how can I say I'm not going to do this, or I'm going to work on doing that, without actually having those scenarios presented to me, in a relationship?"

"First of all, you're not broken. So there's nothing to fix. But let's first make the commitment to change this aspect of yourself that you felt hindered your relationship last time and continue to commit to that change every day. And then, if there *is* a relationship, we can work on those positive changes."

I nodded, fighting against the lump in my throat. "Okay."

He smiled gently. "And if you find yourself slipping back into the habits you're trying to break, then don't beat yourself up about it. Progress isn't always linear, and as long as you're moving toward your goal, you're going in the right direction."

* * *

Jeffrey burst into the office on Friday morning, full of excitement and enthusiasm. After a cheerful "Good morning," he dropped his messenger bag onto his desk and began rummaging inside. "So I was lying in bed last night, thinking about this case, those books, and I had a brainwave."

I held back my childish "Did it hurt?" and went with a calm, "And what was that?"

Jeffrey held up a flashlight and a Zippo lighter. "Invisible ink! Old school, but…your dad was kind of old school. No offense," he added quickly.

Grinning, I shrugged. "He *was* old school. And possibly a dozen more things I'll never know."

Jeffrey babbled on like a nerdy kid explaining his favorite science thing. "So, we know 'invisible ink' was a legitimate communication technique for undercover intelligence officers, and I'm not ashamed to say my school buddies and I used lemon juice to share what we thought was top-secret information as kids."

I smiled at that, then also the mental image of my dad, hunched over his desk, dipping a fountain pen in lemon juice to write some secret message on these books. Though there was probably something a little more high-tech for a legit spy-type person. "It pains me to say this, Jeffrey, but that's pretty genius." I took the flashlight and turned it on, spraying a purple UV beam over my desk. "Let's try the black light first—I don't want to risk damaging the pages with flame just yet." Or worse yet, accidentally setting something so important on fire.

"My thoughts exactly." He held up a hand for a high-five, and I obliged him. "God, you and me, Lexie. We are the dream team." Jeffrey grabbed *Moby Dick* and opened to the first page. He held the book wide open so I could cover the entirety of the spread pages with the black-light flashlight. There was nothing. He turned the page. Still nothing. It wasn't until we got to the next page, where my dad had written the date, that we found something.

A huge something.

There was a neat square drawn around the 10 in 10th January.

"Fuuuck," I breathed.

Jeffrey echoed my sentiment.

So there really *was* a hidden message in my dad's books. Oh my fucking god. Why hadn't I thought of this sooner? It was *so* obvious. I mean, I was sure I would have thought of "invisible ink" once I'd spent some time with the books, but I wish it had occurred to me earlier.

I moved the beam away then back again, watching that marking appear and then disappear under the UV light. When I looked up, Jeffrey's expression seemed as maniacal as mine felt. We moved through another few pages, looking for more hidden markings. And there they were, glistening under the black light. We kept flicking through the book, kept finding random notations in the pages. There was no obvious pattern that I could see, but here and there were lines over certain letters, and periods under others, shining like the North Star. Shit, this was going to take ages, first to make sure we had every single one taken down and then figuring out what it all meant and how to put the puzzle together. But the enormity of it wasn't tedious, it was exhilarating.

I turned off the UV light and Jeffrey calmly closed the book. We sat quietly, just staring at each other. There were no words needed. After a few minutes of contemplating what we'd just found, Jeffrey leaned back in his chair, propping his hands behind his head. His entire demeanor screamed casual confidence. "What did you call me? A…*genius*, wasn't it?"

I leaned over and patted the top of his head. "Yes," I said sincerely. "You are a fucking genius."

After we'd finished being stunned at what we'd found, and congratulating ourselves (or mostly congratulating Jeffrey for realizing first) for figuring out there were hidden markings, we went on a mission to buy two lamps, black-light bulbs, some protective eyewear—mine were a set of very unfashionable clunkers to fit over my glasses—and document-holder stands for the books so we could keep pages open. Photographing and printing out my dad's squiggles would have made it a whole lot easier, but I did not want to take whatever we found outside of these secure walls. I almost laughed. Some of these books had been outside of secure walls for decades.

I could have requisitioned what I needed, but I needed the supplies urgently and didn't want to wait for the slowly turning bureaucratic wheels to eventually spit out my items sometime next week. Meg at the security station raised an eyebrow when we returned from our shopping mission and loaded the things for scanning clearance, but she said nothing aside from polite greetings. Thank god, because I was too amped up to formulate anything plausible to explain why we seemed to be crime scene techs now.

Jeffrey and I agreed that we would both go through every book to ensure we hadn't missed any of the markings, though that seemed unlikely given they stood out like neon under the black light. But before I started, I went into the Zen Zone and spent fifteen minutes meditating some of the vibrating energy out of my body.

When I came back out from behind the privacy screens, Jeffrey had set up a book holder and lamp on each of our desks. "So how do you want to work this?" he asked. "What do you think is relevant here?"

"Obviously any word that's got a marking on it, and whatever letter that marking is on. I think that word should be transcribed in full, with the marking in place over or under the letters as they appear." So far, it seemed there were only two sorts of markings: lines over certain letters, and periods under others. "And the page number that it's on."

"Do you think the surrounding text, like the whole sentence is relevant?" Jeffrey asked. "Or just what's marked?"

"Honestly, I don't know. *But* my gut says that if it's relevant, Dad would have marked it. Let's leave the surrounding text for now, but we have the page number if we need to go back because we can't make whatever we end up with make sense."

"Copy that," he said cheerfully.

It was probably the last cheerful thing he said for the rest of the day… I'd love to say going through endless pages under a black light and carefully writing down the secret markings was fun. But after a while, a very short while, it became monotonous. And very *very* eye-straining. After four hours of my poring over *1984* and Jeffrey studying *Moby Dick*, he stood, slowly twisting from side to side before he bent forward to stretch his back. We were still only about halfway through each book—being thorough took time.

"Do you want me to get you a standing desk?" I asked as I watched him trying to alleviate his back pain. "Because I am a boss who cares about her employees." After living and working with him for six months, I knew his body niggles.

"No, but thank you," he said, the words muffled by his bent-over position. "Standing for too long is just as bad as sitting for too long. Sit and then get up and stretch has worked for me for years. I'm too scared to try something new. And I'm not your employee," he teased.

"That's right. I keep forgetting because it's so much fun bossing you around."

Jeffrey grunted and I couldn't tell if it was one of annoyance or laughter. "What kind of UV-visible ink do you think your dad used?"

"I have no idea. Maybe he got it at a craft store, maybe he made it somehow, maybe the agency has a special spy blend of ink. Does it matter? It works, that's what's important."

"True." When he'd straightened again, he asked, "What are you up to this weekend?"

"Aside from obsessing over my dad's hidden code and the fact I can't work on it?" I mean, I *could* work on it if I came into the office over the weekend. But overworking myself on this would lead to some superfast burnout. Maybe I'd just pop in for an hour or two on Sunday or something.

He chuckled. "Yes, aside from that."

"I'm seeing Sophia tomorrow."

"That's great," he said with genuine excitement.

"Yeah," I said on an exhale. "Nothing exciting. We're just going for coffee and a walk and maybe lunch or something like that." Something in public where there was no chance of spontaneous kissing. Fuck, who was I kidding? If we were going to kiss, being in public wasn't going to stop us. If we were going to kiss, I didn't think anything was going to stop us…

CHAPTER EIGHT

Conversations with your ex can be awkward but, thankfully, this one wasn't

Just a casual meetup with a friend who was also my ex-girlfriend. Nothing more. Coffee. Talking. A walk. Maybe food. Maybe more walking. Maybe talking about our relationship. No big deal. I wiped steam from my bathroom mirror and stared at my reflection. I looked pretty good, considering all that'd happened in the past few weeks and the fact I hadn't slept well last night because I'd been thinking about today. Not that it mattered how I looked because this wasn't a date. But after I put on skinny jeans, a loose linen top and my favorite comfortable-for-walking but also slightly dressy sandals, I added a little makeup. Just because I was going out in public. Nothing to do with seeing Sophia. Then I spritzed myself with perfume. Again, just because I was going out in public. Not because Sophia liked it.

We'd agreed to meet at ten a.m. at a café near a park that had a few miles of easy, lightly forested walking trails. My Uber arrived early and I stood outside the café to wait for Sophia, nervously fiddling with my handbag strap. Being nervous felt ridiculous, but here I was. Nervous. This wasn't a first date—I'd definitely been nervous the first time we met—and it wasn't like conversation between us had ever been difficult. Scratch that. The content of some conversations had been hard, but we'd never had trouble with actual communication. If nothing else, I knew we wouldn't be staring at each other in awkward silence.

Sophia had apparently had the same thought as me about taking an Uber, and a Toyota Camry pulled up to the curb right at ten. My stomach flip-flopped as Sophia slipped from the back seat, smiling at the driver before they pulled back into traffic.

She came right over and as I said "Hi," Sophia opened her arms for a hug. Without thinking, I folded her into my arms, hugging her tightly enough for it to feel good but not so tightly that it was intimate. She inhaled deeply, then released me, taking a step back. She was dressed much the same as me, casual in jeans and comfortable walking shoes, with her hair in a ponytail.

"Well, that went a little better than the last time we hugged," I said teasingly, trying to ignore how even that simple hug made my body ache with want. And I knew right then that I couldn't just be friends with her. It was too hard. There was too much between us.

Sophia came back with a quip immediately. "Or worse, depending how you look at it." Smiling, she deftly redirected the subject away from our kiss faux pas. "It's so good to see you again. How's your week been?"

"Really good. You?" These pleasantries felt tedious and unnecessary, but I also didn't know how to just…jump into easy conversation with her the way we used to.

"Also really good." Sophia hiked her tote higher on her shoulder and gestured to the café behind me. "Should we get takeaway coffees? Maybe some food too? We can eat while we walk?"

"Sounds perfect."

We paid separately, then moved out of the way to wait for our orders. Sophia grabbed a few raw sugar packets and handed one to me.

"Thanks." Flailing for something to prevent an awkward silence, I asked, "How are your fish?"

"They're good. Alive and thriving."

"That's what you want your pets to be."

Sophia smiled. "Very true." She lightly touched my arm, then quickly drew her hand back. "I meant to ask the other night, how has work been since you got back?"

I paused for a moment before answering, "Honestly? Interesting. I've been moved to a new program. Temporarily and in the same building, just a different office," I added when I caught her look of unease. "I'm heading up the team actually."

Sophia's eyebrows rose. "You finally got a promotion after all your hard work."

I almost choked laughing. "Not quite. Just…I have a unique qualification for this job."

"You have a lot of unique qualifications," she pointed out, her voice bordering on seductive.

The shudder that tingled down my back wasn't unexpected. I allowed myself to enjoy the sensation, and though my voice wasn't quite as desire-laden as Sophia's, it was still a little rough when I agreed, "Yes, I do." I cleared my throat. "I'm working with my partner from my overseas assignment again. Jeffrey," I added.

"His name is Jeffrey?" she asked steadily. I'd never told her his name, because with his background in special ops, I wasn't sure how secretive he was about his identity. But mostly, it'd just been one more unnecessary secret in my sea of secrets.

"Yes." My one-word answer held sheepishness and guilt. "We became good friends while we were away. Chalk it up to working and living in close quarters."

Sophia's pinched expression melted into softness. "I'm so glad you had a friend over there." She didn't need to elaborate, and the unspoken remained between us, thick and heavy and smothering.

Our names were called, breaking the lingering tension, and we collected our coffees and food. Sophia had ordered a breakfast sandwich, and I'd gone with a cheese croissant. Once we were outside, away from the crush in the café, she held out her hand for my grease-spotted paper bag so I could add sugar to my coffee. It was such an automatic, natural, in-sync movement and the pang of how easy it was to be with her almost made my breath hitch. I added my sugar then reciprocated so she could doctor her coffee.

We walked quietly down the sidewalk to cross the street into the park. There was so much I wanted to say, and I was sure she did too, but we remained silent. About two minutes along the path, Sophia pointed up ahead to a bench shaded by a bushy maple, set slightly back from the path. "Do you want to stop and sit and eat here?"

"Sure." I lowered myself next to her. Not next-next to her, but close enough that we could converse without raising our voices, yet not so close that it felt intimate.

The traffic on the path through the park was steady, filled with runners, walkers, families, dogwalkers and everything in between. I settled back and crossed my legs, my food on my lap and the coffee on the bench beside me.

Sophia unwrapped her breakfast sandwich, and after swallowing a huge bite, she asked, "Is there anything you still wanted to ask me about what happened?"

I shook my head. "No. I, um, I understand. I hate it, but I understand." I sipped my almond-milk latte, even though it was still too hot to drink comfortably.

"What do you hate about it?" Sophia asked quietly.

"That it happened," I said simply, because that about summed it up. The reasons why, the aftermath, all of it was encompassed in that fact. "That you felt like you had to do that. That someone who had no right interfering in our lives interfered in our lives and lied to you."

There was a touch of uncertainty in her voice when she asked, "Was it a lie?"

"Yes. You don't make me unsafe, Sophia, in any circumstance. You make me safe, you keep me safe, you give me strength and focus and another more personal reason to try so hard." Aware I was speaking in present tense, I paused and reframed what I was saying. "And your family was never in danger." Lennon's transgression had my anger bubbling up again, and I pushed it back down. "I spoke to my boss. Actually, ripped him a new one is probably a better description. It's not going to happen again. Even if we're not…you know. Together."

"What about the government? My dad…" she said uneasily. "I know you promised, and I trust that, really, I do, but it's scary to think about it happening once and I just can't help thinking that it could happen again."

"The government doesn't care about me," I said emphatically. "I'm completely off their radar now. This new thing I'm working on, it's… big." Leaning toward her, I lowered my voice. "Bigger than Berenson big. I'm too important to get offside. That's what I told my boss when I said he had to stay the hell out of my life. And yours," I added, as if it were a given that her life was tied to mine. In a way, it was, even though we weren't together. Yet.

She grinned. "So you've found yourself some leverage. Excellent."

I returned her grin. "A little." I took a bite of my croissant, and we finished our food in companionable silence. Sophia held out her hand for my trash and dumped it in the trash can a little way down the path. We walked closely, keeping to the side to let people who were doing more than just strolling pass by. Her proximity felt comforting, almost too comforting, and I held my coffee on the side closest to her to stop myself from grabbing her hand.

There were so many things I wanted to tell her, to talk about, to clear up, to explain. In the end, I just started talking. "I had a birthday while I was over there. Turned forty-two. I never told you when my birthday is, even after we'd been dating for a month. Who does that? Who doesn't tell their girlfriend when their birthday is?"

"Someone who's used to protecting information," Sophia said diplomatically.

I laughed dryly, almost unable to stand how rational and forgiving she was. "My birthday isn't classified. I knew I'd have a birthday while I was away and I never told you. My birthday is May thirteenth. I've never liked it, it was always more my mom's day than mine, celebrating it how she wanted to, more like it was celebrating her giving birth to her only child instead of celebrating me. But this year I felt like I did want to celebrate it, but for some stupid reason I didn't tell you. And then it didn't matter anyway, and it was just…a day."

Sophia touched my shoulder. "We can celebrate it next year."

"*We* can?" I asked, unable to disguise the hope in my voice.

"Yes, we," she said emphatically. "Friends celebrate birthdays with each other, and they do it in whatever way the birthday person wants to."

I tried not to show my disappointment. "Right, of course they do."

"So do girlfriends," Sophia said, that simple phrase a casual addition to her statement. "If that's where we end up, of course." It sounded so light and breezy, like she didn't really care one way or the other.

I cared. I cared so much it made my chest hurt. And the lingering uncertainty just made me feel worse. There was an eternal pause before I murmured, "I'm still not sure about that."

"Not sure about your birthday or if we should be a couple?" she asked lightly.

"The second thing," I said, aware of the contradiction of my feelings. Seconds before, I'd been disappointed at the thought of just friends, and now I was second-guessing being more than that. "I'm not going to lie, Sophia, and pretend I don't want to be in a relationship with you, because I do. I really do. So badly that sometimes I feel like wanting to be with you is smothering me. And now that I know you didn't break up with me because I'm a terrible girlfriend, I don't really see why we shouldn't get back together."

She nudged my shoulder with hers. "There's a huge *but* hiding behind what you're saying, I can just feel it."

"But…I don't want us to end up in the same place, where you're unhappy with my job and I'm dancing around the truth all the time, and then we break up. What's that saying? About how doing the same thing and expecting different results is stupid?"

A smile edged the corner of her mouth. "I know the one. And I don't want that either. But we're both intelligent adults who have feelings for each other." She stopped abruptly. "Who…love each other?" Sophia's scared, hopeful expression, as if she was terrified it was only her who felt that way, melted some of my fear.

"Yes," I agreed tightly. "I think that's a fair statement." I wanted so badly to tell her I loved her, but the fear that it would fuck everything up held my tongue. Why would it fuck things up? It was obvious we'd never fallen out of love with each other. "I'm just…scared, I guess."

The physical manifestation of her relief was obvious. "I'm scared too," she admitted. She moved slightly to the side to let a group of unswerving middle-aged women pass by, brushing against me as she did.

I took that statement and brought it in close, holding it alongside my fear. We were both scared. That seemed like a solid starting point, both of us being afraid, both of us knowing the stakes and the risks and the rewards.

We kept walking, slowly, neither of us talking. But the silence was comfortable, a thinking sort of silence rather than an awkward one. Once I'd turned my feelings inside out enough, I glanced at her. "What else have you been up to since—" *Since you broke up with me. Since I saw you at the café. Since you came to my house and we kissed.* I frowned and just came out with it. "Since I spoke to you last when I was overseas. Anything exciting?"

"Not much at all. Just working, hanging out with friends, pickleball. Missing you."

"What did you tell your parents and friends? About us?" I'd met her group of closest friends right before I'd had to leave and had been looking forward to getting to know them better when I got back. I'd nixed that thought after the breakup.

"Just that the distance was making it hard and we decided to take a break and then see where we were when you got back." She bit her lower lip. "I thought that was the best thing to tell them, then if you couldn't forgive me we could just play it off as growing apart, but if you could then it really was just distance."

"You think I need to forgive you?"

"Yes," she said instantly. Sophia grabbed my elbow and pulled me to a stop. She tugged me off the path and, still holding on to my arm, said earnestly, "I fucked up, Lexie. I broke up with you without coming to talk to you about what was happening. I shouldn't have done that but I really need you to believe that I thought I was doing the best thing for you and me at the time." She inhaled shakily. "You have no idea how persuasive he was."

"Oh no, I know." I'd been pushed to do quite a few things by Lennon in my time at Halcyon.

"For every one of my questions, he had an answer. Every misgiving, he soothed. I can't explain it. It was almost like he knew exactly how to guide me into doing what he suggested."

The croissant churned uneasily in my stomach. "Because he did. That's his job, Sophia, that's exactly what he was doing." And I'd done the same to Sophia, early on, when I needed to hide. "And I'm so sorry."

"I just…I felt like I didn't have a choice."

"Even if you knew breaking up was going to make both of us utterly miserable?"

"Yes," she said immediately. "Because the way I saw it, being utterly miserable was preferable to being unsafe."

I couldn't argue with her logic, and the relief of her confirming that she'd been coerced, even if it wasn't by the president, flooded through me again. The problem wasn't me. I wasn't a terrible, unlovable person. "But why didn't you contact me when you knew I'd be home?"

"Because I didn't see the point. I'd made enough peace with my decision to have the strength to walk away from us. And I'd left you a message, hoping you would know that it wasn't my decision and the reason why I made that decision, and I had to trust you'd come to me when you found it."

"I'm mad at you," I admitted, hating myself for the emotion. "*So* mad that you didn't come to me with this, that you didn't trust me enough."

"I know." Her voice went soft. "But you're not the only one who wants to protect the things they love, Lexie."

It was such a simple statement, and one that I felt deeply. After all, wasn't that why I'd done everything since I asked her to come with me to Tampa? To protect her. To protect the things I loved? I laughed shakily. "It's hard to be mad at someone when they're trying to protect you."

"Tell me about it," she deadpanned.

I swapped my coffee to my other hand and took hers. Sophia interlaced our fingers, and I started back on the path, bringing her along with me. We walked in silence for a few minutes, both of us sipping our coffee.

The contact between us felt easy and natural, and I decided to not overthink things and just enjoy what felt like a reconciliation. But if

I wanted to reconcile with her fully, I needed to tell her some more truths. "As well as my birthday, there's probably some other things I should share with you."

There was no mistaking the dread when she asked, "Like what?"

"Just…things that happened while I was over there. When I was working overseas in 2016 and 2017, I was with a woman, casually. Not *together*, just—" I felt sick as I thought about me and Elaheh. "Sleeping together. Scratching mutual itches. I told you about her? Kind of."

Sophia glanced up at me. "The one you broke up with not long before your hostage thing?" Her expression was interested, but neutral.

"Yeah. That's the one. It's convoluted, but she'd moved to the same city I was posted to this last assignment, and we reconnected, and *not* in the way you think. This happened when you and I were still together, but I couldn't tell you because it was now a work thing. She, uh…she'd remarried and was involved in her husband's business now. Terrorism," I explained at Sophia's raised-eyebrows silent question.

"Oh," she said flatly. "That's, um…I don't even know what that is. Fucked-up?"

"Yeah," I agreed. "Fucked-up sums it up. So, I had to try to get information from her about her new life, without her suspecting. Every time I'd talk with her, it made me feel dirty. And all I could think about was you. About how the two of you were so completely opposite, and how all I wanted after seeing her was to see you. And after you broke up with me, seeing her became a sick sort of substitute for company. A really poor substitute. And I was obsessed with cracking her, with getting her to spill her deep secrets. She never really did.

"And it made me feel like I'd failed, like the whole assignment was a failure and completely pointless and a waste of time. I think she knew something was off with me, maybe not that I was Intelligence, but just something was off. Or…I don't know, maybe she suspected I wasn't who I said I was. So I don't know why she didn't cut off our contact sooner or even…kill me. I can only think that she wanted to talk to someone who understood who she really was. She was still so lonely."

Sophia rested a light hand on my forearm. "What's her name?" she asked gently.

"Elaheh. *Was* her name," I added, trailing off as I touched my right eyebrow. As soon as I realized I'd unconsciously touched the scar I'd received as Jeffrey dragged me away from the café just before it exploded, I dropped my hand. "She carried out a suicide bombing about a week before I came home, at the café Jeffrey and I went to frequently. The café she knew I loved. And she went there anyway, knowing I could be there, when I *was* there, and detonated a bomb. That's how I cut my face, and broke my nose again."

Sophia stopped abruptly and I did too. She took a few deep breaths, but her words still broke. "I'm so sorry." In one smooth movement, she closed the gap between us and gathered me into a tight hug.

I didn't think, I just held on to her, held her against me, pressed my face into her neck to inhale the warm, comforting scent of her. My throat tightened and I closed my eyes, desperately trying not to cry. If I cried, I didn't think I'd be able to stop. Sophia apparently didn't have the same conviction as me, and I felt the hot, wet tears against my collarbone a moment before the sound of her trying to hold back her sobs.

We stayed like that for a minute until she pulled back, but stayed close. She took my face in her hands and pulled it down. The press of her lips to my temple was brief, but unmistakable. "I'm so sorry, Lexie," she repeated.

I gently wiped under her eyes. "It was weird, being in that moment, months after we'd broken up. The first thing I thought, when I could think again, was how you'd told me to come home safely. Just your voice, saying that, looping in my head. And I'd come so close to not coming home at all."

"What do you mean?" she murmured in a tight voice.

"Jeffrey wanted to leave the café." I didn't tell her he'd seen a person of interest there and had had a weird feeling—that wasn't important and it was classified. An acceptable omission. "So we did. Less than a minute before Elaheh walked in." Less than a minute between life and death. "I bumped into her outside, as she was going in and I know she knew it was me. Knew that I was there." I swallowed hard. "And I still don't know if she would have done it if she'd seen me inside. If there was something about me that made her do it, because she *knew* I went to that café frequently, so she knew if she bombed it she might be murdering me. Me, who she'd been intimate with years ago. Me, who she'd been talking with for months. And she had warned me early on, not to go to another restaurant that was later bombed. So why not warn me about this one?"

I'd been grappling with whys ever since and the only answer I'd come up with was that Elaheh's new life, her new ideals, had turned into the most important thing in the world to her. So important she'd have killed me. So important that she'd leave her son without a mother. And as much as I hated it, as much as I didn't agree, I still understood.

Sophia squeezed my hand tightly. "Oh, Lexie. I'm so sorry."

I squeezed back. "It was the weirdest feeling, because it felt a little like our breakup where I didn't know if it was something about me that made her do that. At first I was convinced our breakup wasn't real. But I didn't hear from you and then I convinced myself that it *was* real and all my fault. The bombing isn't exactly parallel but it felt like it."

"It wasn't you," Sophia confirmed quietly.

"I know that now. But the more I thought about it, the more you made me realize, the *breakup* made me realize, that I hadn't been giving you all of me. And that made me realize that I needed to work on that. I've been withholding things from you without even thinking, just by habit, even as I knew I had to be open with you about personal things. I'm secretive by nature, but I shouldn't have been so secretive with you, with *everything*."

She smiled at the emphasis. "I don't like your secrecy but I know that it's part of your job and it's become part of your nature. I'm grateful you've had time to reflect on things you were unhappy with about yourself, and I'll take it."

"I'm working on some things, on myself. On the reasons why I wasn't open with you."

"Do you know why?" she asked quietly, and I could tell it was part curiosity, and part prompting me to talk about it and confront it.

"Because I'm scared," I said tightly. "Of being open and letting someone in and not having that reciprocated, or worse—of having it used against me. My parents, the hostage event, are just a few things that've made me that way. If I hold some things back, then I've not given away everything that could be used to hurt me. I still have some control." I inhaled deeply. "I need to accept my relationship with my parents and accept my feelings of guilt and shame from the hostage situation, guilt because I…I had to kill a man to save myself, shame because I should never have let myself get into that situation. I need to recognize that nothing about those things had anything to do with my lack of control. They just happened. They just are."

She nodded slowly, but it took her a few seconds to answer. "That makes sense."

I licked my lower lip. "Withholding things from you, the way I was with you, was not intentional, Sophia. I *wanted* to share, I really did. I tried. I did share. But, obviously, I also didn't share. I just want you to know that I truly, honestly, wanted to give you everything you needed and wanted."

"I know you did."

"I'm sorry I couldn't. But my therapist and I have started delving into that, and I'm working on it."

I could tell she wanted to ask if it was for her that I was doing it, and if I were honest with myself—I was. But like my therapist had said, I was doing it for me and then the next woman I chose to have a serious relationship with. I just hoped that woman was Sophia.

Fuck—feelings were so complicated. How could we have put each other through all of this and still want to be together?

Sophia inhaled a deep, slow breath. "I'm really happy for you, Lexie."

"Me too." I frowned, thinking about where my path was taking me. "It'll take a while, but I can see the ending. I think. I don't want to blame my parents, like—the clichéd 'they didn't give me love so I don't know how to love.' They did love me. But not the way I thought I needed. They always felt distant, and I think maybe their withholding affection and information shaped me into doing some of the same things. And I don't want to do that, Sophia. I won't. But I'm a work in progress and I need you to understand that I'm going to fuck up sometimes, but I truly am working on it. I'll be doing what I can to make sure I'm being the best girlfriend I can be, for whoever my partner might be, and I need to know that my partner is with me."

"I can live with that," she said simply. "I want to be with you."

I gestured vaguely. "I still have this job. It's still going to be weird at times. And even with my newfound commitment to sharing, you know there are things I can't share."

"I know. And I can live with that," she repeated. "Remember our promises, in the beginning, about compromise? About it not always being on your terms or my terms?" At my nod, she continued, "If you promise you'll meet me in the middle whenever you can and if you *swear* us being together won't compromise your safety, that my parents and family will never be brought into play again the way they were because of Berenson, then I believe you."

"Why?" What I really meant was "Why now?"

"Because I love you and I trust you."

"You didn't before?"

She looked surprised. "Of course I did. But doubt sucks. It's insidious. Once he suggested that things might not be the way you said they were, I got so…stuck. It was all I could think about. And the more I thought about it, the easier it was to convince myself that I was doing the right thing."

I smiled. "Did you fat-man yourself to save just one other person?" I asked, referencing the trolley/tram moral dilemma of saving one person or saving many.

She laughed. "Of course not. You taught me you only push the fat man to save many people."

"True," I agreed with a laugh that sobered pretty quickly. "And I need you to trust me that regardless of what happens, you don't need to worry about your family. Your dad is safe. Your mom is safe. Brother, sister. You. You're all safe. Because if you don't trust me on that, then I'm not sure this will work. You're going to drive yourself crazy thinking something is lingering in the shadows."

"I know. And I promise I'm going to set it aside. I trust you," she reiterated firmly.

We paused by a clear pond to watch birds splashing and swimming and flocking to the people throwing out the pellets bought for a dollar at the park's entrance. "Being apart from you was miserable," I admitted. "Breaking up with you was miserable. But…maybe it wasn't the worst thing."

"Oh, I don't know," she said, singsong. "It *felt* like the worst thing."

"At the time, yes. But if it forces us to evaluate what we want and things that are a barrier to that, and to figure out how to get over that barrier, then I think it's not a bad thing."

She turned toward me. "That's true." Sophia took a step forward until she was so close I could feel the heat of her body. "I want to kiss you," she murmured, her eyes lingering on my lips. She swiped her tongue along her lower lip as if she could taste a kiss.

"I want you to kiss me," I whispered. My throat ached with the admission.

Sophia paused, the weight of our conversation hanging between us. She waited until I'd nodded and made an indistinguishable sound at the back of my throat before she pulled my face down and kissed me. Unlike the kiss at my door the other night, there was nothing accidental about this one, and as my arms stole around her waist, I felt her sigh at the contact.

Our kiss wasn't deep or passionate—I wasn't about to drag her from the park and home and into bed—but in those few seconds as she held on to my face and showed me again just how much she'd missed me, I felt more connected to her than I had ever felt.

Sophia's eyes fluttered open. "Okay," she said breathily. "So… I'm just going to put it out there. It feels like we both want to try a relationship again. So, can we just see where this goes?"

The relief rushed out of me so strongly my exhalation was audible. "Yes. Can I take you on a date?"

Her eyebrows rose fleetingly as her mouth quirked. "A date?"

"Yes. Not a let's-see-if-we're-compatible coffee or brunch, or dinner. A real, I know how I feel and I'm trying to romance you, date."

"I'd love that." She grinned cheekily. "Just to confirm though, is this our first real date?" I knew exactly what she was implying, and what she was doing—drawing us back to a laughing fake argument we'd had at the start of our relationship about whether or not we'd been on actual dates or just meetups.

"Quiet, you," I said laughingly. Sophia opened her mouth to say something that I just knew would be facetious, so I pulled her against me and kissed her again.

And, for a minute, as we kissed, she was quiet.

CHAPTER NINE

Super Lexie is here to save the world

I arrived at work extra early on Monday morning, determined to dedicate as much time as I could to solving my dad's code. And though I wanted to rush through my usual workout so I could dive into the search, I forced myself to slow down, enjoy the movement and take in the endorphins that would help me through a day of staring at books.

I'd been trying very hard to not just constantly think about Sophia, but as I was making myself up after my shower at work, I decided fuck it—why shouldn't I think about her? Why shouldn't I think about possibilities? Why shouldn't I think about things that made my life more pleasurable, which then seeped into other aspects of my life to make things easier. Like figuring out the most important pass phrase since computers were invented.

When someone knocked on the office door at eight thirty, before Jeffrey had arrived, I braced myself for a Lennon intervention. I switched off the black-light lamp, turned over my legal pad, and closed *1984*.

It was a pleasant surprise to see Derek instead of my other, less pleasant, boss. I exhaled a relieved breath. "Morning, sir."

Derek smiled warmly. "Martin. Good morning."

I opened the door to let him into my office, feeling like a proud parent showing off their workspace baby. "How are you? Feels like I haven't seen you in a year."

"Ten days, to be exact," he corrected, smiling.

"Oh. Well, that's not so bad. What news do you bring me from the outside world?"

His eyes crinkled at the edges. "We all miss your smiling face."

"Aww. I love how that's news."

"Of course it's news. But in news about work, we've found more cells connected to the one headed by Basir Mohammadzai. It's trickling in slowly, but the information seems solid."

"Fuck. I mean, great, but fuck. I did so much work on that while I was overseas and now I can't follow it up." They'd already tagged Mohammadzai, a.k.a The Cleaner, a.k.a Mr. Elaheh, when I'd arrived in country, so I couldn't take credit for that. But I'd been sorting through intelligence, reporting, and then engaging with Elaheh for months, and the misery connected to her made me feel possessive about stamping out everything connected to that terrorist cell.

Derek soothed, "It'll be there for you when you're done here. Speaking of, how goes the new assignment? Sorry I haven't been to see you sooner. It's been crazy downstairs."

"It goes busily, which is why I haven't come down to see the team. But it's also going productively." I wasn't sure how much Lennon had shared with him, or even how much I should share. But given that as far as I knew, Derek hadn't been read in to this program, I didn't want to elaborate.

"Have you learned anything pertinent, or even interesting?" he asked. His posture and tone were casual, strangely so, and he gave off the vibe that he really didn't care about my answer but was just making conversation. It seemed…forced? Or maybe I was just paranoid and looking for things that didn't exist.

So, I paused. "A little, yeah. Mostly that I didn't really know my father at all. I never thought I knew my parents well, but now…I just don't know." I indicated one of the seats on the long side of the I, and we sat next to each other.

"That must be difficult to reconcile alongside the work you're doing," Derek said gently.

"A little," I agreed. "Did Lennon ask you to come keep an eye on me?"

"No. Why would he do that?" I caught nothing false in his words and shoved my paranoia aside.

"Because I'm shitty with him and he knows it." I gave Derek a brief summary of what Lennon had done, keeping *most* of my rage out of my explanation because I was sure he could extrapolate how I felt.

Derek's face went through a range of emotions from utterly still, to shocked, appalled, and angry. His voice was incongruously calm when he stated, "That was entirely uncalled for."

I threw up my hands. "Right? *Thank you*. I'm glad I'm not overreacting."

Derek shook his head. "You're definitely not. I cannot believe he did that. I looked into Halcyon as well as the White House when you asked me to find out who was tailing Sophia Flores, and as I told you, there was zero evidence of anyone connected to the president, Halcyon, or the agency. I just assumed they'd covered their tracks exceptionally well." Sounded about right.

"I got the feeling Lennon might have been acting alone, rather than on official Halcyon business," I said. Derek raised his eyebrows at my statement, but I chose to leave my theories about Lennon's strange possessiveness of me alone for now. I leaned back in my chair and crossed my legs. "Has he been filling you in on my progress?"

"Yes, he has." Derek laughed disbelievingly. "I'd say this classifies as important, wouldn't you?"

I blew out a long breath. "Yeah."

Derek shook his head. "I'm glad I wasn't stringing you along promising you that you were important. Lennon had been hammering on about it since before the Kunduz Intelligence."

"Really?"

"Yes. Quietly at first, but after Kunduz, he grew quite loud about it."

"Mmm," I said noncommittally. "Did you know about my dad?"

"No. I never even met him. But from what I've heard lately, he was an incredible and prolific intel officer. You should be proud of him."

"I think I am. I'm just…I'm a whole bunch of other things as well that are kind of drowning out the proud at the moment. Did you know about him and Lennon?"

Derek's thick eyebrows shot up. "No. What about them?"

Oh boy, breaking the news to someone. How exciting! "Lennon was a good friend of my dad's. I knew him when I was a kid, though we hardly interacted. He was just…there sometimes, you know, my dad's pal when we came back to the States between Dad's postings, nothing to do with me really."

Derek folded his arms across his broad chest. In his midfifties, he looked as fit as he had when I'd first met him on overseas assignment over a decade ago. I was an ops officer managing human intelligence assets and he was in military intelligence. And when he adopted that pose, he looked serious as shit. "I didn't know that," he said. I couldn't quite decipher his tone because he'd carefully masked it behind forced neutrality. "Does this cause a conflict for you?"

I waved dismissively. "*Everything* feels like a conflict for me at the moment. But it's fine. I just want to figure this out, uncover our enemies so someone else can deal with them, take credit for my excellent work, and go back to my old life."

He nodded along with my talking. "I suppose that explains how Lennon came into possession of your dad's work. I was trying to figure out how he got it when he wasn't part of the agency then, nor was your father Halcyon." There was no trace of dishonesty in his words, and I chided myself for thinking he was being disingenuous.

"Yeah…" I said neutrally. "At the moment, I'm still working with more questions than answers, but I'm sure the answers will come."

"I'm sure they will," he agreed. The keycard reader beeped from outside the office and Derek stood. "Sounds like it's time to start work."

I pointed to my desk. "I started an hour ago."

He laughed. "Of course you did."

Jeffrey paused in the doorway for a moment, then smothered his surprise. "Derek. Good to see you again." He glanced to me and, grinning, added, "And in less antagonistic circumstances than the last time the three of us were in a room together."

I rolled my eyes. Yeah yeah. I'd been a bitch during our preparation briefings for our ridiculous overseas assignment. Derek had been tasked with bringing Jeffrey and me up to speed before handing us over to the insertion team. It had been…tense, to put it mildly, but I still maintained I wasn't overreacting. All I knew then was that Jeffrey Burton was a.k.a Mr. Smith a.k.a the fucking asshole who'd debriefed me when I turned myself in after giving the Kunduz Intelligence to Halcyon. He was just doing his job, but he'd been a fucking dick. And now he wasn't.

But Derek just laughed. "I'm just glad everyone's getting along. Let me know if you need anything, Martin." He patted my shoulder, shook hands with Jeffrey, then let himself out.

"All good?" Jeffrey asked.

"Mhmm, fine. He was just checking in. Whatcha got there?"

Jeffrey held up a package. "Replacing all the cookies I've eaten. I'm going to have to let my belt out if we don't finish this task soon."

"I thought *I* was the sweet tooth," I teased him as he unpacked the new cookies into a clean container, then ate one.

"You've rubbed off on me," he mumbled.

"You should be honored that I've bestowed some of my favorite personality traits upon you."

"Believe me, I am." While he busied himself putting his lunch in the fridge, I set up my workstation again after I'd hidden everything from my visitor.

Once Jeffrey had retrieved his laptop, a book to work on, his notepad from the safe, and set himself up for the day, he asked, "No brainstorms?"

"So far, all I've come up with is that the boxed-in number ten might be the shift key for a Caesar cipher, or that there are ten words or letters in the pass phrase. But those few ideas *could* be monumental. Or they could be nothing. You?"

"Still no clue. But I'm sure we're going to have an epiphany soon. How was your weekend?" he asked as he opened *Moby Dick*. "Did you have your coffee-talking thing with Ms. Flores?"

My coffee-talking thing. Just the thought sent a smooth flow of warmth through me. "I did."

Jeffrey sighed loudly. "Lexie, you're killing me. And?"

"*And* it went really well. We talked, cleared the air, and I *think* we're back together again." I wrinkled my nose. "Or, we're on the way to getting back together. We're going on a date this week."

He fist-pumped like he'd just scored a touchdown. "Hell yes!"

I eyed him. "I still find it really strange that you're so invested in my relationship with Sophia." If I didn't trust him so much, I would have thought there was something weird underlying his interest, something related to Lennon or even the president, and it was going to bite me in the ass.

Jeffrey's eyebrows shot up in surprise. "Well, you're my friend, and friends want their friends to be happy. Plus, from both a personal and professional standpoint, I don't think it's fair that someone interfered in your relationship and broke you two up, so of course I'm invested in you giving that the ol' middle finger and getting back together. Plus, you're just nicer to be around when you two are together. I much prefer that to the sadness."

"Those are all valid points," I conceded. "I don't want to get ahead of myself, but I'm getting ahead of myself. It just *feels* like it's going to work out. Like, it's going to take work and time, obviously, and some changes, but I just have a good vibe about it." She'd let me off the hook when I'd withheld some of the horrible things that surrounded me every day overseas because I'd made the decision to shield her from the truth. And she'd let me off the hook after she learned the truth about our road trip. It would be unfair and hypocritical of me to not let her off the hook too. We'd both made mistakes, but what was important now was how we pivoted and moved forward. Together.

Jeffrey waved his hand in front of my face. "You still with me? You look totally zoned out." He gasped theatrically. "Did you just have an epiphany? Have you cracked the code?"

Laughing, I put my glasses back on. "Unfortunately not. Just thinking. Dreaming, really." I blew out a breath. "But now I'm ready to focus on work again."

"Well, the moment it's officially official that you and Ms. Flores are an item again, please let me know. I believe I extended a dinner invitation to you and that offer still stands, for both of you."

"You'll be the first to know," I promised him.

By early afternoon, Jeffrey and I had finished *Moby Dick* and *1984*, respectively, and put our notes in separate folders before swapping books to confirm that neither of us had missed anything. I opened *Moby Dick* and set it on my book holder. "You know, I might actually read some of these once we're done—eBook copies though. I think if I have to go through these physical versions again, I'm going to scoop my eyes out with a spoon."

"That sounds très dramatique."

"That's me." I put my UV-protective glasses back on over my regular glasses but held off turning on the black light again. The intense concentration was giving me a headache. I propped my elbow on the desk, resting my head in my palm to stretch my neck and give it a little relief from the weight of my head. Insert big, heavy, smart brain joke here. "Do you think the letters are going to be the pass phrase, like some massive long thing? Or do you think it's a clue, like…it's going to spell out 'What's the fifth moon of Jupiter?' or be an anagram we have to solve, or some sort of puzzle like that?"

In *1984*, I'd found three letters marked by a line over them and thirty-nine letters with a period underneath, and it really seemed logical that the smaller group of letters were the first letters of words. But that didn't fit with there being ten words in the phrase, because there were only three letters with lines over them, so it would be three words. So I was leaning toward ten as the Caesar cipher shift key. Assuming there was a cipher and it was a Caesar and there wasn't something huge I was missing. At the moment, I was working with nothing but assumptions.

"I have no clue." Jeffrey leaned back in his chair, arching his back. "At the moment, I'm trying not to think too much because if I do, I'm going to get myself stuck on one idea and not keep myself open to all possibilities."

"Nooo. I want you to have a firm idea of what this is leading to." Groaning, I threw a pen at him, which missed and fell to the floor behind him.

Laughing, he leaned over to collect it and calmly put it back on the desk. "Of all the people who might know, with the exception of your father, I think it's you." He held up a hand, forefinger extended. "And, I do think if it spells out a question, it's going to be something only you can answer. Otherwise what's the point of all this?"

"I ask myself that at least once a day. And I think I know the answer."

Jeffrey rested his chin in his palm, all attention. "Please tell me what the answer is."

"Because I'm supposed to save the world, right?"

CHAPTER TEN

Little black dress

My I'm-romancing-you date with Sophia was the perfect interruption to a tedious week, and I approached it with a mix of excited anticipation and anxiety. The obvious day for a date would have been Friday or Saturday night, but I couldn't wait that long to see her again, and after confirming the day with her, I made dinner reservations for Wednesday night at a restaurant near the river.

I'd spent some of my downtime meditating and focusing on my personal goals and relationship behaviors I wanted to change, and I'd had another session with my therapist on Tuesday after work. He'd done an impressive job of maintaining neutrality, but I could see his underlying alarm when I confessed to my upcoming date. But after a nonspecific rundown of how the coffee-and-chat had gone on Saturday, he seemed to calm down and put his "I think you're moving too quickly" away.

Maybe it was too quick. Maybe it wasn't quick enough. I really had no idea, but the only way we would know was if we tried it. I knew, and I was sure Sophia did too, that we were both going to have to work hard to bring us back to where we were. Right back. Back before Tampa, when we were two women moving through an intense connection toward a relationship. Back before she found out I'd used her, out of necessity, to further my mission to keep the world safe. Back before someone else had manipulated her.

It *felt* right. But…so did a lot of things that weren't good for us. I was jumping way ahead of myself. It was just a date, but it was such an important date. No it wasn't. It was just me and Sophia going out for a nice dinner and conversation. It wasn't like anything actually hinged on this event, like whether or not she'd see me again. We were just going out for a good time. And I was going to pull out all the stops.

But first, I had to look good for her. I'd never had such certainty about what I would wear on a date—not that I'd been on a lot of dates that required dressing up—because I'd been waiting for this evening since October. When I pulled the garment bag from my closet, I felt both excitement and sadness. I'd bought this little black dress on a whim during our road trip, and promised myself that I'd wear it for her on a date one day. It'd been one of the things that'd lingered in the back of my mind while I'd been detained, something pleasurable to keep me going—the thought that someday I'd see Sophia again and we'd go on a date and live our fairytale happily ever after, even though during my detention I'd been sure there was no such thing for me.

I left my hair down and added a few light curls, made myself up, dressed, and agonized over heels for five minutes. Take a deep breath. Remember, it's just dinner with a woman you know. A woman you love, who says she loves you too. I drove my freshly washed and vacuumed car to Sophia's building, grateful to find an easy visitor park out front. It felt a little silly to be picking her up—we could have just Ubered separately, or even walked from her place—but I wanted her to feel… wooed.

Sophia opened the door a few seconds after I knocked, as if she'd been on the other side just waiting for me to arrive. And then my thoughts stalled. She wore a dress. A dress that left very little to the imagination. And my imagination took what it was seeing and ran a mile with it.

After our breakup, I'd tried very hard to not think about her. To not think about the sublime body that housed an intelligent, kind, funny, sweet woman. But now that that body was right in front of me, with all its gorgeous curves, dips, and swells? I thought about it.

Her hair was down too, longer than the last time I'd seen it loose. Seven months. I reached out to her, not even sure what I was doing but knowing I just wanted to touch her. Sophia took my hand, gripping it tightly. "Hi," she said softly, a bright smile lighting her face.

"Hi, yourself." I leaned down and Sophia met me halfway for a kiss. "You look amazing." My compliment was high-pitched and breathy, and I fought down a blush at my obvious excitement.

"Thank you. And you beat me to it, because so do you. Is that the dress you bought in Tampa?"

"It is," I confirmed.

Still holding my hand, she stepped back. Her slow gaze swept up and down my body, and she made no attempt to hide her appreciation. A small smirk tweaked the edge of her mouth. "Well," Sophia murmured. "It was certainly worth the wait."

"I'm glad you like it," I said, because I couldn't think of anything else to say. The look she'd given me had sent a thrill through my body and stolen my words. "Are you ready to go?"

She nodded and gently pulled her hand from mine so she could grab her purse. I held her wrap for her to put on, and Sophia took my hand again. "Let's go."

The restaurant was a short drive from Sophia's apartment, located about a block back from the river. I left my car with the valet—told you I was going all out—and took Sophia's hand to guide her inside the renovated 1800s Federal-style house. Thankfully, the note I'd added to the reservation that it was a date meant we were seated in a quiet, intimate corner away from the bar and other patrons.

Intimate...

Don't mince words, Lexie. This is a date, and this is what you wanted. Somewhere quiet and intimate where, for just one night, we could converse like we were the only two people on the planet. Once we'd been promised sparkling water, Sophia looked around. "This place is really special."

It was. The renovation had kept the Federal style on the interior, but modernized it slightly. The walls were dark-paneled without being ominous, the lighting warm and inviting, the artwork tasteful and interesting, and the furniture comfortable yet elegant.

She looked back to me. "I thought you might make a reservation at Manger, just for laughs."

Grinning, I confessed, "I thought about it." I'd been to the upscale French-inspired restaurant a few times, and had always been thrilled by the fabulous vegetarian menu to complement (what seemed to me) a good nonvegetarian menu. "Is Camila still working there?" Her sister and I had met only once, in a strange morning-after encounter, and it'd been awkward to say the least.

"She is," Sophia confirmed, fondness softening her words.

Our server returned with water, took our drink orders, then left us to peruse the menu. I already knew what I was going to order. Checking out menus and making decisions in advance of a restaurant meal was one of my hobbies. Cheese and morel scarpinocc, then basil risotto with pickled chanterelles, and I was going to see if I could twist Sophia's arm to share some roasted brussels sprouts with me. "Anything catching your eye?" I asked after a few minutes of silence.

Sophia bit her lower lip, and I could see her fighting with whether or not she should answer with innuendo. After a sip of water, she calmly said, "A few things."

And it was then I knew I was going to have to be careful with my wording, otherwise the charged vibe already moving between us was going to spark and ignite.

She ordered scallops to start, and then the pork chop with spätzle, but not before checking in that I was okay with her eating seafood and meat. Which of course I was. But the fact she'd asked sent a rush of warmth through me. She'd stopped asking after the first few instances when I'd assured her I didn't mind what she put in her mouth. My neck heated as I thought of her response to me saying that.

Sophia raised her glass of viognier in my direction. "Cheers. To… fresh starts."

"Fresh starts," I echoed, and sipped my sauvignon blanc. The phrase stuck in my head, and it took me a moment to realize why I couldn't shake it. "You said you hadn't dated after me?" I hated the weird upset that laced the question. "I thought for sure you would, after we'd separated." I'd almost driven myself crazy thinking of her moving on, while I was stuck overseas.

Her eyes widened in surprise. Fair—it was a pretty full-on way to start conversation on a date. Her expression eased, except for the little scrunch of her eyebrow that meant she was thinking. "I thought about it. And I almost did it. But then I thought about you. Everything about you. Kissing you, making love with you. And it was too raw. I just didn't want to think about anyone else. So I didn't." She held eye contact with me, and hers softened as she took in my expression, which felt so distressed I was embarrassed. Sophia reached across the table and rested her hand on mine. "Sorry, you asked, but I shouldn't have been so…free with my answer."

"It's fine," I said, and I meant it. She shouldn't have to moderate her truthful feelings to accommodate my hurt ones.

"Besides, who else would treat me this well?" she said, an eyebrow raised as she gestured around the warmly lit space.

I clamped down on the self-deprecating response that burbled up and instead, said confidently, "Nobody else."

The evening was quite possibly one of the nicest, easiest times I'd ever had. It really did feel like a fresh start, but with the confidence of something having already settled comfortably between us. Dinner was delicious, and conversation was easy—she talked about some travel plans she'd yet to finalize. I shared as much as I could about my new assignment. We made tentative plans for the weekend. Underneath the easiness was a constant hum of excitement, every look and word charged with innuendo and desire.

Our drinks were almost done—no mean feat considering I'd nursed my glass of wine over the whole evening—when the server appeared again to ask if she could tempt us with dessert. I looked across to Sophia, who was studying the dessert menu. "Share a dessert?" I wasn't hungry, but I did have a ginormous sweet tooth. More than that, I just wasn't ready for the night to end. I didn't want to drop her at her apartment and then go home to my empty one. I wanted the spell to last for just a little longer.

Sophia's eyebrows reached for her hairline and she puffed out a breath. "I don't know that I could fit anything else in. But damn, I really want the key lime crémeux or pear frangipane tart."

"I thought you'd go for the chocolate option."

"I didn't want to seem greedy by listing three," she said, laughing. Sophia cast a longing look over the menu and, sighing, confessed, "I don't think I need dessert. Next time, though, for sure."

Next time. It was only the promise of a next time that settled my regret that the evening seemed to have come to its natural conclusion. I asked the question I didn't want to. "So, you're ready to go?"

She gave me a thoughtful look. "I wouldn't say *ready*, but yes, I'm done. Thank you."

I suppressed my disappointment and made eye contact with our server so I could pay. After I'd helped Sophia with her wrap, she slipped her hand into mine, smiling indulgently while I opened the door for her. All the stops. We waited on the street for my car, standing close in the warm, early-summer evening. She turned to me, a smile playing about her mouth. "I'm going to borrow from every rom-com ever made, but I had such a good time tonight. Thank you."

"So did I. And you're very welcome. Thank you for joining me."

Sophia tugged my hand to pull me slightly closer. She stretched up on tiptoes and kissed me, not touching anything other than my hand. But I felt the heat of the kiss through my body like her fingers were mapping my skin. She eased back a little, and I followed suit, using the respite to inhale a steadying breath.

Thankfully the valet appeared and, relieved, I let out that breath I'd just taken. Smiling, I quietly said, "Okay. Let me take you home."

Conversation on the short drive wasn't strained, but there was a definite feeling of finality in the air. I pulled into a guest spot in front of Sophia's building and turned on the interior light to help her find her purse. Ordinarily, after a date, I'd have walked her into the building, if not upstairs to her door, but that seemed dangerous given the teasing games we'd been playing all night.

Sophia set her purse on her lap, her thumbs playing along a stitched seam. And then she stepped right over the line I'd tried to draw for myself. "Do you want to come up for a drink?"

Nervous excitement danced in my stomach. "I do. Very much. But…I'm not sure it's a good idea tonight."

"Why not?"

I played along. "I think you know why not."

She laughed lightly. "You mean the weird energy that's been crackling between us all night?"

My laugh was less light and more nervous. "Weird energy…That's definitely one way to put it." I would have said a fuckton of sexual tension.

Sophia rested her hand on my thigh, but even that slight touch had my nerves firing. She withdrew it again as my muscle tensed, her face and voice softening. "It's just a drink, Lexie."

I inhaled deeply, smiling at her expression of mild amusement. "You're right. It's just a drink. Yes, okay, I'd like that." And we were both adults capable of rational thinking. In theory at least.

She leaned over and kissed me lightly, quickly. "I promise it'll be a good one." Then she opened the car door before I could respond.

I followed her into her building, making a point to keep some distance from her. But as in the restaurant and the car, I couldn't move far enough away to temper my raging emotions. And raging hormones. I could smell her perfume, had been all night, but for some reason now, it sent a thrill of excitement through me as I imagined where else I might smell it on her body.

During the elevator ride to her top-floor apartment, I made a point to keep my distance, and it seemed Sophia had the same idea. We didn't look at each other, and the ride was silent, uncomfortably so, because all I could think about was her, naked, me kneeling in front of her, my mouth buried in her slick, wet heat.

I closed my eyes and tried to suppress the goose bumps that'd broken out over my skin.

"You okay?" Sophia asked, lightly touching my arm.

The touch startled me and I opened my eyes again, turning to face her. Her light-brown eyes were wide, and I let myself fall into them for just a moment before answering. "Mhmm. Just…thinking."

"I know the feeling," she murmured.

She exited the elevator just ahead of me and I walked behind, far enough that we weren't touching but not so far that I'd be tempted to stare at her as she walked. If I stared, if I saw her ass, her legs, the soft sway of her hips, then I was going to lose my fucking mind.

She locked the door behind us, fingers passing over the deadbolt and chain a second time before she turned around again. Sophia carefully hung her wrap, then extended her hand for mine. I passed it to her and stood rooted to the spot just inside her door as she walked into her kitchen. "Any preferences?" she asked, kicking off her heels beside the couch and dropping her purse on her kitchen table.

"No," I said quietly, her question breaking past my uncertainty. I followed her.

She turned back, smiling. "Moscow mules it is."

As Sophia began gathering ingredients for cocktails, my undisciplined eyes strayed, tracing the landmarks of the body I knew so well, the shapes hidden beneath a dress that made it easy to recall each and every time we'd been intimate. A surge of arousal was quickly followed by a surge of anxiety, and I realized that I'd made a mistake coming up to her apartment. It was too soon—we still had so many foundations to rebuild. When she turned back around, bottle of vodka in hand, I smiled to hide the upset I felt at running away, and said, "You know, I think I might take a rain check on that drink."

Sophia set down the bottle. There was no argument, no attempt to get me to change my mind. As if she knew exactly what I was thinking, she simply said, "Okay. Sure."

I turned slightly away while she put things back in the fridge and freezer, and as she walked back around the counter, I tried not to look at the way the dress clung to her curves, or the tantalizing glimpse of cleavage that had been teasing me all night. Sophia lightly touched my shoulder. "Are you all right?"

"Yes," I said, forcing brightness into the word. "It's just…"

"I know," Sophia murmured. "It's a lot. But it's fine, really. We'll get there when we get there."

"I know."

When we reached her front door, she asked, "Can we hug goodbye? Is that all right?"

We'd hugged without incident when we'd met for coffee. And we'd kissed without incident too. Kissed tonight without incident. But… this was different. The last time we hugged goodbye at a door, we ended up accidentally kissing and then not-so-accidentally continuing kissing, and I could feel that same charged spark between us now. But I was *so* desperate for connection, for contact, that I set aside the nervous excitement and nodded yes before I hugged her.

The sensation of Sophia's body against me, the full-frontal contact made my stomach twist. I could feel all of her, and it took everything I had to keep the hug as it was and not hold her even tighter to me, to not push her back against the wall.

I disengaged from the hug, trying to think around the energy surging between us, but the moment I saw the raw desire in her eyes, I pulled her close again and kissed her. I couldn't stop myself. I threaded my fingers through her hair, cupping the back of her neck as we kissed. Sophia's hands came to my ass, pulling us even closer together.

Hungry. There was no other word for what this was—it was like we were both starved for each other and knew there would be no satiety. Sophia had slightly more willpower than me, and with a reluctant groan, she pulled away, but her hands never left my body. She groaned again when I bent my head to kiss her neck, her exposed collarbone. "Is this a mistake?" she managed to ask. "Kissing? Getting back together…sleeping together now?"

I was glad she was on the same page as me about where exactly this moment seemed to be heading. Her questions made me abandon my exploration of her skin and I straightened, dropping my hands to her waist. "I have no idea if any of this is a mistake," I said hoarsely. I pushed aside my rational, logical brain, the thoughts screaming that this was too soon, and let my baser instincts take over. "But we won't know unless we try it…"

CHAPTER ELEVEN

Eternal yeses

"Yes," Sophia said breathlessly, and the sound of that consent, the confirmation that she was just as desperate as I was to be intimate, sent a shudder of desire through me.

The word had barely left her mouth before she kissed me again, furious and frantic. It wasn't pretty—the kiss was a needy clash of lips and teeth and tongue, but I didn't care. I wanted all of it, and more. Sophia pushed me backward against the door, holding me in place with her body, her hips rocking against mine as her hands traveled to places that hadn't been touched by another person in months. We were clumsy and fumbly, both of us so desperate that we were clashing against each other. I would have been self-conscious about it if it were anyone but Sophia, but the frenzy of our coming together only amped up my arousal.

Her mouth left mine to kiss my collarbone and she moved the strap of my dress aside to access more of my skin. The soft touch of her lips, the warm caress of her tongue made me shudder, and I held the back of her head, guiding her to where I wanted her mouth. Sophia licked above my neckline, her mouth dipping into my cleavage and when I tugged her hair, she lightly bit the curve of my breast.

With a low, throaty moan, she dropped to her knees in front of me, her hands gliding up my legs, under the tight black fabric, until she'd reached my underwear. Sophia looked up, eyebrows arching slightly, and I nodded, unable to actually verbalize that *yes*, please, I wanted her to undress me. I wanted her to kiss me, put her mouth on my skin, fuck me until I couldn't think about anything except how good it felt, and how much I wanted more.

Her fingertips skimmed the seam of my barely there black panties. "Did you wear these for me?"

As I'd dressed, I'd told myself my underwear was for myself, that I wanted to feel sexy and confident. I didn't want to admit that even though I'd been telling myself that we should take it slow, I'd hoped to show her what was underneath my dress tonight. But I couldn't think of a response, let alone speak with her fingers so close to my clit.

"Answer me," Sophia murmured, her mouth a breath away from my skin.

That whisper of air against my thigh made me shiver. "Yes," I managed. "I did."

"Good girl," she said roughly. "Thank you."

Those four words made me quiver. Jesus…fucking…help.

Slowly…so slowly, Sophia pulled my underwear down and helped me step out of it, leaving the fabric discarded on the floor. She kissed the inside of my thigh, just underneath the hem of my dress, then slowly pushed it up, her mouth exploring newly exposed skin. The touch of her mouth so close to my clit made me ache and I was so desperate for her to explore that arousal, I almost just took her head and pushed her face against my wetness.

She was *so* close. The teasing touch that remained just away from where I needed it was driving me insane, and I fell back against the door again. Sophia's mouth paused and I could feel the heat of her lips against my labia. And though all I wanted was to push her head deeper between my thighs and beg her to lick me, I held back and let Sophia dictate the pace. My pulse beat heavily in my clit, the anticipation sending tingles over my skin as her breath caressed my thigh.

But instead of putting her mouth on me, Sophia stood up abruptly and kissed me—a hot, intense, open-mouthed kiss that almost made me forget how desperate I was for her to touch me. Sophia hitched her dress up then straddled my thigh, her mouth never leaving mine as she grabbed my ass. Our bodies rocked together, seeking familiarity, and welcome heat burned through my belly as the arousal built. I couldn't control the choked groan of desperation that escaped.

She inhaled sharply. "I've thought about that sound so many times since the last time we had sex." Sophia sucked my lower lip before kissing me hard. She broke contact with my mouth to kiss her way up my jawline so she could whisper against my ear, "I want us to fuck right here, up against this door. Hard and fast, rough…"

"Then do it," I choked out.

"Mmm…" she purred. The frantic movement of her hips slowed, and she licked my upper lip before kissing me again, lightly. "But I also want us to go to bed and make love for hours, slow and soft, sweet, long…"

I took her face in my hands, forcing her to stop, to look at me, to see how fucking desperate I was to have her, anyway she'd give herself to me. I just had to have her. "I don't care what we do, just…I want…*something*. Please, Sophia. *Please*." Making a decision about the where and how was beyond me at that moment, and I surrendered control to her.

Without breaking the kiss, she unstraddled my thigh and gripped my hips, pulling me with her as she stepped back. Sophia kept walking backward, her hands guiding me as our mouths danced together. We could have made it to the bedroom faster if we'd stopped kissing, but the idea of losing contact, even for a few seconds, was unbearable. We bumped into the walls and furniture, and when we finally made it, I fumbled for the light. I wanted to *see* her, fill my eyes as much as my hands and mouth.

Sophia reached under my armpit to unzip my dress, then pulled it off my shoulders. My nipples tightened, partly from being bared but mostly from her heated gaze. She looked up at me, an eyebrow arched. "Naughty panties *and* no bra." Sophia bit her lower lip. "You really did come prepared…"

She brushed her lips over a nipple, so lightly I barely felt it, but when I gripped the back of her neck and guided her to my other one, she sucked hard, grazing her teeth over my flesh. I arched into her mouth, my clumsy and ineffectual hands trying to remove her dress. Without taking her mouth from my breasts, Sophia helped, guiding my hands to the zipper between her shoulder blades. I drew my fingers up either side of her spine, felt her shudder against me, then slowly pulled the zipper down, letting my fingertips trail along exposed skin on the way.

She straightened so I could pull the dress down and as I was sliding the fabric from her hips I took that brief moment to step out of my heels. Sophia unclasped her bra and I helped her pull it off before pushing her underwear down, as she wrestled with my dress. After what felt like an eternity, we were both naked and we tumbled onto the bed, her on top of me. I wrapped my arms around her waist, pulled her closer and raised my head to kiss her shoulder, inhaling the scent of her skin, her perfume. Our kisses shifted to languid and gentle but were no less passionate.

Sophia settled slightly to the side but still on top of me, one hand cupping my breast, her thumb doing amazing things to my nipple that sent heat into my belly. Her other hand trailed lightly up the inside of my thigh, brushed over my labia, then down the inside of my other leg. I wanted to reciprocate, to put my hands between her thighs, to seek out her wetness, but I couldn't focus on anything except what that hand was doing.

My excitement and arousal built and built until I thought I might come before she'd even touched my clit. I bit my lower lip, hard, trying to draw my attention away from her teasing, torturous touch. But it didn't work, and I had to squirm away from the hand that was making its way back up again, clamping my thighs together and trapping her.

"No?" she asked, a note of disappointment coloring the question.

I exhaled a shaky laugh and shook my head. Then I realized she might take that as me withdrawing consent, so I hurried to clarify, "Very much yes. I just…I need a moment."

Apparently the helpless look I gave her conveyed my feelings, and Sophia laughed quietly. The hand on my breast stilled and I relaxed my legs, releasing that hand. Sophia grinned, and moved it deliberately up to rest on my hip. After ten seconds, she asked, "Has a moment passed yet?"

I inhaled shakily. "Yes."

"Good," she murmured, a second before her fingers found my heat.

I couldn't even respond, because she was gently pushing through my folds, her fingers knowing and certain. Heat built low in my belly, slowly spreading outward until my body felt molten. When Sophia's fingers finally moved upward and over my clit, I arched into the touch. I pulled her down to kiss her and kept kissing her as she stroked my clit. And the whole time I tried not to hyperventilate. A kiss smothered my "Oh my god," and then another kiss swallowed my "Oh, yes, please, yes."

She kept stroking and, around kisses, she moved to kiss my neck, my chest, my breasts, before coming back up to meet my mouth. I'd known it wouldn't take long for me to come, but it *really* wasn't taking long—I could already feel the first insistent tingles of my orgasm building. I wanted her to lick me until I came in her mouth, wanted to feel her expert tongue on me. But I couldn't bear the thought of her moving. I tried to breathe deeply to soothe the opposing feelings that threatened to overwhelm my pleasure. This wasn't all of it. We had time. And after she'd fucked me to my climax, I'd do the same to her, and then we could do it all over again.

When my breathing hitched, Sophia sped up, increasing the pressure. She knew me. She knew what I wanted. And when I buried my face in her shoulder, my trembling arms uselessly gripping her shoulders as I came, she stayed with me, still stroking my clit slowly until I'd finished shaking and gasping. I couldn't speak. I could barely think. It was so, so fucking good.

"I think you missed me…" Sophia mumbled against my neck.

When I'd caught my breath enough to answer, I said, "A little bit."

She laughed and pushed herself up. "Hi."

"Hi."

Sophia bent down for a kiss. "Thank you for that."

I laughed shakily. "I feel like I should be thanking you…"

"Maybe," she said, an eyebrow raised. "I know one way you can thank me, if you really want to."

My throat tightened at the thought. "I really want to." I rolled on top of her, straddling her leg, guiding my thigh between hers. The pressure against my sensitive clit made me gasp, and I had to take a moment to recenter myself.

Sophia smirked as she gripped my ass, pulling me harder against her.

"Are you trying to distract me?" I asked, increasing the pressure with my leg. I could feel her arousal against my skin, and it made mine swell again.

Biting her lower lip, she shook her head. "No. I just love watching you writhe."

"The feeling is mutual," I said as I leaned down to taste her nipples.

I wanted to take my time and relearn her body with my hands and mouth, but I also wanted to dive in and taste her, feel her. Sophia solved my dilemma by urging me downward, and once I'd settled my shoulders between her thighs, I looked up the length of her glorious, naked body. A light sheen of sweat coated her skin. Her chest rose and fell and we made eye contact, and held it, before she uttered a single word. "Please."

I dipped my head and put my mouth on her. Sophia was soft and silken, exactly as I remembered her, and I swallowed back a moan of desire. A hundred clichés tumbled through my mind. That she felt like coming home. That she felt like a safe place. That it felt like no time at all had passed, like we'd never been separated. And I felt silly, until I realized love was one big cliché. So I let myself fall into it. Fall into her. But even with all of it, as if we'd spent no time apart, there was still a newness to our intimacy.

When I sucked her clit, she vocalized a loud, unfettered groan of pleasure, and I couldn't help it, I let out my own groan. She tasted exactly as I remembered and I had to remind myself to go slowly and not devour her. A flood of arousal filled my mouth when I guided my fingers inside her and ran my tongue around her slick clitoris. I fucked her unhurriedly as I licked her, until her body grew taut and her breathing became ragged and rough. Sophia dug her fingernails into my shoulder, gripping hard as she cried out her climax. The sound made my stomach twist with excitement and I barely held on to my freshly rising arousal, grasping her thighs to ground myself.

As soon as she'd relaxed back down to the bed, Sophia growled, "Come up here." It was part demand, part plea.

I did as she said, peppering her skin with kisses as I went. When I was face-to-face with her so we could lie together, she kept pulling me up until I was straddling her face. Yes please…

What I'd thought was sex was apparently just foreplay, and every time I thought we were done, Sophia would playfully bite my finger, then suck it into her mouth before guiding it to where she wanted my touch. And once she'd finished again, she would take a few minutes to catch her breath, shoot me a devilish look, then push or pull me into the position she wanted to have me in again. Our bodies moved together, finding midpoints between hard, fast, rough, slow, soft, sweet, until I thought I'd come apart from the pleasure.

Finally, we were both sated, lying in a sweaty, tangled, tumbled mess in her rumpled sheets. She'd ended up on top of me with one of her legs over mine. One hand played lazily over my belly and breasts, and it was only that I was so satisfied that I didn't react to the teasing touch by flipping her onto her back and diving back between her legs. The slow, steady movement was so relaxing that I felt myself sinking deeper into her mattress, and I fought the drowsiness, even though I wanted nothing more than to fall asleep in her bed, naked, as I'd done so many nights before.

But… Sex was one thing, staying over was another. I swallowed, took a deep breath, and said something I didn't want to say, but thought I should. "I think I should go home?" My lack of desire to leave her bed made the statement come out more like a question.

The stroking hand paused. "Why? It's late." She took my wrist and turned it to check the time. "Early."

I glanced at my watch. 1:53 a.m. It had been a marathon, not a sprint. I licked my lips. "It feels like sleeping together is one thing but me sleeping over is maybe…too far right now." It sounded like a weak excuse now that I'd said it.

Sophia laughed, propping herself up on an elbow to look down at me. "Hon, I think we've maybe gone past too far." She kissed me, lingering long enough that some of my already fragile resolve wavered. "If you want to go, I won't stop you. But I would rather you stayed, and not just because I don't like you driving around in the early hours of the morning. I'll sleep on the sofa bed if you really want."

Hon…

I was totally stuck on that endearment and unable to respond. It'd slipped out so easily that I didn't think she'd even realized she'd said it.

Sophia's eyebrows shot up. "What? If you want to go, Lexie, I'm not going to tie you to the bed." The smirk hiding in the smile made it clear she was thinking about the times she'd done just that.

"Okay." I lightly gripped her bicep and pulled her back down on top of me. "Then I think I'll stay…Right here."

I made myself leave the next morning, early enough to get home and shower, and dress in work-appropriate attire instead of a rumpled little black dress. Sophia drowsily protested when I extracted myself from underneath her, but didn't verbalize anything other than a mumbled, "Why you leaving?" I'd never met less of a morning person than Sophia. It was like she didn't actually become human until after ten a.m. and just functioned on some form of autopilot until then.

I kissed the edge of her mouth. "Some of us have a commute. And this morning, I technically have two."

I found my dress discarded by the bedroom door, and as I shook it out, I thought about the frantic way we'd shed our clothes last night. I didn't really have to go to work, did I? Yeah…I did. Once I'd zipped up, she shuffled out from under the covers and sat up, her nipples tightening in the cooler air. If it was an attempt to get me to reconsider leaving, it was working. Sophia pulled the sheet up, tucking it under her armpits. "Is everything okay between us?"

After last night, I would say everything was amazing between us. I smiled at the memory of those hours. "Yes, I think it is."

"I don't want this to make things weird."

"It hasn't made things weird for me. What about you?"

"No." She lightly nibbled her lower lip. "I knew last night that it might muddy things a little, but I honestly didn't care."

I grinned. "Me either. But, the muddiness is confusing, right?"

"Yeah. Are we back together?"

I blew out a breath and dropped down onto the bed beside her legs. "Yes, I think so? Or, it feels like that's where we're heading. But I don't want to fail, especially not this. I want to be different. I want to be better."

Her expression softened, and she reached up to cup my face. "I know you're different already, Lexie. And I think that will only make us stronger as a couple."

"I am different," I agreed. "But my job is always going to be a thing. I just don't want it to be The Thing between us. So I need to be sure that my thought process is in the place where my automatic response is to share my personal things, not think about whether it's the right thing."

"You're not a robot. You're allowed to think about things before you do them. You don't have to have auto-share turned on." Smiling, she reached up and hooked her fingers in the neckline of my dress, pulling me toward her. "And as much as I want to sit around all morning talking about the logistics of whether you and I are in a relationship"—I noted her very deliberate exclusion of *or not*—"you're going to be late for work if you don't leave now." She kissed me then pulled back as she gently pushed me away.

Groaning, I got up from the bed. "Okay. We'll do something this weekend? Or dinner again this week? Maybe at my place?" My voice rose hopefully with each offer.

"Yes. All of it. And anything else too."

"Good." I chanced another kiss, relieved when Sophia seemed content to leave it as a quick, not-horny, goodbye kiss. "I'll call you."

"Please do. Have a good day."

"I will. Enjoy going back to sleep."

She stretched luxuriously, the sheet slipping to her waist, and it was only by the skin of my teeth that I managed to not get back into bed with her. As if she knew exactly what I was thinking, Sophia purred, "Oh, I will." Her expression sobered. My heart sank. Then it soared again when she said, "I love you."

"I love you too," I said, only just managing to get the words out without my voice cracking.

A broad smile lit her face and she reached for me, but when I moved forward, Sophia shooed me with both hands. "No. Go! Or I won't let you go."

Laughing, I agreed. She was far too tempting to risk touching her again. It took me a minute to locate my shoes, which lay in a tangle with her dress, bra, and underwear on her bedroom carpet. She watched me putting my heels on. "I think your underwear is near the front door," she said breezily.

"I think you're right." I checked my hair in the full-length mirror on the opposite wall, deemed myself acceptable to walk out to my car—no walk of shame here—then turned back to her. "Thank you," was on the tip of my tongue, but it seemed like a weird thing to say. But I *was* thankful and grateful that she'd been so receptive to us reconciling. The sex was just an incredible bonus. "Have a good day. I'll talk to you after work?"

"Absolutely," she promised. I'd just reached her bedroom door when she said, "Lexie, wait." I turned to see her scrambling out of bed, bringing part of the sheet, which threatened to trip her. She laughed, dropped the sheet, and came over to me. She hugged me tightly and quickly, then gave me a little shove out of her bedroom.

I found my underwear, which had indeed been discarded on the floor near the door, and bundled it into my purse. Once I'd closed the front door, I took a moment to breathe. Last night was not a mistake. Not at all. It was the exact opposite of a mistake, and I couldn't wait to see where we would go now. Together.

CHAPTER TWELVE

Occam's razor sure is sharp

By the time I got back to my apartment and took the world's quickest washing-off-a-night-of-sex shower, I was in danger of being late for work. Though I didn't have a set start time, I still felt like I should get to work at a reasonable hour, not only for work but so I wouldn't have to contend with parking way out in "Parkistan." Plus… when I consistently left work earlier than my "official" end of day hours, arriving late as well felt a little cheeky.

I left home without my morning yoga and meditation, and knowing I was too late to work out at work, promised myself I'd indulge in a long session of self-care tonight.

I hesitated in the elevator before pressing the button for my floor and instead, scanned my ID and pressed the button for the top floor. While I'd readied for work, I'd thought about last night and its implications. It was none of Lennon's business whether or not Sophia and I were a couple. But I didn't want it to come back and bite me in the ass somehow. I needed to control the narrative here.

The agency director was very busy and important, and I had to wait almost fifteen minutes in his office lobby. I was lucky I had an unlimited entry ticket, otherwise I would have likely been told to go away.

As I sat opposite Lennon, the picture of him with my dad drew my gaze again. My dad was charismatic, and that had always felt incongruous with the man I knew as a father, who was gentler, less bombastic. I'd seen him draw people in and charm them effortlessly, and he had always projected confidence. But I now realized, although Dad was apparently laughing at something in the photo, if I looked closer, his eyes hadn't joined in with the laughter and his body language was almost…guarded.

"Alexandra," Lennon said crisply, pulling my attention away from the moment captured in time. Yep, he was in an "I'm busy" mood. Ah well, my thing was important. "What can I help you with? Have you made some noteworthy progress?"

"There's nothing new from my progress update yesterday. As a courtesy, and nothing more, I'm letting you know Sophia Flores and I have reconciled." So your disgusting plan to keep me as a work-obsessed spinster forever backfired. Sorry—not sorry at all.

His expression remained neutral. "I appreciate the courtesy, unnecessary as it is. Especially considering you made it very clear that your personal life was…'No Man's Land,' I believe you said."

"I did say that. And I meant it. But I'm telling you, because I want you to know about my relationship, because I'm going to tell Sophia about Halcyon. In a roundabout and nonspecific way," I added at his aghast expression. I'd expected that reaction, but it still annoyed me that he seemed to think I was acting on a whim, like I was about to blurt out highly sensitive information to impress my girlfriend. Which I obviously wouldn't, because secret division is secret.

Lennon's mouth contorted into displeasure. "Why?"

I could have easily told him it was none of his business and left it at an "I'm doing this, so deal with it" unspoken explanation. But I wanted him to really understand that I was actively working to strengthen my relationship with Sophia, and yeah, again—your plan failed, Lennon. "Because I don't want to withhold things from her that don't need to be withheld. It eats at me. It caused problems in our relationship before. And because there's nothing in our terms of service that forbids it."

It wasn't like agency employees pretended they were going off to work at the shoe factory every morning—their spouses and partners would know their job. Halcyon was no different; it could be broadly alluded to without sharing specifics. It was just that Halcyon agents seemed to see no point in it, likely because Halcyon work was just something that constantly ticked along in the background rather than a physical job we went to.

"I have to strongly advise against that, Alexandra." Though his statement was calm, there was no mistaking his distaste and frustration.

"Of course you would. You seem to think I've become idiotic all of a sudden. No details, Lennon. Simply that I have two jobs that complement each other." I was beyond caring about his opinions—he'd proven that he had no right to anything but the barest minimum of respect and compliance from me. And he was lucky he was even getting that.

"Why is this suddenly so important to you?"

Oh how I wanted to tell him to mind his own business as I had before, but I'd opened the worm can again, so I had to explain why. "Because *she's* important to me. And I want this time to last. I need it to last. I'm not sure why you find it so hard to believe that having someone in my personal life makes my professional life better."

He said nothing. I guess when you're the head of the most important intelligence agency in the country as well as the head of the division that, among other things, keeps foreign operatives from influencing our government, you've earned the right to not comment or answer questions.

"Are you married, Lennon?" I'd noted on our first face-to-face meeting that he wore no wedding ring, but a lot of men didn't—including Jeffrey who, for personal reasons, kept his on a sturdy chain around his neck.

"Widowed. Many years ago."

"I'm sorry," I said automatically. He'd said it completely without inflection, which made me think the point I was about to make about him knowing that companionship is amazing was pointless. So I decided to just leave it and take a different route. A route that was perhaps treacherous. "Look. Clearly you don't understand, or aren't willing to understand, my stance on this. And I'm tired of arguing about this with you. So I'm not going to any longer. Either accept it, or I'll find a new boss who will. For both of my jobs."

"I'm not trying to antagonize you, Alexandra, as I'm sure you're not trying to antagonize me." Well, the jury's out on that one. "I'm simply ensuring the integrity of our agency and other organizations that you touch."

"I accept that. But you need to trust me and my personal integrity, not to mention my intellect. I've made it this far without revealing classified information or compromising my work." I inhaled sharply. "I've done everything you've ever asked of me. And now I'm asking you for this courtesy." I wasn't asking him to "let me" be in a relationship with Sophia. I didn't need anyone's permission. I was just asking that he mind his own fucking business and trust me.

He sighed. "You're right. This is tiresome and a waste of both our time and mental energy. From now on, I'll stay out of your personal business and trust that you know what you're doing as that personal business relates to agency and Halcyon business. But, if you want me to stay out of your personal life, then you need to assume responsibility for it and accept that if it even *looks* like compromising our objectives, then I will have to get involved."

I ground my molars. *Assume responsibility.* Like Sophia and her family were an unruly dog. But instead of snapping back at him, I just nodded and stood up. "Understood."

Jeffrey had beaten me into the office and was already nose-deep in *Don Quixote* when I arrived. I took myself into the Zen Zone for twenty minutes—I wasn't going to get anything done if I didn't take some time to rid myself of my mounting annoyance at my boss before I tried to focus on my dad's code.

If Jeffrey suspected that my date had gone incredibly well, he didn't say anything, or indulge in some teasing or swooning on my behalf. He'd asked how it was, in his usual friends-ask-questions way, and after I'd confirmed it was good, he'd nodded and returned to work. But during a midmorning break he did give me a slightly quizzical look when he caught me staring into space while I drank my tea, ate Combos, and daydreamed about Sophia.

By early afternoon I'd finally finished going through *War and Peace*. After taking a break, I read back through what I'd put down over the few days it'd taken me to get through the book, which had been as cumbersome as I'd imagined. As I read, I began having déjà vu. After swapping to cross-check each of the four books we'd completed, *Moby Dick*, *1984*, *Don Quixote*, and *War and Peace*, Jeffrey and I had confirmed that we'd both found the same notations (yay for consistency). I stared mindlessly at my handwriting, hoping the feeling of déjà vu would solidify.

As well as the box drawn around the ten of the date in each of the books so far, we'd found the same symbols associated with letters on completely random pages throughout—lines over letters and periods under other letters.

Again, the letters with lines over them were far outweighed by the letters with periods underneath them. My hunch was still that the lined letters were the first letters of a word. If I was going to be working with anagrams then it made sense to give me an anchor point for the phrase, that these were the first letters of the word. Or, they could be capitalized letters in a pass phrase? Part of the Caesar cipher? Dad simply being capricious? Unlikely…

I stared at what I had until it suddenly made sense. I hadn't been paying attention to the actual letters, simply marking them down within the words as a whole, and noting on what page they appeared. But now I was comparing book notes, I could see similarities. I flipped frantically back and forth through the pages.

"What are you doing?" Jeffrey asked, as he tore back the foil on a yogurt cup.

"Just seeing if a hunch is more than a hunch."

"Do you need my eyes?" It was asked around a spoonful of yogurt, and sounded perfunctory rather than him being excited to check something for me.

"Not yet," I muttered distractedly.

It only took me a few minutes to confirm my suspicions. Though the letters were marked on different pages in each book, in a different order and spread widely through each text, there were forty-two in total for each book—three line-marked letters and thirty-nine marked with a period.

I looked up to find him watching me as he ate. "I think the letters are the same. The same markings with the same letters in every book. Look." I held up two pieces of paper. "Letters with a line over them. Here"—I pointed—"here and here…All the same letters, right?"

He abandoned his snack to come closer so he could read the notes. "Yeah."

"And it looks like all these other letters with periods under them are also the same in each book. Just found on different pages, but the same? I mean, X is one of the least commonly used letters, just ask any Scrabble player. But there's an X marked in each of the books. Or have I just been staring at letters for too long? Seems like more than a coincidence." And it made me even more sure that there was some sort of shift-cipher, because a word with X seemed unlikely.

"It does. Okay. Why don't we confirm or deny this properly? How about I'll read what we have from each book out to you, and you put them down in a spreadsheet, then we can sort the spreadsheet alphabetically and see if there's any matches, or if there's all matches."

"Good idea." I started foot-wheeling my chair sideways to get to my laptop, but Jeffrey grabbed the chair arm and stopped me.

He spun the chair so I faced away from the desk and toward the kitchenette. "But first…you need to eat lunch. It's almost three."

He was right. I'd been ignoring hunger for a few hours because I was so focused on finishing *War and Peace*. I ate lunch, took a bathroom break, and after ten minutes of stretching and another ten of meditation in the Zen Zone, I was ready to tackle the task.

I made up a quick spreadsheet with columns for lines-over and periods-under letters for each book. Jeffrey slowly read from our notes and I entered the data until I had full columns for all four completed books.

"Okay," I said, "so in the lines-over column we have E, E, and E."

"Consistent," he deadpanned. "The Es have it."

"And in the periods-under column we have..." I rattled off the thirty-nine letters which ranged from A to X. "All vowels present and accounted for, and a lovely array of other letters which, at this moment, mean absolutely fucking nothing to me." I massaged the back of my neck. "I mean, we still have seven other books to read, but this makes *way* more sense, doesn't it? That he's given me the *same* message in eleven books, rather than eleven books being needed to make up one message. So if I lose one, or most or whatever, I still have what I need."

"That does make way more sense," Jeffrey agreed. "And I have to believe your father would have done something that made sense."

"He would have. Logic above all else." I leaned back in the chair and pulled off my glasses, rubbing my eyes. "God, I so just want to call it a pattern and leave it there, but we have to go through all of these books, just in case." I put my glasses back on and pushed them up my nose. "Remember how I said that when we were done I thought I might read these books? I changed my mind..."

Jeffrey snorted out a laugh. "I did wonder about that."

I stared at the letters laid out in the spreadsheet, willing them to make sense. They did not. "So where does the Caesar cipher come in? Or doesn't it? I don't know what's relevant but I have to assume everything is until proven otherwise."

His eyebrows shot up. "You're asking me?"

"Yes. Because the order the letters appear, in both line-over and period-under, is different for every book. So do we have eleven possible variants to try with the cipher?"

"Quite possibly. Maybe one of them, as is, will make perfect sense, or none will and you'll just have to try all of them through a cipher." His eyebrows crinkled. "Or is the pass phrase just the letters as they appear?" Jeffrey frowned. "No, that'd be nonsensical if the cipher shift was consistent for every letter. You'd just have groups of letters the way we do now and they make no sense so they'd still make no sense. Or maybe it's the groups of letters, alphabetically arranged and that's the pass phrase. A long pass phrase but still a pass phrase." The more he spoke, the more he rambled, the more he seemed to go in circles.

Smiling beatifically, I said, "I see you've reached the spiraling-into-madness stage." I swept my arm expansively to the side. "Welcome. I've been here a while. Make yourself comfortable."

Jeffrey raised an eyebrow. "You got beanbags and ice cream?"

I laughed. "We have everything you need to feel at home in your quest to figure out Spy Martin's code." I tapped *War and Peace*. "Look. Occam's razor, right? My dad thought Occam's razor was like…a life motto. So I'm going to go with what I know, and that is that the simplest answers are usually the correct ones."

"Right," Jeffrey agreed. "We just have to get to an answer, any answer, first."

CHAPTER THIRTEEN

The lightness of truth

We were getting faster at our black-light book checking and by Friday afternoon, we had six of eleven books completed. And as I'd discovered the day before—it looked like we had a pattern. Or…a consistent set of letters at least. Aside from that, we'd found nothing else that screamed "this is how you figure it out," which meant it was still just staring at pages until we had a complete dataset to work with. That was next week's task, because if we continued as steadily as we had been, we'd have notations from all the books by Wednesday.

An offhanded, joking comment from Jeffrey reignited a thought I'd already had and I'd been pondering it ever since he'd mumbled, "I really wish your father had Sharpied the pass phrase on the bottom of the hard drive."

I really wished that too. So why hadn't he? Metaphorically, of course. There had to be a good reason, because Dad never did anything without meticulous thought. And so far, for all my brainstorming, all I'd come up with was that Lennon was not supposed to know the pass phrase when Dad gave him the drive, for whatever reason. I wished I knew what that reason was.

After I left the office for the weekend—definitely not coming in to work before Monday, not when I had time to spend with Sophia—I stopped by Lennon's office on my way out to give him a brief status update. There really wasn't much status to update, but checking in regularly would keep him happy and Happy Lennon wasn't nagging me about things I couldn't change.

He listened quietly while I told him what we'd done, and then I wrapped up with, "So yeah, not much going on. Just looking for letters and brainstorming how they might come together to create a pass phrase."

"Do you feel that you're making progress?"

"Yes, steady progress. And honestly, we're further ahead than I'd anticipated. It's just grunt work at the moment, extracting whatever data we can before we start looking at how to turn that into what we need. It's not that we lack resources, just that we're still working out how to get a result from what we have."

"I see. How long until you have a concrete result, do you think?"

"No clue. As I've been telling you in my reports, we *are* making progress. And a result will happen when it happens. There's no way to do this any faster than we already are." Plus, you've waited this long, so…you can wait a little longer until I figure it out.

He steepled his fingers and for a moment I wanted to laugh at the posture, as if he'd been watching men in charge in movies and decided to copy their mannerisms. "Then I'll continue to trust your process. But I must stress again that this is important and time-sensitive."

"Yes, I know. And I'm treating it as important and time-sensitive." I leaned back in the chair and crossed my legs, forcing my upper body to relax. If I seemed relaxed then he'd be more likely to respond in kind and not flare up when I started questioning him. "So, something's been bugging me, and I realized what it is. My dad gave you the hard drive with his work on it. Important work. So why not give you the pass phrase to access whatever's on the drive? I'm assuming he was trusting you to keep it as a backup copy, which means you'd need to access it if he wasn't around."

Lennon didn't falter in composure or voice. "We were to meet the evening of the day he died, and he was going to give the password to me. He'd left the hard drive in one of our safe drop spots for me to collect, but obviously he would never leave a password at the same time, nor would he ever write it down."

"Obviously," I agreed.

"Unfortunately, in this instance, OPSEC has caused a rather large issue for us." Ah yes, my parents dying was very inconvenient. "He never specified the reason he gave the drive to me, but I assume as you do that it was to keep a backup copy."

"That makes sense. It just seemed weird. But thanks for clearing that up."

"You're welcome."

"Did he ever tell you exactly what was on the drive?"

"No. As a rule of our friendship, we didn't discuss our work, even nonclassified matters. It was why we remained such good friends, we understood the rigors of our work, but didn't have to discuss it. He simply told me that the drive was of utmost importance." As if anticipating my next question, which was "Then how did you know the drive contains information about foreign operatives operating on American soil?" Lennon added, "After your parents passed, I decided to see if I could figure it out, and I suspected, when I delved into your dad's dossiers, what it might be. And after speaking with his handler, it was confirmed that he was investigating undercover foreign operatives on American soil."

Oh, now here was something that might help. I would love to speak to the person who, aside from my mom, probably knew my father the best. And yeah, I wanted to speak with them for both professional and personal reasons. So I blurted, "May I speak with his handler?"

"That's not possible."

I held back my annoyance and calmly asserted, "It might help me."

"I'm sure it would. But she died of cancer late last year."

"That's annoyingly inconvenient."

Lennon smiled. "I've found, in our line of work, that a lot of things are annoyingly inconvenient."

That made me laugh. It was so true.

"I've been thinking too." He leaned forward, fixing me with a laser stare. "Would you consider hypnosis to see if something might surface from your subconscious?"

"No," I said instantly, flatly. "Completely off the cards." I had to bite my tongue on unleashing my full feelings about his ridiculous request.

"Why is that?"

"Because I said no," I responded, far more calmly than I felt. *No* was a complete sentence, but I knew he was going to keep pushing until I gave him an actual reason, so I ticked some off on my fingers. "Because it's pointless. Because my father didn't embed the answer in my head, it's in his books somehow and I just need to figure out what it is. Because my thoughts and memories are private, and I don't want you delving into places you're not allowed. And finally, because I said no and you need to trust that the reason I'm doing that is because I know it's a pointless endeavor."

"I hope you'll reconsider."

Smiling tightly, I shot back, "I hope you'll respect me and my decision." I stood up. "And if that's all, I'm finished for the week so I'm going home to my girlfriend."

He displayed no reaction, except for a slight tightening around his eyes. I pretended it was because he was trying not to smile about me and Sophia because he'd suddenly realized he was being an overbearing dick about us, not that he was stopping himself from narrowing his eyes. "Have a good weekend, Alexandra."

"You too," I said cheerfully. Then I got the hell out of his office before I said something seriously disrespectful.

Had Lennon always been such a fucking asshole dickwad? I always knew he was The Boss, and he made no secret of the fact that Lennon's Way was the only way. But I trusted that and him and everything he'd ever asked me to do because I trusted that he knew things I didn't. But now? Now he just seemed like a petty asshole, flexing his power. Maybe his job as agency director was fraying him. Or maybe he'd always been this guy but I'd never realized because all our interactions had been over the phone, and specifically pertaining to Halcyon tasks.

Something just felt…different, and I wanted to put my finger on exactly what that was. But, for now—it was the weekend, and it was time to rest and recharge and forget about codes and secrets and lies and bosses who were being assholes.

It was time to be with Sophia.

We hadn't seen each other since our date-plus-more on Wednesday, but there had been a long call and plenty of flirty texts sent back and forth, which reminded me of the early stages of our relationship when we were just sending out feelers. In a way, this *was* a new beginning, and I was determined to make these foundations even stronger than the old ones.

I started texting Sophia as soon as I'd collected my phone from the trunk of my car. *Leaving work now. Come around whenever you're ready. Huge day, huge week. Mind if we order in instead of me cooking?*

Of course, no problem. I'll eat anything you want to offer me. A swath of naughty emojis followed. *I'll just shower and pack an overnight bag and be on my way.*

Pack an overnight bag.

We hadn't discussed sex, though given our recent history, it was almost certain. But sleeping over? In our short time together, sandwiched between the Kunduz Intelligence trip and my short incarceration and then me being shipped off to a hostile country by our illustrious leader, we'd spent almost every night together. Before it had all imploded, we'd even reached shared keys, and leaving toiletries and clothes at each other's place stage.

But planning to spend the night now? So soon? It felt…scary. I didn't want us to rush into resuming our relationship without considering things. And nightly sleepovers felt like something that should be reserved for some time in the future. Like, maybe…next week.

Once I'd showered off my tiring and tedious week I situated myself on the couch to wait for Sophia and watch the best serotonin boost I could think of—TikToks of deaf babies receiving hearing aids and being able to hear their parents properly for the first time.

Sophia knocked just before seven p.m. and after a quick kiss, I pulled her into my apartment. As I secured the door, Sophia set her duffel and handbag down. I'd barely turned around before she was right there with me again. Sophia wrapped her arms around my waist, pulling us together. "Hello," she murmured before her mouth met mine. She kissed me again, just the lightest stroke of her tongue hinting at her underlying passion, and I met her with enthusiasm. God, I'd missed kissing her.

"Hi," I said breathlessly once we'd moved apart for some air.

She reached up to tuck some hair back behind my ear. "I've missed you."

"I've missed you too. Want a drink?"

"Yes," she said emphatically. "Fridays." Sophia rested both hands on the back of her neck before pushing them up through her hair. "What a ridiculous work week."

"Busy?" I asked as I poured her a glass of water.

"Mhmm. And stupid." She drank half the glass. "I hope you meant a drink drink when you offered. Water's great, but…"

"I'm getting to it," I promised her. "Hydration is important."

"It is. Have you thought about what you want for dinner?"

"Aside from gin? No. But I think I just want like…fries and mac 'n' cheese and soup and nachos and chips and cookies and—"

She interrupted my expanding food list with a laughing, "Comfort foods?"

"Yes," I breathed. "That's exactly it. I want comfort food." Comfort everything.

Sophia grabbed her phone from her handbag which she'd casually left on the kitchen counter. "Leave it to me, babe." She looked up, her eyes approaching saucer size. "Sorry. That just slipped out."

"Why are you apologizing? It's a perfectly normal endearment for people who're dating or in a relationship."

"It is," she agreed carefully.

"And it's not the first time you've called me that," I pointed out as I pulled a bottle of Whitley Neill Blood Orange Gin from my alcohol pantry.

"No, but I didn't want you to feel like I've just…forgotten and bulldozed past everything we talked about, about making sure we're not rushing. Because I haven't."

"Sophia, darling, you brought an overnight bag on what is technically the second, or the third if you count our coffee and walk-talk meetup, date. I don't think 'babe' is problematic, nor do I think that moving forward in a way that feels natural, which includes endearments, is discarding the things we talked about." I moved around to her side of the kitchen counter and kissed her. "And I also don't think you're bulldozing. Quite the opposite. Hell, I just called you *darling*."

"You're right. I'm overthinking it. Totally overthinking." She held up her phone. "I'm just going to order food."

While she did that, I made G&Ts, fussing with rimming the glass with orange oil from the peel and making overly complicated garnishes. My task overlapped hers by many minutes, and she sat at the counter opposite and watched me struggling with my extravagance. When I'd finally made two very passable drinks, I handed one to her. "For you, madam."

Sophia whistled through her teeth. "Fancy."

"Well, yeah." I grinned. "I'm trying to woo you."

Smiling, she shook her head. "Oh, Lexie. It's far too late for that…"

After dinner, which was a comforting girl-dinner spread eaten on the couch, Sophia told me to turn sideways so she could check how many muscle knots I'd gained in the past half year. She wriggled behind me, with her legs outside mine—she was making it very hard to not suggest we go to bed. Though, we could just use the couch. Not like we hadn't done that before. I reluctantly pushed the thought aside. First, tell her about Halcyon, and then maybe sex. Definitely sex.

"How's work been?" she asked as she massaged the back of my neck, her fingers kneading firmly before moving to my shoulders.

I groaned, my ability to speak temporarily stifled by her magic hands. After a few seconds' concentration, I managed to focus enough to answer. "Productive. Tedious. Annoying. A little frightening." I reached back and gripped one of her hands, pulling it forward and turning my head to kiss the butt of her thumb.

She stroked my cheek with her thumb before resuming her attention on my tight shoulders. "Why is that?"

"My new job. It's…I'm investigating some historical dossiers in the hope I'll figure out a key to open something important encrypted on a hard drive. And it's going well, we're making good, solid progress." I inhaled deeply. "But I'm scared of what I'm going to uncover."

"Why are you scared, hon?"

"Because whatever is on the hard drive was created by someone I know. And I've already learned things about them that I didn't know before and everything's kind of up in the air. I just…I don't want to find out something that completely changes how I feel about them." *So you know how we used to joke about me not being a spy? Well, guess what, Sophia…* I held back a smirk at the ridiculous irony.

"I think if the person who created whatever is on the hard drive is a person you know well, then you have to trust that anything you might find out about them won't change how you feel."

"You're right." I reluctantly extricated myself from her massage and turned to face her. "Maybe I've just been spending too much time trying to find hidden meanings in things, but it feels like there's a side meaning in what you just said."

"Maybe there is." She framed my face with her hands, her thumbs stroking my cheeks. "Trust and forgiveness, Lexie. I give those to you, and I hope you have room in your heart to give me the same."

"Yes. I do." My throat tightened. "I love you. I hope you know that."

"I do know that. But thank you for reminding me." She pulled me toward her for a soft kiss.

I leaned my shoulder against the couch. "I was thinking, when things have settled—and I know I say that a lot but I really mean it here—I really want to meet your parents. And Mateo." I'd already met her older sister, Camila, and was hoping we could move on from our…well, *hostile* meeting wasn't exactly the right word, but it wasn't rainbows and sunshine. And I'd met her parents over a video call, but hadn't met Sophia's older brother at all.

"Then we'll do it," she assured me.

"Thank you." I relaxed a little at her easy, open expression, and decided now was as good a time as any to share about Halcyon. "Hey, can I tell you something?"

She smiled. "You can. And you don't need to ask me if you can tell me something. You *can* just tell me," Sophia said teasingly.

"I know. But this isn't just me telling you that I love you, or that your hair looks great tonight."

She faked a pout. "Oh. Why not?"

"Because it's something else that's important. But, obviously I do love you and your hair always looks great."

Sophia leaned over and kissed me. "Nice save." She jumped up off the couch. "I feel like this 'telling me something' needs chocolate. Do you have any?"

"Some." Smiling, I amended, "A little. Hardly any."

"Okay. Then I'll eat what tiny amount remains while you tell me what you need to tell me."

I leaned an elbow on the back of the couch and watched as she rummaged around my fridge for chocolate. She seemed relaxed when she settled back down on the couch, but then again, it could just be the prospect of the banana crunch chocolate bar she'd found.

Okay. Here goes. "So. In the interest of transparency between us moving forward, I wanted to tell you a little more about my work."

Sophia smiled. "Oh I know plenty about your work," she said teasingly as she broke off some chocolate.

I returned the smile. "Yes, you do know plenty about my work. But there's more I want you to know. Most civilians wouldn't know that there are many private, hidden divisions within the government—think of it like branches supporting the tree trunk, which is comprised of the agency I work for, other agencies and bureaus working in intelligence and law enforcement, the military, as well as the actual government. And I work for one of them. The branches that is."

"You're not really an intelligence analyst?" She looked like she'd been punched in the gut, and I hurried to reassure her that I hadn't lied to her about my profession.

"Yes, I'm an intelligence analyst. That's my primary job, the one I go off to do Monday through Friday. But I'm *also* an agent of one of these branches." Smirking, I bragged, "I'm excellent at multitasking."

"Oh," she breathed, visibly relaxing. "Okay. I thought—" She frowned, shaking her head. "Never mind."

I finished the thought for her, hating that she'd even had it. "You thought I'd lied."

"Yes," she said instantly. "I'm sorry."

"I understand, darling. And it's all right." Smiling sadly, I agreed, "It's a logical thought."

"I know. But I still hate that I had it. I, um…So, how long have you had two jobs?"

I blew out a loud breath. "A while. I started at Job Two around the same time as I started at Job One, so…fifteen years or so."

She reached out to curl some of my hair around her fingers, and I relaxed instantly at her touch. "And what exactly do you do at Job Two?"

"Honestly? Not much. Mostly it's really boring, kind of a 'sit and wait for action' gig. Mostly I pass along relevant intelligence from Job One that crosses my path. Mostly I just get paid for doing nothing for Job Two, kind of like…a nightwatchman at a morgue."

"Did the stuff in Florida have anything to do with this other job?"

I paused for a second before answering, not because I didn't want to answer, but because it was habit to weigh sharing information like this. "Yes it did. That started as a Job One task but turned into a Job Two task. We generally don't share that we're employed by Job Two, but…I'm sick of not sharing. And it's not like you know the name, or the purpose of this branch or anything like that. I'm deeming this a 'something you can know' piece of information."

"I appreciate that. But why are you telling me now?"

"Because I don't want to withhold things from you that don't need to be withheld. I've thought a lot about where my loyalty lies. Obviously, it's one hundred percent to my job, and my country. But, it's also to you, Sophia." Her expression softened at that and I reached over and rested my hand on her thigh, squeezing gently. "You already know I can't tell you job specifics, but you can know that I also have this secondary job."

"Thank you." Her eyebrows scrunched together and after about twenty seconds, she looked up, the epiphany clear in her expression. "The blue phone," she said. The phone with a blue case that was only ever used to communicate with Lennon.

"Yes."

Sophia nodded slowly, scraping her upper lip through her teeth. "I'm glad you told me. It makes things a little clearer now, honestly. I just thought…none of this really makes sense, you know? I always felt there had to be something more to the story, but not just a 'this is classified information' something more, because that's always there, but something you really weren't telling me."

"Mmm. I'm sorry," I said earnestly. "It's so secret that only a handful of people outside of us who work for Job Two know about it. So, you're in a very special club. Or…adjacent to the club because you don't *really* know about it."

"I feel so special," she deadpanned.

"Oh you are, believe me. But, I know I don't need to say this, but I need to say it. Even though you don't know anything other than the fact this is a thing, Job Two isn't something we talk about."

Sophia humored me and mimed zipping her lips. "Got it."

"Thank you."

Shaking her head, Sophia murmured, "Which boss…"

I raised an eyebrow. "Pardon me?"

She grinned. "When I told you that your boss had been to see me, that he was the guy who'd been following me. You said 'which boss,' then you breezed past it like you'd never said it. And I thought it was weird, but a lot of things are weird so I just put it aside because you had."

Shit. "I shouldn't be surprised you noticed that. But yeah. Two bosses."

Sophia bounced her eyebrows. "Lucky you." The silliness faded and she sobered. "So, can I ask—Job Two really is just another office job? You're not secretly out putting yourself in physical danger every day?"

"No," I laughed. "I'm not moonlighting around the globe as Jane Bond." I reached up to take the hand that was still playing in my hair, using it to pull her closer. Her mouth was within a whisper of mine as I apologized, "Sorry to disappoint you, darling, but I'm still not a spy."

CHAPTER FOURTEEN

*Is it too much to hope for that the pass phrase is just...
"pass phrase"?*

Reaching milestones in a task was important. They made you feel like you were accomplishing things. They assured your superiors that resources weren't being wasted. But in this case, the milestone of us having read through all eleven books left me feeling overwhelmed. I'd felt similarly when I'd finished reading through Dad's dossiers, which yielded nothing except discomfort that I didn't know my dad at all.

So far, all I had were bad feelings, some notes about my dad from his decades as an undercover intelligence officer, a ten with a box around it, and forty-two letters that neither Jeffrey nor I knew what to do with. We were obviously much closer to the answer than we had been initially but we'd stalled.

"I don't know where to go," I admitted to Jeffrey, after I'd spent twenty minutes just staring blankly at the printed list of letters sorted into their columns. We'd confirmed that every book contained the same set of letters marked with either the line or period, but other than that? Dead end. Were the lines and dots actually relevant as something more than a marking tool?

He'd also been staring at the list, though with perhaps a little less blankness than me. "Okay. We need to move step by step here." He grabbed a legal pad and flipped to a fresh page, writing as he spoke. "Forty-two letters. A ten with a box around it. The tenth of January, which means nothing, but if we take everything that's considered historical on that date and we're logical about our profession, would lead anyone to a Caesar cipher. Your watch with Little Mouse, and XXX for your thirtieth birthday." Jeffrey glanced up. "Am I missing anything?"

"And Frost. As in Robert and his poem, and the person my father mentioned in his dossiers."

Jeffrey wrote it all down and turned the notepad around for me to see. I nodded. "Yep," I said, "looks like a bunch of nonsense."

He rolled his eyes, and pulled the notepad back toward himself. "Let's start at the beginning, the most basic answer, with each of the eleven sets of letters being a password, as the letters appear in order in the books. So that gives eleven possible combinations right there, of just the letters, unadulterated."

"Yeah. I'm just…I don't think this is it. Think about it. Remember, the hardest passwords to brute-force are those with combinations of upper- and lower-case letters, plus numbers and if you want to get fancy, symbols. Even harder to guess are separate words—"

"Purple monkey space helicopter," he cut in.

Laughing, I agreed, "Right, a phrase like that, rather than something like Velociraptor123! with upper and lower case spread throughout the word. And given they've been trying to work this out for over a year, I think these would have come up as 'basic' passwords already in the brute-force attempts. I still think we need to exclude these combinations by trying them, but I don't think this is it."

"That's highly likely. And I agree, but yeah, I think we'd be negligent if we didn't try everything we have."

"I know. But…I'm just saying now, before we start, that I think it's a dead end."

Jeffrey raised an eyebrow. "Are we betting on what'll work and what won't?"

"Let's do it. Winner buys dinner."

"Agreed." He reached a hand over to me and I shook it. "Right, let's get into this."

"Let's," I said, with less enthusiasm than him. I wrote down the book titles. "So, eleven passwords, just straight up. Then we have the fact that we've ended up with forty-two letters that are exactly the same. And then if we move on to a Caesar cipher with those, we have…fuck, I don't even know how many possibilities that is. We need to figure out what number is the shift key."

"But we have numbers here," Jeffrey pointed out, "given to us by your dad. Ten and thirty."

"Okay, so that's another twenty-two possibilities, two lots of eleven sets of letters, using both ten and thirty as the shift key, because I see no other numbers here."

Jeffrey lightly pricked my balloon. "That doesn't mean that either of those are actually the shift key. For all we know, they're completely unrelated."

"Don't bring me down, Jeffrey. If it's not ten or thirty then I don't know what the fuck the shift could be." And how long would it take to calculate a Caesar manually with every possible numerical shift key? Far too long. Dad would have given me the shift key somewhere, I was sure of that.

"In lieu of evidence contradicting our theory, I think those two would be a good start."

"What about the lines and periods?" I asked.

"I think our idea that it's capitals and not is the most obvious so let's start there."

"Right." I tapped my pen against the notepad. "Or, it's an anagram and this is just wasted time." Frowning, I corrected myself. "Not wasted time. Nothing is wasted if it produces a result, even if that result is a failure, but…you know."

"I know. And honestly? I agree that an anagram is the most likely use for these letters," he admitted. "But also the most labor intensive. So let's just take the raw data first and see what we come up with. It won't take long to go through thirty-three combinations, and then those three theories will either be ruled out or confirmed."

I collected the thumb drive from the safe and plugged it in for the first time. All in all, it was rather anticlimactic. It took almost two hours to go through the thirty-three possibilities—you try typing a forty-two-letter password in accurately that many times—firstly just the raw data in the order it appeared in each book, and then working a Caesar cipher, with ten and thirty as shift keys. Every time I entered a combination, a little surge of nervous anticipation mixed with the certainty of failure twisted in my stomach. And every time, I was met with that failure. Not a big flashing INCORRECT PASSWORD, just the prompt resetting.

After thirty-three nopes, I was pretty disheartened. "Well," I said. "At least we know it's not just the raw data in any iteration, and it's not a Caesar with ten or thirty as the shift." Pity there was an infinite amount of numbers that could be used as a shift key in a Caesar cipher. I tried not to think about that. Not thinking about it was actually pretty easy, because now I was sure that these letters created something that would lead me to a pass phrase, rather than some form of the letters *being* the pass phrase.

"Have you tried 'password' as the password?" Jeffrey asked dryly.

Just for laughs, I put it in and was met by the password prompt again. "That's another nope."

"Damn. I was sure of that one." He pretended to cross something off his list. "Let's take a break before we tackle this again."

I made tea. Jeffrey ate cookies. I stretched out the frustration of not knowing what to do. Jeffrey paced around the office. I munched through a bag of Cheddar Cheese Pretzel Combos. Jeffrey snuck more cookies when he thought I wasn't looking, because apparently I was the cookie police and he was weirdly guilty about eating them.

When we reconvened after a thirty-minute break, I felt mildly refreshed, but still without a lightning bolt of inspiration. "What do you think is on the drive that's so important?"

"You mean aside from the identities of foreign operatives compromising our democracy and security?" he asked dryly.

"Aside from that. Don't get me wrong, obviously that's important. But…I feel like there's more urgency to get this open than if it was just a bunch of foreign operatives who've been working on the inside for decades. Which makes me think it's someone or someones big."

He made a musing sound of agreement. "Possibly."

I swung side to side in my chair. "I think it's someone like Berenson. Maybe even the president."

"Aiming high, are we?"

"Mhmm. Shoot for the moon, and even if you fall short you'll still land in the stars."

"That's so profound."

"Thanks. I read it somewhere on the Internet once."

He bent over and wheezed out a laugh. "I honestly don't know what I did for laughs before I started working with you."

"I just think you didn't laugh."

"Not much, no," he agreed. "I've not met many workplaces I truly hated, but working with you is so easy."

"I'm glad." Come on, Lexie, reciprocate. "I enjoy working with you too."

"I know," he said smugly. "So, speaking of enjoyable and friendly workplaces. You haven't mentioned Ms. Flores in a while."

"You need to work on your segues. And haven't I?"

"Don't be coy with me, Lexie. It doesn't suit you." He stretched his legs out, ankles crossed. "I'm simply asking my friend how her personal life is."

"Thank you for asking. Her personal life seems to be going well. We're back together." The blush warming my cheeks wasn't unexpected, but I pressed my lips together and concentrated on getting rid of it.

"How's it going?"

"Incredibly. It feels like…not like we never broke up, that's still a little raw, but it's almost like we've realized we needed to break up to move forward?"

He raised an eyebrow. "Interesting perspective."

"I know. But the breakup has made me more certain that I can't keep unnecessary secrets from her just because the habit is ingrained in my personality. And I've been working so hard on that. We're still not together every day, but when we are, it feels natural to share with her."

Psychologist Jeffrey—I could tell the doctor was in; it was all about the nod—smiled. "Personal growth is amazing, isn't it?"

"It really is. And to start my new sharing resolution, I told her about Halcyon. Or, rather, I told her that I have another, secret job in intelligence that complements my agency job. And that's all."

"Wow. Uh. Hmm. Okay. Does Lennon know this?" It was hilarious how gobsmacked he was, when he didn't even know Halcyon's true purpose.

"He knows. I told him I was going to tell her, in a *very* nonspecific way, that I have two jobs. I didn't ask. He wasn't happy, but there's no concrete rules against it." I pushed out a loud breath. "I can't have something like that hanging over my relationship. Not when she sees the consequences of Halcyon work and it affects her."

"That seems logical," he said. Then unlike Lennon, Jeffrey smiled. "I know you, and I know how much integrity you have, and you're not just out there blurting classified information. Not even to your significant other."

"Thank you. Do you find it hard? I know you said Dominique had learned to accept some secrets from you throughout your career."

"She has. She knows now that if I don't tell her something then either I truly cannot, or it's not something that affects her or us so she doesn't need to know. But her elephant in the room isn't secrets. It's gray moral choices. That's why I left military contracting." Jeffrey smiled fondly. "Compromise, remember?"

"I remember." He'd given me, relationship novice, a few pep talks while we'd been overseas. "It feels different this time, without the Kunduz Intelligence and its aftermath hanging over us."

"I'll bet. And I for one, am thrilled for you."

"I'm thrilled for me too," I said, trying to tamp down the glee bubbling up inside that made me want to do something silly and movie-esque, like leap from my chair and dance around.

"And part of me being thrilled is that I can finally tell you that you *and* Ms. Flores are invited to dinner at my place."

"Oh? Okay. Great! When?"

"Whenever suits you this week. Dominique was very specific that whatever works for you also works for us." He smiled apologetically. "She's been pushing me about asking you and I've been putting her off while we worked on this, and while you…worked on getting back with your girlfriend. But I can put my wife off no longer, so, please come around for dinner."

"I'll ask Sophia after work and let you know right away." I was sure she'd agree without hesitation.

"Sounds good. But for now, are you ready to stare some more at our forty-two letters?"

"Not in the slightest," I answered cheerfully.

But that's what we did.

I formed and unformed letters into words, hoping for something to make sense. But it didn't. An anagram or word generator would have been helpful, if for nothing other than to give us all the words that could be made by these letters, but I couldn't access the Internet in the office and I wasn't going to run back and forth to my car all day to use my phone.

Jeffrey pushed back from his desk to stretch. "Do you know if anyone is still out there trying to break this encryption?"

"No clue. I assume they're still running the brute-force program or whatever it is, hoping something works."

"Is Lennon *sure* there's no encryption key on a flash drive somewhere?"

"No. And neither am I. But, I found nothing in my parents' effects like that, so I've ruled it out for now." I'd finally made time to check their storage unit after work one day and had found it a dead end both personally and professionally. "Why? Do you think we're not being told something?"

He snorted midway through his laugh. "Of course we're not. I knew right away when I was called in for this that huge patches of information were being left out of my briefing."

"So what aren't we being told?" Or what wasn't he being told, more specifically. Actually, no...both of us. I was under no illusions that I had every piece of information relating to my father, just that which had been deemed relevant.

"You're asking me? I have no idea." He shrugged. "But it does make me wonder..."

"Wonder what?" I prompted.

"At the disparity. This is your big important task. A task so important that you escaped prosecution for what you did with the Kunduz Intelligence. A task so important that you were assigned a handsome, physically fit, funny, charming, kind bodyguard when you were sent overseas."

"I was?" I feigned ignorance, grinning at his eye roll.

"You wound me. My point is. It's a big deal. You've had many concessions because of your apparent ability to figure out this pass phrase. It's so important you got a literal 'get out of jail free' card. So why is Lennon not haranguing you more about results?"

"Maybe he knows I work better when I don't have people asking me for progress reports twice a day."

"Could be. Or maybe there's another reason."

"Like what?"

But he shook his head, and I decided I'd leave it alone for now.

"Okay," I conceded. "Let's add this to the 'Lennon does things that don't make sense' column."

Jeffrey eyed me. "Is it a long column?"

"Moderately sized."

"Mm, so...pretty standard for agency directors and the like."

"Yeah," I agreed. *Don't ask, just do* had been the unofficial motto for as long as I'd been working in this field. Problem was, I didn't like doing things without knowing why. "If you had to allocate percentages, how much would you go with gut feeling versus actual knowledge for how you work through something, or choose what to do?"

Jeffrey blew out a loud breath, propping his hands behind his head. "Maybe fifty-fifty? I won't do anything or go anywhere without having all the information possible, but I always trust my gut. I've honed that instinct over decades. But my work is a little different to yours." During his military service, he'd worked special ops, then moved into private military contracting where rules were just suggestions, and then finally to private contracting where he did everything—collecting and analyzing intelligence, debriefing assets or hostile actors, and even physical protection.

"Right. I mean, I'm cerebral, and information is my bread and butter. But I always trust my gut."

"And what's your gut saying now?" he asked quietly, leaning forward.

"That something doesn't feel right. Problem is, I just don't know what that something is."

CHAPTER FIFTEEN

Some things, you just don't want to know

What Jeffrey had said about Lennon's apparent disinterest stuck in my head, so much so that I mulled over it for the rest of the day. And I concluded that he was right. For someone who'd spent the past eight months drilling into me how important this was, how important *I* was, Lennon seemed pretty uninterested in my dad's dossiers now that he'd handed them over to me. Was he apathetic because he was dealing with a million other things since he'd taken over the agency? Or was he apathetic because he already knew what was on the drive and my role was simply to unlock it to provide the evidence needed to go after these bad actors?

The more I thought about it, the more annoyance gnawed at me. Annoyance at his apathy and annoyance at being kept in the dark about things I wanted to know and annoyance at being put in this position. He'd made out like I was the only hope of this being solved, but how did he know that for sure? So, I did something I did best—I went to get answers. I was supposed to meet Sophia for dinner and a movie at her place, which meant I had less than thirty minutes to fit in a chat with the director. Not ideal, but I would make it work.

For once, instead of just turning up at his office, I called ahead, and his secretary confirmed he had some time for me. After filling him in on our progress, which only took a few minutes—hardly any progress takes hardly any time to report, even when you pad it out a little—I got into the meat of why I'd come up to see him. "I've been thinking about this task." Leaning forward, I fixed him with an unwavering stare and asked him, "Are you being straight with me? Because it feels like this isn't high on your priority list, despite both you and Derek constantly hammering into me that I might be the savior of the universe." A little hyperbole never hurt anyone.

Lennon's eyebrows rose fleetingly before settling back to a normal position. "I apologize if it seems as if I'm uninterested in what you're doing," he said sincerely. "That could not be further from the truth. Since taking on the role as agency director, I find myself pulled in more directions than I'm used to. When I add managing Halcyon Division to the new workload, I just don't have time to check in constantly." Lennon smiled brightly. "And I know you're working on it, and that the data is safe, so perhaps it just seems like I'm uninterested when what I actually am is trusting that you have it under control."

"I do have it under control. Mostly. I still feel like I'm missing some major pieces of information. Can you shed any light on my dad?" I asked, annoyed by the childish optimism in my question. "You were his best friend *and* you knew him as an intelligence officer. He was just my dad to me and I don't know if that's enough. Obviously there were aspects of him I never saw, and that maybe my mom never saw. But if you worked with him, spent time with him, then maybe you know something I don't."

"Your father and I were very good friends, Alexandra, but that doesn't mean we always saw eye to eye."

"What didn't you see eye to eye on?"

"You, for starters."

That surprised me. I'd expected something job or friendship-related. Not personal. "What about me?"

Lennon hesitated for just a second, then said smoothly, "Your career, mostly."

I frowned. "My parents never gave any indication they disapproved or were worried about my career choices." The fact he'd hesitated made me think he was holding something back.

"We don't always say what we're thinking, Alexandra. He was worried you might get caught up in something."

"Well, he was right," I said cheerfully. "I have been caught up in some things."

Lennon chuckled. "Yes, you have."

"And what're the other things you didn't see eye to eye on? Anything to do with work?"

For once, the head of Halcyon Division looked uneasy, and he took a little while to answer. "We fought about our private relationships. Your father and I had very different views on marriage, on family. I thought it was simply a necessary step to enable me to work more effectively, having a 'normal' life in society. Your father disagreed, vehemently, despite everything we'd learned and experienced. He thought marriage required love and connection. He...he couldn't understand why I was so opposed to him and your mother getting married."

"You were?"

"Yes. When he was posted in Italy and met your mother, he changed completely."

"Paris," I said absently. "They met in Paris."

"Paris. Yes. Well, he changed. His focus was split from his work." Now where had I heard that before? Oh, that's right...he'd told me that's what my relationship with Sophia was doing to me. Seems Lennon has a theme.

"Really?" I asked, incredulous. "He seemed consistent in the dossiers I read."

Lennon's lips thinned. "He was *so* dedicated to the job, he always had been. Of our class, your father was the best, even our instructors were impressed by him. He got things done, Alexandra. And then..." Lennon made a gesture like he was letting dandelions float away in the breeze. "When we were young men learning our trade, he swore he would never get married, never have children. Before your mother, he never wanted children. It was something he was adamant about, that he did not want to be a parent. But then when they found out that they were going to be parents, like your mother, he wanted to keep you. I was against it."

Keep me... As opposed to the alternative, which was what? Terminating me? I felt sick. I couldn't even make myself say something in response.

Lennon, apparently realizing he'd come across like a completely insensitive dick—nice self-awareness, boss—softened his face and tone, but not the content of his words. "We fought, for weeks, about it. I tried to make him see that having children, in our line of work? It's unfair. But he could not see my point of view."

I, for one, was glad my dad hadn't seen Lennon's point of view. "Why are you telling me this?" The cruelty of it was horrible. Pointless. But something about it niggled, because I could see how me coming along unexpectedly might result in the kind of parents I'd had—cool and indifferent, yet loving in their own way.

He arched an eyebrow. "Because you asked me about your father. And I'm telling you."

"Well. I don't believe you," I said, only just getting the words out through a throat that felt so tight I thought I might choke. My parents weren't role models of overt affection, but I'd never felt they didn't love me.

"That's your prerogative. I'm sorry this hurts you, but I have no reason to lie."

He had every reason to lie. I was sure he lied whenever he needed to. Or felt he needed to. But let's say Lennon wasn't just bullshitting me for…whatever reason he was bullshitting me, which was probably to make me like him more or make me feel he was the person I should turn to, because oh look, my dad wasn't the heroic figure I had in my head. My parents died. Being mad at them wasn't going to change that fact—it was only going to poison me.

"You were married," I pointed out. Oh the hypocrisy.

"I was. But my marriage was a mutually beneficial arrangement for me and my wife. She was also in the same line of work, there were no secrets between us about our professional lives." The unspoken implication hung distastefully in the air—that my father had lied to my mother about his work for their whole relationship, and Lennon disapproved. "We were very fond of each other, but we knew exactly what our relationship was. A necessity, rather than a luxury. Your father thought he could have both."

Wow. Just…wow. Lennon was a fucking insensitive dinosaur. He sounded like some Cold War spy, though, given his age, that probably wasn't too far off the mark. "He did have both," I said calmly. "From what I've read, he functioned extremely well as a diplomat, with my mother and then me by his side, and managed to extract more raw intelligence than almost anyone else operating in the field at the same time."

"Yes." This agreement seemed to pain Lennon, like he hated the fact my dad somehow managed to have a family and his spy gig all at once.

The more we spoke, the more my gut was screaming at me that something was wrong. Maybe it was residual upset from being told that my dad's supposed friend, my secret boss, had told my parents to terminate their pregnancy. The pregnancy that resulted in me. I had to draw on every bit of willpower, every mental trick I knew, to remain neutral in the face of that revelation.

Something told me to keep digging, so I decided to shake the tree a little and see what fell out. "Since I found out who you are, I've been trying to remember you as my dad's friend. But it's hard. I only remember you being at our place a handful of times. Were you hardly ever around because of work?"

"Partly work. And partly because relationships complicate things when you're undercover. They can compromise you. And having both of us, two intelligence officers, as friends, it was not a good idea. But our friendship was important for both of us."

"What did you two do when you were together? Fishing? Barbeques? Golf? Football?"

"Mostly we just talked. Sometimes we'd catch a football game—you would have been asleep—and just take some time out from all of this." He smiled as if remembering a pleasant memory. "Just two friends enjoying each other's company, even with the rivalry of our teams. Giants versus Falcons."

My stomach fluttered uneasily. My father was a Philadelphia Eagles fan. Eagle. Falcon. Both birds of prey. Easy to mix up. "Did you miss their wedding because of work?" I asked hastily, trying to cover my unease. I knew the people in my parents' wedding photos, and Lennon was nowhere to be found.

He grimaced. "Yes. I was supposed to be his best man, and it pained me greatly that I was delayed."

"I'm sure he understood. Just like he understood when he had his retirement party, and you weren't there." Best friends don't miss multiple important events in their pal's life. Do they? Best friends remember things like their pal's favorite football team. Don't they?

"No I wasn't," Lennon agreed. He stared at me, his gaze steady. "Is there a reason for you making me feel bad about things I missed in Richard's life?" It came out lightly. Either he wasn't really bothered or he was trying to seem unbothered because he didn't want me to know how much it upset him.

"Not at all." I wasn't going to apologize if he felt bad. Turnabout is fair play. "I'm just trying to make pieces that feel nonsensical fit together. I wish I could remember more of the times you came by. I just don't. It might have made me realize who you were when I spoke to you for Halcyon business."

"I was just a voice at the end of a phone line, Alexandra, and out of context, it would mean nothing. Your dad and I discussed that you might somehow recognize me, but I was adamant you wouldn't because our interactions were so few and you were so young. Not because it would have been bad, but because you shouldn't have felt influenced or beholden because of my friendship with your father."

"Did you two become friends during training?"

"Yes. We were sharing a room. I was shy, he wasn't," Lennon said fondly. "We struck up a natural friendship that continued even when we separated after finishing our training. Our friendship was… seasonal. We would come together sporadically and it was as if we were still those two young men."

I made myself smile at that. It felt like a rambling, forcefully poetic response.

Lennon smiled too, but he didn't seem as disingenuous as I felt. "We used to give each other silly, pointless gifts all the time. From the most random of places that we'd been working. It was always a priority for me to find something for Richard."

That triggered a memory. I remembered "Uncle Michael's" visit one fall when I was about seven. He'd brought my dad a Dutch clog. And when he'd left, I'd overheard Dad muttering about this thing, something about… I stretched for the memory. That he hated this… What was it that he'd said to my mother? Fuck, why couldn't I remember? I did remember him tossing the clog out and I'd thought it was a mistake and had fished it out and brought it back inside.

Dad had gently turned me back around, giving me a little push in the small of my back to guide me back outside. "We don't need that in our house, Little Mouse. Take it back out to the trash."

Why wouldn't he want a gift from his friend? Even a tacky, white-elephant gift? My father was sentimental about gifts that were meaningful, and didn't like pointless things—events, possessions, and people. But wasn't a gift from your friend the opposite of pointless? Now that I thought about it, I couldn't remember any gifts from Lennon being in our house, not even in Dad's office.

Wasn't that weird?

And wasn't it weird that Lennon didn't know things about my dad? They were supposed to be best friends. Sure, best friends didn't know every little thing about each other, but, important things? I felt like those were the things you remembered about someone. Maybe it was silly, but these small inconsistent details felt like something was off. Like where my parents met. That he hated pointless things. That his favorite football team was the Philadelphia Eagles, not the Atlanta Falcons.

But my dad had given no indication that there was anything other than solid friendship between them. Was I wrong to be suspicious? And wrong to put so much weight on nothing more than just a weird gut feeling and aggravation with Lennon? Suspicion was in my nature, but in this case, it felt silly to suspect Lennon of anything more than a life full of gathering information, and past events that simply didn't hold as much weight in his brain as other things. Just because something was important to me, didn't mean it was important to him.

I forced a nonchalant shrug. "Maybe I'm just feeling sentimental because the anniversary of their death is coming up."

"That's entirely possible."

I glanced at my watch. Little Mouse. My dad loved me. Fuck you, Lennon. "I'd better be going. Thanks for the information. I'll just keep working on it, I guess."

"Are you any closer to a time estimate for me?"

"Hopefully within a few weeks," I said, just to placate him. I had no fucking idea how long it would take to turn forty-two letters into a bunch of usable words and then figure out how those usable words would lead to a pass phrase.

"Very good. Let me know if I can help further."

Oh, you've "helped" more than enough, thanks.

I left the meeting with no answers, just fistfuls of doubt that hadn't been there before and a firmer sense that I just didn't like Lennon. He was controlling and possessive—he'd been that way with my father and he was now trying it with me. And he had some fucking old-school thought processes about operations. I'd never been an undercover intelligence officer, obviously, and my generation was different to his, but I'd worked in intelligence for a while now and I just couldn't see his reasoning. Nor his reasons for being so blunt.

I appreciated forthrightness, but there was being upfront, and then there was being tactless. Perhaps being a man in positions of power meant Lennon gave no fucks about who he might offend, as long as things got done. Maybe I'd be the same if it were me running the show. Nah. I would never be deliberately hurtful, and deliberate is how his words felt.

I had no idea why he was rubbing me the wrong way; I'd worked with him for fifteen years, long enough to know I trusted him to keep me safe. But until very recently, my interaction with him had been solely through voice communication. Being together in person seemed so different. Was he putting on a façade? And if so, which of him was the real Lennon? Halcyon Division Lennon on the phone, or Agency Director Lennon in person?

Sophia was deep in the throes of creating dinner when I arrived at her apartment after stopping by mine for a shower and to shed my work frustrations.

"What's this masterpiece?" I asked, resting my chin on her shoulder as she stirred veggies in a heavy-based pan.

"It will be a veggie lasagna, or something kind of like it. Camila's been teaching me a few things. Said she was sick of me texting her about my cooking, like 'does this look right for sautéed?' and 'I don't have fresh sage, can I use dried basil?'"

"I'm impressed." Sophia was a capable, independent woman. But by her own admission, she was a mediocre cook and had accepted her place on the culinary ladder. "Can you?" I asked, and when she raised her eyebrows, I elaborated, "Use dried basil in place of fresh sage?"

"Not recommended," she answered, turning her head to kiss me. "There's an unopened bottle of wine in the fridge."

"Thanks." I opened the pinot grigio and poured us both a glass. "Why the change of cooking heart? Sick of scrambled eggs and toast?" I teased.

"Partly. And partly because I want to take care of you."

"I appreciate that." I kissed the side of her neck, then her jaw, careful not to distract her from the hot stove. "And I appreciate you."

"I know you do." She checked the heat then turned away from her veggies. "Are Jeffrey and his wife okay with us coming for dinner Wednesday? I know a few days is short notice." I'd called her from the work parking lot about the invitation.

"Mhmm. He assures me it's all fine. He seems exceedingly excited."

"That so sweet," she said, her voice radiating warmth.

"Or weird," I said, laughing. Not wanting to distract her from cooking, I took a seat at the breakfast bar and drank my wine while watching her carefully assembling the lasagna.

After putting a delightful amount of cheese on top, Sophia slid the tray into the oven. "Dinner needs about forty minutes, then we're good to go. Are you hungry now? Need a snacking platter?"

"No, I'm good, thanks."

Sophia came around the counter and leaned against it, facing me. She lightly touched the tops of my cheeks. "You okay? You look exhausted."

"I'm just…I don't know what I am, honestly. Not great, but still okay is probably the best summation."

"Why are you not great?"

I huffed out a loud breath. "Because this assignment is really fucked-up. And it's bringing up all this shit about my parents that I thought I'd dealt with. I feel like I was a disappointment to them." Frowning, I amended, "Not a disappointment, I'm sure, but like…a burden. Like I interrupted the life they had planned for themselves."

Sophia rubbed soothing circles on my lower back. "What makes you say that, sweetheart?"

"Because I think it's true." I blinked hard to push back the tears burning behind my eyes. "This thing I'm working on. It's looking into some things my dad found during his time as a diplomat." A version of the truth, which told her what I was doing, but not the specifics. It would have to do. "And it's…hard. Really hard. Because the guy who was my dad is different to the guy who did this work, and I'm discovering things that upset me."

"Like you thinking you were a burden to your parents?" she asked gently, still rubbing my back.

"Like that," I confirmed in a whisper.

"Did anything about them ever make you feel like they didn't want you?"

"Maybe sometimes," I admitted tearfully. "They just never seemed interested in me." We'd talked a little about my family dynamics, but I hadn't delved deeply into the nuance of my family with her because we'd had so little time. "It was like I was part of the furniture who sometimes needed to be fed, or taken to school, or on play dates, or to the doctor."

I'd spent most of my life thinking that if my parents had been different then maybe I would have turned out differently. But then I kept reminding myself that, for the most part, I like who I am. Still, I couldn't help wondering if having more affection, more openness as a kid would have made it easier for me now as an adult in personal relationships.

Sophia pulled me into her, snuggling close. "Oh, honey. I'm sorry. That must feel awful." She kissed my temple, her lips remaining against my skin as she held me tightly.

I turned my head to catch a soft kiss, but the moment her lips brushed mine, an unexpected surge of desire filled me. When I used my tongue to part her lips, Sophia opened her mouth willingly, gasping when I squirmed an arm free to grip her ass so I could pull her between my spread thighs. The silence was punctuated by the sound of our breathing, the desperate gulps of air around our frantic explorations.

"Dinner…" Sophia protested weakly. It was made even weaker by the fact she had her hands under my shirt.

"Still has plenty of time in the oven," I assured her. For just a few minutes, I didn't want to think about my dad's double life, and secrets, and lies. I didn't want to think about my boss, supposedly my dad's best friend, telling him not to get married for love, not to have children. I just wanted, selfishly, to think about myself, about Sophia. I just wanted to feel something good.

"Are you sure you don't need to talk?" Sophia murmured, and I loved her for checking in with me, even though I'd initiated the intimacy.

"Yes. I'm done talking about my family for now. But I'm not done talking about everything I'm going to do to you." I reached down and pulled the knot in the drawstring of her sweatpants free. "And I'm not going to be quiet…"

CHAPTER SIXTEEN

Addicted to Us

I pulled to a stop at a red light and turned to Sophia. "Is it weird that I'm nervous?"

"What are you nervous about exactly?"

"I'm not sure." I faced forward again, twisting the steering wheel until my knuckles felt tight. "We lived together for six months. He saved my life. We're good friends. We work together now. This is just…an extra step in friendship that I've never done before. Us, a couple, going to another couple's house for a social event." I glanced at her. "I'm totally deficient in normal adult activities, aren't I?"

Sophia turned slightly in her seat to face me, assuring me, "You're not deficient in any way, hon."

"Thank you. It's…I think I want to make a good impression with Jeffrey's wife? And I don't want her to hate me because her husband put his life on the line to save mine."

"Why would she hate you for that? It's not like you caused it. And," she added after a second, "that was his job, so it was his choice."

"I know." The light turned green and I drove on. "Just paranoia I suppose."

"Do you need a secret password for me to come rescue you? If she starts berating you, I can…I don't know, start a wacky interpretive dance or something."

That made me laugh. "It'll be fine. But thank you, darling. And just a heads-up. Jeffrey will call you Ms. Flores."

She burst out a laugh. "What? Why?"

"Because he's weird. And he has this idea that because you're my girlfriend and he's never met you, that you're somehow special and therefore *Ms. Flores*." I couldn't tell her, of course, that he'd known about her from our time in Florida, and that's where "Ms. Flores" had begun, but I didn't feel any guilt about that omission. That was in the past, and we were moving forward.

She laughed again. "Well, we will have to disabuse him of that notion right away, won't we." Sophia reached over and rested her hand on my thigh.

"We will."

Jeffrey and Dominique lived in a beautiful house. A kind of imposing, I-make-a-fuckton-of-money house. Maybe I should get into contracting. I mean, I wasn't struggling, and I liked my apartment, but…this was a really beautiful house. Sophia apparently had the same thought, and as she peered out the window, she said, "Well. I'm glad we brought the Veuve Clicquot instead of the twenty-dollar bottle of sparkling wine."

I assured her, "Trust me. He's so unpretentious. Don't worry. And based on what Jeffrey's told me about her, I'm sure his wife is chill too."

"What does Dominique do again?" she asked once I'd parked.

"Human rights lawyer," I said. "For one of the biggest firms in the state apparently. So I guess she's very good at her job."

"They don't have kids, right?"

"No," I said somberly, recalling the look on Jeffrey's face when he'd answered me asking that exact question. "Not on the cards. But they have a dog-son, which, according to all the photos I've seen is spoiled as hell."

Sophia tucked her arm into mine, leaning against me as we walked up the brightly lit path. In the twilight, I could see the immaculate lawn and garden beds, which, for a moment, made me want a house with a yard. Then I remembered how much I didn't like mowing or gardening. But they probably had a gardener… I could have a gardener.

"Ready?" I asked Sophia, finger poised to ring the bell.

Nodding, she asked, "Are you?"

Laughing, I pressed the bell.

Jeffrey answered the door, holding Benjamin—a medium-small, snow-white puffball (sorry, Japanese Spitz) who wore a navy blue and white polka-dot bow tie. Jeffrey and Benjamin, in person, were a thing to behold. I knew from our time overseas, and time working here, that he really loved his dog. But this was something else. After planting a kiss on the top of his dog's head, Jeffrey enthused, "Someone went to the groomer this afternoon because he was so excited about finally meeting you!" He used his hand to wave one of Benjamin's front paws at us, while the dog's tongue lolled inside a smiling mouth. "Nice to see you both, come in, come in."

He set Benjamin down, and made a gesture that sent the dog running back into the house instead of out the door. As I stepped inside, I was struck first by the aroma of something incredible, and then by the incongruity of inside versus outside. Although it had expensive, tasteful furnishings, the interior felt warm and welcoming. Kind of like the man himself—a contradiction. I made introductions. "Sophia, meet Jeffrey Burton. Jeffrey, meet *Sophia* Flores." I emphasized her first name.

Jeffrey, thankfully, had decided that now he'd been officially introduced to my girlfriend, he could refer to her by her first name. His smile was warm, genuinely beaming as he said, "Sophia, it's so great to finally meet you."

She matched his smile. "You too. I feel like I need to hug you, even though Lexie's told me practically nothing about you." She directed a sideways glance at me.

Jeffrey opened his arms immediately and Sophia stepped right into them. Their hug was brief, but sincere, and I heard Sophia murmur something to him and then Jeffrey's quiet, chuckling response.

I shrugged. "I'm sure he'll tell you anything you want to know about himself. He loves talking about himself."

"He sure does," came an amused response from our right.

Jeffrey's wife emerged from a large living room—it was easy to recognize her from the photographs I'd seen. About Sophia's height, Dominique was an attractive Asian woman, slightly younger than Jeffrey, who I'd always assumed to be early or midfifties (I should really get his file…or just ask him) and all my anxiety about meeting her fell away when she strode right over and hugged me.

She released me, but kept her hands on my shoulders as she looked me right in the eyes, hers creasing softly at the edges. "Lexie. I'm Dominique. It's so wonderful to finally meet you after all these months. Jeffrey has told me so much about you." Her voice was low and warm, with just a hint of New England accent, and my immediate thought was that I wanted her to read me a bedtime story.

I glanced at Jeffrey, who just shrugged, then looked back to Dominique, who smiled and raised both hands as she assured me, "All wonderful things of course."

"Now I really don't believe you," I laughed.

"I tell no lies." Then before either Jeffrey or I could introduce Sophia, Dominique strode right over and gave her the same enthusiastic hug she'd given me. "Sophia, welcome. Come on through to the living room. I've got some platters set out to tide us over until dinner is ready. What can I get you both to drink?"

Sophia handed over the bottle of champagne. "Sorry, before I forget and just carry this around all night like a weirdo, this is for you. Just a small gift to thank you for having us." Thank god Sophia also sounded like a tentative ten-year-old saying "thanks for having me" after a visit.

"Oh wow. Thank you," Dominique said warmly. "Shall we open it now?"

Jeffrey took the bottle. "We shall." He walked off and we followed into a warm, inviting living room.

Sophia went right over to a large abstract oil painting on the wall. "This is a Kerlan original, right?"

Dominique's eyebrows rose in surprise. "It is. I love her work. We have a few of hers. You're an art fan?"

"I am." Sophia's eyes softened. "Graphic design and building websites pay the bills. But I cling fiercely to my art school roots."

I left them to discuss art and went to pay attention to Benjamin who had inserted himself into the gathering without being obnoxiously excitable and annoying. (Sorry, that's the cat person in me speaking.) Jeffrey came over to hand me a drink, interrupting me rubbing a flopped-over Benjamin's tummy. "Told you he's the world's best dog," he said fondly. Jeffrey bent to rub the dog's ears.

"If we weren't here, you'd be baby-talking him, wouldn't you."

"Yep," he confirmed cheerfully. "He's my liddle baby guy, the best pup in the world, isn't that right, my special buddy boy?"

Benjamin wagged his duster-thick tail.

Once we all had a glass of champagne, save for Jeffrey who had a beer, we reconvened on a set of couches in an L-shape around a solid wood coffee table. Dominique disappeared for a few minutes and returned with two platters—one vegetarian and one charcuterie. I shot Jeffrey a grateful look and he winked at me. Dominique handed out small plates and we all served ourselves.

After ten minutes of comfortable small talk discussing Jeffrey and Dominique's house, Sophia's and Dominique's work, the weather, and Benjamin, Sophia stepped right over acquaintance-talk territory and into friends territory. "How did you two meet?" she asked as she assembled a cracker with some brie and a deli meat.

They shared a fond, amused look, and Dominique nudged her husband. Jeffrey set down his beer and leaned forward, resting his elbows on his knees. "We met at a bar, during Led Zeppelin night while the cover band was playing 'Kashmir.' I'd been watching her for most of the night, and thought she was the most incredibly beautiful woman I'd ever seen, so I sidled up to her and stupidly blurted that I'd been to Kashmir. She looked at me like I was a dope, which I was because I was so nervous, and said, 'That's great. I'm going to go over here and get another drink now.' I asked her if I could buy her that drink and she looked me up and down, smiled a smile that stopped my heart and told me sure, as long as I didn't try to impress her again." He straightened up, looking lovingly at his wife. "So I bought her a drink, and stopped trying to impress her, and after we'd had a few more drinks, I asked her on a date, and she said yes. We've been together ever since."

Dominique patted his cheek. "You were very charming. But also very cocky." She looked to Sophia and me. "He's still cocky, but thankfully not around me."

"Was it a good cover band?" Sophia asked.

Dominique made a see-saw movement with her hand. "Not bad. Honestly, I wasn't paying much attention to the music." She turned to Jeffrey again and smiled. "I was too focused on some guy who was trying to pick me up. And when he cried during 'Stairway to Heaven,' I thought he might be the one."

I actually got misty-eyed at that, and I felt Sophia's sigh beside me. I tutted. "Jeffrey. Who knew you were such a charming softie."

"You did," he said, chuckling. He winked at us. "See? I wasn't that cocky…"

The conversation moved easily between the four of us, feeling more like a circle of established friends rather than two couples who'd never spent time together before. Dominique excused herself periodically to go into the kitchen, and always came back to assure us it wasn't long until dinner, and refresh drinks as needed.

Sophia and Dominique were deep in conversation, discussing the art museum and a potential girls' day out. Jeffrey snuck Benjamin a piece of cheese before he passed me the veg platter. Apparently satisfied that his wife was occupied, Jeffrey leaned toward me and lowered his voice. "So I was thinking on the drive home, that maybe we—"

I had no idea what he thought we should maybe do, because it was like a flashing, blaring alarm had gone off for Dominique, and her head whipped around to Jeffrey. "Nuh-uh. No work at home," she chided him. "Why do you think you can get away with it because Lexie is here, Jeffrey Burton? And when we have company too." She turned to Sophia, and asked lightly, "Does she do this to you too? Try to bring work home?"

"Oh no," Sophia laughed. "I think she's very good at work-home separation." She winked at me, and I smiled back at her unspoken teasing. I was almost too good at separation.

That return smile felt a little tight and hollow, and it was only Sophia's gentle reassuring hand on my thigh that relaxed me again. She wasn't being snarky. She was just following along with the conversation.

After we'd eaten our fill from the platters and had our drinks refreshed again—except for the designated driver among us— Dominique excused herself to the kitchen again, promising this was the one, that dinner was ready. She declined all offers of assistance, except for telling Jeffrey she'd need his help soon to carry food to their dining room table.

Once it was just the three of us, Jeffrey turned to Sophia, leaning forward in interest. Here comes the third degree, I thought. "So, Sophia. Lexie has actually told me very little about you. Care to remedy that?" It was a beautiful and hilarious truth, because I *hadn't* told him much about her. But I was sure he knew all the basics about her from when he was trying to track me down while I was hiding with the Kunduz Intelligence.

Sophia dusted her fingertips off onto her plate. "Do you want the everyday stuff, like my job, hobbies, and star sign? Or my deep dark secrets, like how I cheated on a math exam in sixth grade."

He bounced his eyebrows comically. "I want everything."

"Okay then. I'm a Virgo, but I honestly have no idea what that means because I'm not into star signs. In my free time I—"

Dominique popped her head into the room. "So sorry to interrupt, but dinner's ready. Jeffrey, could I get a hand please?"

He jumped up right away, and with a quick grin, assured Sophia, "To be continued."

She nodded, feigning seriousness. "I look forward to it."

I waited a few seconds after he'd left the room before asking her, "You okay?"

"More than," she said, a soft smile lighting her features. "They're both so great."

"They really are," I agreed.

Sophia's expression turned pained. "I'm so sorry about the thing before, about you not bringing work home. I didn't mean it like it came out. I was just playing along with her joke, but as soon as I said it I realized how you might have taken it. I didn't mean it like that, like I'm upset with you for withholding things."

"I know," I said gently.

"Are you sure? Because I know you've worked so hard on—"

I cut off her groveling with a kiss. "Babe. It's fine. I know you didn't mean it like that."

Jeffrey came back, and in an over-the-top French maître d' accent, said, "Ladies, dinner is served. If you'll follow me please."

The place settings were fancy, but not uncomfortably so—I didn't feel like I was in a triple-Michelin-starred restaurant, just at someone's home who obviously enjoyed entertaining. Dominique handed her husband a chilled bottle of Bollinger and he popped the cork and filled the new glasses on the table. I couldn't pass up Bollinger, and accepted a half-glass before turning my attention to the gorgeous enclosed ten-inch-ish pie on the table. So that's the amazing smelling culprit. "Oh wow. What's this?"

Dominique turned the plate around. "Torta Pasqualina." A colorful bowl of roasted vegetables and a fresh summer salad filled out the center of the table. "I know it's not Easter, but I won't tell any Italians if you don't."

"Deal," Sophia and I agreed simultaneously.

The torta was incredible—filled with savory, lemony chard, whole baked eggs, and ricotta, and it took every ounce of my willpower to eat it slowly, savor it. Everything about dinner and dessert was delicious, the company and conversation excellent, and when it came time to make our goodbyes I felt more relaxed and fulfilled than I ever had after a social occasion. It had been so good—understatement—to spend an evening doing something normal, with no thoughts about work. No thoughts until I thought about the fact I hadn't thought about it all night, of course.

Sophia carried the portion of the torta Dominique had sent us home with like it was a precious newborn. Once we were both in the car, we waved to Jeffrey, Dominique, and Benjamin who were standing in the doorway watching us leave.

As I belted myself in, I said, "I think I'm addicted."

Sophia laughed. "To her cooking?"

I laughed with her. "That too. But…I think I'm addicted to *us*. Things like tonight, the normality of us having dinner with friends, being out with you." I turned to her and reached out to take one of her hands. "I want more of this, Sophia. More normality. I want it with you. And I think I want it forever."

CHAPTER SEVENTEEN

So much for bring-your-girlfriend-to-work day

After another morning staring at The Forty-two, I decided something had to change. So far, aside from forming a seemingly endless list of short words like *it*, *set*, *test*, *tit* (ha-ha), *meet*, *tux*, and *tee*, I'd managed to come up with *heterosexual*, *preemptive*, *respective*, *trumpet*, *rectum* (I never said I wasn't juvenile), and *either*. Thinking up words was great and productive, but I still couldn't figure out a way to use all the letters, without using any twice, and oh yeah—what about the line-over Es?

If something didn't change, Jeffrey and I weren't going to figure out the pass phrase any time soon, and that was unacceptable for many reasons. Like foreign operatives undermining our country, and me being so sick of this assignment taking up almost all my waking hours that I felt like yelling. It wasn't like it was hard. Anyone with a brain for anagrams should be able to figure it out. So why couldn't we? Groaning, I pulled my glasses off.

"This is fucked," I said to Jeffrey. "You know, these letters are embedded so deeply in my brain that after I got home last night, I started running the letters through an online word generator. And after looking at a million generators, the longest string I was allowed was thirty-six letters, which left six out so the whole thing was useless really. Not to mention generators overlap letters, using them multiple times to make their lists of words, which I don't think is allowed. It's just fucking gibberish."

"Of course it's gibberish if the pass phrase is words or a phrase specific to you. A standard AI anagram generator won't pick up that nuance." He was so calm I wanted to throw something at him.

"I know, and that's exactly what I was scared of. I'm *so* bad with anagrams. Heinously bad. We know this. You've witnessed it. For the past few days."

He stared at me blankly. I'd witnessed how bad he was with anagrams too.

I put my glasses back on and propped my elbows on my desk. "This is where you tell me you're secretly an anagram wizard and you've been holding out on me all this time because you love this assignment and you want it to last forever."

"I am not an anagram wizard."

"You know who is an anagram wizard? Sophia."

Jeffrey's face fell. "Oh no. You're not thinking—"

"I am *absolutely* thinking. It's an anagram. Not nuclear launch codes."

"It's the equivalent of nuclear launch codes. It could be something classified. Scratch that. It is *undoubtedly* something classified." He wasn't incredulous, but he was clearly thinking WTF?

"It's not like she's going to see anything remotely near the hard drive, all she would need to do is turn the letters into words. I'm willing to take the chance."

Lennon, however, wasn't willing to take the chance, and when I went up to his office to ask him to let me show what I had to Sophia, he looked at me like I'd just asked him to bring down all the firewalls guarding the agency network.

"I need outside help," I said, as diplomatically as I could. "I need someone who's good at figuring things out by looking outside the box."

"Okay, then I'll find you someone."

"I want Sophia. She's a codebreaking mystery puzzle enthusiast. If you want this figured out soon, then you need to expedite the background checks and NDAs and get her working on this ASAP."

"Have you even asked Ms. Flores if she's willing to assist?"

"No. Because I need to make sure she's cleared to assist."

"That would be extremely difficult, Alexandra. Even if I set aside the security clearance issues, she needs to work within a SCIF, but we can't just allow civilians entry to this facility left, right, and center."

"Even security-cleared civilians? The agency allows cleared academic and civic groups to tour," I pointed out.

"That's an entirely different matter, and you know it."

"It's a fucking anagram, Lennon," I said, not bothering to hide my exasperation. It wasn't just exasperation at him, it was at this whole situation. "She won't even see the drive it might unlock. She cannot connect the two things. I've spent days running these letters through my brain and even every Internet anagram maker and word generator I could find at home, and so far, I've gotten nowhere that makes any sense. They're not thinking of phrases that will lead me to figuring out the pass phrase. They're just giving me words. Now, I can spend more days wasting time, or you can clear Sophia to come in and look at a group of letters and I bet you she'll figure it out within a day, if not within hours."

"Why can't you or Burton figure it out?"

If literally tearing your hair out wasn't a cliché, and a painful one at that, I would have done it. "Because neither of us have brains that work like that. You don't think we've tried? That we've *been* trying, anagram generators and brainpower and all?"

"Why not let me look at it?"

"Because you don't know me personally, Lennon. And you're less likely than I am to figure out the specific phrase or question that my father left for me to clue me in to this pass phrase. I'm certain this is an anagram, specifically tailored to me. So even if you could make an AI anagram generator available in the office, one that allowed a large number of letters, there's no time to train AI in Alexandra Elizabeth Martin's life to try to make sense of it."

"I'm sorry, Alexandra. I just can't allow it."

I'd expected the answer. I really was asking for something ridiculous and had been so caught up in the excitement of a possible solution that I'd ignored the obvious reasons why it couldn't happen, but it still annoyed the fuck out of me. "Fine," I said tersely. "Then I'll be back in a month when I've made some progress."

I flounced back into the office, and though I was sure Jeffrey knew why I was acting like a kid throwing a silent tantrum, he still asked, "What'd he say?"

"He said no. I knew he would. I was being stupid asking, stupid even thinking it. But I am so sick of not making progress. I need to figure this out."

Jeffrey could have been a smug bastard about being right, but he smiled sympathetically and nodded. "I know. It's frustrating me too.

And I don't have the added parental connection and all the associated shit."

Oh right. That. I dragged my hands down my face. "It's *right* there. Why can't I figure it out?"

"Because we're missing something, obviously."

"Obviously," I said dryly. "Care to enlighten me on what we're missing."

"The thing that tells us what we're looking for," he said cheerfully.

"Thanks, asshole."

"You're welcome," he said sweetly. "Oh, by the way, my wife adores your girlfriend. She's going to ask if Sophia wants to get together this weekend for coffee or drinks and an art museum day."

"Oh? That's amazing." Sophia was not only an insanely talented artist, but just loved art. "I think she'll love that." And that reminded me—I needed to get her to draw me some new things. Another version of Super Lexie to put up in my office, and then maybe another nude self-portrait like the one she'd given me for Christmas. They were both ash in a wastewater system overseas. Didn't seem right to keep either after the breakup.

"Dom needs more things outside of work." He grinned slyly. "Are our significant others about to become BFFs?"

"It's possible." I leaned back in my chair, crossing my legs. "Who would have thought when we first met that this is where we'd end up. Not only coexisting peacefully, but…friends."

"Who would have thought," he echoed with a teasing smile.

"I had a really great time at dinner, and so did Sophia. Thanks for the invitation." Dominique was intelligent and witty, sensitive and thoughtful—an easy person to spend time with. And Jeffrey was… Jeffrey, but he'd turned up the wit and charm, maybe for Sophia's sake.

Jeffrey's eyes creased at the edges. "So did we. We'll have to make it regular."

"Absolutely. My place next time."

"Done."

Though spending the rest of the day talking about fun, non-work-related things would have been far more enjoyable, we really needed to figure out my dad's pass phrase. The more I tried, the more my thoughts seemed determined to drift. After twenty minutes, I stood up, dropped my glasses on my desk, and declared, "I need a break."

"Like the break you just had when you went to see the director to make your request?"

"Yes. Exactly like that. Back soon."

To clear my head, I went for an aimless wander around the building. I stopped by my old floor and chatted with my team members, half of whom expressed genuine surprise at seeing me. Apparently, despite my telling them I'd been moved to another team in the *same* building, the consensus was that I'd left again for some other overseas thing. Short memories.

Derek's door was open and when I peeked inside, he was reading something inside a manila folder. I knocked on the doorframe. "You taking visitors?"

"Martin," he said warmly, abandoning his folder to the side of his desk. "Making house calls?"

"Something like that." I closed the door and plonked myself down in one of the chairs opposite his desk.

"How're things coming along upstairs?"

"Frustratingly. Which is why I'm taking a break."

"I see." He eyed me steadily. "I had a call from Lennon just before."

Brilliant. "A call about me, I assume, given you're telling me about it."

"Yes. He's concerned about you."

"He's not told me that." So fucking typical. Instead of telling me he was worried—though who knew what about—Lennon was going around me to get Derek to do his dirty work.

"Is there a problem?"

"With the work? No. Aside from it taking time and being annoying. With Lennon? Maybe."

"What's the problem?" he asked. Derek was completely nonjudgmental and nonaccusatory. He just sounded like he wanted to know so he could help me fix it.

He couldn't. But at least he was a safe ranting place.

So I ranted.

"I'm really not a fan of this new dynamic. I want to go back to the one where Lennon and I just spoke on the phone sporadically and he wasn't my dad's best friend, or my agency boss as well as my Halcyon boss, and I didn't know about his personality which I'm finding I really don't like. I think I don't like him as a person." And my gut was going crazy, thinking there was something I wasn't getting about Lennon. Something that was important. Something relating to my dad.

"You don't need to like him as a person to recognize that he's doing an excellent job," Derek said diplomatically.

"I know." I tried to keep the sulkiness out of my voice. "Don't tell him I said I don't like him."

"Oh, I've already emailed him, just now, while you were ranting," Derek deadpanned.

I narrowed my eyes at him. "Funny." Settling back in the world's oldest office chair, I asked, "Did you ever interact with him in person? When he was just running Halcyon?"

"A few times, yes."

"What did you think?"

"The same as I do now. That he's very capable, and things flourish under his leadership." Derek rested his hands on top of his desk, fingers clasped. "I don't need to interact with him in person to know that, but it *is* nice to have him so accessible."

"I know." I bit my lower lip. "Am I being petty? I just…I feel like he's keeping things from me."

Derek laughed. "Of course he is."

I fought the urge to roll my eyes. "I don't mean withholding the usual stuff. I expect that. But things about my dad. Things that might help me with this pass phrase."

Thankfully Derek didn't offer to have a chat with Lennon on my behalf to see if he could figure out the issue—the last thing I needed or wanted was to feel like someone was stepping in to save me yet again. Instead, he said, "If he is, then you have to trust there's a reason for it."

I held up both hands in surrender. "I know. It's just irritating me and I don't know if it's that he's getting on my nerves, or if it's just this whole assignment making everything feel off. And I'm annoyed at the secrecy surrounding the fact he was Dad's best friend." Apparently. Who didn't remember basic details about their best friend? Dad had never really said much about "Uncle Michael" when Lennon wasn't around. Actually, he'd never spoken about him at all that I could recall. Could Lennon be exaggerating how close they were so I'd trust him more and not question his directives?

"Secrets are currency in this business, Martin, and you know that as well as anyone. And if someone like Michael Lennon is keeping something from us, we have to trust and accept that there's a reason for those secrets."

As a peace offering for bailing twice in one day—before we'd even reached midday—and leaving Jeffrey alone with anagram-cracking, I stopped by the first-floor café and bought him a fancy-ass coffee and a cheese danish. And to make myself feel better, I also bought a cinnamon roll. Jeffrey almost melted with grateful excitement when I handed him the treats. "Thank you," he said. After peering inside the paper bag, and after a little exclamation of glee, he asked, "Did you do what you needed to?"

"I did."

"And are you feeling better?"

"A little." And I'd feel even better once I devoured my sweet treat. I glanced down at his page of scribblings. "Made any progress?"

"Not a bit," he said, far too cheerfully for someone staring at defeat. "Just the same story we've been reading for a few days. I can get some words, but I can't figure out how to use all the letters without doubling up on any. It feels impossible."

"Maybe it *is* impossible," I admitted, hating the defeat in my tone. "But let's give it a little more time before we give up completely and try something else."

"We won't give up," he said confidently. "Not until we're absolutely sure we've investigated every angle."

"Are we doing the wrong thing?" I felt stupid for constantly asking questions to which he could have no answer, but I needed some sort of reassurance.

And Jeffrey, bless him, answered the way he usually did and without any trace of annoyance. "No clue. But doing nothing is worse than doing the wrong thing in this case."

So I did something. After I'd devoured my cinnamon roll, that is. I'd added a few words to my list, and had had a few moments where it seemed I might have something, just for me to remember I'd already used that letter. I was struck with an irrational surge of anger at my dad for leaving me with this. And I felt childish and stupid for being angry at him. I should have been grateful that he trusted me with something so monumental.

But he was dead and I was here, flailing around in dark waters. He was dead. I bit the inside of my lip as an awful thought hit me.

"Jeffrey." It came out so quietly he didn't hear me. I cleared my throat and tried again. "Jeffrey?"

He looked up. "Yo."

"Yo? Did we time travel back to the '80s?"

He grinned and nodded. "That was a quality decade, my friend."

"It was my first decade of living," I reminded him, digging it in, though he was only about twelve years older than me. Hardly ancient.

"Thanks for the reminder. What's up? Did you solve it?"

"I wish," I said glumly. The glumness persisted when I thought about what I was about to ask. "I need you to dig up an NTSB crash report for me."

"Consider it done." And though I was sure he knew what I wanted, he asked, "Which report am I getting for you?"

"The one for my parents' light-aircraft accident. Richard and Karen Martin. I gave him the date and location, as well as the tail number of my dad's plane, which I still knew by heart. And I felt sick. "I think it was only completed last year?" They'd died July 16, 2021 and when I'd been contacted by the investigator assigned to my parents' accident, he'd told me accident reporting could take time, even for straightforward cases. "I…haven't had the chance get a copy of the report yet." I wasn't even sure I wanted to read it—my parents' crash was an accident, case closed—but now I felt I had to.

His eyebrows shot up. "Are you sure?"

"Very sure." I think.

"Do you want me to reinvestigate, or are you just curious?"

I paused, not wanting to show my hand just yet. If I even had a hand in play. "I'm just curious. And doing my due diligence as a daughter and an analyst looking into these dossiers of my father's. Covering every angle." And making sure that my dad's supposed best friend didn't have a hand in his death. I didn't want to suspect Lennon of foul play, but I'd be negligent if I didn't follow up with my gut feeling that there was something off with him. "I know it was investigated by the transportation safety people, but…"

Jeffrey nodded. "But it's good to be sure."

"Right." I exhaled, relieved he was with me instead of thinking I was allocating mental resources to something pointless.

"Do you want me to go do that now?"

"Up to you. I'd like to look at it soon."

"Now, then," he said. "I need to reset my brain." Jeffrey slipped some loose papers into a folder, and stood. "I'll be back soon. Just need to go outside and make some calls."

"Hey," I said, reaching out as if I could stop him from moving.

"Yo," he said with a grin.

I swallowed hard. "Our eyes and ears only."

He winked. "I wouldn't have it any other way, Lexie."

Jeffrey came back in a few hours with a folder tucked under his arm. After handing the NTSB document to me, he smiled. "I had to agree to take my guy out for dinner and drinks to get this so quickly. Then he reminded me I could have just downloaded the report from their online accident database…Asshole." He was smiling as he good-naturedly cussed out his contact for taking advantage.

I'm an idiot. "Sorry. I overthought this one. I could have just done it at home. I'll reimburse you," I promised. "Including tip."

"Wow. Generous. Be warned, he has expensive tastes."

I waved him off. "It's worth it, thank you for going to get this." Spending a few hundred on a dinner so I could read about the crash that killed my parents a few hours earlier than if I'd found it online at home, and in the company of a friend, was a small price to pay. I exhaled a long breath, then replenished the air with a deep, slow inhalation. I'd seen some incredibly upsetting things in my career—bodies turned to nothing more than mist and mangled parts, bombed cities, children... I shook the images out of my memories. I'd seen things people shouldn't see and I'd survived. But the idea of being confronted by photos of my dead parents was too much.

I passed the folder back to him. "I need to look at the photos. Can you please go through the report and cover any that have...my parents' bodies in them?" I'd been interviewed by the investigator in charge after their death, and thankfully had been coherent enough to answer questions about my parents' health and mental states. He'd given me some basic information about the crash, but I hadn't delved too deeply into it. And now I had to.

Jeffrey respectfully shuffled through the report and placed some strategic Post-its.

I inhaled shakily. "Thank you."

"You're welcome. Do you need some space while you read that?"

"I'm fine, but thanks for checking." Right, no more procrastinating. I flung the folder open and began to read.

The report seemed thorough, almost forty pages, with maps, diagrams, and embedded scene photos, and was fairly easy to wade through, from a comprehension angle. Not so much from a daughter angle. About two-thirds through, I found their conclusions and findings.

The National Transportation Safety Board determines the probable cause(s) of this accident to be fuel starvation which led to loss of control and the aircraft impacting terrain.

That made no sense. "Fuel starvation is listed as the official reason for the crash. Fuel starvation, impacted terrain." What a horribly simple way to describe my parents' death. "But that doesn't make sense. Dad fueled that plane himself before every flight, kept meticulous logs for fuel and service history as well as his actual flight logs. I've been on the plane with him, watched him with all his preflight stuff where he always looked in the fuel tanks as well as cross-checking with his logs and gauges. My dad wasn't a risk taker, which I know sounds ridiculous given his profession. He always had excess fuel on board. He had the plane serviced religiously. But something stopped the fuel from reaching the engine?"

"Did they have those service and flight logs?"

I looked through the report. "Yep. Nothing that led them to believe anything in the logs contributed to the accident."

"What about at the point of sale? I'm assuming he filled at the airport's pump."

I flicked through the pages and found the information from the small private airport's POS system. "Yep. Nothing unusual." I blew out a loud breath. "I don't buy it."

"Fuel contamination?"

"Possible? But no evidence of that. And why was his plane the only one at the airport that was affected?"

"Faulty fuel pump?"

"No. The pump was apparently in perfect working order."

"Faulty fuel gauge in the plane?"

"My dad was meticulous about his plane. There's no way he'd fly with a faulty fuel gauge." I looked up at him. "They basically said fuel starvation but couldn't figure out *why*. I feel so stupid. Why didn't I look more closely at this before?"

"Probably because you were grieving the death of your parents in a horrible accident and had no reason to suspect it was anything more than an accident."

Sounded about right. Though I didn't want to, I flicked through photos of the crash. It…it was a crashed plane. My dad's crashed plane. A mangled hull of metal and plastic and rubber amongst trees in a semirural area. There were close-ups of the interior. I ignored the blood and leafed through photos until I found the dashboard gauges.

There were photos of the fuel tanks and then the tanks in a lab, pictures of the swabs of the interior of the tank showed nothing except avgas residue as it should. But the fuel lines showed clear evidence of fuel starvation. Something had stopped the flow. I stared at the pictures of the fuel tanks. Maybe they'd been damaged before takeoff and had just…leaked fuel until the fuel ran out? But the fuel gauges would have shown the levels going down, surely Dad would have reacted, turned back to land safely.

But none of my theories explained why the plane had crashed so dramatically. Dad was an experienced pilot. He would have been able to glide the plane to a safe landing, or at least attempted to do so. But it'd crashed, and crashed hard. Maybe he had a medical incident. But he was fit and healthy. The medical reports from their postmortems showed nothing unusual. No drugs or alcohol—not that I'd expected any because Dad never drank before flying, not even the night before if he had a planned flight. He'd even refused to go up one morning when I'd asked him to take me and a friend, because he'd been drinking the evening before. I supposed if you lived the life he did then you felt like you couldn't take unnecessary risks—he took plenty of necessary ones.

"Something's not right here." I rubbed my face with both hands. "But I can't fucking prove anything with this information."

"No," Jeffrey agreed.

"It's too much of a coincidence." I pressed the heels of my hands into my eyes and held them there until the sting of tears abated. But my voice still trembled when I said, "I think someone killed them. I don't know who or how but I feel like I can guess why." And was I now in danger? Did whoever killed my dad somehow know that I was trying to continue his work? Would they try to stop me too, by any means necessary?

Jeffrey reached over and rested a light hand on my shoulder, gently squeezing to comfort me. "I think you might be right. And, if it's any consolation, which I'm sure it's not, this tells you that what you're working on is huge and important. You *have* to keep going."

CHAPTER EIGHTEEN

I did not have that on my bingo card

I woke with a jolt, adrenaline making my heart pound and my breath catch. Nightmares sucked. It took me a second to realize I was alone in my own bed, which also sucked. Sophia had gone to visit her parents and, as she usually did, was staying overnight rather than driving an eight-hour round trip in one day. After learning someone might have murdered my parents, I'd almost driven after her just so I could collapse in a ball for her to pick up. Instead, I spent some time with my freshly opened grief, consoling myself with the fact she'd be home soon.

I rolled over and curled up, pulling the other pillow closer to bury my face in it. I was hoping for a trace of Sophia, but didn't find it. I wanted to scrunch my eyes closed to force the nightmare out of my head, but I kept them open, staring into the darkness until my eyes adjusted and my room slowly came into dim focus. The unease from waking suddenly, and the remnants of my dream lingered. But I needed to unpack what'd woken me so anxiously, and I kept my eyes unfocused until the dream returned.

I'd dreamed about my dad. I'd been dreaming about him sporadically since I'd started working on his pass phrase, mostly those weird dreams that make no real sense and leave no real impression.

But this one had definitely left an impression, and it didn't take a genius to figure out why, and why now. I pulled the covers up over my rapidly cooling, sweat-damp skin.

Dad and I were walking the streets of Venice, dodging crashed planes, and he was talking to me, in Farsi, telling me about a guy he'd tortured for information. Then he was speaking to me in Italian, relating a story about murdering a guy because he thought he was lying during an interrogation. Then Russian, laughing about his plans to assassinate the president, and that's how I became aware that it was a dream because I was horrified by the idea. Then Mandarin as he was pushing me backward into a canal, laughing about how much of a failure I was, what a disappointment as a daughter and an analyst and a girlfriend, while he held me under the water.

What a horrible bunch of scenarios. I closed my eyes and soothed myself with some deep breaths, imagining I was on the edge of unconsciousness, until I felt myself relaxing back into sleep. I hovered in that weird space of thinking random disjointed thoughts right before you drift off, until one random thought hit me like a brick.

It's not English.

The code my dad left in his books is not in English.

That's why we haven't been able to figure out the anagram.

Holy fuck. Why was everything so fucking obvious in hindsight, but not while I was trying to figure it out? Thanks to my years of country-hopping as a kid, and my job, I spoke a lot of languages conversationally and a couple fluently. Dad was fluent in many languages. But he had a favorite.

French.

It *has* to be French. My dad spoke French almost as well as a native speaker and he knew I was fluent because we used to converse in French, alongside English and whatever new language I was learning where we were living. My dad was a huge Francophile. My parents met in France. He taught my mom French. Holy fuck. Oh my god.

I flung myself out of bed, pulled off my sleeping clothes, pulled on some leaving-the-house clothes, and after quickly washing my face and brushing my teeth, grabbed keys, credentials, wallet, and phone, and left my apartment in a flurry.

It was only in my car that I realized it was almost two a.m. On Monday morning. Oops. Ah well, I knew I could get into my office no matter the hour, so what did it really matter that I was speeding—oops again, I slowed down—through the streets toward work. I thought about texting Sophia to let her know I'd ducked out—safety first, letting your out-of-town girlfriend know you were doing something out of the ordinary like driving around the city after midnight—but I didn't want to wake her up.

Without traffic, it only took me twenty minutes before I was pulling up at the front gate. New record. Maybe I needed to become a night owl to avoid traffic and get good parking spaces. The spotlights were a glaring contrast to the usual daytime appearance of my workplace, but the personnel manning the external security stations didn't bat an eye when I pulled up and handed over my credentials. The security arm rose within seconds to admit me. I'd never been in the office past eight p.m. before, and was strangely comforted by the fact that it looked almost exactly the same, just darker. The lobby was lit up as normal but only a handful of offices dotted around the building had lights on.

The most exciting thing was that for the first time ever, I was able to snag a space in the first parking lot. I considered parking in the director's spot right up front, but they'd probably come find me to tell me to get the fuck out of it. I left my phone in the glove compartment instead of bothering to lock it in its special thermal trunk box, because it wasn't going to be left for long, and I wasn't worried about anyone taking it when nobody was around. Though, you'd have to be pretty dumb to break into a car and steal something in one of the most secure places in the country in the middle of the day anyway.

At the lone open security station, Maggie seemed both surprised and pleased to see me. Guess there wasn't much going on at this time of night. Or, early-early morning more accurately. I passed through without issue and almost broke the elevator call button in my haste to get upstairs. The building was eerily quiet, but it had a peacefulness it lacked during regular working hours.

When I stepped out of the elevator, the light above me came on right away, then the rest of the hallway lit up like dominos falling. I rushed to my door, opened it, and then locked myself in. My frantic fingers were fumbling as I unlocked the safe and pulled out my laptop, the drive, and the master folder with my notes—though by now I knew the letters and their notations by heart. If I made no progress tonight, I'd try plugging the letters into French anagram solvers at home.

I almost gave myself an actual forehead slap. I'd been so amped up about figuring out the key to the pass phrase that my brain had completely bypassed the fact I could have stayed home and worked on it, then come in to work to check my theory. Ah well. I was here now, and at least I had all my resources on hand in case I was wrong and needed to check anything again. But I didn't think I was wrong.

I stared at the letters, forming and reforming them in my brain, just seeing what single words I could make first of all and building outward from there. Alongside that task, part of my brain was still going over things my dad used to say to me, questions he'd ask, certain quotes he'd repeat. But now, I was thinking in French.

After about ten minutes, I pulled out two words.

Petite. Souris. Little Mouse.

I almost cried with relief. I was on the right path. I was certain of it. I crossed off all the letters in those two words. They were now off-limits. The Es. Three specially marked Es. They had to be French accents. I decided to leave that aside for now and just work on separating out words from the remaining letters.

The usage of "Little Mouse" made me certain it was a statement or a question and I started looking at the letters with a mind to build a complete sentence. After a ten-minute break in the Zen Zone, I came back with my mind loose and open, and it took less than twenty minutes for something to hit me like a proverbial lightning bolt from the sky.

Tu peux sortir les chèvres cet été, ma petite souris.

Ten words. All letters used. Three Es with an accent. My chest tightened, and I pressed my hand between my breasts as the meaning hit me.

You can take the goats out this summer, my little mouse.

A surge of nostalgic longing washed over me. My little mouse. I'd spent my whole adult life resenting the fact that the love I received from my parents wasn't the love I wanted, and I'd forgotten moments like this. Moments that told me they did love me. Ahhh fuck. No crying. Cry later, once all the foreign spies have been arrested.

The sentence my father had created was strange, phrased in such a way that it might seem nonsensical. No, it *was* nonsensical. But I knew exactly what Dad meant. One of our summers back in the States, when I was… I frowned, thinking. I was seven, and we'd stopped in this tiny town in Pennsylvania and there'd been petting zoo. I'd begged my parents to go in. We'd spent an hour petting and feeding the animals until I'd opened the gate to the goat pen and let all their goats out. Thankfully the entire farm was fenced and they were easily corralled back into their pen. But of course, the owners weren't happy because some stupid kid had let their goats out. My parents weren't happy because I'd drawn attention to us. I wasn't happy because my plan had been thwarted.

After furious apologies, and offers to help round up the goats—no thanks, was the terse answer—we'd headed back to the rental car. My parents had calmly closed the car doors—slamming anything was not in our family DNA—and once we were all buckled in, we sat quietly, my parents looking at each other, me looking at them.

Dad turned around from the driver's seat and asked, "Why on earth did you do that, Lexie? You know better." He didn't seem particularly mad, more…wearily exasperated.

And I'd said something like "Because I wanted to take them for a walk." They'd been following me around the pen (food is an amazing motivator for goats) and I'd thought I could just go out and show them the world, like a little pied piper of goats. I didn't want to admit that I'd been hoping to sneak one into the car to take home, which was a stupid notion no matter how you looked at it, because home at that point was in Belgium.

Mom and Dad glanced at each other and, almost simultaneously, had burst out into hysterical laughter. My dad had actually wheezed, then fallen forward onto the steering wheel and accidentally honked the horn, which made them both laugh even more.

It'd become a joke, in whatever country we were stationed, as we were planning our summer holidays back in the States, my dad would teasingly tell me that we'd find some goats for me to take for a walk. The teasing annoyed me but it seemed to lighten my parents' moods, so I'd laugh along and agree.

The goats were at Forever Home Sanctuary.

I knew the pass phrase.

Or did I?

Was it Forever Home Sanctuary? ForeverHomeSanctuary? Forever_Home_Sanctuary? Was there a reference to goats? Pennsylvania? The year? I cut myself off before I could spiral into all the possible combinations to label the place where I'd let the goats out. Occam and his razor—the simplest answer is more often than not the correct one.

I took in a massive lungful of air and let it puff my cheeks before I let it out again. You know your dad, Lexie. He would capitalize properly and have underscores between words because that's just how he was. When I'd been going through his personal PC after his death, every file was labeled: Taxes_2018, Family_Vacation_1993, Portfolio_2020, etcetera.

He would capitalize it correctly, use underscores between the words, and add a year. This would make a pass phrase that was long, made of three seemingly random words with a mix of uppercase, lowercase, symbols, and numbers. And wasn't that what the Internet had said a secure password should be? Obviously it'd worked by being something basic masquerading as not basic.

Forever_Home_Sanctuary_1988

I forefinger-typed each letter and number and symbol, panicked I'd mistyped, deleted them all, and did it again. The moment I tapped the Enter key, the password prompt disappeared. Give me a fucking drumroll, please, because I have just cracked an uncrackable code. With help, of course. But I'd cracked it. So I guess it wasn't uncrackable. Now that it was done, I felt an unexpected kind of comedown, and my jubilation would have evaporated if not for my excitement at what I saw.

Displayed on my screen were eight folders, seven of them labeled "Project_Sputnik"—my dad always had a weird sense of humor—with a combination of six letters followed by six numbers. A quick glance at the numerical sequences told me they were likely birthdates, but I wasn't sure what the letters stood for. Initials perhaps? Two sets of initials? Foreign name and American name? Whatever, that was Lennon's problem.

He'd told me not to look further once I was in, but it wasn't like I could help it—the folders were right there in front of me. He'd also told me to contact him immediately, but something made me pause before I exited the drive. The eighth folder stood out because it didn't have a Project_Sputnik label. That difference alone had already caught my eye, but the fact the birthdate was *my* birthdate, and the letters AEM—Alexandra Elizabeth Martin—made the back of my neck tingle. I clicked on the folder and was met with another password prompt. Oh for fuck's sake, Dad, haven't I done enough codebreaking? I had to laugh, though, at the text of the prompt.

1993_Vacation_Snake?

Firstly, why would my dad leave me a pass phrase-protected folder, inside a pass phrase-protected hard drive? And what was in that folder that was so important that he felt he needed to add another layer of protection? My gut had a theory, and I didn't like it.

Before I attempted to delve into the ol' memory banks for the snake encounter I'd had in 1993, I ran a malware scan on the folder. I trusted my dad, but this was apparently a hard drive full of intelligence on undercover foreign operatives currently at work in our country, and contained a secret folder. Espionage has done stranger things than fake-out an analyst to introduce a virus into an agency system.

Luckily, being off the network meant nothing would get into the agency system, but...habits and all that.

I dragged my mind back to 1993 and our summer vacation. No goats. After spending two years in Prague, Mom declared she wanted to get out into nature after spending so much time in the city. Dad's and my reminders that we made regular weekend trips to hike or ski were met with an eye roll. So, once back in the States, we'd hired an RV and driven around the Great Lakes Region for three weeks, camping all the way.

Then I stood on an eastern hog-nosed snake and got bitten, which kind of ruined the vacation vibe. Like the goats, it was something only my parents or I would know. In a way it was the perfect password to use within a folder that already had a layer of security in it.

The scan came up malware free. Good job, Dad.

I typed Eastern_Hog-nosed_Snake into the password prompt and the folder immediately opened. Apparently, and thankfully, he trusted that random memory of mine was enough to secure this folder. Over eight hundred files—pictures, audio, documents—were meticulously labeled with first my dad's initials, underscore, then the initials MAL, underscore, then dates ranging from 1980 to 2021. I almost laughed. Yep, my dad and his underscores.

At the top of the folder was a .txt file named !Lexie_Read_First. I opened it.

Lexie,

If you made it here, then know that I'm beyond proud of you for figuring out my pass phrase. I tried to make it easy enough that you would figure it out with a little work, but not so easy that anyone but you would know the answer.

And if you made it here then it means that I am dead.

I won't bore you with the details of how I started this assignment, but this intelligence is the culmination of forty years of work and each dossier is true beyond any doubt. I know you intelligence analysts are allergic to that statement but it's true in this case. I'm sure you'll understand why this particular folder has an extra layer of security. I'm trusting you to do the right thing with it and continue the work I started but haven't been able to finish. I'm sorry that you were put into a position where you had to work with this person, but I wanted you as close to him as I was, for your own safety.

Mom and I love you and we're incredibly proud of your accomplishments. Take care of yourself, be happy, and keep doing good work, Little Mouse.
Dad

I tried to swallow around the tight lump in my throat, but it refused to budge. Thanks for the intelligence and the pep talk, Dad. It would have been nice to know you and Mom were proud of me before now, like maybe you could have told me to my face while you were both alive? I felt like a dick for being angry with my dead parents. But anger was an easier emotion to deal with right now than say…devastation or profound grief.

I shook myself off and opened up the oldest picture file. So, that gut theory of mine about something being weird? I realized the moment I saw the image that my feeling was spot-on. Though the photo was clearly from the late '60s or early '70s, I recognized the man in it immediately. The color and shape of his eyes, the give-nothing-away expression, the neat side part in his hair. And if I hadn't recognized him, the note written in the bottom right corner, in my father's neat hand would have confirmed it. *Michael Lennon, USSR*. As in, Michael Lennon, the current director of this agency, and head of Halcyon Division.

Michael Lennon. A Russian operative.

Oh good. Great. This was fine.

I wasn't sure how long I sat there staring at that photograph while unpindownable thoughts swarmed in my head and sweat trickled down my back. I needed to pin down some of those thoughts so I could figure out what I was supposed to do next, aside from have a mild panic attack about what I'd just learned.

Why hadn't my dad done something with this intelligence earlier, something that could have neutralized Lennon? I just couldn't reconcile it—my dad was meticulous, forthright, moral, and intelligent. So why had he sat on his hands for so many years? Was he afraid? I'd never seen him afraid of anything and as a kid I'd thought he was impervious to fear, though back then I didn't even know what impervious meant. I just didn't think my dad was afraid of anything.

I scratched "afraid" off my mental list of reasons why he hadn't taken his investigation up the chain years ago. Maybe he didn't have hard irrefutable evidence until more recently. But…if he'd been investigating Lennon since 1980, I'd think he should have found something and acted on it, or found nothing and realized this investigation was futile. But he seemed to have done neither of those things.

None of it made any sense, and all I could think was why had my dad played such a long game? Just because he had a gut feeling? Dad didn't deal in gut feelings—he dealt in absolutes. I scrolled through all the files again, hoping something leapt out at me to prioritize before I went back to the first file and investigated my way through to the final file. The last file he'd created was a document labeled RJM_President_Brief_07-14-2021_draft.

I opened it and skimmed the report, surprised by my relief as the words sunk in. Well, that made more sense. It wasn't a fruitless, decades-long witch hunt—Dad actually had receipts for his suspicions. Of course, that relief was tempered by him having absolute proof of Lennon's allegiances. And those allegiances weren't to America. The man I'd thought was most loyal to our country, was most definitely anything but.

Dad was due to brief the president and head of agency two days after he died. Obviously he never made that briefing. Seemed whatever he needed to put the final nail in Lennon's metaphorical coffin had come into Dad's possession about two weeks before his death. Talk about stumbling right as you're about to cross the finish line.

A chill shot through me at the thought of what would have happened if I'd never been brought in to work on this. The chill intensified. I was now certain Lennon killed my dad because of his investigation. And my mom was an innocent victim. He had to be responsible, there was no other explanation. After reading the accident report, I'd been certain something felt weird about their deaths, but the thought that Lennon had murdered two people to cover up his disgusting, duplicitous life was…actually completely possible.

But I had no proof.

I'd grieved my parents' deaths and in the two years since, had moved into acceptance of my life as an orphan. But the idea that someone I'd known, trusted, given information to, for fifteen years had taken them from me made me nauseated. So now it was imperative that I take this all the way to the top and have Lennon removed. I owed it to my dad. And I owed it to everyone in the country.

First, I needed to go over every piece of evidence in this folder and make sure I reached the same conclusion as Dad had. I was sure I would.

Second, I needed to copy these files and disseminate them to trusted people for safekeeping.

Third, I needed to take this as high as I could, like…the president high. Gross. I loathed him. And had serious doubts about his competence.

That part was going to be difficult because people like me did not demand a briefing with the president. And I would need to do it without Lennon realizing, which added yet another challenge. Also difficult, and probably the most difficult part of all? Copying files from a laptop in one of the most secure places in the world.

I inhaled a long breath, puffed out my cheeks, then let the air out. Derek would know what to do, and he would be able to arrange a meeting with the president or at least some of the White House's top security advisors. I had to trust him and Jeffrey to help me with this, because I couldn't do it on my own. Shit. What if Derek was involved? He'd been Halcyon for decades, had known Lennon for decades. Hadn't Lennon been in Derek's office constantly, if Sam's gossip was to be believed? I had to blink back tears at the thought that Derek, who'd saved my ass literally and figuratively, might be the enemy as well as Lennon.

Okay. Step Zero, check the other folders on the hard drive—Lennon's directive to not open them be damned—and make sure there was nobody I knew involved with Russia. I had to make sure I could trust the people I needed to trust.

I could say honestly that I had no idea how I felt about this bombshell, even though I'd had niggling suspicions for a while. I mean, how are you supposed to feel about learning something like this? About learning that every action taken by Halcyon Division in the last twenty-plus years, and every action taken in the last month by this agency, was possibly made by a foreign operative, for foreign gain. That he could have been passing along intelligence to our enemies all this time. Particularly intel I gave him at great personal cost.

Actually, no, now that I thought about it, I did know how I felt. Sick. Sick was a good starting point. I felt sick. Not quite puking-sick, more…soul-sick.

If Lennon got hold of this intelligence my father had compiled, I couldn't even imagine what might happen. It would be classified for eternity, buried deeper than anything any intelligence agency or government had ever buried. Or, more likely, he'd burn it and continue on as the head of two of the most influential intelligence entities in the United States.

Obviously, that wasn't an option. I almost laughed. Once again, it was on me to solve a major national security issue. I really needed to ask for a massive pay raise.

So… Last year, my government thought I was a spy. But as it turns out, my boss is the Russian spy. *Fuck* is the right sentiment to express in this situation, isn't it? I think so.

Fuck.

CHAPTER NINETEEN

Just act normal

I had no idea what to do. Aside from continuing to panic a little. Maybe panic a lot. So that's what I did. I sat in my office, staring at the laptop screen, and I panicked. I panicked so much that I gave myself a full-on anxiety attack and had to crawl to the Zen Zone to bring myself out of it.

I had no idea how long it took me until I could breathe again, but eventually my vision cleared, my heart rate slowed, and my lungs filled and emptied fully. I lay on my back in Savasana, consciously breathing, and gently pushing away every thought. But when I could no longer visualize palming the clouds of thought aside, I rolled onto my side and got up. Thinking was not allowed on the yoga mat. I went back to my chair, and rolled right up to the desk. So many thoughts were tumbling through my head and I worked to separate their strands.

What do you do when you can't trust those you're supposed to trust? One thing I couldn't figure out was why Lennon hadn't just buried this whole thing. That was assuming he knew my dad was investigating him, which he probably did because I believed he killed my parents just days before my father's scheduled meeting with the president. If nobody knew about the hard drive, if he never told me, then nobody could figure out my dad's pass phrase, and there was no threat. So why was he so desperate for me to gain access for him? The only thing I could think of was that there was something in those files that he needed to know. Maybe information on other undercover operatives? Maybe to warn them if they'd been compromised by my dad's work? Or did he want to know exactly what my dad had uncovered about him so he could plug the leaks that had blown his cover?

I might never know the reason and it bugged the shit out of me. It would be so nice if I could just pop into Lennon's office, pass him a list of queries and ask him to please explain all of this. Hopefully he'd be in a cooperative mood once he was arrested. Assuming he was arrested... I shook myself out. He *was* going to be arrested. This was going to work. It had to work. Because if it didn't—we were all completely fucked.

Right, so, first things first. I needed to figure out how to copy the files onto some other drive that I could take out of the building. The major issue with that? Access to any other external drive except for this one had been disallowed on my laptop. What had Lennon called it?

Whitelisted.

This thumb drive was the only one recognized and usable by this laptop. And I couldn't ask for access to another laptop with USB ports—but please don't do any of that whitelisting shit, please—because that would surely tip Lennon off. None of the computers to which we had access at work had USB ports so I couldn't take the thumb drive to another computer, copy the file onto it, then smuggle in another thumb drive to copy it onto before smuggling that drive out again. And there was no network access, so I couldn't just send it to another computer in the building, or my laptop at home. Okay, so it had to be good old sneakernet—moving information without any sort of network access, as in physically transporting media from one computer to another computer.

Except for that one small issue—using sneakernet assumed you didn't have restrictions in place. Which I did. There *had* to be a way to get around the barriers Lennon had erected. Hackers did shit like that all the time. Pity I wasn't a hacker. Fuck, I wished I was a hacker. I laughed at that. I wasn't a hacker, but I knew someone who basically was.

I needed Bink.

How? They couldn't come in, and *wouldn't* even if Lennon hadn't expressly forbidden it. I couldn't get the data to them because I needed their help *getting* the data. And I couldn't explain what I needed on the spot because calling them from an agency phone risked my call being monitored which was a no-go for me, and especially for Bink. They avoided calls like the plague, even from end-to-end encrypted apps. So I'd just have to figure out a way to get them to talk to me so I could explain what I needed and get their help. I mentally added that to the list of things I needed to figure out.

Because if I couldn't figure it out, then I was dead in the water before I'd even left the dock. And if I couldn't restart this engine, then I had no idea what I was going to do. Sure, I *could* just tell people about Lennon. But without proof, that plan wasn't going to get me far. And the moment Lennon got word that I was telling everyone he was a big fat Russian spy he was going to wipe the drive and come after me. And I might not be able to get away.

Shit, could I even copy *from* a whitelisted drive? I had never tried, so I didn't know. Just to be sure I created a folder on the laptop and copied the AEM folder to it, exhaling loudly when it went without a hitch. Success. Okay, so I could move folders off the thumb drive. Stage one was going to work. I *could* copy the files.

Of course, in order to move the files onto something I could use outside the office, I needed to bring a portable drive into a place that expressly prohibited it. No big deal. So maybe first things first was actually devising a plan for getting a portable drive into the building and then out again, undetected. But if I couldn't copy the data onto an external drive, then it didn't matter if I devised a way to get a thumb drive into the building.

Nice spiral, Lexie. Take a breath. These are the things you need to do, and they are all equally important.

1. Figure out how to get a thumb drive in and out of the building, undetected.

2. Figure out how to copy data onto a thumb drive that isn't whitelisted on this laptop.

3. Arrange a briefing with the president so you can turn Lennon in.

But all that brainstorming could wait until I had a clearer brain space and the ability to research. I deleted the test folder I'd created, then deleted it from the recycle bin on the laptop. If someone wanted to trace what I'd been doing, I was sure they could easily do so. But at a glance, nothing seemed amiss, and they wouldn't go looking unless I gave them reason to track what I'd been up to, which I had no intention of doing. And by the time anyone became suspicious, it would hopefully be too late and I'd be clear and the information would be with people who could do something about it.

I closed my eyes and exhaled loudly. What an absolute clusterfuck. There was no way I was going to get back to sleep when I went home, so I opened up the oldest file in my AEM folder, and began to read.

I spent a few hours reading through Dad's work, storing as much information about Lennon's duplicity as I could in my brain before I decided I needed to go home and get ready to come back into work. Arousing suspicion by being in the office in jeans, looking like I hadn't been to bed, was the last thing I wanted.

As I drove home, I thought over Dad's files. I'd barely scratched the surface of what he'd uncovered about Lennon, and I still needed to check the contents of the other seven folders. Maybe I needed to send Jeffrey on a wild goose chase out of the office so I could finish reading the rest of my father's reports.

From what I'd read, Dad and Lennon weren't best friends, at least not from my dad's side. They weren't friends at all, according to my father. It was a ruse for Dad to stay close to his mark, which would explain why he hadn't wanted that clog, or other Lennon gifts in the house. It may have had a listening device in it, and even if it didn't, Dad was right to be suspicious. They'd met during their initial training program, and had indeed been roommates and were friendly, but not besties. So Lennon had twisted the truth about that. My level of surprise was zero out of ten.

Maybe Lennon had approached their "friendship" the same way, and that's why he couldn't remember basic details about my dad. They were in contact because of work, and Dad started noticing things that seemed off. And full credit to my father—these were not things many others would have noticed. I don't think I would have pinged it so early. So he insinuated himself, pushing the friendship to see if he could expose Lennon. My gut feeling was that Lennon may have suspected Dad's true motives, and so he also wanted Dad close. It was like the both of them were just playing the part.

And then my father was killed for it.

I mentally added "by Lennon" even though I couldn't prove it. Maybe, when all this was done and dusted, I'd be allowed to question him. And that was the first thing I'd ask. The sun was just over the horizon when I pulled into my apartment's parking garage. I was so exhausted, mentally and physically, that I decided to skip my usual workout at work and instead, soothed my anxious cells with a stretchy yoga practice. Meditation helped scrape enough of the remaining sharp edges off my anxiety that I felt like I could think and breathe for the first time in hours.

Sophia had texted while I was taking care of my brain and body and I read the text as I walked into my bedroom.

Morning, gorgeous. Sleep well? Hope you have a good day at work. I'll leave after breakfast and lectures from Mom and papi about taking better care of myself and you meeting them ASAP. Tongue-poking emoji. *Still on for your place tonight?*

I decided to ignore the question about sleeping and instead went for light and easy. *Haha, sounds fun. Drive safely, call me on my work landline when you get home? Yep, my place tonight, I'll call you when I'm leaving work. Can't wait to see you. Love you.* I added a few heart emojis and once she'd responded with her own and a kiss-blowing emoji, I set my phone down and dropped onto my bed. The urge to just flop backward and try to sleep was strong, and I sat up again to stop myself from giving in.

I had to keep going. The finish line was so close. And once I'd crossed it, Sophia and I were going to ride off into the sunset and I was going to forget about everything to do with Michael Lennon.

I made it back to the office before Jeffrey. He sauntered in with his usual good humor, and greeted me with a cheery, "Goood morning! How was your weekend?"

"Morning," I said, still surprised by the roughness in my voice. Hardly any sleep and hours of raging anxiety will do that to you. Even Damien at the security station had commented, asking if I was getting sick. He'd leaned away hilariously as he'd asked, and if I wasn't so gaga, I might have laughed.

Jeffrey studied me, an eyebrow raised as if that might help him discern what was up. After a few seconds, he concluded, "Bad night's sleep?"

"No night's sleep," I mumbled. Knowing Jeffrey would push, I looked up and forced a smile. "Sophia was out of town visiting her parents yesterday. She's back later today."

He adopted a babying tone to ask, "Has someone gotten used to having a girlfriend sleeping next to them?"

"Someone has," I confirmed glumly. And god I hoped I wouldn't be caught up in something that would take me away from her again.

Jeffrey worked on the letters, and I pretended to work on the letters until the dot of ten a.m., when someone knocked on the office door, sending my heart rate soaring into the stratosphere. Jeffrey was closest, and he popped the last of his cookie into his mouth and jumped up.

I knew from his posture when he opened the door that it was Lennon, not Derek, and my stomach sank. Simultaneous soaring heart rate and sinking stomach was not a pleasant experience.

"Would you mind giving us a few minutes, Burton?" Lennon asked him graciously.

Oh fuck. Fuck. I was fucked. How did he know I'd figured it out?

Jeffrey glanced my way, eyebrows raised. And though all I wanted to do was frantically shake my head and tell him without words to not leave me, I nodded, and tried to add a reassuring smile to it. As soon as the door had closed behind my partner, Lennon turned to me. I tried desperately to discern his state of mind, but his expression was carefully curated neutrality, even as he said, "I note from my security logs briefing this morning that you came in early this morning."

Okay, this is okay, maybe he didn't know I'd discovered his disgusting secret life. But how had I not known he reviewed security logs? I forced nonchalance, but not too much nonchalance—don't wanna seem like you're trying to hide something with incongruous reactions here, Lexie. "Yeah. I couldn't sleep." I stifled a genuine yawn, which had the added bonus of relaxing me. "Just kept thinking about the pass phrase so I decided to come in and see if anything came to me while I was looking at the letters."

He smiled. "I'm assuming, based on your demeanor, that it did not."

"You assume correctly." There was something about *his* demeanor that had me on edge, and I wondered if he suspected I was lying. Maybe he had hidden cameras and he'd seen me break the pass phrase. When I'd first started this assignment, I briefly considered the fact there might be some sort of keylogger on the laptop, but given it was fresh out of the box and had no network access or strange cables attached, I'd dismissed the thought.

No. There was no way hidden surveillance would be allowed in this building, not even by the director. And surely, if he knew I'd figured it out, he would have come right out and accused me of lying and demanded I tell him, not play cat and mouse with me. He was fishing. And he wasn't going to catch anything from me. I removed my glasses and set them carefully down on my desk. "But I think I'm close. I can feel it."

"We're going by vibes now?" he asked, a playful note in the question.

"We are," I agreed, making sure to answer in the same light tone. For all it mattered to Lennon, I could be going on crystals and woo-woo, as long as I got the task done.

Lennon nodded briskly. After a quick glance around the office, he let his gaze slowly come back to me. "I look forward to seeing the results of those vibes."

"Me too."

Once he'd gone, I leaned heavily against the wall beside the door. The moment I relaxed my tight control, the stress I'd been suppressing came flooding back. If Lennon didn't kill me for what I was about to do, the anxiety just might…

My vibe for the rest of the day was tense and trying not to let Jeffrey see it while I pretended to work on the code. I felt bad for making him stare at the letters all day, because I knew just how frustrating making no progress had become. Well, guess what, Jeffrey? I made progress. And it's not as cathartic as I'd hoped…

I made it to four p.m. before I declared I'd had enough, and that we should start fresh in the morning. Zero complaints from my colleague. As we walked to the elevator together, he teasingly told me to, "Sleep better tonight so you won't be such a useless zombie tomorrow."

Adopting what I hoped was a sly smile, I assured him I would. And I hoped I could keep up this charade for a few more days until it was time to bring him in to the new plan. We said our good nights and wished each other safe journeys home, and I made my way home to wait for Sophia.

I'd barely finished getting dressed when she was knocking on the door. Excitement and relief blurred together. As soon as I'd let Sophia in and locked the door, I pushed hair away from around her face, holding it back as I gently cupped her cheeks in my hands and bent down for a hello kiss. As if sensing that I was feeling discombobulated, Sophia wrapped her arms around my waist and returned my kiss enthusiastically.

When the kiss ended, I held on to her, tightly, trying to regain some of my equilibrium. Sophia hugged me back, letting the hug continue until I felt controlled enough to pull away. She scrunched her nose up adorably, smiling as she told me, "I missed you."

"Me too," I said tightly.

After we both had drinks and some pretzels and dip to tide us over until dinner, we relocated to the couch to catch up.

"How are your parents?" I asked after I'd chewed an enormous handful of dip-laden pretzels. Uncovering secret plots to undermine the country really gave a girl an appetite.

Her face lit up. "They're both really good. Excited about meeting you. Fair warning, there *were* some jokes about you running off overseas for six months because you were scared to meet them."

"From your dad?" I'd picked up on his dry, witty sense of humor the one time I'd talked to them, in that video call before I'd gone overseas.

She grinned. "Yeah. They're ready whenever you've got a little time, but in the meantime, they'd like to set up some more video calls."

"Deal. I'd like that. And I still want to have another, uninterrupted social event with your friends, whenever we can fit that in. And invite Jeffrey and Dominique over for dinner. Shit, you've got pickleball on Friday too, don't you?"

"Do we need to combine calendars?" she asked teasingly.

"I think we do. We have reached peak lesbian relationship." I swallowed down the surge of unease at what I was about to suggest. It was ridiculous to feel uneasy about something we'd already done when we were together before. "And maybe it's time to swap keys again?"

"I think maybe it is," she agreed, with not a small amount of excitement in her voice.

I kissed her again, then pulled my feet up onto the couch, leaning sideways into her. I wrapped an arm around her waist and rested my head against the front of her shoulder. I wanted to bury myself in her, hide somewhere warm and safe.

"You okay?" she asked, gently rubbing my back.

"Yeah. Just…I couldn't do this without you, Sophia. I mean it." I pulled away, and sat back so I was facing her on the couch. "This is going to sound corny and clichéd and I don't give a shit because I love you. I don't know what I would do if you hadn't reached out to start reconciliation. I think I might have just…curled up in a ball and given up."

She rested her hands on my forearm, her long, elegant fingers pressing lightly into my skin. "Luckily we don't need to speculate." Sophia stretched over for a kiss.

I deepened it.

She put a little space between us, just enough for her to ask, "How hungry are you?"

I recognized the tone, and it only took a few moments for me to run the calculations on whether I wanted dinner, or sex first. "I can wait."

"Good." She stood abruptly and pulled me up, then without a word, led me into the bedroom. There was no need for words as we helped each other out of clothing, dropping everything carelessly to the floor before we moved together to the bed. I caught the look she gave me and knew she was about to maneuver us so she was in charge, so she could have me first. But I twisted until I was on top, and she gave in to me instantly. My hands roamed to all my favorite places, softly stroking and kneading, as my mouth mapped the skin of her neck.

I could feel the heat of her against my hip as I rocked into her, and the copious wetness spiked my own arousal. I didn't know if I wanted fast or slow, I just knew that I...*wanted*. I reached up to cup her breasts, and Sophia took one of my hands, bringing it up to her mouth. She turned her head to kiss my fingertips, then took them into her mouth. Her tongue slid over my fingers. I suppressed a loud groan at the slow movement of her tongue, insinuating what she wanted me to do. She bit teasingly, then sucked my fingers before releasing the pressure.

I gently withdrew them from her mouth, and reached between us, pushing my hand between her thighs. Sophia pressed into my hand, her hips rolling in time with my movement. She pulled me down for a kiss, murmuring hoarsely against my lips, "Put your mouth on me."

I still didn't know if I wanted fast or slow, but I did know that I didn't want to wait to taste her. I shuffled quickly down the bed, spread her legs, and dove in. Her breathing grew ragged, her movements restless as I played my tongue through her labia, deliberately avoiding her clit.

"Please," Sophia begged in a rough whisper. Her neediness was so fucking sexy, and I had to swallow the sudden swell of emotion at the realization of how close we'd come to never having this again.

I stopped teasing, and gave her what she wanted, licking and sucking her until she was crying out in pleasure. Sophia urged me on with little moans of encouragement as she writhed and bucked, her hands moving through my hair, over my shoulders, up my neck. Her breathing hitched and I added a little more pressure until she tensed, her thighs tightening around my shoulders as she came. The sound of her climax, the sensation of it in my mouth, the unashamed way she took her pleasure had my own arousal skyrocketing until my skin felt like it was on fire. I stayed with her until she'd relaxed a little, then slowly made my way back up her body.

I kissed her inner thighs, then up the smooth curve of her hip, lingering to indulge in the softness of her belly. Her hands were in my hair, lightly guiding me back up. I took my time, wanting to savor every morsel of skin I could reach. When I made it to her breasts, taking my time to pay attention to each nipple, Sophia sat up. But before she could flip me over, I shifted to straddle her, inching forward until it felt like we were fused along the front of our bodies. She went along with me, cupping the back of my neck, pulling me down for a furious, demanding kiss. The kiss slowed but was no less intense for its gentleness.

Heat built low in my belly, spreading down into my clit, and I rocked forward, biting down on a groan at the sensation of my heated flesh rubbing against her skin. Sophia cupped my ass with both hands, pressing me forward, angling me just right. I inhaled a ragged breath.

Without breaking the kiss, she took her left hand from where it was cupping my ass, pressed me forward and reached off the bed. I heard my bedside drawer opening, and the simmering heat exploded as I realized what she was doing. Sophia shifted slightly, opening the space between us. I missed the warmth of her instantly as the air cooled my sweat-slicked skin, but my skin superheated when she slowly and thoroughly licked the tip of the silicone toy.

Oh fuck.

Sophia turned the vibrator on and drew it up the center of my torso. The subtle pulse against my nipple traveled downward, and my thighs tightened around her hips. I almost whimpered in anticipation.

"Is this what you want?" she asked huskily.

"Yes." I stroked the tips of my fingers along her jawline, slow and sensuous, indulgent. "I want all of it."

"Show me how much you want it."

I guided the vibrator between my legs and gripped her wrist, holding her in place as I slid forward until the shaft was pressed to my clit. The sensation made me jump, and I shifted to a place that was a little more tolerable, a place where I wasn't going to be rushed to climax. Sophia smiled as if she knew what I'd just experienced, and turned the vibration down.

I sighed loudly, settling into a slow rhythm, rocking my hips forward and back. Every stroke sent waves of pleasure through me, and I wrapped my arm around her shoulders to steady myself as I climbed higher and higher toward my orgasm. Sophia tilted her hand, moving the shaft back and forth. "Oh, baby, you're so wet," she said, a small groan escaping at the end of her words. "Do you want me to fuck you with this?"

Instead of answering her, I kissed her and propped up on my knees until I was lifted slightly from her lap. She lightly bit my lower lip as she angled the shaft, and when I felt the head bump up against my entrance, I slowly let myself settle down on it. The sensation was exquisite, and I didn't even try to muffle my moan of pleasure. Sophia was a master with her fingers, and I would take her finger-fucking me any day of the week, but there was something delicious about being filled so completely.

She performed circus-worthy contortions to keep the vibrator angled as I rocked and rose, back and forth, up and down, her other hand between our bodies so her thumb was against my clit. And I was very grateful for her efforts. Our nipples brushed, and the sensation heightened my pleasure.

"This is…tricky," she said. "I need more hands." She kissed me hard, then softened, her lips remaining close to mine as she said, "Maybe we should get a strap-on."

I couldn't stop the shudder that ran through me and Sophia picked up on it immediately. "You like that idea?" she murmured, biting my shoulder. "Me fucking you with a strap?"

"Yes." I swallowed hard. "Or maybe I'll fuck you with it."

"Jesus," she hissed, biting me again.

I held on to the bedhead with one hand, and kept the other around her shoulders for balance. Our mouths remained within a whisper of each other, hot breath mingling as I rode the toy toward my climax. I was so close. So wet. So desperate to come. Sophia skillfully stroked my clit and held the toy steady for me while I fucked myself on it. My entire body felt electrified as heat and arousal built, until my climax came upon me so suddenly and with such intensity I thought I might shatter.

When my legs had stopped trembling, I carefully eased myself from the toy and then her lap, rolling onto my back and pulling her on top of me. Sophia kissed me slowly, and I responded eagerly. I hooked my calf around her thigh as we kissed, long and languid until she pulled away with a quick peck each to my nose, cheeks, and chin. She snuggled into my neck, and I hugged her close.

"Oh my god," I said, still breathless. "That was incredible."

"Mmm," she agreed. "We're incredible." Sophia propped herself up on an elbow. "I know it's not all about sex, but the sex is really good."

"It really is." I'd had good sex before Sophia, but nothing like this. Trusting her was everything, and made intimacy infinitely better.

She settled back down on top of me, one hand tracing meaningless patterns over my breasts and collarbones. I closed my eyes, wanting to relax and come back to myself for a few minutes before we had to get up and think about dinner. But instead of relaxing, I had the most horrible thought.

If I was caught, if Lennon found out that I knew who he really was, then he would probably kill me. But at least I'd have done this. At least we could remember this moment.

CHAPTER TWENTY

Rubber Ducky

How exactly do you sneak classified intelligence out of a secure government facility? I'd spent all day brainstorming that question and so far, all I'd really arrived at was: with great difficulty.

I *could* try to sneak the drive that held the copy of my dad's data out of the office—method as yet undetermined—but that was risky because I would need to bring it straight back to the office after copying the files at home. And it also risked corrupting the data. How to explain *that* to Lennon?

I decided to focus first on how to copy the data to a new external drive when the tech guy had basically blocked that functionality on the laptop. Because if I couldn't actually copy the data, then working out how to move a drive in and out of the building was moot. Rather than waste time Googling and trying to figure out geek-speak, I decided to go right to the person I knew could help me. After dinner, I emailed Bink using one of their throwaway email accounts, from one of my throwaway email accounts.

I need to talk to you. Voice.

I got a response with fifteen minutes. Bink lived on computers so they were either busy, or making me wait just to be a dick. *Voice? No thank you.*

Red alert.

This response came almost immediately. *Get yourself a new secure phone and then contact me. It'll cost you.*

It always does.

Sophia didn't bat an eyelid when I told her I had to go to the store, and after I said I was fine to her asking if I needed company (with a look that told me she was comfy on her couch in post-dinner chill mode and was just asking to be polite), she told me she'd keep the couch warm. It took no time to grab a new smartphone and SIM. I sat in my car and set it up, then downloaded Signal so I could communicate with Bink. I sent them an email with the new number. Then I waited.

The app rang a minute later and I got out of the car to take the call. Maybe paranoid—I didn't really think my car had been bugged, but at the moment, I wasn't entirely adverse to a little paranoia. So I stood out in the parking lot, away from the lights, and answered, "Hello."

Bink's flat, deadpan voice said, "Red alert, huh? Haven't heard that since we were cozied up in a shipping container in the desert and you needed information." Then, with their usual cut-the-bullshit-and-get-to-the-point demeanor, they asked, "What do you need?"

"I have a laptop with a whitelisted thumb drive, and I need to copy the contents of that drive onto another external drive. How exactly do I do that?"

Bink laughed like I'd just told them the most hilarious joke. "That's easy."

"Easy for you? Or easy for me, just a regularly computer-literate person."

"Easy for you, with my help. Okay, time for a quick tech lesson. So, whitelisting. Basically, every external drive has an ID. Following me so far?"

"Yes," I said dryly.

"Good. Whitelisting is telling the computer that it can *only* talk to that specific thumb drive ID, and all others are blocked. So what you need to do is clone a drive with the ID of the drive that's whitelisted and then you can use the cloned drive on that laptop as if it were the original."

Oh, right, of course. Why didn't I think of that? "So how do I do that?"

Bink was silent for a few seconds. "You need a Rubber Ducky."

"A what?"

"It's just a thumb drive with superpowers. I'll send you one, as well as the steps you need to find the ID of the whitelisted drive you have, and then how to clone the Rubber Ducky with that ID." They snorted. "I'll spell it out so even a troglodyte could do it."

I ignored their veiled implication that I was a troglodyte. Compared with Bink, everyone was a troglodyte. "I'd appreciate that." I bit my lower lip. "It's…urgent."

"It always is. I'll have it express couriered to your post office box. It'll be there tomorrow."

"Thanks. I'll email you a Visa gift card for your trouble."

"You'd better." Bink paused. "Something tells me *you* haven't accidentally whitelisted a thumb drive…"

"No."

There was a longer pause. "I want to be excited by whatever you're doing but honestly, I'm worried. Add this to the fact that not long after you came to see me last year, asking me to dig around in one of the most secure places in the world, the vice president was arrested, outed as a Russian-loving fuckwit, resigned, and was imprisoned."

"That could just be a coincidence," I said airily.

"Right. And my IQ is sub one-fifty." I heard their loud inhalation. "Look. Don't be stupid. Nothing is worth getting yourself jailed, fired, or killed."

"Some things are." Then before I could be lectured any further, I barreled on. "Another question. X-ray machines can see through tinfoil and maybe even thin metal like…a lunchbox, right?"

"They can," was the wary response. "That's why they use lead, not tinfoil, to protect against x-ray exposure."

Unfortunately their answer was basically what I'd thought. "Do you think a mag arch would pick up the metal bits in a thumb drive? If I…hide it within my body?"

"Jesus," they hissed. "The ones you go through? Highly unlikely. They're tuned for larger amounts than that, I think. Please don't mention my name when you get arrested."

Highly unlikely. But not totally certain. "I promise I won't. I'll be in touch if I have any problems."

"I can't wait," Bink deadpanned.

* * *

The parcel from Bink was waiting in my post office box when I went out during my lunch break the next day. Inside was a clamshell package with a thumb drive, and a double-sided printed page of detailed instructions. The Rubber Ducky was indeed just a small thumb drive—superpowers obviously hidden—with a tiny rubber duck stamped on the metal. Before I drove back to work, I sat in my car and repeatedly read through the instructions for getting the ID of an external drive, until I'd committed the steps to memory.

The instructions were confusing, but once I'd been through them a few times I was confident I wouldn't fuck it up. I just had to wait for Jeffrey to leave work that afternoon. And as soon as he did, in I went. Within five minutes, I had the ID of the whitelisted drive carefully written down on a scrap of paper, placed in the diary that lived inside my handbag. To the x-ray, it would just look like the paper inside the diary that the machine saw every day. At least something was easy.

Cloning the Rubber Ducky was even more straightforward—one of its purposes was to mimic any thumb drive's ID, and it had a specific command for just that. Man, hacking was actually kind of easy. If you had the right tools that basically did everything for you, that is. And now, I had my tool.

Of course, I still had to figure out a way to hide the cloned Rubber Ducky on my person or in my bag without it being detected. Twice. Once going in. And once going out. Because if I didn't figure it out, well…catastrophe didn't seem like quite a big enough word to describe what would happen. I lay on the couch with my forearm over my eyes blocking out the light, letting my brain wander as it pleased, going through every scenario for getting the Ducky through security.

After an hour or so, I decided that of all my ideas, placing the slim thumb drive in a doctored belt was looking like my best bet, followed closely by uh…storing the drive internally and hoping like hell that it didn't set off the mag arch, because I wasn't sure how I'd explain that one. I got a new IUD that magically fell out by the next day? Bink seemed certain it wouldn't be detected, but I didn't know for sure if the mag arch wouldn't pick up such a small amount of metal stored internally. I didn't want to take the chance if I could avoid it.

Fuck, I wished I'd known I needed to sneak a thumb drive in and out of work sometime in the future, and I would have started bringing in my lunch wrapped in tinfoil or a metal lunchbox to set a precedent that would soon be ignored because it was normal for me.

Yes, it had to be a belt. Belts set off the metal detectors all the time—including my belts when I was in a rush and not thinking about metal content when choosing a work outfit—and the security people were pretty blasé about it now. Or as blasé as you got at one of the securest facilities in the country. Sometimes we got waved through with the belt on, once we pointed at it. Sometimes we took them off before passing through the mag arch, but it was rare that a belt was scanned through the x-ray. Usually it was just handed back to us on the other side of the arch. What a great plan to save the country—a thumb drive in a clumsy hiding place.

As well as my brainstorming about the what and how, I'd been racking my brains for what I would say if I got caught with the drive either on the way in or out. "It's not mine" or snatching the belt and sprinting away were frontrunners. One niggling idea kept popping back into my head—I'd read stories of clothing-factory workers sometimes sewing notes into clothing to alert people to their appalling working conditions. If I printed out a note with a message and some reference to evidence of factory conditions and slotted it into the belt with the Ducky, I could feign complete ignorance, ask to look and, if it was on the way out with the evidence about Lennon already on the drive, "accidentally" break it to prevent anyone looking at it.

And then I'd be back to square one.

So the obvious solution was that I just needed to not get caught. Right. So. I had a plan about how to take highly classified intelligence offsite. Now I just had to execute it. Oh, bad choice of word, Lexie.

I knew Sophia had been aware of my anxious, frantic mood over the past few days while I'd been trying to figure out the sneaky sneaky with classified intelligence dilemma, and when she arrived unexpectedly just after seven p.m., even though we'd agreed to spend that night apart, I almost cried with relief. Without saying anything, she pulled me into a hug just inside the doorway of my apartment.

"I don't know how you do it," I said around a barely withheld sniffle.

"Do what, hon?" she asked, her fingers massaging my lower back.

I dropped my head into her shoulder, inhaling her scent. "Just… know when I need you."

"It's my superpower." Sophia gently disengaged from the hug but didn't let me go. Smiling, she wiped under my eyes. "Do you need anything from me? Aside from being here?"

I loved that she didn't ask if I was okay, because clearly I wasn't. "Yes. Can you stay tonight?"

"Of course." Sophia gently kissed me, before she guided me toward the couch. Once we'd sat down, thighs brushing, she took my hand. "Have you eaten dinner yet?"

I shook my head. "I was going to cook, and then I was going to order in, and then I was just going to have toast, but so far, none of that's happened."

"Okay, new plan then—you need something to eat." She pulled my hand to her mouth, kissed the butt of my thumb, then hopped up and went into the kitchen. Before I could make a joke about her cooking, she did it for me. "I promise I won't poison you. Much," she added with a grin that melted away some of my anxiety. I followed her to the kitchen, settling on a stool on the other side of the breakfast bar to watch. First I thought I was getting a fried egg when she cracked one into a hot pan. Then I thought I was getting egg and toast. Then I was just intrigued.

After she'd set a cheese, tomato, fried egg, spinach, and caramelized onion relish sandwich (thanks for the cooking lessons, Camila) into the sizzling butter to grill, Sophia asked if I wanted a *drink* drink. I shrugged. "I'm…honestly not sure." It'd probably help me relax a little, but I also didn't want to have a drink, then another and another and another which is what I thought might happen in my current mood.

While my dinner cooked, Sophia made us both a half-pour gin and tonic. Once my grilled-cheese-and-more sandwich was done, she set it in front of me, then came around the counter to sit on the high stool beside me. She cupped my cheek in one hand and turned my face until I looked straight at her. "Eat something, hon. And if you want to talk about it once you've got something in your stomach, I'm right here. And if you don't, I'm still right here."

"Thank you. I love you," I said seriously.

"I love you too. A whole bunch."

Sophia sipped her G&T and scrolled on her phone while I ate, just quietly being with me but without forcing me to talk or interact. Did I mention she was a goddess and a saint? After a few bites, I realized a, that I was actually ravenous and b, that she'd indeed upped her cooking skills. I dusted crumbs from my fingertips onto the plate. "I admit, I was dubious about your combination of beefed-up grilled cheese ingredients, but I'll happily admit I was wrong and you were right."

"Oh, I love it when you say that."

"Believe me, I know."

She winked, then turned back to her drink and scrolling. I returned to my dinner. I'd eaten about three-quarters of my sandwich when the dam finally burst. "I found what I was looking for in those files that I've been working on," I blurted out of nowhere. "So my assignment is…pretty much done."

Sophia set down both glass and phone and grabbed my wrist, squeezing gently. "That's awesome, babe." Her excitement was genuine, and wonderful, but also made me feel kind of sick.

"Yeah." I raised my drink to my mouth, realized my hand was trembling, and set it back down. "And I found something that's...it's a problem. I looked at the files, even though I wasn't really supposed to. And now I know why I wasn't supposed to."

Sophia moved closer until she was almost leaning off the stool. Her expression had transformed instantly from supportive pride to intense concern. "Are you okay? Are you safe?"

"Okay?" I made a back and forth see-sawing motion with my hand. "Not sure. But, safe? Yes, we are." I made sure to emphasize the *we*. "It's..." I paused, trying to think of the analogy, and instead thought about how she'd once told me about The Face—the look I got when I was doing mental gymnastics as I worked out how to tell her something without telling her something she shouldn't or couldn't know. I smiled, knowing I totally had The Face right now. That brief smile was the respite I needed to ease some of my anxiety. "...complicated," I finally managed.

She smiled knowingly. "Isn't it always?"

"Yeah," I admitted on a defeated breath. "But this one is...it's *big*, Sophia. Think of it like, um, in terms of nuclear disasters. If the situation with ex-Vice President Berenson was Three Mile Island, then this is Chernobyl and Fukushima *combined*, and multiplied by one hundred."

"So it's a big deal," Sophia deadpanned. "Got it."

"A really, really big deal," I confirmed, trying to ignore the queasiness rolling through my stomach.

"Are we going on another road trip?" she asked lightly, her hand stroking soothingly up and down my back.

"Honestly, I wish it could be fixed with a road trip." I'd fallen in love with her on that "road trip," despite everything I was subjected to trying to unravel the Kunduz Intelligence.

She straightened up, but kept her hand on my back as her voice took on a firm, fix-it tone. "So what do you need to do?"

I was so ashamed of what I was going to admit, I couldn't look at her. "I need to do something that's questionably legal at work but I'm not going to tell you about it because of plausible deniability. And I'm feeling more than a little anxious about it." Questionably legal, and maybe even criminal, but this intel really was life or death for the country.

She smiled, but it was tight around her eyes. "I appreciate that."

I leaned over and kissed her. "You're welcome." Swallowing hard, I added earnestly, "Told you I'd always keep you safe, didn't I?"

Her eyes softened. "You did," she murmured. Sophia lightly gripped the back of my neck, keeping us connected. "I know you would have thought of every option already, but I'm still going to ask—is there no other choice than to do this questionably legal thing?"

"No."

"Then you're doing the right thing, Super Lexie."

I nodded, exhaling loudly. Once I'd let the breath out, I realized how much tension it'd been keeping inside. "Super Lexie," I repeated quietly. "Thanks for dinner, sweetheart. Now, if you'll excuse me, I have a small craft project to work on for about an hour." Craft project. There, that sounded totally chill and not espionage-y.

"Then I have about an hour of wasting time on the Internet to do." She kissed my temple. "Let me know if you need some glitter for your craft ventures."

I grinned. "Will do."

To keep Jeffrey from catching me copying the data—not that I thought he'd tell on me, but I needed to keep him out of it so he'd be clean and free and able to take care of Sophia for me if I couldn't—I called him before starting the belt massacre and told him to take a day off tomorrow.

"And do what?" he asked. "I'm a contractor. I don't get PTO."

"You get paid by the day regardless of how much work you do, so we both know that's a dumb whine. Do you really want to spend another day staring at letters?"

"No."

"I thought so. If you need something to do to justify your paycheck, then…I need you to go to the library and…look at books about Caesar's conquests for me. All day."

"Really? I thought we were well past that and it wasn't relevant."

Read the fucking context clues, Jeffrey, and stop arguing. I pulled out a trump card. "Drinks," I said evenly.

"You're right," Jeffrey said immediately, "I do need to brush up on my Roman history. I'll see you the day after tomorrow?"

I added extra cheer into my, "Yep." Then I turned my attention to my craft project.

It took me three ruined belts before I managed to create a slim thumb-drive-sized pocket on the inside of one of them. The trick, I'd discovered after much mental engineering, was to not only make the little hiding place in a spot that wasn't immediately obvious but that could also be "sealed" to keep the drive from falling out at an inopportune time. Like when one of the security people was handling the belt. If they broke their usual unwanted-belt protocol and x-rayed it, which would be incredibly unlucky because I frequently set off the mag arch with belts, I'd just have to employ some serious diversionary tactics. Surely something would come to me in a flash of brilliance if I needed a diversion.

Sighing, I held the belt up, examining it from all angles. It looked like dogshit. They all did. Anyone with eyes would see that my belt had been tampered with. And I couldn't keep ruining belts for the same outcome. This wasn't going to work. I needed to figure out another way to get the Rubber Ducky in and out of the office. A tinfoil-wrapped sandwich or a metal lunchbox was the easiest solution, but neither was strong enough to block x-rays—they'd see the Ducky. So…it looked like I'd have to employ the ol' "prison pocket." I'd kind of wanted that to be the absolute last resort. But it looked like I'd reached the last resort. And the last resort needed a few supplies. I thought about what a smuggler would do. Just…shove it in there, I guess. But I wanted to protect the Ducky, so maybe a menstrual cup would help? I did have a large one, for those few period days when my body felt like it was trying to kill me.

When I came back from the bedroom, Sophia said nothing about the "craft project," but she did comment on the fact I was dressed for a run. "Nighttime cardio?" The way she said it was similar to the way someone might say "eating dogshit?"

I laughed. "I just need to go to the store. Be back in about twenty minutes. You need anything?"

"Chocolate."

I kissed her gently on the mouth. "Done. Lock the door behind me?"

She nodded.

I jiggled a quick warm-up in the elevator down, then ran the three blocks to the twenty-four-hour convenience store on the corner. The pimply teen clerk barely hid his smirk when I dropped nonlubricated condoms, lube, and chocolate onto the counter. Get over it, you immature idiot. I'm saving the world here.

I made it back home in eighteen minutes and after delivering Sophia's chocolate, I put my stuff in the bathroom cupboard and took a quick shower to wash off my espionage-supplies run. Sophia looked up as I came back, and held out her hand to me. I took it and plonked down onto the couch, leaning into her. She stroked my thigh lazily. "Why don't we have an early night."

"I'm not tired yet," I said, with more petulance than I meant to. The thought of what I had to do to get the Ducky in and out of the building tomorrow had put me in a sour mood.

Both her eyebrows went up. Oh. Right. Clearly she wasn't tired either. I'd been planning on initiating sex once we were in bed, because I'd been craving that connection with her, craving the comfort. Especially if Lennon found out what I'd done and decided to punish me. I reached for her, pulling her on top of me. And for a few hours, I forgot about everything but her.

CHAPTER TWENTY-ONE

I am really not cut out for espionage

It'd taken me a little while to fall asleep, because I'd been going over my plan for the Ducky smuggling. I'd decided to put it inside a condom, and tape that to the inside of the menstrual cup to keep it secure and protected. Sure, I could just leave it free-floating in there, but that felt icky, and honestly—I was already icked-out enough. Icked-out and hoping I didn't get an infection—I didn't care that it was in the name of national security—from inserting a foreign body, even if it was safely stowed inside two things that were allowed to go inside that part of my body.

I'd decided to skip my morning workout at work, wanting to get into the building and get the Ducky out ASAP. And to cover my ass against the mag arch picking up the Ducky, I'd decided to wear one of the belts I knew set off the detector. Some quick talking with Kevin should push him toward "Dr. Martin forgot belts set off the detectors" rather than "Dr. Martin has a thumb drive in her vagina," and hopefully he'd let me go through with the belt on.

Once I fell asleep, I slept surprisingly well, considering what the following day held for me. But when I woke an hour earlier than usual, the butterflies began swarming again. I closed my eyes and concentrated on the weight of Sophia's limbs slung over my body, on my breathing, and on the fact there was nothing more I could do. I was going to be as prepared as I could be, and ride out the consequences as they happened. If they happened.

I set all the what-ifs aside, slid out from under Sophia, and went into my yoga/meditation room to calm myself down. I had no idea why I was so anxious—aside from the whole "if you fuck up, Lennon will probably kill you, and a Russian operative will continue running one of America's intelligence agencies as well as an influential department" dealio. I was good at manipulation, at appearing to be something I was not, at operating covertly. But this was different. This was catastrophic if it failed.

I indulged in an extra-long yoga and meditation session to center myself before the big event. Sophia slept while I crept around the house, pawing through my first aid supplies for sterile wound-closure strips, checking I could still fold the menstrual cup for insertion with the Ducky against the side (thankfully, yes), and putting some more wounds strips and another condom in my purse. They'd show up on the x-ray, but it wasn't like condoms and something like a Band-Aid were contraband. Sure, a condom was slightly odd for me, but not something that would cause any further scrutiny.

I put the Ducky in a condom that I knotted tightly, before taping it inside my menstrual cup. You're the hero we need today, menstrual cup, don't let me down. I had to push down the hysterical laugh that bubbled up.

And then I got on with the job.

I would have loved to take the lube to work to assist with…uh…reinsertion, but that was going to seem *really* weird on the x-ray. So, I was just going to have to conjure up some nice thoughts of Sophia, while hanging out in a bathroom stall, for some natural assistance with getting the menstrual cup back in on a non-menstruating day.

Sophia woke as I was almost finished dressing, mumbling something incoherent before she sat up to mumble something slightly more coherent. "Why didn't you wake me?"

"I was going to just before I left," I said, threading my belt. "Wanted you to sleep as much as you could."

"I appreciate you so much," she said hoarsely. "But I don't want to be in bed without you." She threw back the covers and kissed me on her way to the bathroom. By the time I'd put on my jacket and heels, and gathered my stuff, she was dressed and ready to go home.

If she noticed I held our hug a little tighter and a little longer than normal, she didn't comment. Sophia framed my face in her hands and kissed me soundly on the mouth. "You're staying at my place tonight, right?"

"Yeah. I just need to go home quickly after work, then I'll come around. Love you."

"Love you too." She kissed the right side then the left side of my mouth. "And I believe in you."

During peak morning and afternoon periods, all the security stations were manned. I was my usual relaxed, not-doing-anything-nefarious, no-sir-not-me self as I made my way to my regular station. "Morning, Kevin," I said, smiling as I held out my ID badge.

He smiled back. "Good morning, Dr. Martin."

I set my handbag on the x-ray belt and strolled to the metal detector arch. My heart pounded like I'd been sprinting for a mile and I focused on just breathing and not looking like I was doing something bad. You're not doing something bad. You're saving the country. Maybe the world. Super Lexie.

As expected with me wearing the belt, the mag arch blared an alarm. And I froze. I just…froze. Kevin looked up from watching the screen as my bag passed through. "Anything unusual on your person that you think might have set off the detector, Dr. Martin?"

Oh yeah, that may be the thumb drive I've inserted into my vagina, a thumb drive that I've cloned to be the same as the thumb drive upstairs that holds some of the most classified intelligence I've ever seen, that I'm going to use to copy the intel and then sneak it out because the director of the agency is a Russian operative. No, wait. It's just a belt.

I frowned, pretending to think it over. I held back a forehead slap, but made myself laugh, inserting an extra dose of hilarious disbelief. I tapped my belt buckle. "I'm so sorry." I forced another laugh. "God, I really need to just stop wearing belts. Or they need to stop putting belt loops on suit pants and skirts."

Kevin stared at it and I could tell that he was going to ask for the belt and then send me through the arch again. No, Kevin, don't do that. "Happens all the time. Gives me something to do," he said jovially. "Now, the folks over at the eastern district office where I used to work? They'd forget phones and personal hard drives in their bags and on their person all the damned time. It was a shit show."

Oh my god. Did he know? No, Paranoia, of course he doesn't know. I laughed again, relieved when I sounded normal. He still hadn't asked for my belt, so I kept talking. "Sounds like it. And we don't talk about those other people at those other offices." I winked, hoping he was in on the joke about the mild rivalry between this central office and the branching agency offices. And finally, finally, I made my legs work and moved away from the arch. If I wasn't near it, hopefully he'd forget that he wanted to send me through again sans belt. "Oh, hey," I said quickly. "I've got a really great fact of the day for you today."

"Yeah? I'm all ears."

"The shortest flight in the world is in Scotland, between two islands, Westray and Papa Westray. About one-point-seven miles and lasts ninety seconds. But the record is fifty-three seconds."

He chuckled. "Must have had a damned good tailwind that day."

"Must have. Wish I had that for my commute."

Kevin laughed as he passed me my handbag from the x-ray belt. "Have a good day, Dr. Martin."

I might, if I don't die of panic-induced cardiac arrest. "You too."

I walked away with my stomach trying to climb up my throat and my lungs resisting air. Thankfully some mindful breathing resolved both issues. Jesus fuck. One hurdle cleared. Now I just had to copy my dad's files, get the Ducky back into its hiding place, and make it back out again without anyone catching me in the act. Easy.

I made it up to my floor uneventfully and after a quick stop in the ladies' room to extract my "tool"—thankfully nothing had gone awry—I went about the rest of my usual workday routine: checking emails, making coffee, eating breakfast, then a cup of tea. Another part of the plan I'd had to factor in was when I was least likely to be interrupted during the act, because that was second on the list of bad stuff that might happen, right underneath "Security catching me with a thumb drive."

Another reason I'd chosen today was that Lennon had weekly briefings with the White House on Thursdays between nine and ten a.m. but they sometimes went until ten thirty if there was a lot of heinous shit going on that Lennon needed to share with the president and his advisors. I wondered how much heinous shit Lennon had been personally responsible for. Some weeks Derek sat in on the briefings, but I couldn't be sure if this was a sit-in week or not. Lennon ate lunch at midday on the dot every day, and always in his office, for about half an hour. Then he was usually in-office or in briefings for the rest of the day, with the exception of the few minutes when he sometimes came to bug me.

I knew the longer I left it, the more it was just going to hang over my head and make me stressed and anxious, so I decided to copy the file as soon as I'd finished my first, calming, cup of tea. My calming cup of tea wasn't as calming as I'd hoped, and if I wasn't so accustomed to overcoming (okay, suppressing) undesirable emotions, I probably would have just fallen into a heap. Full credit to my dad and all undercover intel officers and assets who probably operated at this level, or higher, of stress most of the time.

First, I copied all the folders from the thumb drive to the hard drive of the laptop. Then I held my breath as I inserted the Rubber Ducky into the port. It was so uneventful, I almost cried. Thankfully copying data wasn't arduous, but I still watched the progress of the data's movement from the laptop to the Ducky like it was the most precious thing in the world. I double-checked the folders had copied without issues, and for one of the first times in my life, told the laptop to safely remove the hardware instead of just yanking it from the port. Though I wanted to keep the Ducky on (no, not in) me for safekeeping, I locked it in my desk drawer, not wanting to contaminate the electronics with my stress sweat all day.

I'd just pocketed the drawer key when someone knocked on my office door. Cue aforementioned stress sweat. The sound sent a thrill of panic through me and I quickly pulled out *Moby Dick* and opened it, before double-checking there was nothing on the laptop screen that screamed "I just copied files onto a hacker-thumb drive!" Irrational fear made me clammy and nauseated. On my way to the door, I wiped my damp hands on my pants, then pressed both palms to my belly. Not caught in the act. Just caught after the act.

And of course, of all the people it could be, it was the one I didn't want to see. Lennon stood with his hands clasped in front of him, an impassive expression on his face.

"Hey," I said, noting the anxious breathlessness in my voice. I smiled, inhaling and exhaling through my nose. "What's up?" Shouldn't you be in a briefing with the White House right now instead of coming to see me when I'm doing something I don't want you to see?

"Good morning, Alexandra. May I come in?"

No way. "Of course."

I sat back behind my desk while Lennon took up a position to my right on the long side of the I. I'd never really thought about the change in power dynamic when he was in my office vs. my being in his—logically whoever owned the office should have the upper hand, the alpha position. But now that I was hyperaware of every moment, every expression, every nuance, every tone of voice, I realized that it felt like he had the upper hand everywhere.

He settled himself comfortably and I suppressed a groan. Why, today of all days, could he not just want a quick chat? "Just checking how you're progressing. I'd like to report something to the president soon."

"I know. And I'd like to have something for you to report to the president soon. But I can't produce results out of thin air." I swung back and forth in my chair and looked at my watch. "Speaking of the president, shouldn't you be briefing him now?"

"He's in the air and we had comms issues so cut the briefing short, to be resumed this afternoon."

"Ah." Of all the times for Air Force One comms to crap themselves, now was probably the worst. Okay, maybe in wartime or assassination attempts or something else was worse. But this was pretty bad. "Annoying."

Lennon made a gesture like he didn't really care either way. "I didn't know you followed my schedule so closely, Alexandra." He smiled, and his eyes crinkled with it. But I still didn't know if it was a genuinely amused smile, or if he suspected something. Let's be honest—I didn't trust him at all now I knew who he really was, and every action felt false.

I kept my response light and breezy. "It's my job to have information. You follow the same schedule as the previous director to whom we reported and provided intelligence with which to brief the president." I grinned like the smart-ass I was.

Lennon nodded. "Of course." He stood and rebuttoned his suit jacket, and I rocketed to my feet too. "I'd best be off," he said. "Have a good day, Alexandra."

I responded with an automatic, "You too." *Because once I go public with your real identity, your good days will probably be few and far between.*

I locked the door behind him and sank to the floor, leaning against the doorframe. Holy shit. I pulled my knees into my chest and lowered my forehead to rest against them. Closing my eyes, I deep-breathed out of the stirrings of an anxiety attack. Fuck. I am *not* cut out for espionage.

With no actual work to do, and no access to the Internet, I alternated between lengthy meditations and handwriting a letter to Sophia in case things went south. Then, sweating the whole time, I opened the Project Sputnik folders and looked at the names and photographs of the subjects. I didn't recognize any of the seven other foreign agents Dad had been investigating, and the relief was so strong my adrenaline let go in a rush of shaky limbs. Derek wasn't involved. I wanted to read through those dossiers and my dad's files on Lennon, but was too scared to look deeper into them with so many people around and the possibility of another drop-in by the main subject himself.

I made it to three p.m. before I decided I'd waited long enough. Anxioused long enough was probably more accurate. The security stations would be starting to approach the peak afternoon busy time, which would help in the sense the security staff would be focused on moving a lot of people through. I packed up, grabbed the Ducky from the drawer and popped it in my handbag, then locked the office.

Nobody was in the ladies' room, and after washing and drying my hands and the cup, I shut myself in a stall, reassembled my package and prepared to smuggle it back out again. But my body was *not* having it, despite thinking about the other night with Sophia and my vibrator, and the way she'd had me last night. So…with those images still in my head, I helped myself out for a few minutes until I had enough lubrication to insert the cup. The things I had to do for this job.

Oh, if only I had kids. Wouldn't this make a great story? Sit down, children, and let me tell you about the time I masturbated at work. I washed my hands twice while I checked my appearance to make sure I looked normal, and not like a woman who'd just had to pleasure herself quickly in a work bathroom stall and didn't even get to orgasm.

On the way down to the lobby, I gave myself a pep talk. No reason to worry, it's all going to be fine. I smiled at Warren, Rita, and Grace, who were manning the other security stations, but deliberately made my way to Kevin's. He smiled at me as he moved over to the x-ray scanner. "Did they let you out early for good behavior today?"

I set my bag on the belt. "Doctor's appointment." I walked through the mag arch, which of course blared again because of my belt. Tapping my belt buckle, I added an unnecessary but kind of necessary detail, wrinkling my nose as I clarified, "Annual check of all my lady parts."

He flushed. Good. That little bit of extra information made him uncomfortable (try actually *having* those checks, Kevin) and hopefully he'd want me out of there right away, no lingering, no dawdling, no questioning why I didn't take off the belt that I knew would set off the metal detector. "Right," he mumbled.

I collected my handbag. "Have a good afternoon, I'll see you tomorrow."

"That you will. And good luck with your…appointment."

"Thanks." I smiled cheerily, waved, then walked outside to have a tiny heart attack.

Could have gone better. Could have gone worse. But! I had the files outside the building, and I hadn't puked or peed myself. All in all, a win. Now I just had to get the Ducky home and out of my body safely, and use the information it contained to bring down one of the most dangerous men in the country.

Easy peasy.

CHAPTER TWENTY-TWO

Clearly none of us had this on our bingo cards

When I removed the menstrual cup at home, I discovered again that, thankfully, everything I'd put in it before leaving work came out along with the cup. Mission success. Let's not speak about this again.

I made copies of the Ducky on four separate thumb drives—checking again that the data had copied successfully—before encrypting each copy with a pass phrase and locking the original and two copies in my safe. I was going to take one copy with me to Sophia's and keep it on me as much as was practical before I could deposit it in my lockbox at the bank before work in the morning. I would have liked to sprinkle safe copies around the city in secure locations, but for now, this would have to do until I could get three copies to the three people I trusted the most—Jeffrey, Derek, and Bink—to either keep the data safe, or act upon it.

I could have passed the drive to Jeffrey tomorrow in the work parking lot, but not only would the parking lot cameras see us, but it would necessitate one of us keeping the data in our car all day. Not ideal. Neither was me stressing about it all night and day. So I texted him: *I need a drink. ReBar in 40 mins?*

He answered almost immediately. *See you then.*

I changed out of my work clothes, tossing the damp, sweaty mess into my dry-cleaning pile, then took a hot shower to wash off some of the ickiness I felt. A shower *and* sex, under Sophia's rainforest showerhead would have been idyllic, but I couldn't wait to feel clean. Once I'd packed up tomorrow's work clothes, I texted Sophia. *I'm home but I just need to do something before I come over. Shouldn't be more than two hours. Instead of cooking, I'll stop on the way and get takeout?*

Sounds good. Be safe. I love you.

I sent a heart emoji then collected my bags, my copy of the data and the thumb drive for Jeffrey, and finally—my courage. I was going to need it.

The bar was just a bar. Not secluded. Not big. Not tiny. Just a regular, slightly upscale bar between Sophia's apartment and mine where people gathered for drinks and apps after work. There was nothing about meeting Jeffrey here that would attract any attention. It was the perfect place for a clandestine meeting where I might blow my partner's mind with what I was going to tell him.

I double-checked both thumb drives were still safely inside my zipped inner jacket pocket—yes, I know it's paranoid and irrational, but knowing you have paranoia about inanimate objects spontaneously jumping out of their safe space doesn't stop that paranoia—glanced around the parking lot, then got out of the car.

Jeffrey was already inside, seated at a small table near the back of the bar. He must have been there for a while, if the half-eaten plate of fried pickles and almost-empty glass of dark beer was any indication. As I approached, he finished his beer, then stood and pulled the chair to his right out for me. "Hey, good to see you." He indicated the bar with a tilt of his chin. "What'll you have to drink?"

I wasn't going to have an actual drink, but now I thought about it, a cold beer would really hit the spot. "A Boxcar please."

He patted my shoulder and went up to the bar. I ate one of his fried pickles and looked around the warmly lit room while I tried to suppress my rising unease. Nothing unusual, which I was sure Jeffrey had already clocked. He came back with two beers and set mine down in front of me before taking his seat again. "Post-work drinks like normal people. This is amazing." He raised his fresh beer and when I was too slow to raise mine, he clinked my glass with his. "And I didn't even work today, so it's even better!" He wasn't drunk, but he was definitely relaxed.

"You're not driving?" I asked, trying to walk the edge of concerned friend and hey I'm not your wife, Jeffrey, but I will absolutely take your car keys.

"No. I Ubered. I figured whatever you had to tell me would necessitate time. And if not, I figured I'd hang around and have a few drinks, eat some grease, watch some ball. It's been a while since I did that."

A server appeared with a basket of fries and set it between us. I loved magically appearing fries.

"Help yourself," Jeffrey said, holding the basket out to me.

"I already did, with your pickles." I ate a few fries because I'm not a sociopathic fries hater. "But I'm going to Sophia's for dinner after this."

"And you decided to fit in a social event with me. I'm flattered." Jeffrey leaned his elbows on the table. "Did you miss me today?"

"I did. What'd you get up to?"

He shrugged. "Not much. Took Benjamin for a walk. Watched a movie. Realized how much I like not working through the week. How was your day?"

I turned my glass around and around on the table, then grabbed a coaster to blot up the condensation. "Stressful." I took a big mouthful of beer, enjoying the cool crispness of the lager. "Um. Hmm. I, uh…" Shrugging, I just let my inability to formulate an actual response speak to how my day was.

"Was so stressful you forgot how to speak?" he finished for me, teasingly.

"Something like that." Okay, just start talking and it'll come out eventually. "A few nights ago, I figured out the pass phrase."

"That's amazing!" He held up his hand for a high-five, and I obliged. "Go, teamwork." In the next second, Jeffrey's face fell. "So we're all done with this assignment then?"

I exhaled noisily. "Almost. Sorry, it's not quite Tuscan villa time yet."

He brightened. "Oh. Good. I mean, Dominique and I want the villa year, but I'm also enjoying this assignment." After a long swallow of beer, he asked, "So, are you going to tell me how you did it? Did you sneak Sophia in under your jacket?"

The image made me laugh and settled some of the tension tightening my muscles. "Not quite. I realized we were working with the wrong language. It *was* an anagram, but it was in French."

"French? Fuck me. Well I would have been completely useless. How'd you figure out it was French?"

"Don't laugh. I had a dream in the early hours of Monday morning. My dad and I were talking in a bunch of different languages and I woke up freaked out because it turned nightmarish. Anyway, I was trying to fall back to sleep and I was in that weird space right before you're out, you know, when your brain's all loose and you're thinking weird disjointed thoughts. And it just hit me that it wasn't English. My dad loved French, we used to converse in it a lot. So I went straight to the office and sat with it for a while until it hit me."

"I'm dying to know what it was."

"A ten-word sentence, leading me to the answer, which was the pass phrase. Once I saw it, it was obvious what he meant, but it wouldn't have meant anything to anyone except me. And he called me 'Little Mouse' in French, so I knew I had it right." I drank deeply to push away the emotion that still welled up when I thought about it. My parents loved me, even if I hadn't been able to quite see it until now.

"Well, I'm impressed." He held up his beer and I touched my glass to his. "So, what's still left to do? Now are we working with the data you unlocked?" I loved that there was no mention of the fact I hadn't told him the moment I'd unlocked it, that he just accepted I knew what I was doing.

"No." I only just held in the nervous laugh that was threatening to spill out. "I didn't think it was relevant to tell you when we first started, but Lennon was explicit that when I figured out my dad's pass phrase, I wasn't to look at whatever was on the drive. But when I entered the pass phrase, the contents were just…there. It's a bunch of folders. *But* there was another folder in there, labeled by my dad in such a way that got my attention."

"Go on," Jeffrey said slowly. His posture or tone hadn't shifted, and yet he suddenly seemed more alert.

"It was also pass phrase-protected and the prompt was, again, something only I would know, and therefore how to access." I drank a quick mouthful of beer, smothering my burp.

Jeffrey's eyebrows shot up then came down so quickly it was almost comical. "And?"

"I accessed it. And it turns out my dad was an intelligence ninja." I fiddled nervously with the edge of the fries basket. Leaning closer, I lowered my voice, though there was surely nobody here who even knew us, let alone what we were talking about. "He discovered Lennon is sideways." As in corrupt, foreign operative, working for the enemy etcetera.

Jeffrey's expression didn't change. "Certainty?"

"I still haven't examined everything, but from what I saw? Beyond doubt." The intelligence analyst in me shuddered at the use of the expression "beyond doubt," but this was one thing I didn't want to fuck around with by calling it "probable." Lennon was a Russian operative operating in the USA. Simple as that. After a quick check that nobody was paying attention, I extracted one of the thumb drives from my zippered pocket. I tapped Jeffrey's knee under the table and when I felt his hand touch mine, I slipped the drive into his palm.

"Well. That's unfortunate," he said drolly as he closed his fingers around the drive.

I almost laughed at his dramatic understatement. And then almost applauded at the deft way he maneuvered the drive into his pocket. If I wasn't watching him so closely, I would have never realized he'd just done it. "Just a little, yeah."

He tipped his glass toward me in salute. "I don't even want to know how you got this. Actually, yes, I do. I *really* do. But not here."

I gave him a summary. "It took a call to a cyber expert, a bunch of failed ideas, something I don't want to talk about, and a whole lot of forcibly suppressing my panic."

He laughed. "They should get you in to teach a class on espionage. Just don't tell them what you were doing sneaking thumb drives in and out of the building."

"Maybe they should," I agreed. I felt a small tinge of guilt at what I was going to reveal, but given Jeffrey already knew about Halcyon, and this new information was essential to him understanding just how fucked the situation was, I just told him. "There's more." No deep breath, no preparing myself, I just said it. "Lennon is also the head of Halcyon Division. And Halcyon is far more powerful and involved with the government than I think Lennon let on to you. Think, 'goodbye Berenson' powerful."

"Oh god." He didn't need to say anything more, his expression conveyed everything. It was one of the few times I'd seen him shocked or lost for words. But if there was ever a time to be shocked, the moment you found out the man in charge of the country's most powerful organization *and* its main intelligence agency was a Russian spy was probably a good time.

"Yeah."

After a frantic mouthful of his beer, Jeffrey asked, "How far back does this go? When did your dad realize? They were friends, right?"

"They were friends"—I air-quoted—"but not *friends*. Dad was operating under a keep-your-enemies close mantra, and I don't know about Lennon's real feelings on their friendship. But talking with him these past few weeks, I don't think he cared about my dad at all, maybe didn't even like him. But I definitely remember Lennon from my childhood, it seemed like whenever we came back to the States, he'd come around to see my dad, until maybe the midnineties? Dad started looking into him in 1980. I know Halcyon was formed in 1962, and Lennon took over as its head in 2001. So I think it's safe to say he's been compromised this entire time." Was it also possible that Halcyon had been compromised since its inception? That thought was almost too horrific to contemplate.

"I think that's a safe assumption." He gestured at the food, as if reminding me that leaving it almost untouched seemed suspicious. Or maybe he thought I looked pale and in need of fried goodness.

I picked at a few more fries, chewing thoughtfully while Jeffrey demolished a pickle. After wiping my fingertips on a paper napkin, I leaned in. "I'm going to speculate about what happened." At his expression, I laughed. "I know, the horror. So, I've been wondering. My dad obviously suspected Lennon for decades. These files go back to almost the beginning of his career. So why not do anything?" It was a rhetorical question—I knew Dad needed more to take up the chain if he wanted anything more done than watch and wait—but I wanted to hear Jeffrey's take.

"Best guess? He didn't have the concrete intelligence he needed. So he kept digging until he did. And maybe he didn't know who to trust up the chain."

"Mm. That's my best guess too. Jeffrey, you're not going to believe the amount of work he put into this. I've only skimmed through part of it, but it's incredible. The problem my dad had wasn't lack of access or information. It's that Lennon's smart and canny, which I suppose is part of the job description. You can see how my father gets so close, constantly, but just can't quite nail down what he needs. But he found that concrete evidence a few weeks before his death, and he'd drafted a brief for the head of the agency and the president. And then a few days before that scheduled meeting, he died."

"So it really looks like someone might have helped him to dead." He frowned, shook his head. "Sorry, stupid wording. Very little shocks me, Lexie, but you've managed to shock me so much I've forgotten how to formulate sentences."

"Don't blame me," I said. "*I* didn't shock you, the news I brought you did. And yes, that's exactly what it looks like. I also think he refused to reveal his suspicions to anyone, even his handler, because he was afraid of what would happen when he did." I gripped the glass hard with both hands. "And it did happen. I'm sure Lennon murdered my parents."

Jeffrey's expression softened. Instead of telling me I was jumping to conclusions and I needed to dial it back, he reached over and took my hand. "If he did, then I'm so sorry."

I shrugged. "They're still dead, so how they died doesn't really matter." I shook my head. "Wait. No, it does matter. If they weren't murdered then they'd still be alive." I rubbed both hands over my face. "Argh. This is fucking with my head."

"Do you need to take a step back?"

I looked up, aghast. "God no. I need to charge forward. I'm still just…I'm confused. Why did Dad give me the key to unlocking it all? And he didn't give it to me recently—the first book was twenty-two years ago. This started over forty years ago. Was he worried someone was going to murder him over this? If not Lennon, then someone else in these dossiers who discovered that he knew about them. Maybe there's more than one Lennon…"

"I think it's entirely possible. Once someone goes through the other folders in detail, we'll know for sure. But that would be my fear if I were doing that work. People with big secrets can do incredible things, crazy things, immoral things, to keep those secrets. Maybe your dad gave you the key because he wanted you to have a choice he felt he didn't have—to unlock the intelligence or leave it buried and never read."

"But do I have a choice? Really? Dad would have known I'd never just ignore this. Even if he'd given it to me himself, hard drive and pass phrase, I would have looked into it right away. It's one fat man or a whole station of people. I have to do it. It's been drilled into me my entire career, really. Didn't you ask me while we were overseas why they keep asking me that trolley question every psych eval? Maybe this is why. Because someone knew I would have to make a choice like this, that I would have to put myself in front of the trolley to save everyone. They've been hammering it into my subconscious for fifteen years."

"Okay. So what's our move?"

I loved that he said *our*, that I wasn't doing this alone. "I don't know. But I can't stall Lennon forever. He knows I'm close to figuring out what the pass phrase is." Curse those status updates. "I can't string this out for too long, and I don't want to. It's too fucking stressful. So…I need to get a briefing with the president. Or…try to." I shuddered. "Won't that be fun."

"I assume Derek is clean? Can he brief him? The president might be more amenable if it's someone higher up the hierarchy."

"He is and he could. But I'd rather it be me. This is my thing. And it'll be nice to rub this in the president's face, that I found out yet another monumental thing and I deserve a Presidential Medal or something."

"Are you sure the president can be trusted? I mean, his vice president was working with Russia. How do we know the president isn't compromised as well, either the same way Berenson was, or"—he looked utterly disgusted—"the way Lennon is."

If our president was a Russian operative as well, I was just going to move to the moon and forget all about this shit show. "I honestly don't know. I suppose I could demand that others be present—advisors, Derek, you, maybe some high-up military intelligence officers? If I have credible witnesses when I present this evidence then he can't bury it."

"That's a good point," he said. "Whether or not he agrees to allowing others into a briefing is another matter."

"The president rarely briefs security matters in a vacuum, one-on-one. He always has advisors there, probably because he's too fucking dumb to understand briefs and needs someone to explain them. And I really think he's not going to want to be briefed by just me, so I'll have Derek, and you if you're allowed." I frowned, thinking. "He had a briefing scheduled with my father in July 2021. And Dad was obviously someone of note within the agency, which means, theoretically, that the president would be inclined to take what he said seriously. If I tell him this relates to what my father was bringing to him, then it might make him more amenable. Or it might have no effect at all and I'm going to have to beg and grovel to get an audience with him."

If he refused to see me, then I'd have Derek run the briefing—my pride wasn't important here. And Derek could put me on the list as his advisor. There were ways and means, but I hoped I wouldn't have to resort to subterfuge and shitfuckery to arrange a meeting with the president to tell him the very fabric of our national security was in grave danger.

Jeffrey nodded. "Okay. Do it. Get it set up. I'll go through all of this as soon as I get home, and I'll be ready for any questions that might be asked about our work." At my eyebrows-raised look, he held up both hands. "I've only had one and three-quarter beers, Lexie. I'm perfectly capable of doing my job." He smiled widely. "Even after I finish this second beer."

"What about your drinks and food and sports evening at the bar?"

He gave me an *are you kidding me* look. Yeah, it was a dumb question, but he still answered. "I can do that any old day. This is time-sensitive. A rapidly ticking clock."

"And you have a secure locat—"

"Of course I do," he reassured me. "Secure location and device."

I blew out a noisy breath. "Okay, good. Oh, before I forget…" I lowered my voice and pointed to his pocket. "Purple monkey space helicopter. Capitalize the first letters."

He laughed. "Got it."

"I guess I'll go over it in detail tonight if I can, but I need to spend time with Sophia." I could just work on it while she was watching television or something, except… "Shit, I didn't bring any devices with me, and I can't use her laptop. God knows what security holes she has wide open on it. Okay. I'll be in late tomorrow. Or maybe I'll take a sick day. I don't know."

I'd go home tomorrow morning and spend a few hours looking through the files on a secure offline machine, the way Jeffrey would tonight. Unfortunately, every room in my apartment had windows—not secure. But my closet could double as a SCIF if I closed the door to keep anyone from seeing inside. Lennon would have no idea that I'd broken the pass phrase and was looking at Dad's files.

He nodded calmly. "Contact me and let me know when you're headed to the office. Just in case there's something we need to discuss beforehand."

"Sounds good." I finished my beer and nabbed a few more fries. "Okay, I need to get out of here before Sophia starts worrying."

Jeffrey grinned. And kept grinning when I stared at him, waiting for him to spill what had him looking like a kid who just got an allowance increase.

"What?"

"Nothing. Just that I love being right."

"What are you right about specifically this time?"

His eyes crinkled. "You. Saving the world. I knew you were going to do something amazing. And you are."

I looked down into my empty beer glass, both surprised and unsurprised by the insistent press of tears. It'd been a high-octane few days, and I'd been smothering a whole rainbow of feelings. "Thanks, cheerleader." After a deep breath, I asked a question I didn't really want to have to ask. "Will you take care of Sophia? If something happens, just…keep an eye on her. Keep her safe."

"Of course," he said, not hesitating for even a microsecond.

I had to swallow my upset at even needing to ask that of him. "Thank you."

"And if she needs anything, even if you're around but maybe incommunicado, for whatever reason, she can come to me and I'll protect her, and her family, to the best of my ability."

"You're a good man, Jeffrey Burton," I said, my voice tight with emotion.

He smiled beatifically. "I know."

I gripped his hand hard, squeezing. There were no words to express gratitude as monumental as I felt for him putting himself in possible danger to protect the woman I loved.

"You know…my dad used to tell me that courage isn't the absence of fear. It's knowing fear, but having the strength to face it." I bit my lower lip. "It seems pretty apt now, doesn't it? Because I'm pretty fucking terrified."

His expression softened when he repeated, "I know. But it'll be okay. I'm here. Derek's here. And I know Sophia is here too. Between all of us, we'll make sure everything is okay."

Sophia… I had to get home to her.

Jeffrey reassured me that he was going to call Dominique for a ride as soon as he finished his beer and the remaining apps. I hugged him bye, clinging tightly. It was still so strange that the man who started out as an antagonist was now one of my most trusted friends.

Once I was sure I had my things, and the other thumb drive copy was still zipped inside my pocket, I said, "I'll let you know if I'm coming in tomorrow. If you need to talk to me about this, let's not do it inside the office. Just in case."

"Good plan," he agreed. "Now drive carefully. Don't die in a crash now and leave me to deal with this on my own."

"Good to know your priorities are in place. I will," I promised.

And I did drive carefully. Like a grandma, all the way to the Thai takeout place, and then to Sophia's.

After a day running on adrenaline, I felt a surge of relief when I opened Sophia's door and found her sitting at her breakfast bar, drinking a glass of wine and reading on her phone. She hopped down from her stool and came over as I was securing her door. "Hi," she murmured, stretching on tiptoes to kiss me.

"Hi." I stole another kiss, lingering just enough to soothe down my roller-coaster emotions. "Sorry I'm late."

"No worries." She took the takeout bags from me and set them on the table so I could divest myself of my jacket, handbag, and overnight bag. "Did you do your thing at work today?" she asked casually as she opened the cutlery drawer.

"I did, yes. All fine." Copied highly sensitive information. Snuck it out. Didn't get caught. That's the very definition of "fine" isn't it?

Her eyes softened. As she passed by to set the table, she kissed me, pausing to say, "I'm glad."

"Me too. But"—I blew a noisy raspberry—"I now know I'm really not cut out for the stress of super high-stakes things. Just…medium high-stakes stress like what happened in Florida." I held up my arm to show her the fresh sweat under my armpits. "I've been stress-sweating *all* day. I'm still sweating, even though I took a shower at home and I was in a cool place before I came here. My dry-cleaner is going to think I ran a marathon in my work blouse. I haven't stress-sweated this much since Florida. Not even when I was overseas working with constant low-level work and personal stress."

She paused pulling food from the takeout bags. "You were stressed in Florida?"

"Beyond."

Sophia smiled, her expression going faraway for a moment before she seemed to return to the present. "Well, you hid it very well."

I'd hidden a lot of things. "Didn't want you to worry that something was going on." I winked and was relieved that she laughed in response.

"I appreciate that. Thank you, hon." She folded the reusable paper bags. "Do you want a drink? Beer or wine?"

"Just a small glass of wine, thanks. I had a beer at the bar." Frowning, I thought about it. "Actually, no, I'll stick with beer. No wine. Just a beer. Thanks. And sorry, I'm a little broken up, all over the place at the moment."

Sophia came over to me. She took my hand, twining our fingers together. "Then let me help you get put back together."

CHAPTER TWENTY-THREE

The Three Musketeers

I woke up on Sophia's couch, and after a brief moment of panic about not being in a bed I recognized, realized where I was. I wasn't in custody. I was free, and with my girlfriend. Kind of. She'd obviously left me to go sleep in her bed, but I'd been covered in a blanket and I fought with it until I managed to free myself. It took a minute or two for my eyes to adjust, and I noted the time on the oven. 2:17 a.m. God. I didn't even remember lying down.

After a quick bathroom stop, I padded quietly into her room and stood by the bed for a moment, just looking at her. She hadn't closed her curtains fully, and the moon shared more than enough light for me to see her. Sophia lay on her stomach, sprawled as usual across the mattress. Some of her dark, wavy hair had come loose from its ponytail and spilled over her shoulders. In repose, she lost some of the intensity she had when awake. Maybe intensity wasn't the right word. It was just that she was always so in tune with me, so focused, so willing to share, that sometimes it felt like intensity. It felt like love.

I took my watch off and set it on the bedside table with my phone, then pulled the curtains together. Sophia stirred when I eased myself into bed, and sleepily snuggled into me. "What time is it?" she mumbled.

I covered us both with the duvet. "Almost two thirty."

She burrowed back under the covers, squirming until her calf rested between both of mine. "Sorry," she said, yawning halfway through the word. "I wanted you to come to bed, but you looked so exhausted so I left you there."

"Thanks." I kissed her temple, then closed my eyes and tried to sleep. It didn't come easily. All I could think about was how in a few hours, I had to tell Derek that the man he'd known for longer than me was a traitorous, disloyal fraud.

My alarm was still twenty minutes away when I suddenly awoke. I lay still, my body almost indistinguishable from Sophia's, and let myself feel heavy against the mattress. I hadn't woken because of a nightmare, or panic, and I let myself enjoy the sensation of being able to just lie here with Sophia, not needing to spring from bed to *do* something. I thought about my father's note in the folder he'd left for me and reached for my watch on the bedside table, turning it over. Tilting the band, I could see the engraving in the dawn light.

Little Mouse.

Maybe I had been unexpected, or even a mistake. But my parents wanted me. My father had even fought with Lennon about it. My parents loved me the best way they knew how. And maybe their version of love was trying to protect me. Now it was up to me to protect myself, and the woman I loved.

Derek was an even earlier riser than I was, so I sent him a text knowing I wouldn't wake him or his wife, Roberta. *Need to talk to you this morning, outside of work.* I named a café that was easy to access for both of us, and received *I can be there in 30min.* in response. I loved that I didn't have to explain myself, or beg—he knew if I was asking for something then it was important enough for him to come to the party.

I disengaged myself from Sophia's slumbering limbs, rolled out of bed and slunk quietly into the master bathroom. I wasn't going to have time for yoga or meditation before going out into the world to meet Derek this morning, and the way it was going, I probably wouldn't get to work out either, unless I broke up my reading with a run. Yes, I was going to do that, because the thought of sitting in my walk-in closet for a whole day reading Dad's files made my body scream. I added "Fucking up my morning routines" to the list of reasons why I would be glad to have this debacle in my rearview mirror. I mean, yeah, sure, it wasn't up there with "Removing a Russian operative from positions of power" but it was still important in *my* life.

Sophia "Not a Morning Person" Flores still hadn't stirred by the time I'd showered. Nor did she stir when I dressed. I slowly packed up my things and only once I was ready to go, did I wake her. It took a couple of shakes before she groggily acquiesced. Blinking slowly, Sophia smiled lazily as she stared up at me. "You going to work early?"

I bent down to kiss her. "I have an early meeting. I'm probably not going to work today, so you can reach me on my cell. But I'll let you know if I go in."

"Mmkay. Let me know what we're doing tonight."

"I will."

She reached up and pushed some hair away from my face, her light fingertips brushing over my skin. "Be safe."

"I promise."

We said our goodbyes and our I love yous, and I left her to go try to put one more piece of this mess in order.

When I arrived during the prework rush, Derek was already at the café, seated at a table for two in the corner, drinking coffee. He didn't get up when I came over, but he did smile as he asked, "What's up, Martin?"

"I need some air," I said pointedly.

"Then I guess it's a good thing I got this coffee to go." He followed me outside, and fell in step with me as I made my way along the sidewalk.

We dodged joggers and people on their way to work, and it was only when we'd walked for a few minutes that either of us spoke. "I'm assuming you don't want ears?" he said.

"You assume correctly." There was no good way to say it, no easy way, so I just came right out with it. "I figured out the pass phrase, and among the folders containing information about foreign operatives Dad was investigating, he left another folder just for me. In it is incontrovertible proof that Lennon is a Russian operative, and he's been operating as such in this country since at least 1980, probably earlier."

Derek's step faltered, and when I looked over to check if he needed steadying, he looked utterly stricken. "Fuck," he breathed. "You're sure?"

"That's what incontrovertible means, so yes. I'm sure."

"Okay, I"—he shook his head—"I have never been this shocked before. Ever. In my life. We need a plan. What's the plan? Is this information safe?" He shook his head again. "No, of course it isn't.

Okay, I'll think of something. I might have to override some protocols, but—"

I interrupted his rambling to assure him, "It's safe. I have copies. Jeffrey has his, and there's one for you. I have it with me now. They're all pass phrase-protected, with a different pass phrase to the original." The thumb drive would have to stay in his car for the day, unless he sped home to secure it, but I still considered cars in our parking lots at work more secure than the average home. "And I'm sending one to Bink, which is the safest place I know. But I'm not sure they should have the pass phrase."

"Why not?"

"They haven't been read in to this program." It did seem pedantic to be following protocol in the middle of a crisis, but what was it Lennon said when I'd told him I was going to use Bink, and been shot down? *Extreme is what keeps us safe.* None of this felt the slightest bit safe. But hell, Derek hadn't been read in either. Bink had clearance to work with Top Secret programs and things none of us knew about. I could trust them if everything went pear-shaped.

"If you send it to Bink for secure storage, they can contact Burton or me for the pass phrase." He stared at me. "You *will* give the pass phrase to us, yes? Otherwise this drive is as useful as a screen door on a submarine."

"Of course I'll give it to you." I repeated the pass phrase I'd put on these copied drives, and he nodded as he committed it to memory. "Also, I need you to set up an urgent briefing with the president. Yesterday. I've already been sitting on this for a few days while I worked out how to proceed with securing the data, and Lennon is starting to get pushy about results."

"I'll do that." Derek pulled me to a stop next to a florist that was just starting to put out the day's flowers. "You should have come straight to me."

"I didn't know if I could trust you," I said honestly. "No offense."

"A little taken. But I understand."

"I'm sorry," I said, genuinely feeling bad for suspecting he could be part of Lennon's Little Russian Circle. "But my priority was the information. Once I knew it was safe, *then* I could share."

"Do we need to review security procedures?"

I grinned. "I don't think so. The laptop had a USB port so they could bring my dad's data over on a cloned drive for me to work with. They disabled access to any drive except that original clone, which in theory is a perfectly acceptable security measure. But Bink helped me get around that. Then I just had to get a drive in to copy the data, and out again."

He looked intrigued and concerned in equal measures. "How'd you do it?"

"A thumb drive in a place I don't want to talk about."

Derek blushed. Then he cleared his throat. Then he cleared it again. And then thankfully, we said no more about it. "Goddamn, Martin. I don't know how you've done something like this again, but good work. You might have just exposed the greatest security breach in US history, no exaggeration."

"Can I have a pay raise?" I asked, which was my usual teasing response whenever he complimented me on doing a good job.

For once, he didn't come back with his usual "That's above my pay grade." Instead, he assured me, "I'll see what I can do."

"Thanks. And it wasn't me. Full credit to my dad. God I wish he'd lived long enough to see the result of all his hard work."

"I know it's a terrible cliché, and I wouldn't presume to put words into your father's mouth, but I think he would be so so proud of you. Any father would be. I know I'm so proud of you."

"I hope so. And thanks," I added hoarsely.

"So what now? I'll go through the files, set up the briefing with the president, and then we go from there?"

"Yep. And until then, we all go to work and act like the leader of the two most influential intelligence organizations in the country isn't a Russian operative…"

* * *

I spent the rest of my morning at home, hidden in my closet (no jokes, please), reading the rest of Dad's Lennon dossier and sketching out a brief for the president that I'd give to him along with my father's draft. I discovered "Frost" was actually Lennon's wife, an American intelligence officer who obviously suspected her husband wasn't as he seemed. She had been passing along information to Dad. I had an enormous amount of respect for a woman who'd discovered who her husband truly was and yet remained married so she could continue to funnel information about him.

I had to send Bink their copy of the data and deposit a copy in my bank lockbox, and thought I should make an appearance in the office to avert any suspicions Lennon might have, so I decided to go in to work for the afternoon. Maybe I could pester Derek into speeding things along with the president.

On my way in, I stopped at the bank then dropped off the thumb drive to be couriered to Bink. The package contained instructions to hide the drive on Mars or somewhere equally as secure for safekeeping, and to look for an email telling them what to do with it.

I'd barely had time to say hi to Jeffrey and flip the kettle on when Derek knocked on the door of our office. He passed me a note that said simply *The three of us need to talk tonight.*

Jeffrey pointed to his chest, then wrote his address on the note. Derek nodded, held up six fingers, then pocketed the note. Okay, so we were meeting at Jeffrey's house at six p.m. Plenty of time for me to have a quick bite to eat so I wasn't running a brainstorming brain on empty, then get to his place—especially if I dipped out of work at four p.m. like I usually did. God it was going to be so hard to go back to regular working hours when this was all done.

I pretended to put something in my mouth and chew it, pointedly looking at Derek with an eyebrow raised.

He rolled his eyes at me, and mimed flushing a toilet. Good enough.

Not good enough was the fact Derek suspected someone might be listening. I didn't really think the office was visually or audibly bugged, because Lennon would be all up in my face about lying to him, but caution's good, I suppose.

"So how's it coming along?" Derek asked casually.

"I think we've made some good progress," I answered. "It's right at our fingertips, I think. Hopefully it'll reveal itself next week."

"Excellent," he said. "Well, I suppose I'll let you get back to it."

"Have a good weekend."

Derek nodded, gave us a thumbs-up, then left us alone to pretend to work.

Jeffrey and I left a little before four p.m. and he waited until we were in the first parking lot before he spoke. "I guess it's on like Donkey Kong."

"I guess so," I agreed, hating the simultaneous anxiety and excitement that surged through me. "You still have your copy?"

"Nah, I tossed it out."

I bumped him with my shoulder. "Just for that, you're not getting your name on the brief for the president."

"Oh you tease. What about my accolades?" He grinned down at me. "I'll be good, pinkie promise."

"Did you read through the files last night?"

"I did. Excellent work, undisputable. Your dad was an amazing man, Lexie."

I'd had that same thought while I'd been reading this morning. "Yeah. I'm pretty proud of him."

"Why don't you bring Sophia with you tonight, if she's amenable? I'll ask Dominique to pop out for a few hours. They can go out for Friday dinner and drinks, which is far nicer than me just kicking my wife out so we can discuss the fate of the country."

He delivered the last part so dryly that I had to laugh. "Sounds like a great idea. I'm sure Sophia will be into it. Just let me go collect her, or let her know I have to go out, and then I'll come around."

"Perfect."

Sophia was very into it, and after she'd changed to go out and packed a bag to stay the night at mine, we were off to Jeffrey's. His place really was the best meeting spot to discuss our next moves, because he assured us nobody knew where he lived and also he had the tools to ensure nobody would be listening. Ex-Special Ops guys are pretty cool.

Derek was already there when Sophia and I arrived, playing with Jeffrey's dog. Dominique greeted me enthusiastically, and confirmed that pizza would arrive any moment. She tucked her arm into Sophia's and they left in an Uber for their impromptu girls' night, but not before we'd been told that we shouldn't expect them back for at least a few hours, and we probably shouldn't expect them back sober.

Jeffrey gestured for us to follow him, and after opening a door at the end of the hall, ushered us into his large office.

"This your man cave?" I asked.

"Yup," he confirmed. "Gotta have a cozy place to plot the downfall of Russian spies." He pointed to the leather seats and told us to get comfortable while he fetched drinks. He came back with a beer for Derek and him and a glass of wine for me, then left again almost immediately to answer the door. Benjamin followed him back into the office and sat expectantly by Jeffrey's desk, clearly hoping to share dinner with us.

Jeffrey flipped the lid on a vegetarian pizza, and passed out plates and paper napkins. Once we'd eaten—including Benjamin, who got some crust for doing a trick—we all settled into one of the buttery-soft brown leather library chairs to finish talking things over.

Derek swigged from his beer bottle. "How're you holding up, Martin?"

"By a thread," I admitted.

"A strong one," he said, smiling fondly. "So I've scheduled a briefing with the president for first thing Monday morning. It's the earliest he could meet with us, because he's in Australia until Sunday night."

The earliest wasn't early enough for my liking, but I had to take what I could get. I'd already spent a week sitting on this secret, what was another few days of the same in the scheme of things? "And you'll be there with me?" I asked Derek.

"Both Burton and I will," he confirmed.

"Okay," I breathed. I wasn't nervous about briefing the president. But I was nervous about his reaction. Not to mention his animosity toward me. Me telling him that he'd nominated a Russian operative to head up the agency—a.k.a you fucked up, Mr. President—probably wasn't going to go down too well. "And you've insisted on some aides and military and intelligence advisors being present? We need witnesses so the president can't bury this if he's involved."

"Yes, I know and yes, I've asked for aides and advisors. We went through the plan, remember?"

"Did you tell him that this relates to the director, and he mustn't be brought in on the briefing or tipped off?"

Derek was very gracious about me questioning him like it was his first day on the job. "Of course," he soothed me, resting a hand on my shoulder. "Relax, take a deep breath. It's going to be fine. We'll be right there with you."

I did as instructed and felt marginally better for it.

"We'll be like the Three Musketeers!" Jeffrey exclaimed.

"*Unus pro omnibus, omnes pro uno*," I murmured. At their raised eyebrows, I shrugged, and translated the Latin. "One for all, all for one. Close enough."

We sat quietly for a minute, slowly lowering the levels in our respective drinks. Shaking his head, Jeffrey said, "You know, I just keep thinking about this whole situation, and the level of fucked-up that this is has no measurement. It's beyond comprehension." He silently raised his beer bottle in my direction and, with a smile, drank deeply.

Derek agreed, "This is going to blow up the Intelligence Community."

I nodded. "Yeah. But I still have so many questions, and no answers. If Halcyon leaked the Berenson Russia connection, why? It makes no sense."

Jeffrey set his beer down, leaning forward with his elbows on his knees. "It does if you look at it not from the angle of Halcyon, but *Lennon*."

A lightbulb winked on in my brain. "Right. Because exposing ex-Vice President Berenson as being aligned with Russia shifts blame and suspicion from Lennon. So I have to assume that Berenson knew or suspected who Lennon was?"

"That's my theory," Derek said. "Maybe Berenson threatened to expose Halcyon because of his own Russian connection. Maybe Lennon wanted Berenson gone in case he leaked who he was. That is if Berenson even knew about Lennon. Maybe he was just a sloppy operator that put what might be a large cell in jeopardy."

"Maybe…" I mused. "Or maybe Berenson had no idea and Lennon's spent his whole life tying up loose ends so they didn't trip him." Whatever the reason, I was sure we'd have answers soon enough.

Just before nine p.m., Sophia and Dominique came back, and as they'd promised—they weren't exactly sober. Derek had left not long before that, promising he was going to read through the files again and start working on his own framework for the presidential briefing. Jeffrey had chimed in that he was going to do the same. What a fun weekend we were all in for.

Dominique hugged me gleefully, and wished me good night before turning to Sophia to hug her too. Smiling, I turned to Jeffrey. "See you Monday," I said, hugging him tightly. "Let me know if you need anything from me."

"Will do." He lowered his voice. "Don't forget—you have power. Don't be afraid to use it." Then he raised his voice to normal levels to tell me to, "Drive home safely."

"I will," I promised him.

Sophia wasn't falling-down, pass-out drunk, but she *was* relaxed, talkative, and very affectionate. After more effusive goodbye hugs—Dominique had clearly had as good a time as Sophia—I wrapped an arm around her waist and guided her out to the car.

After checking she'd belted herself in properly, I started the ignition. "Did you have a good time?"

"I did," she said brightly. "I'm so glad you introduced me to Dom. It's nice to make new friends. I love mine, but different circles of friends are really nice."

"That they are."

"Did you guys figure out your thing?"

"Some of it, yeah." I exhaled loudly. "I have a briefing with the president next week, so hopefully that'll be the end of all this."

She blew a loud raspberry. "Gross. I'll have a bath full of Lysol ready when you come home."

Laughing, I pulled out, and drove us back to my place.

Sophia sobered up a little on the drive and after downing a few glasses of water, lost the stumbly, fumbly portion of her inebriation. I waited on the couch while she finished hydrating. She joined me, plonking down heavily. Sophia slipped her hand behind my neck, massaging the tense muscle, running her fingertips through my hair. "Do you want to talk about it?"

I tilted my head back and to the side, effectively trapping that massaging hand in place to keep working its magic. "So much. But… you know." I'd already shared as much as I could, in as roundabout way as possible.

"Yeah, I do."

"This helps, you know."

"I know." Sophia leaned over and kissed my temple, lingering for a moment before her lips moved to my cheekbone, then my jaw, then my ear. She shifted slightly until she straddled me, and I cupped her ass, pulling her closer.

I shuddered, and tilted my head back to expose my neck to her wandering mouth. That wandering mouth journeyed down my neck as Sophia cupped my breasts, squeezing gently in time with the kisses that were now approaching my collarbone. She was still tipsy, which meant she was really horny, made more evident by the fact she was grinding against me. "I want to go down on you," she said, her voice rough with desire.

"Well I'm not going to stop you."

Grinning, she slid off the couch and knelt between my spread legs. She unbuttoned my pants, and slid the fly down, but didn't shift the fabric at all. Instead, she pushed my top up and began to lick and suck my hipbones, which had me pressing my hips up, begging her to pay attention to parts of my body that were starting to notice things were happening.

A most unwelcome knock on the door made her pause, and for a moment I considered just ignoring it. Nobody would come to my place except for Jeffrey or Derek, or a food delivery which we didn't have incoming. When I didn't get up, Sophia continued her progress downward and I let my head fall back against the couch.

The person knocked again. A little louder this time. "Fuck," I hissed. "Sorry, baby, probably someone ordered food and they've fucked up the apartment. Give me one sec to get rid of them and I'll be back."

She sat heavily on the floor, groaning in frustration not pleasure. I bent down and kissed her apologetically, then strode to the door, fastening my pants, straightening my clothing, and smoothing my hair. I was going to give the delivery person a snarky monologue about the correct thing to do when nobody answered the door for a wrong delivery because their girlfriend was thirty seconds away from starting oral sex.

The peep through my peephole made my stomach drop. Not food at the wrong door. Not Jeffrey. Not Derek.

Lennon.

I swallowed hard, my arousal dissipating like fog burned off by the sun. I couldn't just back away and ignore him. He would have seen the flash as I'd looked through the peephole, and even without it, I was sure he knew I was here. Lennon didn't do anything wasteful. Hell, he would know I was here with Sophia even without the damned peephole because knowing was his job. I glanced back at Sophia to check she was decent, sure my emotion was plastered all over my face, before turning back to the door.

Act normal, everything's totally fine, the guy you've trusted for fifteen years is just a foreign operative working to undermine the government and you're still trying to figure out how to deal with that. After a deep breath, I put on my most neutral, pretend-your-boss-isn't-a-Russian-spy face, and opened the door to him.

Lennon smiled, *seeming* totally relaxed, though he couldn't quite mask the tension around his eyes. "Hello, Alexandra."

CHAPTER TWENTY-FOUR

Time to stop the trolley; wish me luck

"Hi. This is a surprise." Ten points for steady, calm voice. No stress here, nope. "You've never been here before." That I knew of, anyway. For all I knew he could have been in here snooping around my shit whenever I was out.

"No," he agreed. "But I wanted to talk face-to-face and thought it about time I visited your apartment. I apologize for the late hour, but this is important."

I kept my face and body neutral. Maybe if I didn't answer, he'd just…evaporate?

"May I come in?" Lennon asked when I said nothing, nor made any movement like I was going to admit him.

I held tight to the door, like my grip might actually stop him from getting in. "Actually…now's not a great time. I have company. Can we talk Monday in the office? Or meet for coffee or something tomorrow?"

Lennon peered over my shoulder and smiled, probably because he'd just seen Sophia. Fuck. "Ah yes. I won't take up much of your time, Alexandra. I'd prefer we did it now. I just wanted to discuss your father's work with you. I believe our timeline is growing more urgent and I'm not sure you understand the importance of us getting this information in a timely manner."

Oh no, I understood the importance very well. As calmly as I could, I nodded. "Of course. Come on in."

As I ushered him into my apartment, I scanned him for a weapon as inconspicuously as I could. Nothing obvious, but that only meant I couldn't see anything, not that he was unarmed. Unfortunately, I could confirm I was unarmed. Except for my wits and my smarts and my good looks. None of which were any match against a gun or blade, alas. Sophia had tidied herself, and was sitting on the couch like we'd been doing nothing more than just talking. She appeared mildly confused, but that confusion quickly turned to an expression of distaste. I'm right there with you, darling.

I gestured to my traitorous spy boss, though technically they'd already met, even if Lennon hadn't given Sophia a name or anything beyond his role as it pertained to me. "Sophia, this is Lennon, my boss." Good enough explanation. "I believe you two have already met."

Lennon chuckled. "Sorry, you must think our constant usage of surnames somewhat odd. I'm Michael." He offered his hand for Sophia to shake. "It's good to see you again, Sophia."

"Ms. Flores," she corrected him firmly, waiting for just a moment longer than polite to take his hand.

And despite the tense gravity of the situation, I had to bite back my laugh at her telling him in no uncertain terms not to use her first name. If I started laughing, it was going to spew out of me in hysterical bursts and Lennon would suspect something was wrong. I mean, something was very wrong but, poker face and all that.

Lennon didn't react to Sophia's unsubtle point that she was having none of his shit. He placed his hand on my back. "Can we speak in private, Alexandra?"

No no no, absolutely not. I fought the urge to squirm away from his treasonous disloyal hand, and instead of declining as my brain was screaming at me to do, I said, "Sure. I just need a minute to pee. We've been out at a brewery and I am so full of beer."

He looked like he was going to object—who the fuck are you to tell me I can't even pee in my own house, Lennon?—but he nodded. "Of course."

If he assumed that I was still working on figuring out the pass phrase, he wasn't going to do anything to jeopardize my work or upset me. Like hurt my girlfriend in any way. So I left Sophia out there with a man I no longer trusted so I could get something to protect her. Protect us.

Quickly, I opened my safe and pulled out my HK P30 handgun. I double-checked the safety was on before I pushed the gun into the waistband of my jeans at the small of my back. Sophia loved my ass, and shooting myself in it wasn't an option. Now, look casual, look cool, look like you don't know a huge national secret about the man you thought was one of the good guys actually maybe being the baddest of all. I flushed the toilet, ran the water in the sink, took a deep breath, and went back to make sure nothing had happened.

The moment I stepped back into the living room, I realized my error. I should have texted Jeffrey or Derek while I was in the bedroom. Fuck.

Sophia was still on the couch, and Lennon had moved beside the window, thankfully nowhere near her. They were engaging in typical small talk of two people who had nothing in common, and one of whom had done something terrible to the other, and I rescued Sophia with a cheerful, "Sorry, darling. This might take a while. Why don't you head home?" I tried desperately to convey with my eyes that she needed to leave. Because now I was certain Lennon was here for one thing. He wouldn't come around at ten p.m. on a Friday night just for a chat. He was going to force me to give him the pass phrase, and then he was going to kill me. And if he killed me, he would kill Sophia too.

But before she could answer, Lennon interjected, "Not that long. Stay. I'll be out of your way in a few minutes. Surely we can talk in your bedroom or something, Alexandra?" His smile was relaxed, easy, and all I could think was fuck off, you're not seeing my bedroom.

Lennon's smile would have disarmed anyone. Except those who were suspicious types, or who already knew his secret. And also Sophia, who was, by now, clued in to the intricate dances that I did with my work. But she smiled back at him. I glanced between the woman I loved and the man I thought I might hate, and saw something on Lennon's face that sent a cold shiver through me.

Scratch that previous thought. He was going to use Sophia to force me into giving him the pass phrase. Not if I had any say in it. I had to get her out of there. And, as a bonus, I had to get her to contact Jeffrey and get him here right now.

I reached out and lightly touched her arm to get her attention. "Didn't you say you still had to confirm tomorrow with Dominique?" I asked casually.

She paused for only a fraction of a second before understanding dawned on her face that I *really* wanted her out of here. Hopefully it was also understanding that I needed her to contact Dominique's husband. "Right. Shit." Laughing lightly, Sophia picked up her phone from the coffee table. "She'll be pissed off if I don't. I'll just duck out into the hall. Uh…I'll be back in a few minutes?"

"Thank you, babe," I said, smiling when it was the last thing I felt like doing. But I didn't want her to panic, so projecting a calm exterior was top of my list. "We shouldn't be too long."

Surely Lennon suspected that I was sending Sophia out to contact someone for help, though he hadn't reacted to my veiled message to her. He was probably so confident that nobody would get here in time that he didn't stop Sophia from leaving.

Once the door had closed behind her, Lennon pushed away from the window and began a slow trek around my living room. He studied my artwork, photos, and bookshelves with great interest before he asked, "Have you made any more progress?"

"No," I said evenly. I'd spent so long hating how good I was at lying, but now I was grateful for that warped skill set.

Lennon sighed heavily, then walked over to lean back against my kitchen counter, arms folded over his chest, expression totally inscrutable. "When did you figure it out?"

And here I was thinking I was acting totally normal. I was tempted to pretend I had no idea what he was talking about, but there was a reason he was the head of both Halcyon Division and the agency, and it had nothing to do with the Russian thing. So I told him the truth. "Monday."

"Hmm. I thought it was only yesterday."

"How did you know?" I was dying to figure out what had tipped him off, what my tell was.

Turns out, I didn't have a tell. Thank god. "You're not as stealthy as you think, Alexandra. Meetings with both Burton and Wood outside of work? That's not usual. And when something is not usual, I'm suspicious. I didn't know for sure, but thankfully you confirmed my suspicion without even trying to deny it."

I shook my head disbelievingly. "Of *course* you've been tailing me. I'm not even surprised, but I am disgusted."

"Thank you for not lying, and pretending that I'm just imagining things. I've been playing this game a long time, Alexandra. I'm disappointed you didn't do as instructed. I told you to leave those files alone if you broke the code."

"I would have," I said indignantly, "but my dad was smart, and left me a whole-ass fucking novel on your disloyalty. It was left for *me*, my folder, so I opened it. And I have to say, it's a lot of disloyalty. Once I saw that, I thought everything on the drive was fair game."

"I'm sure you see it that way. So, where do we go from here?" He asked like he was checking where I wanted to go on a vacation or something.

"Well, I kind of have to turn you in."

"No, you won't."

Won't. Not don't. I fought against the trembling realization that my suspicion was correct. He was going to stop me. And there was only one way he could. By killing me. I just needed to buy myself some time. Time for Sophia to call Jeffrey, and for Jeffrey to call Derek and Derek to call 911, or something. Time to talk Lennon down from whatever he had planned for me. I inhaled a steadying breath. I still had the upper hand—he wasn't going to kill me without getting the pass phrase.

"Is your name really Lennon or was it like some play on Lenin?"

His smile was incongruously convivial. "Maybe I just like the Beatles."

I almost laughed at that. Back when our relationship was conducted purely through calls, I'd wondered idly if the head of Halcyon, an organization steeped in secrecy, employed a cover name, and if he'd picked his the same way I'd picked mine—because we liked something. In my case, Ellen Ripley from the *Alien* movies, and Jackson fit well as a last name. But if he'd been here since childhood, he couldn't have named himself after a Beatle. Pity, I could use some humor about now. "And Michael? Or is it Mikhail?"

"Does it really matter?"

"It does to me."

But he said nothing. Okay, Mikhail Lenin it is.

I backed up so I could rest my butt against the back of the couch. Crossing one ankle over the other completed my mirage of relaxation. "I'm curious, do you have a Russian accent underneath that American one?"

His forehead crinkled. "I came to this country a decade after the Cold War began, before you were born, Alexandra. I was a child when my mother country sent me to begin my mission. So, no, though I speak Russian as a native speaker, I do not 'have an accent' underneath this one."

I felt like a foolish kid, but I had to know, and my question came out meek and childish. "Can you at least tell me why? Why you do this."

Lennon radiated surprise, as if the answer should be obvious. I supposed, if I set aside the underlying distress, I could maybe see why. His expression changed to one of mild pity, which felt really shitty. "For the same reason you do what you do. Because I was ordered to, and it was my duty. Because I believe in what I'm doing. My work is no less important than yours just because we're on opposing sides. In some things, we have worked together. Not all of Halcyon's tasks have been for my side."

His side. The Russian side. "How did you do any…Russian work under the Halcyon banner?" It should have been obvious, shouldn't it, if Halcyon was working in opposition to the government because they were acting in the best interests of a foreign power?

"Because Halcyon Division is a tool used to benefit my country. And Halcyon knows how *this* country, this government, works, and thus how to operate the tool without suspicion."

Oh god. The thing I'd sort of suspected but had tried not to suspect was true. "Was it just you? Or was there someone before you heading up the Division?"

"It's always been us." The underlying *and it always will be us* was clear. "Halcyon was formed *by* us, to work *for* us. Halcyon, as an ideal, has been here far longer than just the existence of the actual physical Division." So a foreign entity had been working its way through our government like a cancer this whole time, for sixty years, maybe longer.

I had to swallow bile. That meant every major political event that'd been enacted by them, by…us via Halcyon, had been not for the benefit of my country, but his. Assassinations, resignations, impeachments, civil unrest. All of it. For them. Our enemies. Halcyon, *Lennon*, was a puppet master, pulling all our strings. It made me furious. Sick. Upset. But now I could do something about it. I could stop it. "How much damage have you done?"

He shrugged. "Enough. Not as much as I would have hoped, but more than what was originally asked of me."

"Well," I said slowly, "you won't have the chance to do any more."

"An interesting theory," he said musingly. "Now, you know what I want."

"Yes, and I'm not going to give it to you."

"I'd urge you to reconsider your stance."

"Obviously you would. If I give it to you, then you'll delete the files and all traces of your treachery. But, you should know that other people know about you. And they don't know the original pass phrase, so there's no point in squeezing them for it so you can delete the original."

"I taught you well." The note of pride in his voice was disgusting. "But how exactly did you get the files out of the building?"

He'd taught me nothing, but I chose to ignore that in favor of not antagonizing him further. "I copied them to a special thumb drive and walked out with it on my person." In my person. Whatever.

His nose wrinkled and he quickly glanced down, toward my waist. "You're dedicated, Alexandra. I'll give you that." He sighed. "I should have known it was a mistake to give you access to your father's hard drive. I went through every scenario in my head, imagining what might happen if you saw the data. I concluded you had enough integrity to not look. But not once did I ever imagine you would be able to make a copy and leave the building with it."

"You should have done something better than whitelisting the drive," I said, with a not small amount of smugness. "Thankfully you obviously realized that taking away too much functionality hinders our ability to actually work."

"Evidently I should have done something better. I thought keeping the laptops away from any network would suffice, and that blocking access to any other drive was enough. How *did* you get around the whitelisting to copy the files onto external media?"

"I utilized Scott. Just like you told me not to do."

His jaw bunched. "I thought you would respect my directives."

"I don't respect you at all."

"That's unfortunate. Because I respect you a great deal. I've never met anyone as loyal to your country as you are, Alexandra."

Oh my god, the irony. My loyalty against his disloyalty. It'd be delicious if it wasn't so toxic. "Thank you."

"It wasn't a compliment."

Too bad. I'm taking it as one. "You know what I think?" Without waiting for him to answer, I continued, "I think maybe subconsciously, you knew this might happen, and you were okay with it. Are you tired, Lennon? Tired of being a fucking horrible person?"

"I am tired, yes. Mostly of your games, and your incessant questioning."

I held up my hands. "What can I say? I'm curious about a lot of things."

"Of course you are," he said wearily.

"My dad didn't willingly give you the drive, did he…"

Lennon shook his head.

"How did you get it?"

"I took it from his safe when your parents went out for their flight. I needed it more than he did." The unspoken "Because he was about to be dead" lingered distastefully in the air.

Yeah, no, I don't think so. I tried to take in a deep breath without looking like I needed a deep breath to work through what was happening. "I really need to know how you knew I might know the pass phrase. How could you, when even I didn't? I know my father would never have told you that willingly. Did you take that from him without his permission too?"

"I…overheard many of your father's conversations with his handler, and—"

"Overheard?" I interrupted. "You mean you bugged something or someone you weren't supposed to."

"Doing things I'm not supposed to so I may know things I'm not supposed to know is my job, Alexandra." Lennon waved dismissively, like he could simply wipe away one thought to move on to the next. "He would never tell her the pass phrase, nor where it was located, at least not verbally that I ever heard, nor in any written communication. He simply told her that the pass phrase for his drive was with the safest, most capable person and that they would know what to do. It took me a little while to figure it out, but after taking some time, I realized it could only be you. As I told you—logic."

"Logic," I agreed bitterly. "I've called you Lennon from the day I joined Halcyon, but then when I found out who you really were, you took any form of personal address off the table. I called you 'Uncle Michael' as a kid, so why not now when we're away from work?" Not that I wanted to, of course, but I wanted to know why he'd shut it down.

"Because I am *not* your uncle." His lip curled slightly. "And I always disliked how your father insisted you call me that and that I simply… had to accept it."

"Why would he do that?"

"I always suspected he was trying to make me form a connection to you, in the event things went wrong, so that I wouldn't harm you."

"Are you going to harm me?"

He didn't answer. That's a yes then.

"I have a briefing with the president on Monday morning. He knows that I'm bringing him something highly sensitive and urgent."

"And?"

"And, don't you think he'll think it strange that first my father dies right before a briefing and then me?"

Lennon laughed sardonically. "The president will simply assume that Martins are prone to dying unexpectedly, especially with me in his ear." He shook his head. "Have you really learned nothing in all the time you've been under my wing?"

Under his wing, like he was some sort of deranged mentor. "You taught me nothing. Except deceit. And if you tell me I'm actually a

Russian sleeper operative, who's just waiting for activation, I'm going to go fucking nuclear."

His lip curled. "No, you don't have the mettle to do what is required of us by my mother country."

And thank fuck for that. "Did you plant the Kunduz Intelligence?"

"No. I heard about it, of course, and I simply made sure that it came to us. That it came to you through one of your previous assets. I needed Berenson gone and this was the perfect vessel to carry that plan. I don't like loose ends."

"What about Hadim? I tried to contact him afterward, but he slipped back into the shadows. Did you have something to do with that?" The asset I'd known for a decade had disappeared after contacting me with the Kunduz intel, and it'd made me beyond suspicious, but I'd had no way of finding him.

"Loose ends, Alexandra."

So he'd killed him. I shoved down the disgust. "God, you're even worse than I thought. Is this why I had to deal with the Kunduz Intelligence on my own? You were trying to…what? Get me emotionally invested in this chain of events so I'd just look the other way when I realized who you are?"

"You're one of the best analysts we have, and you helped me achieve my goal of removing Berenson. Nothing more."

"Oh my god, this is too rich." I almost choked on the incredulity. "Let me get this straight. You enacted the protocol to remove the vice president because he was in bed with Russia, and yet here you are, Russia incarnate. Tell me, Lennon, did he know your secret?"

"He knew nothing, but he's an idiot. I had to remove him before he found something. I couldn't risk it. Do you think I've survived this long by being sloppy?"

"I think you've survived this long because you're a cunning bastard. My dad was so close to finishing this and you got scared, so you killed him. And my mother." It was a fishing expedition, but I was sure I'd find him at the end of my hook.

"I did what was necessary." Zero emotion. No remorse.

"How did you do it?" It was nothing more than morbid curiosity, and the moment I'd asked I wanted to pull the question back, tell him never mind, I don't need to know. But I didn't want him to think I was weak.

"I had dinner with your parents the night before their accident. It wasn't hard to introduce something, slowly absorbed, that would interfere with their breathing and circulatory systems. I knew he was taking a flight the next day, because he'd invited me to join them. Of course I had to decline because I knew what would happen in less than eighteen hours. I imagine that an hour or two into the flight they both began to feel very unwell. It wouldn't have taken long for them to pass out once they noticed they were feeling sick. No way to deal with the faulty fuel system. If it eases your distress, they wouldn't have been conscious at the time, if they were even alive. Quite an easy way to pass, really. We should all be so lucky."

That's why Dad hadn't been able to glide the plane with fuel starvation. He was already close to dead. Or he was dead. "The toxicology didn't show anything in their systems. Nor was there evidence of a faulty fuel system."

"Of course not. You forget who you're talking to, Alexandra. You've seen the…medical consequences of someone acting against Russia. As for tampering with the fuel system? Child's play." At my eyebrow raise, Lennon lifted his chin defiantly, almost as if he was personally insulted by my disbelief. "We have tools you could not even dream of."

"Jesus. Fucking with the fuel system *and* inducing a fatal medical event. You really wanted to cover your bases didn't you? It must be so nice to be a sociopath who just doesn't fucking care about anything or anyone except himself," I spat out.

"I care about my life's mission. And despite what you think, I did care about you. But you've proved yourself unworthy of that."

"Why did you wait so long to involve me? All the bullshit with me being unable to work on this, the president's absurd six-month assignment aside, because if this was so important, why not bring me in right away? And spare me the lies about my mental state after my parents died."

His gaze was burning. "Because I didn't want to draw your attention to it so close to your parents' death. Because I feared you might do exactly what you've done—look in places where you're not wanted. But in the end, I had no choice. I needed to know exactly how much damage your father might have done, not just to me but to all of Halcyon and where I might need to do damage control."

"And you figured you could just do damage control with me too if need be?" Damage control sounded so much nicer than murder.

"Exactly."

"Did you murder my father's handler?"

"No. She died of cancer, just as I told you." When I gave him a dubious look, he sighed. "You can check her records if you really must."

Oh! Maybe I was going to get out of here alive after all. "While I'm asking questions about murder, I just have another one."

It looked like it took enormous effort for him to not roll his eyes. "If you must."

"The previous head of agency. What happened to him? Did you murder him so you could take over?"

"No. He was persuaded that his time at the agency had come to an end, that he could do no more good in his position and it was time for retirement. He's happily playing golf in Florida. The president agreed with the decision and my appointment. It was all too easy."

Persuaded. I could just imagine what form that persuasion took. Oh wait. The president… "Does the president know about you?"

Lennon looked both appalled and amused. "That buffoon? Of course not."

Well, that was one thing for the positives column, I supposed. We didn't have a Russian spy for a president. "Sorry. Just one more murder question. Did you murder your wife because she found you out and was passing information to my dad? I bet she wasn't too happy about sleeping with the enemy."

His jaw bunched, but he said nothing.

"Okay, uxoricide it is."

"This is ridiculous, Alexandra. *Enough!*" The movement of his right hand toward his left armpit had me reaching behind myself and we drew guns on each other simultaneously. I would have laughed at the movie synchronicity of us both drawing weapons, if not for my fear and anger. I held my weapon in a two-handed grip, while his was more casual in just one hand, almost as if he was overconfident.

"Well, if I'd known this was going to turn into a shootout, I would have gotten in some range time this week." I didn't shoot much, but was fairly certain of my ability to at least hit him, especially at close range, and was surprised to feel the slightest curling of doubt in my belly.

What if I had it wrong? But…then why was he here, with his gun trained on me? My doubt was just fear talking. I knew what I'd seen, the classified information I'd uncovered. Jeffrey and Derek knew too. Lennon couldn't leave here unless he was in handcuffs. Or maybe on a stretcher. Or in a body bag. I wasn't fussy.

He tilted his head mockingly. "You do know I don't really need you. I have ways of getting information from…reluctant subjects."

Yep, I did know that. But I hoped the insurance of hiding it with one of the best hackers in the world, as well as two moral men would help my cause. "Let me guess, you're just lazy? Can't be bothered doing the work to figure it out on your own?"

His chuckle was less amused, more menacing. "Not lazy. Impatient."

"But people know," I reiterated.

"Yes. And I know who those people are. It won't be hard to take care of that problem. Without evidence, it's nothing more than a rumor. And when you do what I do, you get used to rumors. I've been fending them off almost my entire life. I'm very good at it."

"I keep wondering. Why not just ignore it? Throw the hard drive out if you knew it had information about you and Halcyon on it?"

"Control. If you don't control the information then you've lost. I *will* control the information, Alexandra." After a deep breath, he said, "Now. The pass phrase."

"No."

"I'm not going to ask you again."

"Good, because then I won't have to keep coming up with new and exciting ways to tell you no."

Lennon smiled at the gun I held on him. "You know, we both have firearms, but I have another weapon. Sophia Flores…"

"Don't you fucking dare," I snarled, taking a step toward him. The movement of his trigger finger made me step back again.

"You're being dramatic."

True, but sometimes a situation called for a little drama.

His finger moved back against the trigger guard, and I relaxed a fraction. Lennon stared at me. "I don't think you realize the importance of this data, especially to me."

"I'm not an idiot. I know exactly how important it is to you, and exactly what this means for the security of our country, past, present, and future. But Sophia doesn't know anything. I don't know how many times I can say it. I'm so sick of keeping secrets from her, but I do, because I have to. But you'd know all about that, keeping secrets, wouldn't you?"

Lennon sighed. "Don't be coy, Alexandra. It doesn't suit you at all. I don't *want* to hurt her, I just want her to help you see reason." He flicked his wrist, using the gun to gesture vaguely.

He stepped forward, I stepped back, and we kept up the dance, both of us trying to lead. The knock, then sound of the key turning sent a shard of dread though me that was so sharp I almost winced. I'd hoped Sophia would just call Jeffrey and then run, go home or do something, *anything*, other than coming back here.

As soon as I heard the door open, I asked, "Did you get hold of Dominique?" I turned my head slightly so I could look at her without having to take my focus off Lennon.

Sophia froze in the doorway, taking in the scene, her head whipping back and forth between us at almost tennis-spectator speed as Lennon and I calmly played cat and mouse around the room. "Yes. She said… she'll come get me."

"Good." God I hoped that meant she'd spoken to Jeffrey and he was on his way. To further the subterfuge, I said, "Then I won't have to drive you."

"What's going on?" she asked, unable to disguise the tremor in her voice.

I shuffled backward to her, hoping to get in front of her before Lennon grabbed her. "Just a small work disagreement, darling. Nothing to worry about." I would have run and shoved her out the door if I didn't think Lennon would react badly. I needed to convince him to let her go again willingly. Good luck with that, Lexie.

From behind me, Sophia said, "Have to admit, I'm kind of worried. This is the most aggressive work disagreement I've ever witnessed."

"It's okay, I promise," I said, still racing Lennon to get to her.

"Yes, it's okay," Lennon agreed calmly. "But Alexandra has something I need, and I think it's in all our best interests that she gives it to me." He side-stepped, but I moved diagonally, finally managing to position myself right in front of Sophia, blocking her from Lennon's view. And his gun.

Light fingers touched the back of my shoulder. "Lexie? Can you just give it to him?"

"I cannot." And suddenly, I knew nothing with more certainty than I did right then, that no matter what I did, this scenario was going to end with me and then Sophia dead. Unless I shot first. But if I shot and missed, it was all over. So I just couldn't miss. Easy. I stepped forward and raised the gun a little higher, sighting on him.

"Lexie," Sophia said urgently. "Don't, please. You don't have to do this again." *Again.* I'd killed a man in self-defense once, and it'd fucked with my mental health something fierce. But I'd take a mental health crisis over being dead, or her being killed too.

Lennon's voice was sharp. "This is the last time I'll ask, Alexandra."

I exhaled slowly, and my words came out long and breathy. "Okay. I give in."

"Good."

"I have one condition though. She's not here to see it."

Sophia lurched into me, choking out a "Lexie!" that bordered on a scream.

I held out a hand to stop her from moving, not wanting her panic to spook him. "Sophia, please. Trust me. Please. I don't want you to see this. You're going to go now." Because I'd either fail and be dead, or I'd have to make a mess in order to succeed. I didn't want her to see a mess, or be left alone afterward with him.

Lennon scoffed, "I can't let her leave, Alexandra. That's ridiculous. She knows who I am."

"So chase her down and take care of her later," I snapped. I felt Sophia's wince at my blunt statement. But if I could get her away now, Jeffrey would protect her.

I could see he was considering it, and I pushed him a little further along by reminding him, "I'm not cooperating if she's in danger. You let her go, or we're both dead and you're up shit creek, without a paddle."

After an eternity spent deliberating, Lennon agreed with a firm, "Done. She can go freely now, you have my word." He even lowered his gun. I wasn't sure his word was worth anything, but I had no choice but to trust him. Sophia's life depended upon it.

Sophia's sob split the room, and I turned to her. As best I could while still holding a gun and keeping an eye on Lennon, I pulled her into a hug, still keeping myself between her and Lennon. Against her ear, I murmured, "It's okay, darling. It's okay. You'll be okay." And she would. Lowering my voice to a whisper, I told her, "It's time for me to be the fat man."

She shook her head, tears tracking down her cheeks as she sobbed out, "No. No…"

"Hurry up," Lennon said, and surprisingly, it wasn't unkind.

Though it disgusted me to let him see it, I kissed Sophia. I had to satisfy myself with nothing more than a quick press of my lips to hers, and I could taste the salt of tears and snot. She clung to me, her arms tight around my neck and her face buried in my shoulder.

I disengaged her as best I could with one hand, and raised her chin, forcing her to look at me. The raw fear on her face sliced through me but I shoved my emotion aside. "I love you," I said, injecting every ounce of truth I could into those three words. "Meeting you, being with you, loving you, has been the best thing that ever happened to me."

"I love you too. I—"

"I know," I cut her off, wishing I could kiss her again. But I had to hope she felt my love. I gently pulled away and turned her toward the door. "It'll be okay," I said, forcing a wobbly smile. I'd lied to her so many times before to make sure she felt safe, so, in the scheme of things, what was this lie at the end for the same purpose? "Jeffrey will protect you," I whispered, barely able to get the words out around the massive boulder in my throat. And though it was the hardest thing I would ever do, I pushed her away from me, toward the door.

"Wait," Lennon barked. "Give me your phone."

She looked to me first, and at my nod, handed it to me. I dropped it on the kitchen counter. Fuck, I wished I'd thought to sneakily record the conversation we'd just had. Oh well. Jeffrey and Derek had the files. It'd work out the way Dad and I wanted it to. And Sophia would be safe.

Sophia.

Beautiful, kind, funny, caring, compassionate Sophia gave me the most heartbreaking look before she went through the door to safety. The fear I'd been shoving down started to rise up again, and I had to fight to get it away, into a place where it wasn't dictating my actions.

Lennon nodded when the door closed behind Sophia, a short, sharp nod of satisfaction. "I've given you what you wanted, now give me what I want. The pass phrase, Alexandra."

I inhaled a deep, soothing breath. Sophia was safe. The data was safe. That was all that mattered. "Okay. It's 'go fuck yourself sixty-nine,' uppercase on the first letter of each word, numeral sixty-nine."

He briefly raised his eyes to the ceiling. "Perfidy," he scoffed. "Of course. You think you're so cute. I am beyond tired of your obstreperousness."

"You know what? So am I. But it's all you're getting."

"Fine. Have it your way." Lennon raised his gun.

The instant I saw the movement, I raised my firearm too. I had just mentally committed to pulling the trigger, when there was a deafening crash and a bright flash. Then pain.

So. Much. Pain.

CHAPTER TWENTY-FIVE

*All's well that ends well,
even if that ending is you being shot by a Russian spy*

When I heard the footsteps at the door, I turned away from staring at birds in the trees outside the window. I expected to see Sophia, wearing the tentative smile she always did when coming into my hospital room, like it was some sacred space of healing. She'd ducked home to shower and change into fresh clothes, and had promised she'd be back soon. The only time she hadn't been with me was when hospital staff kicked her out, she needed to eat or shower, or because someone else had stopped by to see me.

Not Sophia. But almost as good. Smiling, I croaked out, "If it isn't my two favorite rescuer guys."

Jeffrey held up a Ziploc bag of cookies—from Dominique no doubt—and a book that was thankfully contemporary fiction instead of his joking gift a few days ago of the thick *The Lord of the Rings*. I'd had enough of long books for now, thank you. "Here to rescue you again," he said cheerfully. "From boredom and bad food this time." He closed the door, then followed Derek over to my bed.

Derek rested his hand gently on my left shoulder, careful of all my wires and tubes. "How're you feeling?"

"Shitty," I answered honestly. "Remember that last time I was in the hospital when I said don't ever get stabbed repeatedly?" In 2017, I was recovering from the six-stab-wounds hostage incident. At his nod, I continued, "I'm adding don't ever get shot in the chest." Yeah, it wasn't like getting-shot-in-the-heart bad, but the upper right chest still messes with some internal body stuff, and I'd been recovering in the hospital for nearly a week, with no jailbreak in sight. Like being stabbed, getting shot is a terrible thing to do. Zero out of ten stars, do not recommend.

Derek winced. "Again, I'm sorry. We got there as soon as we could."

"Better late than never, right?" I struggled into a slightly more upright position. "But why is it that you always seem to break in and save my ass, but only ever *after* I'm wounded." I now had several additional scars on my torso after this adventure.

Thankfully, Derek took the teasing and just smiled, shaking his head.

Jeffrey puffed up in mock indignation. "Hey, we saved Sophia, didn't we? And technically saved you too. Please give us some credit."

"Yes," I breathed. "You did. Thank you. All the credit." I shifted uncomfortably against my pile of pillows, and adjusted the bed so I could sit up properly.

Jeffrey and Derek moved chairs around to both sit on the same side and keep me from having to look back and forth between them. The last time they'd visited, the movement had produced nausea so strong that I'd barfed all over myself before I had time to ask for a puke receptacle.

I'd been desperate to know what happened, and now I finally felt well enough to quiz them a little on what'd gone down. All I remembered was getting Sophia safe, pulling the trigger, noise, pain. Then nothing. "How'd you guys even know he was there?" Sophia had steadfastly refused to talk about it while I was in the hospital, telling me this time was for healing my body and we could heal my emotions later.

Derek answered, "I put him under surveillance on Friday morning. When he went to your place, I got a call. Then Sophia called Burton in a panic. We mobilized as quickly as we could. Sorry it wasn't quite quick enough."

"You're a terrible shot," Jeffrey said dryly.

"I'm a fabulous shot. I was going to shoot him in the head. Or…try to. Maybe I should have, then he wouldn't have gotten that shot off at me. But then I thought of all that knowledge in there. We would have lost everything he might know. So I went for the stop-but-hopefully-not-kill, right-side-of-chest shot." I had to take a breath before asking, "Did it hit where I thought it did?" Lennon's shot had hit me where I wanted mine to hit him. Irony.

"A little high and right. More shoulder-arm than chest. But effective enough. Except for the reflex of his trigger finger while he had a gun aimed in your direction," Jeffrey said. There was a little teacherish admonishment in his answer, like he was desperate to school me on how I could have done it better. "Luckily I was there to finish it for you."

"Thank you," I said sincerely. "But I'd like to state for the record that your flashbang startled the shit out of me which is why I missed my intended area."

"Nuh-uh," he teased. "That was thrown a millisecond after the first shot."

"Ohhh, so it was actually your flashbang that made him shoot me then? Not his reflex to me shooting him?" I attempted an eye roll, which just sent a dull pain through my skull. "Thanks, guys." I sipped a mouthful of water from the kiddie-straw sippy cup by my bed before asking, "Where is he?"

They exchanged a look before Derek answered, "In a secure, secret location. Recovering well, apparently."

"What about his handlers? Assuming he even has any. But he'd have someone he's been reporting to, for sure. Oh god, unless they gave him complete autonomy to run riot through our agencies." I held out a hand. "Pass me the puke basin, please." I didn't think I was actually going to hurl, but the thought made me feel sick and I'd been caught out before.

Derek handed it to me, and I held it on my lap.

Jeffrey answered, "We're still working through all the details, and once Lennon's recovered sufficiently, we'll be debriefing him. We need to know how many of him there are. And who…"

"I doubt he'll talk," I said. There was enough information in Dad's files to have Lennon tried and incarcerated, but it would be nice to have his side of things.

"Me too," Jeffrey agreed. "But that doesn't mean I'm not going to try…" His toothy grin was part gleeful, part feral.

I suppressed a shudder. The debriefs I'd had with him had given me a glimpse of what he could, and would, do. And he'd never even touched me. "I assume someone will be debriefing me too?"

"Yes. How's your memory before the shooting?"

"Crystal clear." In my less painful, more lucid moments, I'd been making notes on the laptop I'd begged Sophia to bring in, typing with just my left hand. I wanted to make sure I had what he'd told me written down so it wouldn't be lost.

"Good," Derek said gruffly. "The president is having conniptions. You might get some sort of award." He and Jeffrey had taken Dad's intelligence to the president on Monday, as intended, and apparently heaped credit upon my absent butt.

"Can't wait," I mumbled. Then I brightened. "Maybe that idiotic fucker will really leave me alone now."

"Maybe," Derek agreed laughingly.

"Do you think I'll get an apology for all his bullshit, like 'Sorry, Dr. Martin, I was wrong to send you to a hostile zone last year, hoping you'd get killed just because I'm a petty man-child who couldn't deal with you telling the truth'?"

Jeffrey hmmed. "I think that might be pushing the boundaries of his vocabulary."

Derek added, "And his decency."

"Yeah," I agreed. "Oh my god, I can't wait to brief with him. It's going to be so satisfying to tell that fuckstain that I saved his ass. He's going to owe me so hard." I laughed, then winced hard at the pain, which made me cough, which set off a spasm that had Derek and Jeffrey scrambling. "Oh god, no," I finally managed. "Don't let me laugh." When I'd caught my breath again, I asked, "What about the other dossiers on Dad's hard drive?"

Derek leaned forward. "They were passed along to the relevant team to investigate. I've only had one briefing, but it seems they were all low- or mid-level employees in private companies and government departments. As far as we can tell, the damage has been minimal, but it's possible we'll uncover more once the team delves further. But all seven have been…contained."

"Good." I inhaled a shallow breath, trying not to induce another spasm of pain.

Jeffrey grabbed my sippy cup of water while Derek made sure my supportive pillows were fluffed, and once I could breathe normally, we resumed our conversation. We spent ten minutes just catching up, and Derek promised me he'd talk to my colleagues about the overwhelming amount of flowers that kept arriving to my hospital suite, while Jeffrey assured me that none of the investigators had messed with my Zen Zone.

Derek shot my partner a pointed look. "Mind if we have a few minutes, Burton?" Ohhhh, it's time for a secret discussion.

"Course not." Jeffrey stood up, then leaned over and kissed my forehead. "Rest up, and heal. Let me know when you want me to come visit again. And as soon as you're feeling up to it, Dom wants to see you too."

"I will. And sounds good. I'll be out of here soon." I reached out a weak hand to him and he squeezed it. "I owe you. Again."

"Well…you *were* the key to uncovering someone who had the power to give me orders that might endanger my aliveness even more than regular orders, so I'm gonna call us even."

"Deal."

Derek stood and clapped Jeffrey on the shoulder, then got up to make sure the door had closed. When he sat down again, he leaned close, his voice a near-whisper. "The Division has been dismantled and will not be replaced. They've completely lost faith in its utility. Understandable, when you know it was established as a Russian initiative."

"I'm glad, and I can understand that. Learning you've been played by the enemy for sixty years will do that to you."

"Mmm," he agreed. "After the investigation and a secret congressional hearing it will be classified to the deepest level, buried forever. If word of it ever got out, well…I'm sure you can imagine what would happen."

"I can." After a cautiously deep breath, I asked, "So we're just going to let the government function as normal without Halcyon pulling the strings? Shocking."

"Well, we still have lobbyists and regular corrupt congressmen and women and senators, so…" He raised both hands, indicating his sense of helplessness.

"What happens to my lovely offshore retirement account?"

"It'll continue to be lovely and offshore, as will mine, and every other Halcyon agent who doesn't want to move their funds onshore. We earned that money as legitimate employees of what was thought to be a legitimate government branch with budgetary freedom."

"Good. So, after what I did, you know…basically being the key to unravelling all of this, we *really* need to discuss that raise. I'm sick of single-handedly saving this country."

This time Derek didn't disappoint. "That's above my paygrade." He grinned as he added, "But I promise I'll see what I can do."

"Thank you. I need it because I'm going to use up some of my masses of personal time and Sophia and I are going to travel. Visit every continent." And I thought about proposing to her in Antarctica, because neither of us had been there. Seemed like as good a place as any.

Derek smiled. "Lexie, I really hope you do. She's a good egg." I knew they'd talked a little at the hospital, and it felt stupid to be pleased that Derek liked Sophia, but I was.

"I know. Now if we could just stop having crazy shit happen so we could get on with our lives as normal, that would be great."

"Surely there's nothing else that could happen."

Oh he did not just tempt fate like that. "You never know," I mumbled. "But I hope we've had enough bullshit for one lifetime." Sighing, I closed my eyes. Just needed a quick moment to recharge.

Derek took my unspoken cue and stood up. "I'll let you get some rest. Call me if you need anything. I'm looking forward to you coming back to work."

"Me too. *Normal* work," I reiterated.

Derek patted my shoulder, gave me a clumsy hug, then left me to wait for Sophia to return. I definitely felt better when she was around. I closed my eyes and relaxed my body, imagining sinking down into the bed. One thing I wasn't anxious about was this latest round of bodily harm, which was a nice change from the last time I'd been in a hospital. The safety of having Sophia by my side took all that away.

I heard the footsteps of someone trying to be soundless and opened my eyes. Sophia paused like a cat burglar caught in the act. Wrinkling her nose, she offered a quiet, "Sorry."

"What for? I was just thinking about you."

She put her laptop case and handbag down, then went through her usual routine of smoothing my hair back, wiping crud from my eyes, and straightening my blanket. "How are you feeling?"

"Same as I was when you asked me before you left," I answered. She shook her head good-naturedly, and I threw her a bone. "I'm tired. But no big pain." Just little pain and stiffness. The anticipation of how good it was going to feel once I was cleared for some real movement, for yoga and a hike or run, was one of the things keeping me from losing my shit.

"Good." Sophia checked the time on her phone. "Did dinner come while I was gone?"

"Not yet." Not that I'd probably eat much. Scratch that—I would if she was here, because I needed "nutrition to heal," according to Nurse Sophia. "But Jeffrey and Derek did, they left not long ago."

"I know," she said, smiling. "I bumped into Jeffrey paying for his parking as I was coming in. He's asked me to come around for dinner and some company while you're in here."

"That sounds like a great idea, sweetheart. I feel bad that you're spending so much time stuck with me."

"It's where I want to be," she said firmly, but without any trace of annoyance at me questioning her choices.

"I know. I just…it makes me feel…" I fiddled with the controller that moved the bed up and down. "Actually, I don't really know how it makes me feel. I talked a little about what happened with the guys."

Her expression blanked, and I braced myself for her brush-off. When she didn't say anything, I reached for her hand. "Can you tell me what happened?" Her mouth opened, her expression already telling me she was going to sideline my query. So I gently asked, "Please?"

"I, um—" She drew in a deep breath. "It doesn't feel nice to think about it."

Squeezing her hand, I quietly agreed, "I know."

Sophia's cheeks puffed up with air, and she expelled it noisily. "I have to work through it, I know that. But at the moment it's too hard, too raw, especially with you being in a hospital bed."

"Okay," I said gently, not wanting to upset her. "It's fine, we can just leave it."

Her forehead wrinkled, and I could see her working through her internal torment. After a minute, she said, "Jeffrey filled me in on a few things, mentioned that Lennon was corrupt, and alluded to some other underlying stuff that's classified, but it just…it was fucking *scary*, Lexie."

"I know," I murmured, hating that she'd been put into this situation.

"When you told me to go talk to Dominique, I thought you were insane because I'd just seen her. But then I realized what you really meant. I called Jeffrey, well, Dom, who told me he was already on the way."

I smiled tremulously. "I'm so glad you figured out that I wanted you to contact Jeffrey."

"The look on your face when you answered the door to…him was kind of terrified, so I thought maybe something was up." She laughed humorlessly. "Scratch that, I *knew* something was up. I was going to call the cops, but it felt like you were telling me to contact Jeffrey, so I did." She waved a dismissive hand. "Anyway. I'm just glad it's all over and you're okay."

"Not as glad as I am that you're okay. I was right there on the scared with you." I didn't want to tell her that Lennon was going to use Sophia to make me comply, but I had to. And I *would* tell her, but she seemed so fraught from the tiniest amount of recollection that I decided it could wait until we both felt a little less fragile. I cleared my throat. "You know I didn't mean it, what I said about him just 'getting you later,' right? I knew if you got away then Jeffrey would protect you."

Her expression softened. "Yeah, I got that. But it felt pretty fucking horrible at the time."

"I know," I murmured. "I'm sorry."

"Always keeping me safe, aren't you," she said softly. Sophia leaned over and kissed me gently, just a light brush of her lips against mine.

"Always," I agreed. The thought of what had happened welled up in my chest, and before I started crying, I changed the subject. Crying hurt—I'd learned that early on. "Being hospitalized is so tedious. I really want to go home." I raised an eyebrow. "Ever played nurse?"

Sophia grinned. "No, but I'm a fast learner."

"Good." I swallowed hard. "Can I just say one thing?"

Her eyes crinkled at the edges. "You don't need my permission to talk, hon."

"I know, but…" I left-shoulder-only shrugged. "I love you, and I want you to know that what happened on Friday night was an anomaly. That part of my life is definitely history, never to be repeated."

"I kind of got that vibe, but thank you for confirming it." She cleared her throat. "I can't go through that again, Lexie."

"Neither can I," I said dryly. Then, unable to help myself, I said, "I'm running out of places on my torso to get penetrating wounds."

Her laugh had a cough of disbelief at the start, before it turned to genuinely amused at the fact I was joking about something so serious. She carefully tucked my hair back behind my ears. "I love you. You're such a weirdo."

"A spoonful of levity makes the medicine go down. Or something like that."

"Something like that," she agreed teasingly.

"I, uh, I hope you really do love the weird because…" I licked my lips. "Do you remember our brunch date, right before everything went crazy and we went to Florida?"

"Of course I do."

"I think I said something like you'll know if I ask you to move in with me, because you made the U-Haul joke when I turned up with a bunch of bags. This is me asking, Sophia. Move in with me. I want every morning and every evening and every weekend with you. I want to know you're at home, in our space, working during the day before I come home to you. I want to share my life with you."

Her voice rose an octave as she asked, "You want me to move in with you?"

"Yes. Or I'll move in with you. Or we'll buy a house together somewhere in the burbs. I want to make a life with you. I want to make a family with you. You, me, your fish, a cat or three. Whatever you want. I just want it to be us, together."

"Okay," she said simply, a smile twitching the edges of those gorgeous, soft lips. Sophia leaned forward and kissed me, softly, lovingly. She stroked light fingers down my face, then cupped my cheeks in both hands.

I could feel the joy I felt reflected on my face. "Yeah?"

"Yeah. Let's make a life together, my Not-Spy."

Bella Books, Inc.
Women. Books. Even Better Together.
P.O. Box 10543
Tallahassee, FL 32302
Phone: (800) 729-4992
www.BellaBooks.com

More Titles from Bella Books

Hunter's Revenge – Gerri Hill
978-1-64247-447-3 | 276 pgs | paperback: $18.95 | eBook: $9.99
Tori Hunter is back! Don't miss this final chapter in the acclaimed Tori Hunter series.

Integrity – E. J. Noyes
978-1-64247-465-7 | 28 pgs | paperback: $19.95 | eBook: $9.99
It was supposed to be an ordinary workday…

The Order – TJ O'Shea
978-1-64247-378-0 | 396 pgs | paperback: $19.95 | eBook: $9.99
For two women the battle between new love and old loyalty may prove more dangerous than the war they're trying to survive.

Under the Stars with You – Jaime Clevenger
978-1-64247-439-8 | 302 pgs | paperback: $19.95 | eBook: $9.99
Sometimes believing in love is the first step. And sometimes it's all about trusting the stars.

The Missing Piece – Kat Jackson
978-1-64247-445-9 | 250 pgs | paperback: $18.95 | eBook: $9.99
Renee's world collides with possibility and the past, setting off a tidal wave of changes she could have never predicted.

An Acquired Taste – Cheri Ritz
978-1-64247-462-6 | 206 pgs | paperback: $17.95 | eBook: $9.99
Can Elle and Ashley stand the heat in the *Celebrity Cook Off* kitchen?

Milton Keynes UK
Ingram Content Group UK Ltd.
UKHW010627290424
441924UK00001B/59